ASHES
TO
HUEVOS

Also by Susan Emshwiller

DOMINOES
a play (Dramatists Play Service)

DEFROSTING POPSICLES
a play (Playscripts)

THAR SHE BLOWS
a novel (Pinehead Press)

ALL MY ANCESTORS HAD SEX
a novel (Pinehead Press)

HOPE IS A THING THAT'S MOLTING
a conglomeration of short writings (Pinehead Press)

In praise of Susan Emshwiller's writings

Susan Emshwiller surprises and delights with a brilliantly written novel, *ASHES TO HUEVOS*. She invites her readers into the lives of Tango, a veteran without a home, his dog Captain, and Prestonia Cheswick, a woman in search of her authentic self. Emshwiller weaves a complex tale which shines a spotlight on Fate's fickle whims. Her witty dialogues, intense and often amusing internal monologues, and her deft intertwining of her characters lives delivers a captivating read from beginning to end.

ANNE ANTHONY, author of
A Blue Moon & Other Murmurs of the Heart

Susan Emshwiller's *ALL MY ANCESTORS HAD SEX* is not like anything you have experienced before—unless you're an eighteen-year-old girl named Izzy and have kidnapped your monstrously privileged little brother and driven off in a reconditioned Metro Van to criss-cross the U.S. on a wild road trip, pursued by private eyes, and seeking a way to integrate the fragments of your broken personality. Oh, yes, you'd also have to contend with a half-dozen of your squabbling ancestors, all of whom trail their own tragic histories. In other words, baggage. Find out how Izzy manages to unload it all in this funny and very serious novel—with a heart. Then go and do likewise.

JOHN KESSEL, award-winning author of
The Dark Ride and *The Moon and the Other*

Susan Emshwiller's new novel, I'm happy to say, lives up to its stellar title in every facet. It's a rollicking, rocket's blast chase caper, jammed with rich characters and affecting insights into the human condition. *ALL MY ANCESTORS HAD SEX* delivers a delightfully inventive cross-country thrill ride loaded with surprises and PTSD.

RICHARD KRAUSS editor/publisher of
The Digest Enthusiast

If you are holding this book in your hand, congratulations. If you have chosen to buy this book, chosen from all the books you could have chosen to buy, HUGE CONGRATULATIONS. You are in for a wild and heartfelt ride. What can I say about Susan Emshwiller's writing, except that there is no one like her. She is truly an original.
                      NANCY PEACOCK, Piedmont Laureate, author of
The Life and Times of Persimmon Wilson

Susan is afraid of nothing in her writing…Full stop. Hilarious! A mother/son fiasco/journey wrapped in love, grit, and impossibility-be- damned!! I promise you will love this wild ride into the inner workings of one whale and one mother.
                      AMY MADIGAN, actor, producer

Susan Emshwiller wears all her hats in this remarkable and satisfying novel. A page-turner adventure, well-researched and exciting, *THAR SHE BLOWS* is equally as strong for its human drama of a mother and son searching for each other and also themselves. Characters so genuine, flawed, funny and true, they win you over to this improbable premise from the first pages. Enjoy the ride!
                      GREGG CUSICK, author of
My Father Moves Through Time Like a Dirigible

Remember when you used to get lost in a book, and forget to stop to eat? *THAR SHE BLOWS* is that book. Susan Emshwiller has crafted a romp of a tale about Ann, a woman defined by the color beige, and her 19-year-old, screen-addicted son Brian. When Brian is swallowed by a whale, Ann escapes both her suburban home and her senses in a valiant and delightful journey to rescue him. Make your meals in advance, because once you start reading THAR SHE BLOWS, you're going to want to keep going straight to the end!
                      MIMI HERMAN, Piedmont Laureate, author of
The Kudzu Queen

A wickedly smart story of a mother losing patience and a son finding direction in the most unusual way possible, *THAR SHE*

BLOWS by Susan Emshwiller is a deep dive into the tenderness and tension of mothers and sons. Pushing the literary boundaries of magical realism, this one-of-a-kind novel is a bizarre tale of losing, seeking, and finding...inside the belly of a whale. The tongue-in-cheek prose offsets the serious issues at hand, while the premise teeters perfectly on the brink of allegory, parable, and farce. With whip-smart characters, exceptional comedic timing, and high emotional stakes, this book is a surprising read throughout, balancing an outlandish premise with relatable insight.—SPR

Brush Strokes engages with wit and warmth. Emshwiller sensitively establishes the mystery of a situation, and knows precisely when to sever the action—realizing what needs to be revealed and what doesn't.

Pick of the Week, LA Weekly

In *Brush Strokes*...the spectacular results are due to Emshwiller's ingenuity in extracting scenarios ripe with drama. Emshwiller also brings enviable economy and precision to her scripting. There isn't a wasted word in dialogue that reveals entire histories without recourse to expository narration.

Los Angeles Times

A truly original creativity and imagination are apparent throughout *Brush Strokes*. Emshwiller's spare dialogue and virtual absence of exposition—her humor and solid construction skills extend each visual vignette into a startling, believable and complete mini-play.

Larchmont Chronicle

Emshwiller has—talent, discretion, and affection for her characters.

LA View

ASHES
TO
HUEVOS

a novel by
susan emshwiller

PINEHEAD PRESS

ASHES TO HUEVOS
© 2026 by Susan Emshwiller
Santa Fe, NM

www.susanemshwiller.com

PINEHEAD PRESS
www.pineheadpress.com
ISBN: 979-8-9880528-7-6 (paperback)
ISBN: 979-8-9880528-8-3 (ePub)
Library of Congress Control Number: 2026900285

The following is a work of fiction created by the author. All names, individuals, characters, places, items, brands, events, etc. were either the product of the author or were used fictitiously. Any name, place, event, person, brand, or item, current or past, is entirely coincidental.

All rights reserved. No part of this publication may be reproduced, stored in a retrieval system, or transmitted in any form or by any means, electronic, mechanical, photocopying, recording, or otherwise, without the prior permission of Pinehead Press or the author.

Image of Colorado Street Bridge used under license from Shutterstock.com
Other incorporated photographic images from Susan Emshwiller

cover design
by Susan Emshwiller © 2026

Author photo by Chris Coulson

for Chris, who inspires me daily,
and for all those finding their huevos

ASHES TO HUEVOS

THE LAST DAY

IN THE DARKNESS, Tango slips off one of the duplicate military tags from the chain below his beard. He kneels, pulls his matted dog close, and works at securing the tag to the filthy collar.

"This will keep you safe. They'll know you ain't a stray."

The dog whines softly.

"Don't worry, Captain. You're a mix of many, but folks accept that in dogs more than they do in people. You'll be okay."

Tango hugs the dog, pressing his nose into the familiar fur, and whispers, "Stay." Turning quickly to keep the tears from coming, he starts the climb up the steep, overgrown embankment. He can't see the red pit bull/border collie/whatever mix, but knows the dog is alarmed. Still, he won't let that dissuade him from his mission. This has gone on for too long and today feels as good as any for the end.

It's never easy to climb out of this gorge and it's harder in the darkness. His baggy army jacket snags on a branch, he stumbles, and a thorny plant stabs his knee. Tango pushes away the pain and with calf muscles aching, hauls himself up the last yard of scrubby hillside and crawls onto the dark road. Lifting himself upright, he pauses to catch his breath and looks for signs of life. Seeing no cars or people, he lumbers toward the bridge—head low, shoulders hunched. He's only twenty-eight, but he's stooped as one who has been ostracized, marginalized, and every other form of *ized* there is.

It's early, so still cool, and the traffic on the bridge hasn't started yet. There's a gentle glow lightening the sky in the east beyond Pasadena but the sun is still far off. All along the Colorado Street Bridge, the old-fashioned lights on their decorative posts glimmer in the morning mist—looks like a vintage postcard.

Bullshit. It looks like a good place to die.

Unlike most straight-line bridges, this ancient bridge curves sideways across the massive ravine in a graceful arc. In the middle of the long span, Tango looks down. One hundred and fifty feet below, he can just make out the stream winding its way through the Arroyo Seco Park. A stream that started up in the San Gabriel Mountains. Tango leans over the railing. Way, way down there is his dog, but he can't see the mutt. As if sensing this, Captain barks, urging his man to say the command *Come*. Tango wipes his calloused hand down his beard and tries not to think of what will happen next and how his dog will manage. Captain barks again but the man shakes his head, mumbling, "This time I'm coming to you. Just stay out of the way."

He pulls a wrinkled scrap of paper from his pants and holds it under a bridge light to read the words. Satisfied, he spreads the note across the railing, then places his pocketknife over it to weigh it down.

A car is approaching. Can't appear suspicious. Tango quickly pockets the paper and knife and looks up at the dark blue sky. He's surprised to see bright morning stars.

The car stops beside him. An old ragtop jeep, its roof made of vintage thick-striped canvas.

Tango ambles away in the direction the car came from.

"Sir?" A woman's voice.

Fuck, no one calls him that.

"Sir?" the voice says again and there's the sound of a car door opening.

Tango turns. With the glowing sky and bridge lights, he can see she's older. Maybe late sixties. Wild blond-gray hair that's not short like most women her age. Plaid shirt, jeans, cowboy boots.

If he can see her, he knows it is light enough for her to see him. His ragged clothes. His unkempt hair and beard. His mixed-race features. In a moment, she'll realize her mistake and leave.

"I'm in a bit of a quandary, sir. I wonder if you might help me."

Fuck, fuckity, fuck. "I can't help you or nobody," Tango hisses.

"I have a pending appointment and realize I've got things I can't take. I hope you might relieve me of these items."

"Damn it, lady, I told you already, I—"

"From the looks of it, you've hit a patch of hard times. Is that right?"

Far below, Captain barks once.

Tango leans over the railing. At the bottom of the ravine, his dog is now slightly visible in the growing light. "Stay, Captain."

"Your dog? In the arroyo?"

Everyone's always gettin' in his business. "What of it? You want to see his tags? You want to see his license?"

She takes a step toward Tango. "When was the last time he had a full stomach?"

"We eat okay, and it's none of your goddamn—"

"I"m sure you do right by him, but if you would just—"

Tango snarls at her. "*You* want to do right by him? I tell you what. You take him. Take care of him and give him that full stomach and a cozy bed. You can do that for *me*?"

"I can't take him. I'm—"

"I thought so. So don't make it my fuckin' fault!" Tango turns, marching angrily toward the far end of the bridge.

He hears the car door slam and the engine start—*GOOD*, he thinks—and the jeep screeches, racing backwards, passes him, and slams to a stop a few yards in front of him. The woman steps out and starts toward him, then stops, clutching her lower gut. She winces, takes a deep breath, straightens, and stomps up to block Tango's path. She squints at him. "What's your name?"

Fuckin' woman won't quit. The anger rises in him, as it always does. "What's it to you?! What's your name?!"

"I'm Agnes Sloan and you look overdone."

A hint of a smile wriggles behind Tango's mustache. This woman has huevos. He likes that. "S'pose I am overdone."

They stare at each other long enough for Tango to exhale and feel slightly less threatened. "I'm Leon Thibodeaux," he says. "But everyone calls me Tango."

The woman smiles and holds out a padded mailing envelope. "Please take this, Leon."

It's been years since anyone used his first name and the sound of it moves him to take the envelope.

Relief spreads across her features. "Thank you, Leon." And she puts out a hand.

Tango is stunned by the gesture. He wipes his palm on his grimy jacket, unsure if it's leaving behind dirt and sweat or gathering more, and takes hers.

She gives him a warm, firm shake. "I'm grateful to you. I'm sorry to interrupt your reverie. The morning stars are indeed beautiful. Now, please excuse me, I've got a lot to do before my appointment."

And the woman steps back to the ragtop jeep, revs the engine, and speeds off.

Tango watches her go, his hand still tingling from a human's touch. The light is bright enough now to make the colors of the ragtop visible. Red and yellow stripes. Reminds him of a circus tent.

He returns to the center of the bridge and looks down over the railing. Captain, still waiting, seems tiny so far away. Tango places the envelope the woman gave him on the asphalt.

Is it time?

It's time.

He resets the paper and pocketknife on the railing and takes a deep breath. Pauses. Looks down at the envelope.

Tango retrieves the envelope and peeks inside. He inhales sharply and turns to squint to where the jeep had disappeared. Takes another glance into the envelope. Looks up at the stars. They are beautiful. Focuses on the knife holding down the paper. Now what? With sudden resolve he scoops them up and calls down, "Come, Captain. We're eatin' good today."

And the matted mutt charges across the stream, hurls toward the steep embankment, slaloming around trees, leaping over boulders, scattering birds, galloping through thickets, up and up and up and hits the road, tears around the railing, races down the curving pedestrian path of the bridge until he reaches the man—LEAPS, paws high, tail wagging—and Tango circles his arms bearlike around the ecstatic dog.

When the stores in Pasadena open, Tango edges through the morning shoppers. People see him—his filthy clothes, his dirty beard and hair, his angry eyes—and quickly move to the edge of the sidewalk or step into the street. No one wants to get near the wild man stomping through the world with his vicious-looking dog.

    He pauses at the shoe store window. It isn't crowded inside. Good. He ties Captain to the hose spigot outside and steps in. The electronic bell announces his entrance and two referee-clad dudes quickly converge on him.

    "Help you?" one says with a decidedly un-friendly tone.

    First impulse is to punch the fucker in the nose to see the red run down his stupid black-and-white striped shirt. "Gonna get sneakers," Tango growls.

    "Today isn't free-athletic-shoe day," the second referee intones through his nose.

    "I got money," Tango says, waving the envelope in front of Tweedle Dee and Dumb. He walks toward them threateningly and they part like the sea for Moses. Drops himself in a chair and waits. Frantic whispers behind him. Tweedle Dumb steps up with, "What size?"

    Tango toes off a dirty, worn sneaker and lifts his equally dirty bare foot. "Measure it with the thingamajig."

    "You can't—you can't put your foot—it's unsanitary—contamination—there are rules. You have to leave."

    Tango stands and leans close to the man's face. "I will get a new pair of fuckin' sneakers, or I will contaminate every fuckin' item you have in here."

    The two Tweedles get moving. One opens a sanitary package with nylon booties and the other brings the foot-measuring device to Tango. He grabs the booties, slips them on, and has his foot measured.

"What kind of sneaker are you looking for? Hiking, jogging, sports—"

"Walking, asshole."

He tries on a pair and, to the relief of the referees, finds they fit.

One of the clerks holds open the box. "I'll pack them up for you."

"Wearing them."

The two Tweedles glance at each other, each undoubtedly hoping the other will chase the culprit when he runs. But Tango lumbers to the cashier counter holding his old shoes.

"We can dispose of those," one of the two says, holding up the wastebasket.

"These are still good, fucker. Don't you know anything?"

After paying, Tango steps outside—the startlingly white sneakers contrasting sharply with the rest of his aspect. He unties Captain and the two walk to the next stop, the Outdoors store. Again, he's confronted at the door and again, it's a fury-inducing encounter. Once he waves the cash, the clerks treat him like a dangerous Bigfoot and avoid confrontation. He leaves with a sleeping bag, sweatshirt, pocket knife, and renewed hatred for mankind. A visit to a grocery store is next. He chooses Whole Foods on purpose. He's ready to fuck with someone and everyone who shops there is fuckable and fucking deserves it.

The sliding door entry brings a coded loudspeaker announcement and a security guard hurrying to greet him. The man is his size but Tango knows no one is a match for his anger.

The guard puts a hand on his belt as if he has an invisible holstered gun. "Can't be here, man."

"Gonna buy shit. Got a problem with that?"

"We can refuse service to anyone deemed—"

Tango lifts the envelope of cash and pulls out the remaining bills. "I HAVE MONEY. YOU CAN'T KICK ME OUT! I HAVE RIGHTS!"

A gaggle of white women convene their shopping carts to watch. Something to tell their friends about later.

The guard steps closer to Tango. "Get the fuck out or—," he stutters trying to think of something original, then goes for the old standby, "—you're in trouble."

All of the women hold their cell phones high, recording what they hope will be something to post. Tango wants to smash their phones and bash their faces, but something about that old lady that gave him the money flicks into his mind. "You're overdone," she'd said. Old broad had huevos. The memory makes him smile inside, so rather than fighting, Tango gives the filming throng a guttural roar, gives the guard all ten fingers held up as a greatly augmented *fuck you*, and stomps out.

As Tango unties his dog from the lamppost, he shakes his head. "You don't know, Captain. You have no idea how fucked up this world is."

Lugging his bags, Tango leads his dog across the wide boulevard and down a side street to a little mercado. They won't have security. He can see they're suspicious but they just watch, keeping track of him from the convex mirrors over each corner. He buys a steak sandwich sub, several toiletries, and a dozen cans of dog food.

One more stop. The liquor store. Another bell rings his entry. The man at the counter takes in his visage and assumes he's been pan-handling enough to get a fifth of rotgut. No surprise there. Tango picks out the bottle of Scotch that will wipe out the rest of the cash. Takes it to the register.

"That one's not for you, bud," the man says.

Tango drops the last fifty on the counter. The bill is held up to the light and swiped with a marker, and the guy shrugs and gives Tango the few dollars and coins in change.

Pushing the cash back across the counter, Tango says, "Use this for the next fucker who ain't got enough." He slips the expensive Scotch into the middle of his new sleeping bag and snarls, "And don't fuckin' judge people, asshole."

He lugs out all his items, unties his dog and starts home. With the cash spent, Tango feels relieved. Now he doesn't have to figure out what to do with it all. But it's been an ordeal. A reminder. Stay the hell away from the world.

Staggering with his shopping bags, as he nears the Colorado Street Bridge again, Tango looks for the ragtop jeep, but doesn't see it. If he did, he'd thank that woman for interrupting his morning mission in such an unexpected way.

Checking that no one's watching, particularly cops, Tango edges down the steep embankment, switch-backing when the going gets tough, makes it down to the park's trail, hurries alongside the stream to just below the bridge, hops his familiar stones across the water, getting angry quacks from *Ducky* and her ducklings, hauls his bags up the rise, slipping through the thriving native trees and brush to edge behind the cement footings holding up the span. There in the cool, dark shadows, he sorts through his new accoutrements. Folds the plastic bags for later use, saves the receipts for bits of writing paper, lays out his toiletries, and unrolls his new bedding. What a bounty!

After feeding Captain, relishing half his steak sandwich sub, and resting luxuriously, he rolls up his old sleeping bag with his old sneakers. Next trip into town, he'll tote them to All Saints Church for use by others like himself.

The money didn't change his life, but—maybe it did. Tango pulls the wrinkled note from his pocket, reads it again, then tears it into tiny pieces and sprinkles the scraps into a green dog-poop bag. "Happy?" he asks Captain.

Captain thumps his tail against the new sleeping bag.

The day passes with no more drama. From his hideaway, he watches people come and go down on the trail. He sees a bobcat he doesn't recognize carrying a squirrel in its mouth. He snacks on wild plums. Evening brings the second half of his steak sub and another can for Captain. When he finally settles down for the night, Captain trotting in dreams beside him, he lies back with a real feeling of contentment. And in the far, far distance, up beyond the bridge, up through the deep canyon of the Arroyo Seco, there at the Rose Bowl, a concert is starting. He recognizes the beat as the wind carries the sound up and back, up and back. He knows this one and sings along, "You can't always get what you want—but if you try sometimes, you just might find, you get what you need."

THIS IS THE LIFE

IT'S DARK when I drive my Audi down into the Avalon Apartments' underground parking lot. Motor off. Visor mirror light on. Check my makeup. Smooth those too dark, too angled Liz Taylor eyebrows. Gotta do something with them someday. Re-do the lipstick and eyeshadow. Touch of concealer on my cheeks as the freckles are starting to show. Quick brush of my dark red hair that's sagging from the long day. Exit the car and take the elevator up. Cross the pool area, empty in the dark. Step upstairs. Put on my smile. Open the door to our apartment and toe out of my heels. Been too long with my feet crammed into a tortuous point. But it's part of the package. Drop my purse on the cream carpet, slip out of my blazer and drape it over a dining room chair.

Brent, across the apartment in the living room, coughs. He's in his day-off attire—white socks and shorts and Beta Alpha Psi t-shirt. His long body lies stretched out on the white couch watching the Bloomberg business report on TV.

In response to his cough, I say, "I'll put it all away in a sec. Let me just chill out."

Artisan bubble-infused glass from World Market goes under the fridge spigot.

"Water dispenser," Brent reminds me.

I dump the fridge tap water into the sink and set my glass under the spout of the expensive delivered water.

"We pay for it, might as well use it," he adds.

I move beside him and he lifts his socked feet so I can sit, then lowers them onto my lap.

A long drink and set my glass on the retro luggage-sticker

coaster. Look at the TV and the numbers that mean money. Look out to the balcony. We never sit out there. I wonder why. Maybe it would be nicer if there was a plant there.

"I should buy a plant," I say.

Brent clicks off the TV. "Tell me about your day."

I spent all day doing it, so I'd rather not relay it. I let out a slow, exhausted exhale. "Just another day making money—"

Brent drops his feet from their perch, twists his body to sitting position, places his rock-hard arm over my shoulder, and gives me a squeeze. "Damn straight!"

I twirl a ostentatiously demure, pink manicured finger in the air like a dull *whoop-de-do*.

"Don't gimme that," Brent says. "You're doing great. What happened last week?"

"I know, but—"

"What happened?"

"I got a promotion."

"You got a promotion *and* a bump in pay. You should be happy."

I should be happy.

"It took me longer to get that same promotion," he reminds me.

Maybe that's because I'm better at this than you, I think. I decide not to say this, choosing instead to say, "Maybe, just 'cause you're good at something, doesn't mean you're meant to do it."

"Yeah, do something you're bad at instead. See where that gets you."

"But is this really *me*?"

"You *create* you. And in my estimation, you've created a wonderful, successful you!"

He bends in and gives me a kiss on the side of my head. For some reason, this annoys me. He's trying to be nice and supportive, and I'm annoyed. What's wrong with me? It's from a long day. A long week. A long—nevermind. I should smile and talk about something else. "I got home kinda late. You already have dinner?"

"Uh-un, you can't wriggle away like that. I'm here to make sure you know how great you are. Remember what you told me about when you were in college? You couldn't focus. A semester of this, another of that. You were all over the map. You changed your major like changing your underwear. And now look at you. You aced the CFA. You know how many people don't pass? Eighty percent! And now you're a fucking Chartered Financial Analyst! And who, I ask you, at age twenty-five, has such an impressive investment portfolio and 401K? You're kickin' ass and building wealth. You've created a high-octane, girl-power career!"

Does he think high-octane, girl-power is what I aspire to? "But what if I don't want—"

Brent puts a finger on my lips to stop me saying more, then looks to the ceiling, pleading wordlessly for help. Probably looking to the heavens for assistance, but in the apartment above us lives a pretentious dude in I.T. Maybe my boyfriend's pleading for I.T. help.

Brent slowly removes the finger squashing my lips against my teeth. "Baby cakes, you want to, you go right ahead and give up your career. See if you can afford this incredible apartment. See if you miss the pool and jacuzzi and gym downstairs. See if you can afford to get the haircuts and manicures and fancy clothes and shoes and eat out at your fav spots. You'll have to give up living in Los Angeles. People leave this town in droves, because why? Because it's UNAFFORDABLE! Yet you afford it! You don't worry about money. Wonder why that is."

Why does he always have to talk this way? Why can't he listen for one minute? I'm just talking about a feeling. It's not like I would quit my job. "I know, but—"

"But nothing. You know what you need? You need TLC ASAP." Brent pulls me into a musclely hug and rubs his knuckles across the top of my head hard enough to hurt. His version of TLC, I guess. Holding me back at arm's length, he looks into my eyes with compassion, or condescension, and, altering his expression once again, WILLS ME to come around to his view of reality.

He's being supportive. He's being positive. Be grateful. I strike up my best agreeable smile. "You're right. I've got everything a person could want. This is the life! You're the best, Brent."

He spreads his arms wide so I can take in all that is Brent.

I stand and step to the balcony sliding door. It would be nice to get a plant. We could sit out and look down at the pool. Do something other than the usual. I turn and collect my purse, blazer, and heels to sequester them in their rightful places. Stop to smile at my boyfriend. "On my day off Monday, I'm gonna go to a nursery and get a plant. Wouldn't that be nice?"

Brent stretches out again. "Maybe not a good plan 'bout the nursery, babe. The carpets are pristine, and we don't want to bring in dirt, and leaves, and bugs. Go to IKEA and get an artificial one. It'll look the same but with no muss/no fuss."

THE LAST NIGHT

IT'S LATE when Agnes Sloan parks her circus-striped ragtop jeep in the narrow driveway of her Eagle Rock house. She considers the mission to be a complete success. She especially liked that scraggly-bearded man, Leon, early in the morning on the bridge. He was trying hard to be belligerent, but she saw right past that. He'll make good use of the cash, or at least numb himself for a while. *He looked about to do something rash,* she thinks. *Hope he didn't.* But then she remembers, what might *look* rash, isn't always rash.

Cross the tiny lawn. Touch the Bird of Paradise plants guarding the walk to the house, unlock the front door and step inside. Look around the room. Lots to see and remember.

There isn't much left to do. She double-checks the top drawer of the bedside table. All good. Waters the plants. Straightens the handwritten will and the business card on the formica kitchen table. Pours a glass of wine and sets out the pills. Hopefully all will go as planned.

Turning on the little burro lamp, she toasts the world and starts taking pills.

SUNDAY MORNING SOUNDS

SUNDAY MORNINGS, Tango likes to sleep in. He calls it that even though he's *out,* not *in.* Since that night of hell as a kid, he finds sleep difficult indoors. The terror always comes back.

Before he arrived on the streets, when he was in those locked rooms, he'd hum or talk or scream to drown out the chaos in his mind. The sounds in his head carried the house splintering and the water rising and terror. Sounds in his head also carried explosions and screams of pain and zip/pop of bullets. But mostly the sounds in his head carried Mama yelling. Berating him. Telling him how bad he was. There was no drowning that out.

Here, under the bridge, he has the drone of traffic and rustling leaves and gurgling water and singing frogs and quacking Duckie and crickets and owls and coyotes yipping. Here, there's enough soothing noise that it keeps most inner sounds away.

And as he lies in his new sleeping bag, drifting in and out of sleep on this Sunday morning, he's got Captain snoring beside him, a taco truck playing Mariachi music in the distance, and all is right with the world.

SUNDAY AND WE'RE FREE

I WAKE with renewed energy to make the most of this life. It's Sunday, and Brent and I both have the day off, so let's live! Hop out of bed. Slip into my new mid-calf black capri pants. I bought these recently and love the beatnik look. If my red hair was black and cut short with ragged bangs, I could be playing bongos and talking about poetry with Jack Kerouac. Do my makeup and hair and step out.

Brent is at the kitchen counter loading his Keurig coffee maker. I put my arm around his waist and bump hips.

He looks at me like something's wrong, so I ask, "Something

wrong?"

"What are you, a boy in jolly old England?"

"Huh?"

"The knickers."

"Capri pants."

"I don't care where they're from!" Brent SLAMS down the lid of the coffee maker. Something cracks. He turns to me. "You look ridiculous. Change."

I go back to our room and shove the capri pants in the back of the closet and slip into the short dress he bought me.

"There's my best girl!" is the reaction when I return.

I give him my best girl smile.

The Keurig sputters and coughs, dribbling dark liquid into the cup while spreading sideways droplets over the white marble countertop.

"Damn it! These fucking machines never work!"

I see his fist clenching, so step in to fix things. "Let me make you a cup. I'll bring it to you."

He stomps away and I refill the Keurig, slowly close the lid and lower the cracked handle to gently pierce the little cup of grounds. The machine valiantly performs its task but I pick up my phone and order another just to be safe.

Bring the cup of coffee to Brent, sulking on the sofa. Still lots of ways to make this day great. Let's try one.

"Brent, how about we go to the beach? Santa Monica or Venice. Watch people. Swim. Soak up the rays."

Brent sips his coffee and looks at me as if considering the options. "Watch people. Swim. Soak up the rays. Can't we do that down at the pool?"

"But it's not the ocean. No vast horizon. No sound of waves crashing—"

"No gulls squawking and shitting overhead, no children, no trash, and SAND EVERYWHERE! Not to mention the drive. You want to spend two hours getting there, two hours back, slogging on the 405, finding parking, trekking across the beach to do what we can do here?"

Of course, he's right. "You're right," I say. "Let's watch people, swim, and soak up the rays here. I'll get my suit on. It'll be fun!"

"I'll see you down there, post java."

The pool is crowded, as it's Sunday. Or the pool *lounge chairs* are crowded. I pass several of my neighbors on the way to an empty spot. No one looks at me. Everyone living in the Avalon apartment complex is the same. We're young professionals with probably *everything* in common, but none of us acknowledge each other. Guess we have that in common as well.

I stretch out on a lounge under one of the sun umbrellas. Spending most of my time at the firm or in the apartment, I'm quite white and burn easily.

Of all the people out, no one is actually *in* the pool. In fact, I've only ever seen Erika swimming—SPLASH!—*speak of the devil.*

I watch her doing laps. Erika's different from everyone here at The Avalon. Number one, she's older. Probably in her fifties and with a body like someone in her fifties. She looks like that Picasso painting of Gertrude Stein. I wouldn't be out in a bathing suit if I were her. Number two, she's, like, not American. She's got an accent. And, most different, she's the only person here who isn't afraid to be friendly. She introduced herself one day and ever since hasn't stopped attempting to chat. Whenever I see her, I always feel guilty. Like she knows something secret about me and whatever it is, I'm letting her down. I've managed to avoid a conversation so far, as I've been either on the way somewhere or on the way back. Now, poolside, I'm trapped if she sees me— Damn!

She climbs out of the pool smiling and heads my way. Rubs her towel over her short-cropped hair, dries her stout arms and legs like she's not in public, then drapes the wet cloth on the lounge next to me and lies back. "Dinnae see ye partakin' o' this recreation on a regular basis, luv. T'is grand to see ye sheddin' the toil."

She sounds like she's from somewhere like England or Ireland or one of those places they speak English but with accents.

She pats my arm. "And yee'r smart tae be oot o' the sun. Wi' yer red hair, fair skin, 'n—hold on—"

Erika squints at me intently, then grabs a corner of her wet towel and reaches it toward my face. I jerk back.

"Oh, luv, I were nae plannin' tae assault ye. Just cleanin' off the—"

She daubs my cheeks.

"Ach, there they be. I suspected as much. Beautiful ferntickles."

"Ferntickles?"

"Freckles. Where the fairies touched ye. Yer blessed. Do nae cover 'em. Sech a bonnie look f'r a lass."

I don't know what to say to that. It feels strange, her pointing out things I've always hidden and saying they're beautiful. Could freckles be beautiful?

I glance around. People are looking at us. Because she's weird. Weirdest person here. I wonder why she chose this apartment complex with its young professionals.

"Erika, what brought you to The Avalon?"

"Massive feckin' mistake. Had a young friend make the arrangements for me rental. I'm picturin' a nice spot in the town o' Avalon on Catalina Isle. Me mate finds me this Avalon. Sure, she thinks it's grand as she's aboot your age. She travels all the time, toilin' for The Guardian, so I thought she'd be the one tae make me plans."

I don't know what she's talking about. Is The Guardian a foreign term for God? "That's nice," I lie. "Do you like it here?"

"Bleedin' awful. No one says naught t'me but you. I'm invisible. And the town is stifling. You canne walk anywhere. No cozy shops for tea, or a pint and a bit of gab. Everyone's off making their mark. Still, I shouldnae gripe. The isolation gives me time to focus on me work."

Her work. Knitting. Crossword puzzles. Solitaire. I hope Brent comes down soon. I'll be able to excuse myself. "What work is that?" I ask mindlessly.

"I'm an artist."

That's a surprise.

"What kind?"

"Sculpture, assemblage, painting."

I wonder what she paints. Kittens? Gnomes in flower gardens? I ask her.

"Abstract expressionist figurative work. De Kooning mashed with Mary Cassatt."

My one semester as an art major was enough for me to know the painters she's talking about, but not to imagine the result.

"You fancy it?" she asks.

"Painting?"

"Living here."

An awkward flush rises on my skin. This feels personal and threatening, and if I answer wrong, I'll be judged. I stutter out, "Well—I—it's perfect for my life right now."

"Then grand for you, luv. Enjoy that perfection whilst ye can."

And not-in-his-bathing-suit, Brent walks up and declares he's got us tickets to a movie at the Arclight.

I hop off the lounge, wave to Erika, and step beside him. I'm excited to see a film. Brent never wants to participate in what he calls *inconsequential dreck.*

"What are we going to see?" I ask.

He presses his knuckles against my back to get me moving and leans close. "I made that up. I'm not spending my day poolside with that old hag."

A surge of anger moves over me. I vow I'll talk to Erika again and see her art. But how does she paint and sculpt with the cream wall-to-wall carpets that all the apartments have?

EVERYTHING GOES PERFECTLY

THE VARIOUS MOVING PARTS of Agnes Sloan's plan quickly fall into place. She efficiently orchestrated every detail. Years of working within the motion picture industry had made her aware of just how swiftly things could be done if they were arranged correctly. Her neighbor does as she asked and completes his task. That sets in motion the Sunday pickup at the Eagle Rock house she paid extra for, the subsequent paperwork and procedures, the overtime at the funeral home and crematorium. She had anticipated everything, and everything is taken care of with efficiency and speed. Were she still around, she would be quite pleased.

IS THIS A SCAM?

THE PLANTS AT IKEA are quite nice. Better than I imagined. Brent's right. No muss/no fuss. I get two. A tall faux Kentia palm that'll be perfect by the balcony and a tabletop Monstera Deliciosa facsimile.

Back home, I park in our underground lot and take the elevator up to the lobby for mail. Of course, there's nothing but junk adverts and FINAL NOTICE scam bills. Who writes letters anymore? Several neighbors are checking their boxes. We ignore each other.

Pass the pool to get to our apartment stairs. Erika is doing laps and calls out, "Hello!" I pretend to stagger under the weight of my bags of plants as a reason I can't stop. She pretends to laugh.

One thing I like about having my day off on Monday is having a day on my own. Brent works Mondays. He gets to have a day on his own without me on Saturday. Sunday, we're off together. On my Mondays, I get to put my hair in a ponytail, wear jeans and a t-shirt, and spend only minutes on the makeup.

As I test my faux-botanical acquisitions in various spots around the living room, my phone rings. The boss. I have to take it. He doesn't understand personal time. I put him on speaker. He reminds me for the zillionth time about next month's derivatives conference and what I need to do to prepare. As if I don't know. I'm the one presenting the analytic modeling. It's not like he has the first clue of how to even do the math. As I listen, I try the small Monstera Deliciosa plant on the coffee table beside the Van Gogh book and Saveur magazine. Have we ever looked through these publications? I haven't, and I bet Brent hasn't. Why are they here? I guess to make the plant look at home beside them. Looks like it was artistically placed by the interior decorator of IKEA.

My phone beeps over the boss's monotonous monologue. Another call. Maybe I can take it and not miss a thing. I'm about to try when I hear a timid female voice in the background on his side. "Mister Gromley? You wanted to see me?" I recognize the voice. The new young intern. No surprise that my boss quickly ends our "discussion." I answer the incoming call.

It's someone "Joseph," and something about a person I don't know, and now someone's supposedly dead. Is this a scam? Or maybe I'm supposed to know them. I'll play along.

I tap into my semester as an acting major. Voice quivering, halting, nearly sobbing—"Oh, god—this is terrible! So sorry. You have my sympathies. Sorry for your loss."

The voice on the phone is perturbed. "No, you don't understand. You have MY sympathies. I'm sorry for YOUR loss."

This *must* be a scam. I'll string them along until I get the request for a gift card. In my most vulnerable, naïve voice I say, "I don't know who I lost."

"I've been telling you. Agnes Sloan."

No one I know. I'd like to fuck with this asshole, but how to do it? "I think you have the wrong number—"

"Are you Prestonia Cheswick?"

Okay, he knows my name. But that doesn't mean this isn't a scam.

"Hello? Are you indeed Prestonia Cheswick?"

Should I say yes? They advise us not to say that word in a scam call 'cause they can record your 'yes' and use it to sign up for things.

"That's my name."

"And I'd venture to guess there aren't a lot of Prestonias out there, so I'm sure I have the right number. I need to meet with you to go over the papers and get your signature to finalize this. I'm downtown and it looks like you're in Studio City. I'd prefer not to drive up, so let's meet halfway."

I don't like that he knows I'm in Studio City. "You can't just call here asking to meet."

"Ms. Cheswick, please listen to me. This is about your inheritance."

"Yeah, and first you want me to put down a deposit as a goodwill gesture and then you fucking disappear. Get a life."

"This is not a scam. I'm with GitRDone Concierge Service. Agnes Sloan hired us. Look up GitRDone.com. Git with an R and Done."

"Anyone can make a fake website. Fuck off," I say and end the call.

Asshole thinks he can pull one over on me. Might as well be a Nigerian prince.

My phone rings again. I swipe to ignore it.

I look up GitRDone.com. The website has lots of pages. Five star Los Angeles Concierge Services. Peace of mind. Lifestyle Assistance. It has good design. Clear writing. An address in downtown Los Angeles. There are quite a few pictures of men and women in business attire. Check Google entries about the firm. It's on Yelp and other business sites. Could this be legit? But who is—what was the supposed dead person's name? *A* something, *S* something. Alice Stone? Angie Shore? Annie Snore? I can't remember, so I can't look her up to see if *she's* real.

My phone dings. A picture of a paper written in neat cursive script titled: *The Last Will and Testament of Agnes Sloan.* Ding. Another picture with a close-up of my name written in that same cursive writing. Ding. Text says *Astro Diner in Silverlake. Half an hour.*

Fifteen minutes later, makeup and blow-dry-styling done, in my grey pantsuit with white shirt, exuding the *serious-and-confidently-competent* demeanor, I'm curving past Warner Brothers Studios on Forest Lawn Drive to meet this scammer fellow at the Astro Diner.

Pull into the parking lot and I gotta expound about the architecture. The diner is like Godzilla stepped on it, bending it in the middle and making the roof touch the ground like a big broken grin. There are impressive metal columns of green with big holes cut in them. This is the Googie space-age style favored by Los Angeles diners of the mid-century. I know this as pointless trivia from my misspent semester as an architecture major.

It's cool inside and I'm greeted by an old-fashioned revolving cake display. A waitress suggests I sit anywhere, but a young businessman in a window booth waves me over. He's also in his s*erious-and-confidently-competent* attire.

As I approach, he holds up his phone. There's the picture of me as the firm's financial-analyst-of-the-month. I mostly like this picture. They gave me a day's warning, so I did my best makeup and styling job. Except, the picture doesn't look like me 'cause they photoshopped my eyebrows so they weren't so Liz Tayloresque. I mean, it makes me look more normal, but they should have asked first.

The man closes his phone. "Image searched you, so I'd know. I'm Joseph and this meeting is gratis for you now, but once I'm past fifteen minutes, the retainer begins."

"So get talkin'."

"First, I need to see your I.D.."

"Not showing a thing to a scammer."

He sighs heavily and checks a very expensive-looking watch. "Okay, listen, I get that everyone is a scammer and you don't trust a soul, but this is legit and I'm not having you sign these papers if you aren't Prestonia Cheswick. Not to mention, I have to notarize the contract, so please give me a break.

"Show me yours and I'll show you mine."

Joseph pulls his wallet from his jacket and slips his license across the table. I take a picture of it with my phone. *Ha! Take that!*

He wriggles his fingers for mine. I hand over my license and he pushes an app on his phone, slides the screen over the card, scans the other side as well, and hands it back. "Can we get to business?"

I flash him a fake smile as my indication to proceed. He explains that my first cousin twice removed, Agnes Sloan, died and, as she had hired GitRDone to navigate several logistical issues pertaining to her passing, once I sign the papers, he's able to release the inheritance. I nod and he opens a briefcase, removing that handwritten piece of paper: *The Last Will and Testament of Agnes Sloan.* It's in that neat cursive script and there's my name as sole beneficiary. I'm thinking—*Why did this woman I've never heard of put me in her will?*—so I ask, "Why did this woman I never heard of put me in her will?"

"Ours is not to wonder why, ours is but to fulfill the agreement." He sets two contracts before me. "Sign, please."

I look through the papers, and they seem quite legitimate, and I feel his watch ticking, so I sign the two copies. He signs them as well, gets from his briefcase a stamp pad and stamp and fat leather-bound book and he takes my thumb print and gets my address and signature, then with his official stamp, notarizes the bottom of both contracts, packs all that away in his briefcase, stands and places on the table one of the copies, a shoebox-sized cardboard case, and a key.

"What's the key to?"

"Your house. Address is there—last page of the contract. No mortgage. Taxes and insurance have been paid through the end of the year."

"What's in the box?"

"Part of the inheritance."

"Hold on, hold on—"

"I'll hold on if you want to pay $500 an hour, fifteen-minute increments."

I wave for him to get lost.

I haven't been to the funky neighborhood of Eagle Rock before. It's next to Pasadena and I guess it used to be full of artists and immigrants. I've heard it's getting hipper and has some cool foodie restaurants, but Brent and I usually go to the West Side of

LA for our eating excursions.

It's late afternoon when I turn onto Los Robles Street. The houses are a mix of different architectural styles: a 1970s stuccoed Ranch with terracotta Spanish tiles, a Gothic Revival with steeply pitched roof, a Mid-century-Modern with topiaried box shrubs, a Pueblo Revival with viga beams sticking out from adobe walls, and a Minimalist concrete box. No consistency on this street. It's clear there's no HOA directing people what to do with their property. One little yard has been converted to desert xeric landscaping of cacti. One has several cars on the front dirt patch. One has toddler toys scattered across a dry lawn. This is not my kind of neighborhood.

I park in front of the small house this lady Agnes Sloan bequeathed to me. There's a crazy looking jeep in the driveway. Looks like it belongs in a circus. The house is a 1920s Craftsman bungalow right out of the movie *Chinatown*. Birds of Paradise plants guard either side of the minuscule yard's walkway with orange beaks that threaten interlopers. Am I interloping?

I tentatively ring the bell. No response, so try the key.

It's very weird to open a door to a stranger's house that's now supposedly mine. Push and enter, and it's a dark room but beyond is a bright kitchen glowing with the sun's western light. I step in and close the door. Take in Agnes Sloan's smells. Perfume. Talcum. Old wood. Furniture polish. Maybe smoke. Marijuana? I thought this house would at least be cleared out and thoroughly cleaned and disinfected. She might as well have stepped out for groceries.

Move into the kitchen where the setting sun's western light pours through the slatted-glass window and glass panel door. The kitchen is what someone might charitably call old-timey. Or maybe an art student'd call it funky. Nothing is modern or updated. The toaster and blender look as if they're from a mid-century magazine-advertisement. The light hanging over the 1950s formica table is a wide, saucer thing, like that space-age Googie style. The place seems clean but there's something creepy about the lack of slick, shiny surfaces. How clean can it be? The cabinets look like they've been painted a zillion times. Bumps and ancient drips. They're an ancient avocado green and the walls are a haystack yellow. No white anywhere. Totally bizarre.

On the formica table, I set the shoebox part of the inheritance beside a ceramic dog toothpick holder, chicken and rooster salt and pepper shakers, retro plastic napkin holder, and a small clock. The time is correct. I thought clocks stop when people die.

Open the cabinets to dishes and glasses and bowls and platters and pans and towels and pot holders and absolutely everything is mismatched, one-of-a-kind. Not one set. It's a chaos of colors and patterns and sizes. How could someone live like this?

I unlock the back door and step onto the balcony. It's a nice-sized space with two mismatched wooden chairs and a wicker table between them. A metal roof covers it and stairs lead down to what I guess is a backyard. I can't really see down there because dense wisteria vines coming from below surround the stairs and balcony and have been trained to frame only the distant view. Hanging below this frame of wisteria leaves and flowers is a strand of a few colored lights that look like plastic hot air balloons. They must be pretty in the dark. Beyond them, the view goes on and on, over what must be many neighborhoods, all the way up to the curved hills of Griffith Park. There are trees blocking where the Observatory would be, but maybe in the winter when they lose their leaves, it might be seen—the place where James Dean fought in *Rebel Without a Cause*. An incidental factoid I remember from the one semester as a film major. Yes, I had a lot of disparate majors before finding my way.

I'll have to go down to see the yard another day. Right now, I want to see the rest of the house. Close and lock the door and turn to take in the kookiness of Agnes Sloan. The furniture is from a wide mix of eras. Probably some is inherited, and some is from thrift stores or antique stores, and it's all eclectic. There's no sense of a motif or style through-line. The walls are different colors—Turquoise, Dusty Rose, Robin's Egg Blue, Lilac—even within one room! There are paintings and art that look like real people made them, and not all are good. Photos, books, knickknacks, doilies, lamps, pottery, cushions, little rugs—a serious overabundance of stuff. And way too much personality. It looks like a lived-in mess rather than something from *Architectural Digest*. Her houseplants seem healthy but there are too many of them. Still, I grab a glass from the kitchen and, as I can find no delivered water dispenser nor spigot in the old-style refrigerator, I fill the glass from the sink and soak every plant. I'll try to keep them alive until I can replace them with a select few faux ones.

Now to the next part of the inheritance. Using an ancient bakelite-handled steak knife to cut the tape, I open the box on the kitchen table. Inside is a clear plastic bag closed with a twist-tie. A bag of gray powder. What could this—Oh. This must be Agnes Sloan.

Makes me think we're all going to die. We're all going to die, and who is going to be there to unpack my ashes? Brent?

I lock the door of the house and drive back in the last of the rush-hour traffic to the apartment in Studio City. The clean white textured walls and marble countertop and recessed lighting and silver appliances and matching dishware are a welcome relief from the chaos of Agnes Sloan's home in Eagle Rock. Everything here is clean and sleek and minimalistic. It's peaceful. Nothing here has personality. In fact, even our personal items don't have personality. The pictures on the wall are from World Market and one is the ubiquitous museum exhibit poster. An exhibit we never attended. But that's why it works! There is no emotional baggage to anything. Nothing is overlayed with a memory or event. It's easy living. It makes me comfortable. If I go to my neighbors' apartments here at the Avalon, I'll see the same things. Maybe we really are completely the same, but what's wrong with that? We're a tribe and that works.

It's almost seven so I slip out of the pantsuit and shimmy into a tight, low-cut blouse and designer shorts. Do a quick styling to bounce the hair around the shoulders. Mascara, lipstick. About to put a touch of concealer on the—what did Erika call them?—where the fairies touched me?—something tickle. I hear the front door slam and decide to let the freckles be. As I put everything away, Brent comes into the bathroom dripping from the gym. He gives me a slap on the butt and peers at me in the mirror. Taps my cheek.

"Your spots are showing."

"Kinda cute, huh?"

"Make you look like a snot-nosed waif. Better without."

Okay. Back to the concealer. So long, fairy touches.

When I return to the living room with my approved face, Brent compliments my choice of plants. He's already eaten but offers to microwave a Whole Foods chicken pasta meal for me.

"Thanks. Not hungry."

"You okay? You seem off."

"Just tired."

"That's what happens when you have time off," he quips like he does every Monday.

And Brent talks about his day at the firm, as if I always want to be caught up on the goings-on taking place when I'm not there.

I pretend to listen, and in a while we go to bed with the dual alarms set for seven. I lie staring at the textured ceiling, listening to the air conditioner, wondering if Agnes's house has this frigid air.

Why didn't I tell Brent about the inheritance? I'm just tired. I'll tell him tomorrow.

I replay what I remember of the house and try to picture what I can do with it. I could hire *Got Junk?* to clear it out. Get the inside stripped and painted white. It could probably clean up well and sell for a lot. Tomorrow I'll check out the backyard and see what work it needs!

MORE BOUNTIES

TANGO LUMBERS through the quiet Pasadena neighborhood.

He's in his usual outfit. T-shirt. Khaki cargo pants. Green crushable hat and army jacket. The brown beard is scratchy in the heat but he's used to that.

Beside him, Captain ambles at pace. Sun is high now. It's way past the early livable part of the day but this street is cuddled with huge shading trees. These were no-doubt planted back when Pasadena was an aristocratic realm of old money, far away from the acting riffraff of Hollywood. Despite the cooling canopy, Captain pants heavily by Tango's side. He needs water. Tango eyes the stately porches, searching for an offered bowl, or anything.

A small glass-fronted mini-library suspended on a post faces the sidewalk. People sure are strange, thinks Tango, but he reckons he'll take advantage of that strangeness. He slips quickly up to the structure, opens the little latch and pretends for a moment to peruse the contents. He knows exactly where the second-hand bookstore is and figures this will be quite the windfall. A glance to the house and the street and he scoops up the books, slides them into his duffle bag, shuts the door—

"What the hell are you doing, man?" comes a male voice from the house.

"Checking out books from this mini-library," answers Tango.

The man on the porch is wearing pressed tan pants and a pastel pink button-up shirt. He's white and soft and entitled but barefoot, so doesn't look like he's about to venture onto the hot walkway. Captain barks to make sure of that.

The man puts his hands on his hips to assert his authority. "That's a free library for people in the neighborhood. Not for you."

Tango takes a step toward the man. "I'm neighborhood," he growls.

"Bullshit and you took them all. You're not letting other people read these."

Tango takes several more steps toward the man. "YOU DONE, MOTHERFUCKER?" He will beat the shit out of this asshole if he says another word.

The man backs up, stumbles over his WELCOME mat and slips in the door. He pauses and then says, "There are ways to survive besides stealing. *Food for thought.*"

Tango stomps up the stairs, and the man slams and locks the door.

"Yeah, well, fuckface, in selling these, I trade *thoughts for food!*"

Tango gives the door a kick and because there is a horrified gasp from inside, he does it again, then turns away. He rejoins Captain on the sidewalk, but after a few steps the anger gets so high that he returns to the man's yard and grabs the mini-library and yanks it back and forth violently until the post cracks at the base and he lifts it by that post and swings it overhead and smashes it to the ground, scattering pieces across the pristine lawn. *That'll teach the fucker,* he thinks.

Going to the bookstore means trekking quite a stretch of Colorado Boulevard in the sun but it'll be worth it.

"This will bring in a pretty penny, Captain."

Captain gives his matted tail a single wag to acknowledge his name but doesn't look up.

The bookstore is cool and dark, and Tango is sorry to leave Captain tied to the bike rack in the sun.

Tango has been in this shop several times to drop off his finds. It's surprising how many books can be found in the city. The train station. Bus stops. Coffee shops. And these bizarre giveaway yard libraries. As he steps in, the few patrons look up and their alarm shows. DANGER! He will never be able to get away from this reaction and it infuriates him. *Fuck them! You want danger? I'll show you danger!*

But the clerk Mario steps up. He knows Tango and smiles in a real way and waves the homeless man to the register.

Mario's a brown-skinned young fellow. He's a different shade than Tango, but neither could pass for white. Mario's Filipino. Lots of those folks in the neighborhood. Always welcoming. Tango suspects they treat him with respect because of his being a

US veteran. Is it because of that horrible Bataan Death March during WWII when so many American and Filipino POWs died together? Mario told Tango that his great grandfather Felix was on that march, and after surviving and moving to the USA, ended up at 99 years old marching up and down his driveway, tapping his cane to ring out each step as a defiant, *I'm still here!*

Tango unpacks the books for Mario. As he passes one across, the face of a buzzcut-haired woman smiles up from the cover. He pauses, staring at the photo.

"Pema Chödrön," Mario says. "She's cool. Some righteous Buddhist wisdom in her. Might wanna keep that one."

"I don't fuckin' read, Mario."

"This one's worth it."

Tango shrugs and, to make one of the few people who treats him well happy, he slips the book back into his duffle bag. Besides, this Pema woman's friendly looking and he can use that.

"Eight dollars and fifty cents."

"Done," agrees Tango.

Now loaded with a more livable amount of cash, he exits to untie his dog. "You still have cans of the good stuff under the bridge, Captain, but let's keep to our routine, eh?"

Half an hour later, Tango emerges from the market with a small bag of dry dog food and a box of cereal. He crosses the parking lot to check the dumpster.

Dumpster diving brings forth usable vegetables, fruit, and slightly moldy cheese. "Lots of good stuff, Captain."

Tango slips the goodies into his duffle bag, crosses the lot, walks two blocks to the bridge, winds his way down the embankment into the park, steps across the stream and scrambles behind the cement footing to his home. He drops his gear on his new sleeping bag, pulls out the book with the warm face of Pema Chödrön and props it against the dog food bag.

After serving Captain, Tango cuts a strip of mold off the cheese and tosses it to his dog. "We'll piece on things tonight."

With slices of mold-free cheese, an apple, a brown banana, and a sagging cucumber, he sets down to eat and opens the Pema book. "So this is Buddhism." In a moment he exclaims, "What the fuck! This is bullshit! You're demented! Thoughts and emotions are real! They are!!!" And he flings the book deep into the darkness where the ground meets the bridge.

EVENING AT HOME

THE INVESTMENT FIRM JOB is the same as usual but I can't seem to focus. I'm excited about what can be done with the house in Eagle Rock. I look it up on various real estate sites and all the estimates say it would sell for over a million dollars. Last time it sold, probably to Agnes Sloan, was way back in 1986 for $190,000. Nice profit!

I should tell Brent about it, but I've decided I'm going to wait until it's fixed up and ready to sell. He wouldn't see its potential in the state it is now.

The minute I'm off work, I hurry to Brent's office and tell him I've got to pick up some feminine products and will be home later. That always works to avoid any questions.

Drive to Eagle Rock. When I pull up to the curb and step toward the front path, a short, muscular Latino man on the next-door patio stands from his chair. He's wearing a white t-shirt and black shorts and his head is shaved. A gangbanger. Fuck. Oh, no—he's stepping through his gate toward me. Should I try to get back into the car or rush to the house? Why didn't I check out this neighborhood! He's almost here! I turn toward the car and—

"Hola! I'm your neighbor Alberto." He's got a hand out and a warm smile.

I don't know what to do, so I shake his hand. "I'm Prestonia. Uh—glad to meet you."

"We wondered who would move in after Agnes died. Such a sweetheart, that woman."

I try to smile in a way that will end the conversation and step up the path to the house.

Alberto walks with me. Is he going to try to come in? I should buy pepper spray.

"You need anything, or anything breaks—I fixed just about everything in Agnes's house—sorry, your house, so help is a door away. Later, I'll introduce you to mi esposa Teresa, and niños Yasmina and Luis—only when you've got a moment. Buenas noches."

He walks away with a wave.

As I unlock my door, he yells across our little yards, "I hope you won't mind repetitive music. We'll be having teens over for a few weeks. Rehearsing for Yasmina's Quinceañera."

He waves again and pops back onto his patio chair. Damn! That wasn't what I expected. Maybe this is what they mean by *neighborly*.

I go into my house and take in the scents. What would be cool is to spend the night here. I could make lists of how to remodel. I'll make something up. It's after 6:00, so Brent'll be down at the gym and won't answer. I dial and leave a message.

"Hey, honey, I ran into an old high school friend at the drug store. I introduced you to her once a while ago. Maggie Sheamus? Remember? Anyway, she's just moved out from a long relationship and is in a new condo and feeling vulnerable, so I'm gonna stay over at her place tonight. I'll see you at work tomorrow."

Now I've got the whole night to myself in this crazy house! I turn on all the practicals—another term from my filmmaking class. Regular household lights are practicals as opposed to movie lights. The practicals are completely bizarre but they make an inviting warm glow. There's a western-style lamp with a burro carrying little saddlebags and the shade is translucent plastic with scenes of the desert. There's a bright red triple-layer shade that's very mid-century modern. Everything in this house is eclectic and mismatched, no single style, no motif, no time-period, no color-scheme, but it kinda works because it's from one person's taste. Nothing like my apartment. My apartment tries to look like a pristine space in *Architectural Digest*. I try *not* to have my space reflect my personal taste. Actually, I don't even know what my taste is. Do I have any taste?

I step onto the balcony and walk down the steep stairs to the backyard. Whoever this Agnes Sloan was, she sure liked fruit trees. I recognize fresh figs and oranges and grapes and plums and walnuts, but there are lots of exotic-looking things I don't recognize and I'm not about to take a bite of anything strange. Maybe I'll learn what they are before I sell the place.

My dinner is fruit bounty from the trees I know. Okay, time to dictate notes of what to do to remodel the house. I get my phone out but wonder if there might be anything to celebrate with. Poke around in the cabinets to find a few bottles of red wine, one has a post-it note with that same cursive writing saying *Cheers!* I locate her Yosemite souvenir corkscrew to open that bottle. Pour a glass and step out the back door. I sit on the balcony overlooking the yard. I should get started on the remodeling list, but the sun is beautifully inching close to the mountains. Take a sip of wine. Oh! Nice.

Maybe I could just put a hold on thinking about remodeling. Watch the sunset for once in my life.

I turn off my phone.

The sun glows orange and tickles the top of Griffith Park. A great swarm of birds swirls overhead, green feathers sparkling in the light. They look like parrots. Could that be? I thought that was just an old LA legend.

I find the switch for the strand of little hot-air-balloon-shaped plastic lights and they glow orange and green, framing the view, as the wisteria blooms flutter in the cooling breeze. The hills of Griffith Park cut a black silhouette against the pastel bottom of the darkening sky. There's the first star! Hello! Mmmm. Night-blooming jasmine!

This is the life! Thank you, Agnes Sloan!

DUMPSTER DIVING

TANGO ENJOYS PAWING through dumpsters unless he's

confronted by assholes while treasure hunting, but he's always got his antenna up and is ready to bash someone. What he likes about the dumpsters is the surprise, the anticipation, the mystery of it all. Like when he was a kid, he liked listening to the radio rather than playing his Mama's few CDs. It was much more thrilling to have a favorite song come on when it was unexpected, than to put that song played by choice.

This evening, he's behind the Goodwill store. They throw out shit that people don't want. Stuff that's broken or not working. Lots of coffee machines, snapped DVD discs, torn clothes, cracked plates. Tango retrieves two twisted spoons and bends them back into shape. He saves a fake yellow carnation, several National Geographic magazines, a pair of sunglasses, and a chipped serving bowl. Lifting the top of a busted hamper, he finds a silver metal container. As he pulls it out, he's surprised it's heavy. Turning it, he reads the engraved writing: Clayton Robert Linley. 1957-1979.

"Fuck. Hello, Clayton. You were young. Someone cared enough to have you cremated. So why are you in the trash?"

Maybe someone didn't know this was in the hamper. Maybe they did and didn't want to deal with a person's ashes.

He looks at Captain. "You know we can't leave young Clayton, don't you? Leave no one behind."

Tango slips the urn and the other treasures into his duffle bag and heads back to Colorado Bridge. Before stepping down that steep ravine into the Arroyo, he scans the traffic in both directions.

Give it a moment, he thinks. *That lady in the jeep may be about to pass.*

Tango waits and watches. He really wants to thank her. The sun is gone and the sky glows blue. As he scans each approaching car, the lights along the bridge spring to life. Surely now she'll appear as she did that morning. But that ragtop jeep with its red and yellow striped canvas is nowhere to be seen. Captain moans his impatience, and Tango heads into the brush to step and slide his way to the bottom.

There, nestled below the bridge in his hidden home, he sets the found urn to perch on the highway footing, carefully facing the engraved words toward him. "Clayton, this here dog is Captain, and I'm Tango. Good to meet you."

LOOKING FOR AGNES SLOAN

AFTER THE SUN SETS, it gets chilly, I go back inside to look around Agnes Sloan's house and find out more about my benefactress. Her bedroom has a bureau, small bookshelf, two bedside tables, and a closet. It feels creepy to even think of opening them. Like I'm snooping. But she's dead, and this is my house now, so I guess I should get over that feeling.

I open the closet. Pinned to a shirt in the center is an envelope. I remove it and pull out a folded note. Across the top, in cursive writing: *Are you snooping!?*

Yikes! It gives me a jolt. Is she a ghost watching me!? If she can write this note, what else can she do?!

Open the fold to more writing—*Ha ha, just my silly sense of humor. Have at it, Prestonia! It's all yours.*

After I collect my nerves, I continue my snooping. She wasn't a fancy dresser. Mostly jeans and plaid button-down shirts. Several cowboy boots. Bureau has the usual underwear, socks, and bras in the top drawer. Next drawer holds a selection of flannel pajamas. Fun ones like for kids, but adult sized. Cowboys roping steers. Bears and buffalos. Elephants and clowns. Since my staying the night was a spur-of-the-moment decision and the satin nightclothes Brent bought me aren't here, I borrow the cowboys and slip into them, hanging up my work clothes as carefully as I can so they'll be okay for tomorrow.

Agnes's books are a mix. There are mysteries and westerns and bird identification and techniques of grafting fruit trees and a well-worn massive book of the films of Paramount Pictures. I immediately open it to the index just to check. *Sullivan's Travels* is listed and I go to that page. There's a picture of Joel McCrea and Veronica Lake but that's it. Too bad.

On my phone, I google the name Agnes Sloan and find there is a crystal glass named Agnes from the Sloan Glass company. I find an Agnes Sloan lived in Texas and died in the nineties. Social media has several Agnes Sloans but they're alive and living in places like Scotland and Australia. There's one on Facebook who hasn't posted in a while and was a researcher for Paramount Studios but retired a few years ago. Being local, along with the Paramount Pictures book, I suspect this might be my Agnes Sloan.

In the bottom of the hutch in the living room, I find a photo album. Baby, child, teen—a kid growing up in their family. The cars are old-fashioned, like from the early 1960s. Teenagers with long hair and bell-bottoms. I don't know what Agnes Sloan looks like, so I'm not sure who's who, but there's a high school senior picture I assume is her. She's got strawberry blond hair and smiles with her mouth closed. Who doesn't at seventeen? Pages move through the years. She's dancing at a party. Toasting to the camera. Blowing out candles on a birthday cake. In front of the Ferris wheel at the Santa Monica Pier. With students in a classroom. Pretty much the same pictures we all have. Here's a picture of a group of women standing in front of the Paramount Pictures Melrose gate. That must mean she was a researcher there. Another picture, she's got her arms around a woman, both holding up champagne flutes. A great picture of her by her ragtop jeep, arm on it, with a wild grin. A picture of someone cutting roses from a bush. Another of a carousel and another of her sitting under a tree by that carousel.

I power on the old-fashioned computer in the second bedroom-turned-office and look around the desk drawers to find a password. The screen opens to the weather in Eagle Rock. She didn't use a password! Old people are so clueless! I almost turn around to warn Agnes about the dangers of Wi-Fi. Still, it makes my search easier.

Look through the history in her browser. Amazon. News. Amazon. Ancestry.com. Weather. Estate Planning. Concierge

Services, GitRDone.com. End-of-life care. I click on Amazon. What she bought should tell me a little about her.

Wool socks. Western novel. Fountain Pen ink. Lined journal.

Hmm.

If she wrote in a journal, maybe I can find it and really learn about her. I find it in a very obvious place—the top drawer of the bedside table.

Last entry written in that same neat, old-fashioned cursive script as her will:

Hello. If you're reading this, i'm dead. I'm going to take a wild guess—ha, ha—and assume you're Prestonia. I know you're wondering why you, but all I can say is, there were no kids in my life, nor relatives I wanted anything to do with, (they hated my so-called 'lifestyle,' ergo fuck them) so I went to Ancestry.com and found you. My brother was your grandfather. So I'm your first cousin twice removed. I think! I didn't google you as I thought I might find out something about you that would make me second-guess this and I'm tired. All I know is you're young and probably could use an inheritance of this sort. The house is paid off, and the insurance and taxes are paid through the end of the year, so enjoy! The jeep in the driveway works and is fun to drive. Keys in the bowl by the door. What little cash I had I've donated or passed along to folks.

I have uterine cancer and am not willing to spend my days being ill, so I set up everything with a concierge service. Your neighbor Alberto is a great guy and I'm sure he got the wheels in motion the next morning, like I asked. After all, I didn't want to fester too long after taking the pills. Might smell up your house.

If you're reading this, everything went as planned.

Now to my request. They are supposed to have cremated me and I'm guessing you have a box of me. I'd like you to scatter my ashes by the carousel in Griffith Park. I met my wife Tracy there. We didn't have long together but it was loving, and when she passed, I scattered her by the tree beside the carousel. I want to mingle with her.

If you have a camera on your phone, please take a video of the scattering of the ashes and say these words: Darling Tracy, I'm joining you now in substance and in spirit. With you forever. Love and peace, Aggie.

Then post it on your social media and mine. (The computer manages my passwords.) At least someone should know. Thank you, Prestonia, and enjoy your house!

Your distant relative and benefactor,

Aggie. (Agnes Sloan)

Oh, boy. I do not want to do this. I don't want to deal with dead-people ashes or being out in public in a park doing creepy stuff and supposedly filming creepy things and especially saying those words and then posting it! Posting it! What are people going to think!? I'll just slip her box into the back of the closet. She'll never know.

I turn the page.

P.S. Don't you dare think of not doing this. I'll haunt you.

I guess I have a mission.

GETTING HUMAN AGAIN

TANGO WAKES EARLY. He stares up at the underside of the bridge. There's something niggling at his brain. He's so mad all the time. So angry. Could that be—not real? He wiggles out of the sleeping bag and scrambles above his camp into the dark space where the bridge meets the ground. Paws through the dirt for the book he threw. There she is. Still smiling.

"You gotta explain this, or I'm done with you," he warns and slides down to hunker back into his warm bed. Opens the book and starts reading and mumbling, "Man, oh, man. You're shitting me."

After an hour of reading things that make no sense, he packs Pema's book into his duffle bag with his clothes and the expensive bottle of Scotch, then tucks his sleeping bag lower in the space behind the bridge footing, and whistles for Captain, but pauses—what if someone comes and discovers his spot? What if they take Clayton? "Better safe than sorry," Tango reminds Captain. He packs the urn in the duffle bag and they make the difficult climb out of the ravine for town.

The walk is cool in the early morning and he and Captain move quickly, as the shops and stores aren't open yet and no one's on the street to mess with him. As they turn down the open expanse below the massive power lines, Captain squirms with excitement, but Tango is preoccupied.

"Book is a bunch of bullshit," Tango says to his dog. "I can tell you're happy and that's real. Fuckin' Pema lady makes no sense."

Reaching the dog park, Captain hears a familiar bark greeting him.

"Your girlfriend's already here, Captain."

Inside the fence, Tango unclips his dog's leash just as a Dalmatian races up wagging and spinning.

A scraggily, old man makes his way slowly to the newcomers. Hand out, smile ready. "Glad to see you, Tango."

"You too, Bob."

Tango notices that Bob is looking the worse for wear. At eighty, his tall frame is stooped, unable to support those once-broad shoulder and he seems more frail than ever. The sacks under his eyes, normally large, now look like they're bulging—full of tears. His white jagged hair juts up as if reaching for some god, pleading for release, and the white beard looks like it was descended from a porcupine.

Tango puts a hand on Bob's shoulder. "You look tired, friend. What's going on?"

"Put my house on the market. Hard to be there after—everything."

"Can I do anything to help?"

"No. Maybe later after it sells. You'd better get going to snag that first spot. We'll talk after."

Tango looks around the vast dog park. "Where's Captain and Daisy? I can't see them."

Bob squints and then puts two fingers and a thumb together to form a triangle and puts his fingers next to one eye and peeks through the hole.

"What are you doing?" Tango asks.

Bob shows him the configuration, saying, "If you make a tiny pinhole, it becomes like a small camera aperture and makes things in focus. Try it."

Tango does and—"I can see them! That's very cool, man!"

"Now get going or you'll be late."

Tango holds out a finger and reaches in his duffle bag. "Came into a touch of cash. Got you a present."

He hands Bob the bottle of scotch.

"Now hold on," Bob says. "I can't have you spending your money on this."

But Tango's moving away, a salute-wave to his friend, and he steps out of the dog park.

Twenty minutes of walking past nasty people looking frightened of him and abruptly avoiding him, he's at All Saints Church and joins two men waiting at the door. Tango glares at the men, daring them to make eye contact. Neither does. They focus on the pavement or something on their hands. Tango wishes one would meet his eye so he could take out his frustrations on him.

Frustrations, Tango thinks. *I know why I'm frustrated, but aren't frustrations feelings? That stupid book says what I feel isn't real. I don't believe it.*

As it nears eight, more men arrive. They are all ages and races, shapes and sizes. Some stagger from drink. Some stumble from the years, or conditions no one is treating. Some walk with the bounce of toughness, but none looks proud or happy.

Exactly at eight, the door opens and the men go in. They know the way to the basement laundry room, where they load dirty clothes into the machines from their sacks or bags of possessions. Then it's the showers to luxuriate in the warm water and pine-scented soap and silky shampoo. As the clothes wash, the men sit for their weekly haircuts and shaves. The volunteer barbers are young and they tend to move on quickly, as they are practicing on the men before they get out in *the real world*. Tango always has to explain that he wants the beard tidied, but doesn't want it shaved off. "It's easier to keep whiskers than it is to find a place and razors to shave." And no making the hair short. "I'm not a grunt anymore, man."

The outreach guy comes in as usual and reminds them that housing is possible and there are programs for mental health and substance abuse issues. Tango nods like he's thinking about it, but that's just to be polite. He likes his spot below the Colorado Street Bridge.

After slipping into clean, lovely-smelling clothes, folding the rest and stacking them neatly in the duffle bag, he collects his sack lunch and thanks everyone. This next bit is the part he likes best. Stepping out into the world and feeling human. No one looks at him like he's an untouchable. He holds his head high and walks with the steps of a man at home with himself. A song pops into his head. A refrain from olden times. The only words he knows are "Just direct your feet to the sunny side of the street."

Someone slams hard into his back, causing him to lunge forward and catch the fall with knees and palms hitting cement. The duffle bag drops and is snatched up by the teen boys swerving around him, laughing and shouting, "Get a life, bum!" racing down the sidewalk screaming with their victory. Tango struggles to his feet and runs in a limping lope but can't get close to catching them. He stops. People stare at him like he's done something wrong, and the joy and peace of the morning have vanished. His pants are torn at the knee and he's bleeding at the spot and his hands are scraped and there's no way he'll find his belongings. Unless they toss everything as they paw through it. It's damn annoying but it's only clothes—

And Clayton!

"FUCK!"

He's got to find Clayton!

Looks down the next perpendicular block. No sign of anything. The next. There's some trash in the street. Tango moves toward it. A brown paper bag and other litter. Closer, and it's a smashed apple, a sandwich torn apart with a dirty boot-tread embossed into it, scattered potato chips, and a crushed, leaking can of soda. Couldn't just discard it, had to destroy everything. Tango knows the feeling. Destroying everything is cathartic, even if it fucks up your life. He picks up what he can of the mess and throws it in the next trash barrel he sees.

Keep limping down the street. Another something in the road. Might be clothing. He makes his way toward it. It's an army-green t-shirt and he recognizes the stain down the front that never comes out. Okay. Gather that up and keep on. A block later, the second pair of cargo pants. A block later, his thick socks, still balled together. He tucks them into the pocket of the jeans. Next, his new sweatshirt. Maybe he'll find all his clothes, but what about Clayton?

The street ends with Pema's book in the middle of the T-intersection. Tango picks it up and gently wipes off the grit. The woman on the cover is still smiling. Maybe that's Buddhism.

The street has ended, so which way to go?

Scanning left and right, his eye catches a silver glint by the gas station across the street. He crosses and it's clear—Clayton's urn. On the ground. Top no longer on it.

Fuck.

Closer now. The top is near the air pump for tires. And beside it is a swath of gray ash across the asphalt.

Fuck.

"I'm sorry, buddy. Give me a sec and I'll see what I can do."

Tango kneels, rips the title page from Pema's book, uses it to scoop up ashes and slide them into the empty urn. Over and over.

"What you do, fella?" a heavily accented man says.

Tango turns to see a Middle Eastern man in mechanic's overalls approaching. Shit. What to say.

"I spilled something and want to clean it up."

The man comes closer, eyes squinting at the urn. "I see what is." He shakes his head.

Tango gets back to his work.

"No, no, no," the man says adamantly.

"I have to," Tango insists.

"No. I spray." And the man marches away.

Fuck, the guy is going to spray Clayton's ashes away. Tango gets to work furiously. Page-scoop after page-scoop goes into the urn, but there is still a lot left. Footsteps behind him.

Tango stands abruptly and puts a fist up as a warning. "Stay the fuck back, man. You ain't doin' that."

The man holds a big green trash bag up to Tango. "You hold, I spray."

Tango shakes his fist again. "I'm telling you, get outta here!"

The man puts four quarters in the tire air-compressor machine and the rumbling starts. He pulls the black hose nozzle toward Tango.

"I'll fuckin' bash your head in, man."

"I help. It work. You hold, I spray."

Tango looks at the man and finally understands. He grabs the trash bag and carefully spreads it behind the bulk of the ashes and holds it open. The garage man sets the nozzle in front of the ashes and slowly squeezes the lever. The stream of air pushes across the ashes, swirling them into the bag.

Grins erupt across the faces of both men. It works!

Spray after careful spray sends all the ashes they can find into the bag. They work together to gently pour those ashes from bag to urn.

Tango presses the top of the urn down and stands. He shakes the hand of the mechanic. "Thank you."

"No problem."

Tango bundles the urn with his clothes and Pema. The mechanic hands him the garbage bag. "To carry."

With his belongings together in the bag, Tango starts toward the dog park. It's amazing how different humans can be. Some hurt and some heal. He always expects the former. He's always surprised to encounter the latter. And because of that expectation, he always reacts with hostility. With that garage man, he expected the hurt, but his feelings flipped from anger to confusion to surprise and finally gratitude. The anger wasn't based on reality, but expectation.

Fuck. Maybe feelings *aren't* real.

A block away, he finds the duffle bag. Damn kids. A whole lot of messing with him for nothin'. He loads his belongings into this last discovery, then adds the urn on top.

"I'm sorry if I missed any bits, Clayton. We'll have to figure someway to take care of you. Can't have this happen again."

Limping, hungry, and tired, Tango keeps walking and thinking. "You're one of the lucky ones, brother. I'm not gonna even be dust. I'm gonna be rotting under that bridge. Picked apart by ravens or coyotes. Cause I ain't worth shit. No, worse, a jogger'll find me when they leave the trail to pee and I'll be dumped in a mass grave with the rest of the unwanted and forgotten. No one'll give a fuck. But you, Clayton, someone gives a fuck about you. *I* give a fuck."

Tango hobbles up to the dog park fence. Once inside the gate, Bob hurries to him. "What happened?"

"Bunch of hooligans had fun with me," Tango says, dropping onto a bench.

"Let me take you home. You can shower again and clean up."

"Nah, it's fine. I'm done for today. *Overdone* as some might say."

"I'll keep Captain and you go back to All Saints. They don't close all that 'til three."

"It's gonna be packed by now. I can't face it."

Bob shakes his head. "You gotta let a man be your friend, Tango."

"Damn it! Leave me alone! I don't want any fuckin' friends!"

Bob leans close. "You're angry and that's okay. But I'm not going away just 'cause you yell. You're bleeding and I bet you lost that bag lunch. The lunch you always eat here and share with your friend. The friend you spent money on for a nice bottle of scotch that I know you won't partake in. You can be as angry as you want, but you're coming with me, and I'm not taking no for an answer."

Tango blows out a slow exhale. "Okay."

They clip Captain and Daisy to their leashes and Bob leads the way to his Volvo wagon. It's a short drive up to Sierra Madre in the foothills of the San Gabriel Mountains. Inside the modernist home, Bob starts the water boiling for pasta while the clothes swirl back and forth in the washing machine and under the shower's strong blast, Tango tries to hold back sobs. How can life be such a mix of good and bad?

DINNER WITH BRENT

TWO MORE NIGHTS spent caring for my imaginary friend Maggie. Rush to Agnes Sloan's house after work, but now I plan ahead and bring financial-advisor clothes, high-heels, makeup, and hairstyling supplies. I also bring jeans, t-shirts, socks, and sneakers to change into after work. The cowboy pajamas are so fun and comfy I keep using those.

The evenings are spent deliciously carefree. Sitting on the back balcony, watching the sun set over Griffith Park. Reading *Riders of the Purple Sage* by Zane Grey by the little burro lamp. Snacking on mulberries and figs directly from the trees in the backyard.

Brent must be missing me because he taps on my office door at work and suggests dinner at the Water Grill. The restaurant is downtown, so it's convenient. It's time I paid attention to him, so I give him that best-girl smile and agree. We both drive our separate cars the few blocks and use valet parking.

Inside, he takes my arm and escorts me behind the maître d' leading us to our table. I know he likes to impress me, so I act impressed. When the waiter comes for our order, he turns to me with, "Allow me." It's not a question.

I nod my acquiescence.

Brent makes a big show of pointing out various items on the menu to the waiter and closes it with a hard SNAP.

I can only hope he hasn't ordered a revenge-meal to get me back for staying away for a few days.

We're served a tiny dish with olive oil floating a brown circle of balsamic vinegar and the waiter lifts a roll with silver tongs and moves it toward Brent's bread plate.

"Whoa. Dude! Ladies first."

The waiter moves the roll to my side of the table, deposits it gently, then sets Brent's roll carefully on my boyfriend's dish.

For some reason, I don't feel happy. Is it the cost of this place? The rolls probably cost twenty dollars. Brent thinks money is for this. Maybe it is. I don't know what money is for, but it isn't to prove how much you have to throw away on tiny portions.

The waiter arrives with a dish. "Artichoke stuffed with wild mushrooms in a pomegranate glaze."

Two inch-wide artichoke hearts with the stem attached, a smidge of dark mash that might be mushrooms, and a brushstroke of red across the plate. Undoubtedly costs more than the rolls. I take a bite. It tastes like—nothing. How can something taste like nothing?

"Everything copacetic, baby cakes?"

I smile the usual one.

I'm sure some people sitting across from Brent would find him *The One*. He presents himself as an Alpha Male. He has the right clothes and skin color and demeanor. He has gelled hair that covers his fear of balding, which he's preoccupied with, despite reality. He works out every evening, so he's got an unnaturally cartoonish muscular form. In a suit and tie, he looks like he'd be an expert at just about everything. Realistically, he is only slightly proficient as a financial advisor to investment clients. He's an advisor in the very capitalistic sense. Meaning, he's making money for the firm rather than the investors.

I look at him, wondering why I don't feel a lot of love right now. He fucks pretty well, proud of his ability to give the requisite attention to my side of the bargain. He doesn't complain if I want to forgo meat or processed food every once in a while. But why are we together? No, I don't mean that. There are reasons. Lots of them.

We met at work and went on a date, and had sex, and talked of bull markets and hedging strategies, and we have a lot in common. We work at the same investment firm. And he wants to help me. He understands my moods. He knows how much time I've wasted pursuing frivolous interests. Semesters even! He keeps me focused.

I don't like his opinions. I don't like the way he treats waiters and waitresses. I don't like his anger. I don't like his stroking of his black American Express card. I don't like who I am with him.

I poke the artichoke heart and remember we each drove here from work, so I have my car, and without even planning I say, "I've got to sleep over again at my friend Maggie's tonight. She's really been sad."

"You haven't seen her in how long, and suddenly she's usurping all your time."

"I want to be there for her."

Several veins sprout on Brent's neck. If they move up farther, he'll be Medusa, with a head full of snakes. No, I remember from that semester in Art—Medusa was a woman. Probably her anger made her a monster. But this is a man's anger. Not monstrous. Normal.

Brent presses the anger down and whispers across the table, "If you're fuckin' someone else, just tell me."

"I'm not fucking someone else. This is an old friend who needs me. It's only been a few nights."

Brent rips his roll in half, smashes it into the balsamic/olive oil mix and jams the dripping clump into his mouth.

"Ree-ite-n-oo-ite-n-omey-or?"

"What?"

My boyfriend swallows and rinses with thirty-dollar gulps of wine.

"Three nights and tonight and how many more?"

I'm not liking this. Best defense is to move on. "I told Maggie I'd be there by now. I'll pay for—"

"I don't want your money! This is a fuckin' date. Like romantic and shit. You're spoiling it."

I get up but he grabs my wrist. Hard.

"That hurts."

"Are you really going to leave now?"

"Let go, Brent."

He lets go.

I'm shaking. Is it fear or anger or both? I hope he doesn't notice. "I'll see you at work tomorrow."

Brent's veins tell me that Medusa is imminent. I leave.

The drive to Agnes's Eagle Rock home is tense. Or rather, I'm tense. I don't know how to deal with Brent. Should I ask for a hiatus? I should have taken a semester of psychology. Or martial arts.

At the house, I pull in front of the narrow driveway built for cars from 1921. They never anticipated SUVs or massive Prickup Trucks. Agnes's jeep fits nicely, but my Audi doesn't. I should try driving her car. The wild red and yellow stripes of the ragtop are way too flamboyant for me, but maybe I should be flamboyant.

I let out a very vocal sigh that tells me just how tense I am. But I'm safe now.

Inside Agnes Sloan's home, I turn on the burro and red, mid-century practicals—

A knock on the door. I freeze. I don't want to talk to that neighbor Alberto, or meet his wife, or children, or—

"Open up, Prestonia. I know you're in there. This isn't your friend's condo."

I open the door to Brent but don't invite him in.

"Who's house is this?"

"Mine. I inherited it last week."

"Bullshit. Who lives here?"

"I live here. I live here and no one else."

Brent pushes the door trying to squeeze past me.

"Stop! I don't want you coming in! Leave!"

"Who's house is this!?"

"It's mine! I inherited it!"

"From who? Your parents aren't dead."

"From a person who wanted to give me something."

"Bullshit."

"I inherited it from a stranger. She willed it to me."

"A stranger gave you this house."

"Yes. I don't know her and never did, but she willed it to me."

"No one does that. Move over—I'm gonna see who you're sleeping with."

"You're looking at her and she wants you GONE!"

A man's voice comes from the sidewalk. "Everything all right?"

I click on the porch light over my head. It shines down on Brent's angry face and, behind him, the gleaming shaved head of my neighbor Alberto.

Brent grabs my wrist hard as he turns. "It's okay, she's my girlfriend."

I pull at my wrist but he's got it held tight. "No, it's not, and I'm not," I say. "Not okay, and not your girlfriend. Let go of me!"

"You need to let go of her, man."

Brent glares at Alberto and flings my arm away, slamming it into the door. The pain shoots up to my shoulder. I try to keep my voice steady. "Leave, Brent. You and I are over. I'll pick up my things tomorrow."

Brent stares at me, shaking with rage. Those veins are coiling, poised to start rattling.

I peer around him to Alberto. "Do you mind waiting until he leaves?"

"I'll wait."

And Brent gives a guttural ROAR and his fist flies over my head to SMASH the porch light. Glass shatters and rains over me as Brent stomps to his car, gets inside, slams the door, and screeches off. He's probably glad to have the last word—soundwise.

Alberto hurries to my side, gently brushing my hair and shoulders free of glass. "You did good," Alberto says. "I've got an extra porch light. Click off the power at the switch, and I'll fix that tomorrow."

"Gracias, Alberto," I say, trying not to cry.

"De nada," he answers, raising a fist, which I find incredibly comforting.

ANOTHER MOON

A SOUND WAKES TANGO. What was that? He sits up listening. No concert or football game at the Rose Bowl but even Captain has his ears cocked. There's muffled yelling and a woman screams.

Something bad is happening and Tango better investigate. He slips out of his silky new sleeping bag, into his jeans and sneakers, and flips his army jacket over his t-shirt against the coolness. Another distant scream. Tango clicks Captain's leash to the dirty collar, looping the end around a tree. Tied there, the dog can't follow, but even so, to retain the illusion that there's a choice, Tango puts a palm up, whispering, "Stay."

Inching down to the trickling river. Dappled light sparkles on the water. Dappled light where there should be darkness. Light from a full moon, only in the wrong part of the sky. Tango creeps along the path, and through the treetops—there it is. A large, brilliant moon. Step closer and several silhouetted figures stand in the path. Whispers between them. An electronic double beep and someone yells, "That's a cut. Moving on."

The figures get bustling. Tango inches forward. By the open meadow, several white trucks gleam in the light of a massive white orb held by a crane and lit by spotlights—the artificial moon. The reflected glow illuminates the entire movie crew. Everyone is moving fast, carrying cables, chairs, props, clipboards.

A young woman with a headset notices Tango. "You can't be here."

This is exactly what he always expects. *Get lost. Go away. We don't want you here.* The anger rises in him and the screaming words move across his tongue. But he stops. This is one of those moments he's been reading about, isn't it? He breathes out the rage and says, "Sorry."

"No—we're turning around now. This set is hot. Go back to Extra's Holding and we'll call you."

When Tango doesn't move, she points. "Where you checked in. By Kraft Service."

Tango follows her finger. People rush past him. Any moment someone will grab his shoulder and holler at him—but there must be a hundred people here and none of them are paying him any mind. As he moves toward a kneeling man undoing thick cables, he stops. Does he dare be seen?

"Excuse me. Kraft service?"

The guy looks up and there is no anger in his face. No judgement. Just a man looking at another man.

"By the genny," he says.

"Genny?"

"Generator. Follow the hum."

Tango thanks the man, listens, isolates a hum, and heads for it. In the circle of several movie lights, homeless men stand around a table laden with food. Cheese, red vines, bagels, chips, mini-sandwiches, coolers of sodas, and large coffee dispensers. The homeless men make way as he moves into the light. They don't look right. Dirt smudges have been haphazardly smeared across cheeks or backs of hands. A shirt has a pocket ripped. Jeans cut at the knees but not fraying at the slice.

These men are talking and snacking, but it's clear they're not hungry. Does he dare? He grabs a few squares of cheese and pops them in his mouth. No one says anything. So far, so good. As he gets himself a cup of coffee, he listens to the men. They ramble on about agents, and notices in BackstageWest, and sides, and a friend who got Taft-Hartleyed into SAG. Tango curls his palms around the thick, paper cup and takes a sip of the hot liquid. Hot fucking liquid. Man, o'man. When was the last time?

"You look really good, dude."

Tango turns to a young man in a plaid shirt and ripped sweater with a streak of black grease across his forehead. The kid grins, shining his perfect white teeth in the artificial moonlight. "You look like the real thing."

Tango nods, knowing he should be embarrassed, but hell, he looks like the real thing, so—"I do my best."

A young guy with a headset steps up to the group. "They're ready for you. Same as last time, only it's the reverse."

Tango follows the men to a wide spot on the path. A blond, impossibly thin woman in a torn white t-shirt and panties stands as several people apply makeup and tease her hair.

"Not too messy. Keep her beautiful," a male voice yells from the dark trees.

An older bearded man steps up to the group of "homeless men" and leans close. "Remember. Energy. Terrify her."

"Last looks!"

And the hair and makeup people rush to the men, touching up grease and dirt. One looks at Tango, raises his hand with fingers dripping with some dark goo, but Tango catches his wrist. The guy looks bewildered. "You're good, honey, but this is CAMERA. Gotta play it big." Tango shakes his head and the man moves on.

"Roll sound."

A thin kid darts in front of them with a board with lit electronic numbers racing by. "Scene 28 Baker, take one." and he smashes the top of the board down and races away.

"And ACTION, KIM!"

Tango doesn't know what to do. But the thin woman wearing almost nothing does. Kim screams and races down the path.

"ACTION, HOMELESS!"

And the men take off after her. Tango follows. The guys sound like raging monsters. Pounding feet and guttural yells. Kim screams in terror. Tango pushes himself, wills himself, passes the others, closing the gap between him and the terrified woman. Any moment and he will be at her. Just when he can reach out and touch that bare shoulder, he spins to face the raging men and, arms wide, roars his fury at them. They freeze. Kim stops and turns. Tango roars again, fists swinging toward the gang. The men back up. A moment of stasis. Tango strips off his jacket and puts it around Kim's shaking shoulders.

"CUT! What the fuck was that?!"

Kim stares at Tango.

The older bearded man marches angrily into the group. "Who the fuck is this fucking—"

Kim turns to him—a hand up. "Tell Mark I want to see him. This is exactly what I was talking about. We need to change the script. Not every man is an asshole. We need to have someone step in like this. Just like this man did. I'm not being placated this time."

The bearded man grumbles into his walkie, "Everyone take five."

Kim whispers, "Thank you," to Tango as a woman rushes up to exchange his ratty army jacket for a long, down coat. Kim smiles at Tango and marches off to the director.

Slipping back into his army jacket, Tango hurries toward the genny's hum. Kim was happy with what he did, so maybe he deserves a special treat. Like these cheeses and a bagel and mini-sandwiches and—*ooo, now there's salami!*

With his army jacket loaded, Tango trots away. He passes a man arranging cables by the humming generator. A loop of tape rolls hangs from the guy's belt.

Tango leans over him. "Hey, man, can I get ten or so inches of the strongest tape you got?"

"Gaffer's tape okay?"

Tango nods and the man noisily peels a wide grey strip from a roll.

Tango holds the tape dangling at arm's length and takes a last look at the fake homeless and their shining teeth and the hanging moon and the sick story and turns to trot back to his secret home at the bottom of the bridge. Captain growls a scolding greeting and watches Tango carefully curl the wide tape around the top of Clayton's urn, sealing it shut.

"Guess what, Captain. Time for Kraft Service!"

And a feast of cheese and bagel and salami and three mini-sandwiches is shared between them.

CLEARING THE AVALON APARTMENT

I WAKE UP to birds singing instead of an air conditioner's hum.

I'm late for work but don't care. Slip into jeans and a t-shirt. Got lots to do. Call my boss and tell him I'm not there because I'm feeling sick today.

Mister Gromley sighs over the phone. "Your boyfriend Brent looks pretty bad as well. You think it's catching? I'll send him home—"

"No, no, I just have really bad menstrual cramps. Don't think that's Brent's problem."

Mr. Gromley mumbles something unclear and quickly hangs up.

I open my front door to leave and come face-to-face with Alberto's belly. He's on a step stool putting in the new porch light. "Hola, just finishing. Flick the switch and we'll see if it works."

I flick the switch and the light pops on.

"Thank you so much, Alberto! This is so amazing of you!"

"De nada. I picked up the big pieces of glass but you'll need to sweep to get everything. Hasta luego."

Wow. I can't understand this kind of behavior. Why would someone do something for someone else for no reason?

I lied to my boss about being sick but as I drive to the Studio City apartment, I start to feel sick. I know it's because I'm returning to where I don't ever want to be again.

I step into the Avalon Apartments' office and tell them I'm leaving. Give them the Eagle Rock address for any mail and borrow their rolling cart. Cross the pool area. No sign of Erika. Oh well. I would have liked to say goodbye.

Up in the apartment, I don't have a suitcase or any kind of luggage because I don't travel, so I pack three huge garbage bags with clothes and toiletries and load them and the three boxes of my college stuff (from my different semesters), and one box of childhood memorabilia onto the cart. Take a walk around the apartment. I don't need any of the kitchen stuff or any of the decor, but I grab one of the artisan glasses and hurl it into the sink. It shatters wonderfully.

Look around the living room. If only these were not faux plants, I could spread some real DIRT around. I grab the large

IKEA Kentia palm and bring it to the bedroom, slide it under the covers on my side and tuck it in. Your new partner, Brent. As faux as I was with you.

Guess that's it. Wheel everything out and, crossing the pool area, I see Erika.

"Hey, Erika." I step up to the water's edge. "I'm going to be leaving The Avalon. Got a little place in Eagle Rock I'm moving into until I sell it."

"Oh, luv, I hope it's a grand relocation. You and yer fella?"

"No. Just me. We broke up."

"Ach, I'd say I'm sorry, but that'd be lyin', so I won't. Good riddance t'im."

I nod. Good riddance indeed. "Bye, Erika. Great to meet you."

"You likewise, luv. Best o' luck t' ye."

And I turn away, getting choked up. *What makes her so fucking nice all the time? Who does that?*

I go to the underground lot and load the boxes and garbage bags into my car and wheel the cart back to the office. Then step again out to the pool and Erika.

"I wondered if I could see your sculptures and paintings before I leave?"

She is clearly overjoyed. I just hope I can say something nice about them.

Her apartment layout and furniture are the same as ours—but everything is entirely different. As Erika changes out of her bathing suit, I look around. The white couch is covered with a brightly colored South American tapestry. The lampshades are draped with flowery silk scarves. There are colorful area rugs over the wall-to-wall cream carpet and many REAL, LIVE PLANTS. It's dramatically vibrant.

When Erika emerges, she's dressed in striped bell-bottom jeans, a colorful Hawaiian-style shirt, and a vest with clouds painted on it. I've never seen her except beside the pool in a bathing suit. Now she looks wild and eccentric. She takes me back into the bedroom/studio. The floor is covered with paint and plaster-spattered tarps. The bed is pushed against the wall, and the remaining space is for painting and sculpting. One after another she shows her work.

The paintings are incredible! They really *are* a mashup of de Kooning and Mary Cassatt! Large canvases of homey scenes, mothers and children, people sipping tea, reading books—but with vibrant swirls and slashes of paint. Very active and warm and loving.

The sculptures are wild. She takes existing objects and incorporates them into plaster shapes. One is a heavy green glass ashtray with sculpted vultures perched around the edge.

I like everything she shows me. I should say something. Can I give a compliment? It's not cool, but should I?

"Erika, these are, I don't know—they're—like—wonderful."

Wow, that was dangerously over-the-top. Bad move.

Except, she's clearly pleased and asks if I "fancy a cuppa." I nod and soon learn a "cuppa" is hot tea. She makes it in an actual teapot with bag-less tea and serves it in delicate teacups with saucers and little spoons and matching cream and sugar containers on a tray. I could be in a Masterpiece Theater show. The tea is much stronger than any kind I've had and wonderfully flavorful. We sip and talk and I tell her about inheriting the Eagle Rock house and Agnes Sloan. When I finally have to go, we exchange phone numbers and I add, "I work Tuesday through Saturday but give me a call and come visit any time I'm off. There's probably a teapot hidden away in one of the cabinets, so I'll buy tea like this without the bags and we can have another cuppa."

"Or e'en a pint wi' a bit o' the gab."

She gives me a hug and kisses each cheek with, "Glad your findin' y'r way, luv. Keep at it." As I leave, she swats my behind.

THAT RAGTOP JEEP

TANGO CROSSES Colorado Bridge with Captain. It's not the time of day to go walking, but his VA disability check is arriving in the next town over from Pasadena. He sometimes thinks of switching the P.O. box, but notifying all the government agencies of the change of address would be a real drag.

It's a 45-minute walk along Colorado Boulevard, and he's sweating by the time he reaches the post office. Probably shouldn't have taken his duffle bag again, but he's really protective of Clayton after those damn teens.

He loops Captain's leash to the bike rack and steps in. It's cool and there's no one by the boxes that'll object to him being there. Turn the knobs of the combination lock and open. Just the one piece of mail.

Inside, the check's the same as ever. He doesn't get much because he went bonkers. OTH Discharge. Other Than Honorable. Ineligible for the pension, but the VA counselor got him a small amount for disability. Disability because he went bonkers. Just enough to keep him and Captain in cereal and dog food.

He closes the box and turns the lock.

"You need somethin', buddy?"

He turns to see a security guard facing him. Anger instantly rises. Responses rage through his head: *I got a right to be here! I'm a veteran! You can't kick me out!*

And then, the smiling Buddhist woman's face comes to him. *I dare you,* she seems to say.

Tango breathes in and smiles. "No thanks, man. 'S all good."

The man nods and walks away.

Fuck me, Tango thinks. *This Buddhism shit works!*

The check-cashing place is three more blocks. They know Tango, so it's not a hassle. He stands in the line, staring up at the television. Once a month he gets this dose of the small screen. It's always a pretty young woman standing in front of a map of the United States, pointing out the weather as she smiles. Sometimes she's a blond, sometimes she's a brunette, but they're all the same. Pretty, immaculately groomed, and vacuous.

After he collects the cash minus the commission, he steps out into the sunlight and zipping by on the street is that lady's ragtop jeep with those red and yellow awning stripes. Tango leaps to the curb, raising his arm, waving wildly and yelling, "Hello! Hello!" But the jeep keeps going.

He slips his dog's leash from the light pole. "Captain, this proves she lives in the area. Eagle Rock or Pasadena. We'll keep an eye out for that lady."

And he watches the jeep grow smaller—then slow—and turn.

There's a sign, but it's too far away to read, so Tango lifts his dirty hands and makes the tiny triangle of space that Bob taught him and peers through it. Little adjustments and that pinhole focuses the view. Trader Joe's.

"Let's boogie, Captain."

And they both trot down the sidewalk. Tango's duffle bag bounces against his back, and he worries about Clayton in there but hopes that movie tape will keep the urn sealed.

One more block. Will that lady recognize him? What will he say to her to let her know how important she was? At least he can say thank you for his life. And tell her that Captain thanks her also. And Clayton. If she hadn't given Tango cash, he would be dead, and he would never have found Clayton, and Clayton would be in a landfill by now. She helped more than just him.

At the driveway, they hurry into the Trader Joe's lot.

The jeep is parked near the store's entrance. Unbelievable! He's found his benefactor lady! Out of breath, Tango steps to the driver's side. No one's there. Captain groans. They move to the sliver of shade against the building. Now what? He knows he looks bad. Sweating from the run, too dirty, too scraggly, and with a panting, matted pit bull mix by his side, he's gonna look scary. But he remembers this woman wasn't scared of him. She called him "over-done." She called him Leon. She even shook his hand.

How will he start? *Ma'am, I don't know if you remember me, but I want to thank you.*

Captain lies flat, mouth open, tongue dancing on the hot pavement. As Tango presses his palms over his hair, trying to tidy it, a young woman steps up to the jeep carrying two grocery bags and a bouquet of flowers. Red hair expertly styled, nails a sophisticated pink, conservative but fashionably expensive clothes. She looks like those television weather women. Pretty, immaculately groomed, and vacuous. This won't go well.

"Miss?"

Prestonia turns and Tango sees it all. The scan, the judgement, the repulsion. She immediately shakes her head. "Sorry, I don't have change."

He hates her for that. Wants to scream and charge but that won't get him closer to thanking the old lady. He pushes down the anger and as she opens the passenger door and sets down the groceries and flowers, he steps toward her. "Miss, I'm not asking—"

Her eyes widen and she puts a hand up for him to stop. "Stay away. I told you, I don't have anything—"

Fucking woman won't even listen! She's like all the others. Can only see one thing.

Tango tries to picture the smiling Buddhist lady on the book. He breathes in slowly and wills a stiff smile behind his beard and mustache. "I saw this jeep and wanted to thank the older lady."

"I don't know what you're—"

"This is a very recognizable jeep. The older lady drove it and she gave me an envelope of cash last Saturday. I want to thank her."

"Last Saturday?"

"She saw me on the bridge and stopped. Said she had an appointment and—"

"She's dead."

Tango blinks and turns away, surprised at how hurt and shocked he feels.

Prestonia adds, "She committed suicide last Saturday. Had cancer."

"Suicide? I was going to—she gave me cash—helped me and my dog." Tango shakes his head. "Sorry. Sorry to bother you." He pulls Captain to his feet and they start out of the lot.

"Wait!" the young woman calls after him.

Tango knows what's next. The guilty conscience. She'll hand him a dollar and wish him good luck. Tango turns back, ready to give the young woman his middle finger.

Prestonia asks, "What did the old woman look like? Act like?"

Tango squints, confused. "You don't know her?"

"We never met. She also gave me something. This jeep and—uh—a house."

Tango tips his head sideways as if trying to imagine such a thing. "You got a good deal."

The woman nods, somewhat embarrassed.

Tango pictures that dark morning on the bridge. "Old but different kind of old. Not stuffy or square. Long gray hair, cowboy outfit, drove like Steve McQueen—backwards, tires screeching. Stomped up to me like she was one-tough-cookie with huevos. Called me 'over-done.' Strong, determined, but kind. Called me sir and then said my name and shook my hand and when I took the envelope you could tell she was happy."

"Thank you," Prestonia says, turning away.

"Miss?"

The way she turns back, Tango knows what she's thinking. She's thinking—*now that we spoke, he'll ask for money.* She turns back with *NO* written across her face.

Tango pushes the frustration aside again. "The woman told me her name, but I can't remember it—"

"Agnes Sloan."

Tango nods his thanks and he and his dog walk out of the lot to Colorado Boulevard, heading for their bridge.

"Agnes Sloan, Agnes Sloan, Agnes Sloan." He never wants to forget that name.

Tears back up in his eyes. That young woman couldn't see him at all. The whole world is nothing but people judging him and finding him disgusting. Except for Agnes Sloan. She called him *sir*. She called him Leon. She shook his hand. And after all his hope and wanting, he finally found that jeep only to learn, he's too late. Could her death have been his fault? No, doesn't make sense. That's old thinking. Still, it feels terribly sad. But it's also, maybe good? That lady, Agnes Sloan, because she was taking her life, she gave him cash, and prevented him from taking his own. It feels like a circle and a mystery and—"Captain, you never know what may come of your actions. I hope Agnes Sloan knew she saved me."

THE CAROUSEL

I WATCH THE HOMELESS GUY and his dog walk away. God he was creepy. So filthy and his eyes seemed manic. Probably on drugs. Trader Joe's shouldn't let those people accost customers.

I get in the jeep and pull out to Colorado Boulevard. The man and his dog are still walking up ahead. I don't want to pass him and turn on my street and have him know where I live. Pull over and wait.

I've not driven Agnes's jeep before and thought I'd do it to get flowers for doing that thing I don't want to do. But I'm not going to drive this anymore if there are a lot of bums that Agnes gave money to. Can you imagine? Like a horror movie with hordes of them running after her, trying to thank her. Yuck! It'd be like the zombies in *28 Days Later*.

What that man said about Agnes Sloan—a tough-cookie, not square or stuffy, a woman with huevos—no one would ever use any of those words about me. I'm exactly like everyone else in my age group and demographic. I *am* square and stuffy. Not a tough cookie with huevos. Or even kind, if I'm honest. And if I don't have to interact with people like that man, I'll be very happy in my little bubble and ivory tower, thank you very much.

Finally the dog and man get far enough away that I can drive back to Agnes's home without being seen. For this mission, I change into black clothes. Maybe that's a cliché, but clichés work.

Mexican music blares nearby. Loud. I hurry to the balcony and peek through the wisteria. In the backyard of Alberto's house, young teenagers are paired up, dancing. The music abruptly stops and a woman steps into the middle of the group, grabs a partner and, explaining in Spanish, demonstrates the correct moves. She restarts the music and the choreographed dance resumes.

Back inside, into my backpack goes the cardboard box of Agnes Sloan, the flowers, the photo from the album of the tree by the carousel, and the words I'm supposed to say. During my short time as a film major, I bought a small Go-Pro camera that can attach to my clothes—like a police camera. So, perfect!

The music next door stops again. More Spanish instructions. The tune starts at the beginning again. It's enough to drive a person crazy. Good thing I'm leaving.

Drive my car, not the jeep, to Griffith Park. The carousel rotates and kids scream and the calliope plays circus-type music. I think I came here once when I was in grade school but not since then. It's so retro!

I attach my go-pro camera to my lapel, take the flowers and box of Agnes from my backpack, and start toward the tree that Agnes's wife was scattered under.

"What d'you think you're doing?!" a gruff voice yells.

I turn to see the uniform and badge. A young Latino man with a thin black mustache and the top of a tattoo peeking up from his crisp collar. The set jaw and hands on his hips tell me that he will stop this from happening. Do I return another day? Do I put Agnes Sloan in the back of a closet and hope she doesn't haunt me?

"Hello, officer. I'm, uh—we're shooting a scene. I'm pretending to be scattering ashes—really just barbecue ashes—not hot—and my director and cinematographer are filming me."

"Do you have a permit?"

"We're film students. It's for school."

"You need a permit."

I could try to get tearful with some sense-memory stuff from that acting semester, but the truth is, I *feel* tearful. Everything is too hard and I want to get back to the investment firm, working with numbers and money and not dealing with death and people.

I mumble, "I thought it would be okay."

"It's not okay. Get your director and cinematographer over here."

"They're far away. They're on an extreme long-distance telephoto lens."

I turn to the south and make the T-shape—time-out signal.

The officer squints at me like he knows this is bullshit. "Why are they filming you from a distance?"

"It's like a point of view from someone spying on my character."

"So why are you filming with this little lapel camera?" he asks.

"Then we can intercut between the telephoto-spy-view and my point of view."

The man glares. He's not buying it. Can he arrest me? Maybe I should run. Why do I have to do this? I was living a perfectly fine life and now I've got trouble and—

The officer shakes his finger. "You can't intercut the telephoto shots and your POV. You need to be in the frame or the viewers won't understand."

We're in Hollywood, so of course he knows this.

"You should be directing this short," I say.

A slight smile wiggles his thin mustache.

"Please, sir," I say, trying for ultimate deferential-ness. "This is the last shot. I'm supposed to scatter these ashes and then say some lines. Maybe when I wipe my eyes like I'm crying, you could step in and ask what I'm doing. You could be a character in the movie. Add conflict."

I see this intrigues him, so I continue. "We can't pay, but we can get you a link to the streaming and put your name in the end credits."

"I took some acting classes a while back," the man says proudly.

"A professional! We'll need your contact information."

He pulls a business card from his uniform pocket. Claudio Espinosa—Private Security, Event Security, Motion Picture

Security.

"Thank you, Mr. Espinosa. You ready?"

Claudio takes off his hat and slicks back his hair. "I come in when you wipe away the tears?"

"You got it. I'll see you and run away. After that, you should turn and look up toward—see that tall tree at the top of the hill? —now, look down—see the brush below? Look at that. They'll zoom in for a close-up when you face them."

"What's my motivation?" Claudio asks.

"Maybe even though you're security and should probably arrest me, you also identify with my character 'cause you had a sister like me."

"Sister back home. Got it. Can do. Where's my end mark?"

I move a rock to a spot on the ground. "Okay? Now back up a little so you're not in the shot at the beginning."

"What's the name of the film?"

Shit. The name should say what it's about. What's it about? A successful young woman who has her life messed up by inheriting a stranger's house.

The officer stares at me, waiting.

Improvise, damn it! It's about—I look down at the box of ashes in my hands. "It's called *Ashes to Ashes*."

This seems to satisfy the man. I quickly crank my hand to the imaginary crew in that silent film era/charade signaling them to start rolling and gesture for Claudio to back up. Turn on my Go-Pro. Take a deep breath. Step to the tree and—all of a sudden I *do* feel Agnes and Tracy and I say the words Agnes wanted. "Darling Tracy, I'm joining you now in substance and in spirit. With you forever. Love and peace, Aggie."

And the carousel plays a slow organ tune and I don't know exactly how to scatter her, but I carefully open the box and then the bag and shake it over the ground, gently spreading the gray particles across the grass. And the wind kicks up and some bits swirl and dance and somehow it feels sad and wonderful and poignant. I'm crying for real but careful not to wipe my eyes. With the bag empty, I set down the flowers, blow a kiss to them and whisper, "Thank you," and when I feel Agnes Sloan would be happy, I wipe my eyes.

Claudio steps forward with a fervor that wasn't there for his previous real-life entrance. I act terrified and hurry away as he turns to do his closeup for the imaginary camera.

I had figured to keep running to the jeep, but I don't. I step back to Claudio.

He's grinning. "How was I?"

"Fantastic. I really was scared. How did it feel for you?" I ask.

"Stupendous! Thanks for letting me be part of this. It was fun and I'm thinking—I'm gonna get back to those classes."

"You do that, Claudio. You've got talent."

He gestures to the tree. "Time to clean up the fake ashes—"

FUCK!

Claudio shrugs. "Oh, never mind. It'll get washed in with the next El Niño rains. Just take the flowers."

"You take them for your great acting."

Claudio gives me two thumbs up with, "Let me know when I can see the finished film!"

Driving back, I feel energized. That was so much fun! It felt like I was back in both the acting and film-school semesters.

At Agnes's house, I set up my laptop and import the go-pro footage and put in images from her photo album and add public domain music that's warm and soothing but not cheesy. I turn on the practicals in the house and film parts of Agnes's home. Seeing it through the lens makes me realize how cheerful and cozy this place is. It's homey. Out on the balcony, sunset streams through the wisteria and everything looks magical. I edit everything with slow dissolves and the film comes out really great and I post it on my sites and Agnes Sloan's. I really think she'd like it.

WASHED AWAY

MAWMAW AND PAPAW scream at the boy as the water rises in

the small living room. The lights have gone out in the hurricane, and the grandparents crouch on the mantle crying and gesturing for help as the waves lick their ankles. When the lightning flashes, the boy can see their eyes hold terror and recrimination. *How could Leon let this happen? Why isn't he saving them?*

A rush of water pushes against the wall. They hear it groan and whine and things bend and crack and splinter and water rips the front of the house away into what might have been their street, if it wasn't now the Gulf.

Mawmaw and Papaw are whooshed off the mantle and they bob in the water for just a moment until it pulls them out into the blackness of the storm. Their screams of "Save us, Leon!" disappear under the thunder and crashing waves.

Tango jerks awake. There are no crashing waves or screams, just the occasional *shhh-sh* of a car crossing the bridge overhead. He touches the matted fur of the dog at his side and Captain growls, annoyed at being wakened for nothing but a dream.

On the cement bridge footing rests Clayton's urn, taped securely now. What happened to Mawmaw and Papaw's ashes can't happen again on Tango's watch.

Tango points to the urn. "I vow—and you know I ain't shitting you, Clayton—I vow I will get you home."

ADVISOR

TWO WEEKS AFTER the adventure of Agnes's ashes in Griffith Park, my routine has settled back to normal, minus the Studio City Avalon apartment and Brent. It's comforting to relax into the predictable flow of life. One thing is way too predictable—the afternoon session of Yasmina's quinceañera rehearsal. It's the same song, stop and start, stop and start, for an hour. But still, I'm enjoying my house and living alone and have more energy to focus on my work.

At the investment firm, my windowed office looks down on the 101 freeway, but I keep my back to the view so I can watch the goings-on of my co-workers. Us high-powered analysts get windowed offices. These surround the large middle-zone of the room—a maze of the lowly clerk nobodies working at matching desks. The windowed offices have glass walls on all four sides, so the analysts and advisors can keep tabs on each other. An attribute that fosters a fierce competitive spirit.

I pick up the office phone, pretend to be listening to someone who is very funny, and glance through the glass wall to the office on my left. Josh's typing furiously on his computer. Is it a show? I can't see his screen. Maybe he's trolling someone on social media. Change the phone to my other hand to pretend to take notes while glancing into Sylvia's office on my right. We have glass desks, so I can see she's taken her heels off. Dangerous move. I'd love to, but that isn't an option. She's got her nose nearly touching the screen, scribbling on a pad without looking down. I never liked her.

Look out the front of my office, all the way across the cavernous room, to the offices on the opposite side. Peeking from around his computer, Brent is glaring at me. I scratch my temple with my middle finger and hang up the phone.

Mr. Gromley taps on my open glass door, smiling. He only smiles when he's with a potential client. This one has a long beard and tidy hair in that trendy, hipster mode, with two visible tattoos curling out from under his plaid shirt sleeves. Add the khaki pants and Timberline boots, and I can safely predict he drinks local brews, or maybe grog, at ax-throwing pubs. Wannabe lumberjack.

Mr. Gromley welcomes him to enter my office. "Ms. Cheswick, this is Mr. Greggor Burnam."

The guy balks, his eyes clearly telegraphing his mind's message: *This chick can't know shit.* He sees a red-haired woman who must be clueless. He mumbles something to Gromley and gestures with his beard back across the massive room, to Brent's office.

Gromley smiles and ushers the man into my space with, "Ms. Cheswick has been our financial-analyst-of-the-month several times now. She'll treat you very well."

The lumberjack reluctantly sits in the client chair, lays out a bunch of papers on my desk, and gives me a real challenging glare. "I inherited a chunk-o-change from my mother and figure to make it grow via investments. You got that kinda know-how in your wheelhouse, Miss?"

Oh, this guy is asking for it. I smile benignly. "As your advisor, I would have the fiduciary responsibility of implementing trading and hedging strategies that include the use of IPOs, stocks, bonds, currencies, commodities, derivatives, options, forwards, futures, and swaps to increase yields in your portfolio both domestically and across Global Capital Markets."

Greggor shrugs. "Yeah, well, anyone can throw around industry-specific jargon to appear more competent than the mark."

"The mark?"

"Sucker who gets taken in by the scam. I just want to make some cash. Set me up and I'll do the rest."

This guy thinks I'm a fucking scam-artist.

"Do you know why they call us financial advisors?" I ask.

"Let me guess, you advise."

"Yes, and why do people take our advice? Because we studied at a university to get a degree in finance so you won't have to." (Here's where I neglect to tell him about my inordinate number of semesters studying anything but finance.) (I also neglect to tell him that financial advisors are predators and are not above manipulating data to instill a sense of urgency, but that doesn't make us SCAMMERS!) "Where'd you go to college?" I ask, a little too snarkily.

"University of Wisconsin at Madison. BA in Wildlife and Forestry Conservation."

No wonder the lumberjack getup.

Brent slowly ambles past my office, staring in with a look of contempt. I smile to make him mad.

Back to Greggor.

"Let me show you some possibilities that will allow you to

experiment with high-risk transactions while keeping the bulk of your investments in fixed-income index funds."

The lumberjack leans back in the black leather chair with the look of a dare. "Go ahead. Show me what you got."

There's a ding on my cell phone, and normally I would never investigate it while with a client, but this Greggor is making me mad. I pick up my phone. It's a Facebook Messenger notification. Ha, I'll make him wait for some stupid meme about a cat.

"I'm terribly sorry, I have to respond to this. Some of these movie stars just think they own me. Won't be a sec."

Greggor's beard and mustache shift. Does he believe me?

The message is from a woman named Maureen. *A lady in my book club forwarded me your post and I saw the memorial scattering of the ashes that you performed by the merry-go-round. Do you have time to tend to my dear beloved? I am unable to travel, let alone stand or walk. I'm in Wyoming. I can't keep Lyle waiting forever. Please.*

Ha! She must be a kook to think I'd consider this. What kind of person scatters a stranger's ashes? I know. But Agnes Sloan was different. With everything she gave me, I couldn't very well say no. But I don't know this Maureen woman. Just because she can't walk, doesn't make it my responsibility. And Wyoming? I don't even know where that is. All I know is it's some wilderness of cowboy-buffalo-Grizzly bear-Marlboro-Men.

I pretend to text something, set down my phone, and return to Greggor. "This movie star, you'd know her but I'm not allowed to say, wants to make sure she has access to her accounts while she's filming in Wyoming. I texted back that I believe they have internet in that state."

"Wyoming's awesome. You ever gone?"

"I've been as far north as Six Flags Magic Mountain in Castaic, as far west as Santa Barbara, as far south as Long Beach, and as far east as Anaheim for Disneyland."

Greggor looks at me with horror. "You never left Los Angeles? No plane trips? No foreign excursions? No visiting relatives—"

"My folks were from here. My friends also. I went to UCLA.

And this city really does have everything anyone could want."

Greggor stands and collects his papers. "How can you even *pretend* to advise *me* if you have no life experience? You may have a fancy degree and a lucrative job, but you don't know shit."

And he stomps out.

After Greggor leaves, I slip into the ladies' room. I'm shaking. That prick! How dare he! I have experiences! What about all those semesters in Acting, Architecture, Filmmaking, and Art!? Those were experiences! And just because I never left Southern California doesn't mean I'm clueless. Prick. Asshole.

My phone dings. Another Facebook Messenger notification. Maureen again. *Sorry, I forgot to say I'll pay you, of course. I can fly you from wherever you are. Put you up in a motel. Take care of expenses. Please say yes.*

I dial a number. "Hi, Erika, it's Prestonia, the one who lived at the Avalon, talked to you by the pool—"

"'Ello, luv. You can be sure I remember the only Prestonia I've ever had the pleasure of acquaintin'. T'is a joy to hear from ye."

"I'm at work and can't talk long. Can I ask you one thing?"

"Fire away, luv."

"If you had an opportunity to do something really strange and pointless and off-track from what you should be doing, would you—"

"Pick the strange, pointless, and off-track every time. Ye cannae go amiss."

I thank her and step out of the restroom. Mr. Gromley stands facing the door as if he's been waiting for me. "What happened with your client? He left abruptly."

"I got an emergency call. A family emergency. I have to fly to Wyoming tomorrow."

Far across the room, Brent leans out from behind his computer to spy on what's going on.

"But what about the client?" my boss asks.

"He understood and generously promised he'd return."

Mr. Gromley says that I'll need to catch up on any missed

opportunities. "No slackers on my team," he warns.

I employ that acting semester to give him a tearful, chin-quivering nod. Not Oscar material, but he gets flustered and adds, "Hope your family emergency works out."

As I pull up to my curb, Alberto steps out of his house to meet me.

"Prestonia, four people came by while you were gone. They knocked on the door and peeked in the windows. When I came out, they questioned me about you, who you were, how you knew Agnes Sloan, how long you'd lived here."

"Did they leave names or anything?"

"No names. They were white. Like super, not-from-LA kind of white."

"What did you tell them?"

"No hablo ingles."

"Probably Mormons or something. Thanks, Alberto."

I go inside and Facebook message the Wyoming Maureen person and tell her I'm interested. She replies immediately and asks to talk on the phone. I'd prefer texting, but she writes that her phone isn't that type. Oh, my god, she must have a landline.

Moments later, I'm listening to an old sounding voice with a cartoon, witch-like cackling laugh and odd accent. She wants to know how much I'll charge beyond expenses. I really don't know what to say. I don't need the money.

"Two hundred dollars?" I suggest.

"Oh, no. Lyle would be horrified. I couldn't do it for less than five hundred."

I agree and, after a bit of logistics, we hang up. An hour later, a round-trip ticket to Casper, Wyoming pops into my email. I'm flying tomorrow. This is so weird. Maybe this is a scam. Maybe Agnes Sloan isn't dead and she and this woman Maureen are really con-artists and created a whole scenario and they're going to get me to sign over my 401K and stocks and bonds...

But Erika suggested I do it. Except, why the hell am I paying attention to what Erika says? We only just met. For all I know, she's in on it, too.

I shouldn't do this, I think. I'll message back to Maureen that I'm sorry, but—

Lumberjack Greggor's words come back to me. *How can you even pretend to advise me if you have no life experience?*

I lay out my black funeral-type outfit, two pantsuits, jeans, extra shirt, video camera, laptop, and my warmest jacket. But my backpack can't hold it all. A quick look through Agnes's closets and I'm soon filling a cool, retro, leather suitcase. Snapping the latches produces nice *clicks* and makes me feel this might not be a bad adventure after all.

WYOMING

NEXT THING OF INTEREST, I'm at LAX, going through security and taking off my suit-jacket and heels and watching everyone else to see what to do. Though I'm a newbie, I know most of the drill from television and films.

On the plane, I'm nervous as we take off but it's very cool nonetheless. From my window seat I can see the never-ending expanse of houses and pools and golf courses and parking lots and malls and freeways. But never-ending does end and the vastness of Los Angeles switches to a vastness of desert.

The desert goes on for a long time and then gives way to reddish canyons and my ears are doing weird things. We pass slowly over massive circles of green that must be irrigated crops. It looks like a patchwork quilt sewn by someone drinking too much Chardonnay. We go over a great swath of mountains that gets quite redundant and suddenly it changes to absolutely zero mountains and a never-ending flatness as we descend into Denver. Denver, Colorado. My first state other than California! Now I'm a traveler, Greggor!

So this is Colorado. I can't tell much about it from the runway. Or the terminal. Or the gate.

Eventually, I get off the plane. I read the departures board to find my next flight and start for that gate. And keep going. And going. The airport is huge! When I finally get to the gate, I relax a bit and sit watching people. Everyone looks very different from LA people. Not as thin or stylish. What do they think about here?

Soon I'm bouncing down the suspended accordion walkway onto the next plane. This one is much smaller. We take off and there're lots of bumps and jolts and the wings look about to break off and the whole thing is really scary but we finally land safely in Casper. Now, with Wyoming, I've been to three states!

A taxi takes me on side streets away from the business district. It seems like everyone has an RV parked in front of their house. We park by the driveway of a suburban ranch-style home. There's a wooden handicap ramp beside the cement stairs leading to the front and large weathered wagon wheels on each side of the entrance. I wonder if I can back out now, but the driver has already stepped out to the trunk to get my suitcase.

As I walk to the house, I see an old lady perched on the seat of a walker behind the glass storm door. She un-clicks the latch and pushes it open with slippered feet, then wheels back as I let myself in. She's probably nearly eighty with a bright auburn wig and pink flannel housecoat. I've never met anyone who looked like her. She looks like someone you'd see in a sitcom.

"Prestonia! I'm Maureen. So glad to meet you! My word, look at you—all dressed to the nines. One might mistake you for a bank president. Ha!"

Is she making fun of me? I wonder.

"You've got to be tired from the journey, so I won't get to blabbering. You're welcome to stay at the house or I can set you up at the Motel 6 down the way. Let me show you the room to help you decide."

She scoots down the hall. We pass a living room and dining room and I peek into other rooms. There are patterns all over. Like everywhere! The walls are full of flowers or curlicues or little houses or covered wagons. Wallpaper. I've never seen wallpaper. How can anyone live with such visual chaos?

Maureen leads me down the pine tree wallpapered hall. "Had

to pull up the wall-to-wall carpet on account of it being hard to do wheelies on it." She stops in front of a door. "You take a look and see if it suits. Don't mind me, I shan't be put out if it ain't to y'r likin.'"

The room has a bunk bed with stuffed animals, a hanging mobile, picture books, and Disney-character posters over the unicorn wallpaper. "Grandkids useta stay here. I understand if you're not partial to unicorns. I should re-do the place as they're all your age, but who has the gumption?"

I tell her it's fine, figuring I won't spend much time here.

Maureen insists that I change out of my bank-president clothes and get comfy. When I return in jeans and a sweatshirt, she shows me pictures of Lyle, her husband of fifty-two years. He's what you'd call built-like-a-truck. Wide shoulders, wide torso, wide neck, and wide smile. He looks like someone who knew his way around a tractor. Should I say that? Is it friendly or insulting?

"He looks like he knew his way around a tractor," I say, hoping for the best.

"He knew his way around just about everything. Could fix any engine but he wasn't one of those macho man types. He would cup a flailing bee out of the birdbath and set it on a rose to catch its breath. Never got stung."

The smell of food permeates the air. Not in a bad way. My stomach growls and Maureen laughs. "That pot-roast has your tum-tum pinin' for it. You help me cut the taters and we'll have Lyle's favorite meal for dinner."

She zips around the wide kitchen with her walker, remaining on the seat and navigating with her slippered feet. Points out where I should find the "company" china. I set the dining room table for us. The table is large enough for eight people. "You have grandchildren, so you must have children. How many?"

"Four. Three hellions, an' one princess, as Lyle called them. And I know what you're going to ask. Why aren't they scattering their father's ashes instead of you? Well, at first I wanted him home with me. Now it's been five years and I don't want to leave this earth without him set where he wanted to be. Four kids and they're spread across the country and world like I'm afflicted with cooties. They got the mortgages and the cars and the events and the jobs takin' all their time. Grandkids got their own lives. I don't begrudge them that. Mostly I get a call on my birthday from the wives and group-calls on Christmas. Those are a pain in the butt if you ask me. Too many folks talking at once with nothing to say."

It strikes me as familiar. I haven't talked with my parents since the scheduled quick call over the holidays. Do my parents feel like Maureen? Are they resigned to me not giving anything to them?

"I think I lost you, Prestonia. Did I say something wrong?"

I pop back to her. "I was just thinking of how I don't talk to my parents much. Seems like it is easier to do this ceremony for you and Lyle than it would be doing something for my mom and dad. That's kinda sick."

"It's normal, hon. Every kid has to skedaddle sometime. For some, it's easy t' come 'n go. For others, they need to make a real hard break. I didn't talk to my Mah for years and then she died young. Back when I could walk without this contraption, I would go to her grave and talk for hours. Making up for lost time, and—she couldn't disagree with me!" Maureen cackles like that cartoon witch.

Maureen shoos me out to the backyard to pick green beans from the garden. There's another ramp down to a large circle of rose bushes of different colors. The scent is much better than what the makeup women spray on you as you walk past in the department stores. Maureen has a raised box with beans and squash and lettuce and tomatoes. I don't know how to pick beans but I figure it out.

Back in the kitchen, Maureen talks me through making gravy and sautéing the beans with butter and garlic. This meal may be my first time actually cooking anything besides toast and microwave meals. We sit in the large dining room as the sun sets. There are pictures on the wall of kids in graduation caps-and-gowns, clusters of families, vacation waves, but they seem old and dusty. I wonder what picture of me, if any, is up in my parents' Florida condo. Probably me as the financial-analyst-of-the-month.

We have the pot roast with mashed potatoes and beans and, sorry, Lyle, but this is now my favorite meal, too. I should express this to Maureen, but it's always embarrassing to give compliments, so I don't.

After dinner, I help stack the dishwasher and we move into the den. Maureen hands me a VHS tape. I've never seen these except in old movies. So clunky. I have to be told how to insert it in the machine. As I sit beside her on the autumn-leaves-patterned couch, Maureen lifts the remote, but pauses.

"Lyle gave up his dreams to provide for the family. Our kids went to college and have their careers because of him. I know he'd have liked to pursue music but you have to be realistic when you have four kids."

"What kind of music?"

"Like Steely Dan."

I smile and nod like I know who she's talking about.

She continues. "Real good on the guitar, but he worked for BLM."

My quizzical look makes her explain.

"Bureau of Land Management. Lots of travel, lots of meetings, lots of engineering. Worked hard and socked away cash for retirement, when he'd be able to play guitar and fish for the rest of his life. Rest of his life happened too soon."

Maureen pushes play on the remote and the tape starts. It's Lyle with a guitar. Singing and playing. And he's good. I should tell her that of course, but what do I know of this kind of music?

After a few songs, Maureen tearfully warns I'd better get to bed. "Rooster will be calling early."

"You have chickens? I didn't see any when I was picking the beans."

That witch cackle again. "Oh, no, sweetie, Rooster is my husband's fishing buddy. He'll take you to the special spot where

Lyle wanted to be laid to rest. It's about a three-hour drive up into the mountains. 'Spect Rooster'll be here around five. It'll still be dark and cold, so be sure to bundle up."

"You're joining us, of course."

"Not a chance," she says, patting her thin legs.

This is more than I can handle. I can manage an evening with a strange old woman in a Wyoming suburb but I'm not going out into the wilderness with a Rooster.

Maureen must read my thoughts. "He's a teddy bear in a Grizzly costume. Or is it the other way around? Anyhoo, he's the only one who knows Lyle's special spot, so I had to enlist him and he is none-to-happy bringing a stranger, let-alone a female, up to their sacred space. But you'll be fine."

And with that, she sends me off to the land of unicorns.

Maureen wakes me at four-thirty. I dress in my black outfit and warm jacket, get the camera set and step out into the kitchen to coffee and strudels.

"You fixin' to catch your death. That may do in sunny California, but you'll be freezed up here. Come, I'll fetch you somethings set you right."

In her bedroom, she points for me to slide open the mirrored closet door and has me put on a down coat with a hood and felt hat and gloves and heavy boots.

"Now you'll be right toasty."

Maureen hands me a small spiral notebook. "First page has what I'd like you to say. If'n you can make it sound nicer, do y'r best. I jes want him to feel respected and loved."

I nod and a horn blows outside.

"Don't forget Lyle!" And she hands me a shiny wooden box with his name and dates engraved on the side.

With her husband in my backpack and several strudels in a brown paper bag, I head out.

An ancient red pickup truck smokes exhaust into the cold air at the curb. I step to it and open the door, lighting up the cab. Rooster's probably sixty. Short brown hair, close-cropped grey-speckled beard, dark eyebrows longer than any of the rest. He squints at me in a judgmental way and jerks his head for me to get in. When I climb into the passenger seat, he pours me a cup of coffee from a thermos, takes the bag of strudels, and we start off. He's clearly the angry-silent type and perfectly cast as a murderer. I won't have one sip of this coffee unless I see him drink some.

It's a few hours of highway driving with no view but headlights, then we head into the mountains as the sun rises. I'm so glad Maureen gave me other clothes to wear. It's freezing the higher we get. The glow of day pierces through the thick pine forest. As the light flickers into the truck, I look around the cab. A jolt of adrenaline hits me seeing the rifle hanging across the back window, its barrel behind my head. I turn away from the sight and a glint of something pulls my eye to Rooster's waist. Peeking out from below his seatbelt clasp—the shining handle of a huge knife in a leather holster thing. Oh man, now I'm really scared. And I bet there's no cell service out here. I'm so screwed.

We turn off the paved road onto a dirt one. Not a good sign. He needs isolation to kill me. Maybe if I talk, he'll find me a real person and have sympathy for me and spare me.

"So, you were good friends with Lyle?" I ask.

"Twenty or more years. I would've done him right. But Maureen didn't ask me. She doesn't believe I have an ounce of sentimental to me, but she's wrong. Lyle and me were different sides of the fence but we got along. Kept silent when we couldn't."

Maybe he's trying to tell me to keep silent.

I won't say another word.

Rooster turns us down a smaller dirt road. "We're gettin' deep into the Medicine Bow-Routt National Forest. Don't go wandering. People don't make it out. Should be another ten minutes or so."

We're in an alleyway of pines now. I could scream all day and no one would hear.

"You pretty used to death, eh?" Rooster says.

Fuck. I could fling the coffee that's gone cold in his eyes and jump out. He'd jam on the brakes and pull the rifle and he's probably a good shot.

"You do this often?" he asks.

I want to ask if he means going into the mountains with a murderer, but I don't. "Do what?" I ask.

"Scatter dead people's ashes."

I already know he's mad about me doing this. I can't tell him this is the second one or it'll look like I'm clueless and taking advantage of his dead friend.

"This is my first one out-of-state."

"I guess there's a service for just about everything."

Rooster pulls into a grassy spot beside the dirt road and turns off the truck.

"You'll have to help tote things."

I make a sound that could be interpreted as acquiescence.

Rooster unloads the truck bed. Fishing poles, several rolled bundles, an ax *(great!)*, a cooler, a duffle bag. I slip on my backpack and take whatever he hands me. Instantly break a nail. Damn! Why'd I agree to this?!

We start off toward a white-noise sound, which slowly becomes river-sound.

Have to admit, this is beautiful. We drop everything under the trees and step toward a wide, sparkling river.

"Our spot. It's a beaut, ain't it?"

"Hmm. Where should I set up for the scattering?"

Rooster shakes his head. "First things first. Lyle wouldn't stand for us not fishing."

Oh.

Rooster makes me climb into thick wader rubber pants. Definitely won't be able to run in these. He gets me a pole and a handmade "fly" and shows me how to swing the line and make it rest on the water but I'm unable to do it. The fly doesn't go anywhere I try to make it go.

I suggest, "How about you fish, and I shoot what we call B-roll. It'll make the memorial film better, giving the setting and ambiance."

"Get to it."

Whew. Now I can do something and not have him watching me. I get the camera ready and test it and push GO and tilt down from the top of the pine trees to the lichen-covered boulders below. I zoom into the water and make it out of focus so it's just sparkles of light, slowly rack focus to reveal the clear water and undulating pebbles underneath and a fish goes by right then! I frame a squirrel holding an acorn in its tiny hands and munching on it. Get the swirl of Rooster's fishing line as it floats through the air, clouds picturesque behind it against deep, blue sky.

"Yeah! Get this big fella."

I turn from a little lizard to see Rooster lifting a fish out of the water. Spin the camera, zoom in—it's beautiful. I bet if I slow-mo this in post, it'll be gorgeous.

Rooster reels the fish in and holds it out for me to get several good shots, then lets it go and goes back to casting.

I take more shots and rush to the water's edge whenever he catches one.

"We'll keep this one."

I get footage of a huge bird swirling overhead. Could that be a buzzard? Hopefully not an omen! That'd be such a cliché!

I shoot a dragonfly perching on a leaf. Another comes by and I capture them fucking! This is so cool!

Under a tall pine tree are many huge pinecones. These are bigger than two side-by-side Venti coffees. Massive. I take one and put it with my stuff for a souvenir.

Rooster catches another trout and I move close to get its gleaming scales and muscular body and he says we'll keep this one as well.

Taking a break, I lean against another pine tree and I close my eyes to listen as the birds sing and the river murmurs and the sun is warm and—

"Time to wake up." A gravelly voice pushes into my brain.

I open my confused eyes to a view that isn't my home in Eagle

Rock or my old apartment in Studio City. It's a view of what they call big sky country, because of—the big fuckin' sky. Rooster leans into my POV. He could have killed me, but hasn't. That's a good sign.

"You want to start the fire or clean the fish?" he asks.

I've never done either of these. I'm a fucking present-day kid and we can't do shit. He's from a time and place when people did shit.

Seeing my lack of response, he asks, "Would you like to film me while I do those things?"

"Yes, please," I answer.

I film him making a tepee shape of tiny twigs, then medium twigs, then an outside of thick twigs, with branches standing by. A match is set to the swirl of dried grass and leaves in the center and those catch the flame, and it grows and moves up to the twigs, creating a little fire tornado.

"Always try for one match."

"Why's that?" I ask.

"'Cause you did it with one match! Something to be proud of!"

Next filming is the fish cleaning. It shouldn't be called cleaning, but fish killing, gutting, and de-boning. First bit involves Rooster pulling that long knife from its holster and cutting the head off. The fish head is gasping even after being separated from the body. I'm not going to put this in the final film.

Rooster opens a cooler and retrieves butter, white wine, capers, lemons, and spices. A metal thingamajig is set up over the growing fire and a cast iron frying pan hung from it. Rooster slabs in butter, glugs in wine, slides in fish filets, and sprinkles in spices.

"Oh, that smells good!"

Rooster smiles. His eyes twinkle in the firelight. "You had really fresh fish before?"

I shake my head. "I've never had anything before, Rooster. Everything is new."

"That's the way it should be."

And he sautés greens I've never heard of and shallots and garlic and adds a chestnut puree and I wonder aloud, "Are you a chef or something?"

And he tells me he worked for a super famous restaurant in Paris with stars from the tire-guy and brought his know-how to Wyoming and started a prestigious place and it became well known and now he's retired, but still likes good food. So, yes, he *is* a chef. I'm starting to feel okay. He's not scary at all!

And the food is wonderful. I flash back to eating with Brent at the Water Grill in LA and how ostentatious it was but tasted like nothing. This is not that. I'm not good at complimenting people but I give it a try.

"This was the best meal I've had in—maybe forever, Rooster."

"Thank you."

I guess that's all that's needed.

Rooster stands from the log he's sitting on. "Sunset's coming. You want to do the thing for Lyle now. The water is calm and everything is backlit."

Backlit? Fuck, does everyone know about filmmaking?

I jump up to get my gear. Get the camera ready. Get the box of Lyle ready. Get the words ready.

"Where was his favorite spot, Rooster?"

"I'm gonna say where you see the twinkling of his eyes on the river."

Scan the water. Sunlight flashes. A spot by an exposed rock jiggles with activity. Fish or sun or river, it's a center of glittering light. I lift Lyle's box, and the notebook, and the camera—it's gonna be hard to scatter and read and film at the same time.

Rooster puts out his hands. "Hand me Lyle. I'll scatter and you can film and do the reading."

What a relief!

We step into the river, and even through the waders, the cold is a jolt. Move to the spot. The sunlight sparkles get more so. Turn on the camera. I nod to Rooster beside me. He carefully opens the box and slowly shakes out the ashes. I move to get them backlit by the sun. They flash and shine and swirl.

As I film, I watch Rooster. His face is red and I see him choking back tears. Lyle meant something to him. That never crossed my mind. This was a friend of his. His grief hits me and I realize this isn't make-believe. It's real.

I hold the camera steady and do all I can to capture the moment. The ashes become a cloud and a curtain and a reminder of a life.

I read what Maureen gave me. "Dearest Lyle, I love you. Your kids love you. Your grandkids love you. Your friends love you. You did so well in this life and I thank you for every moment we had. This place has held your joy for years and now will hold you forever, dear heart. Till soon. Your M."

My voice breaks saying it and I don't understand why because I didn't know him, but I let that be and pan to film the ashes swirling down the river and tilt up to get a majestic row of tall pines with the orange glowing mountains behind them. It's perfect!

After I cut, we step back on the shore. Rooster rolls out one of the bundles from the truck and starts building the tent. A tent! I've never been camping.

"I know you don't know me," he says, "so if you don't want to share this big ol' tent, I can sleep in the truck."

"Rooster, I think I know you better than most of the people I work with, including an ex-boyfriend. I'm okay to share the tent."

We share wine first. I spend the evening listening to Rooster talk of why he loves cooking and fishing and how one honors the other and how to watch for trout and what constellations are visible at this time of year and what bird is making what call. How do people know all this?!

I get really tired and the next thing I know, Rooster wakes me as the sunrise lights our tent. I don't even know if I can say I've experienced camping 'cause I went to sleep immediately. Birds are chirping all around. Rooster knows what they are just from the songs! After I get up, Rooster insists I make the fire, and it takes three matches to get it going, but I do it! He cooks cowboy-coffee and sage butter biscuits—which we eat with syrup. When I ask Rooster why it tastes so different, he smiles at me like he's amused by my naiveté and explains about it being real maple syrup. From a Maple tree. Who knew?

While eating the biscuits, I get all teary. I don't know why. It feels like—I don't know—like I've been missing something I never knew existed. Part of me wants to stay here and keep camping with Rooster and be in this wide expanse of beauty talking about things I never heard of. But then breakfast is over and we start packing. I bundle the huge pinecone in a t-shirt to keep it safe.

We drive toward Casper, and Rooster doesn't talk, but it isn't scary like before. I keep having to turn to the passenger window so he won't see me crying. As we descend to the plains, he clears his throat and speaks. "I was twenty-five in Paris. Didn't understand French. Apprentice to a world-renowned chef. Scared shitless. Monsieur Duraque said, 'Everything from now on is unknown. Embrace it. Embrace not knowing.' I learned that lesson and haven't stopped applying it. I'm sixty now. Hope to have another thirty years. Still, Death *is* coming, and I want to face it like all the rest. I want to embrace the not-knowing."

I don't know what to say to that, so I don't say anything.

Rooster parks the truck by the curb. I step out and he helps me with my backpack. With a soft palm to my cheek, he looks into my eyes more than is normal. It's almost painful. "Embrace it," he says, and he pats my shoulder, and a moment later the muffler roars and the truck diminishes to a vanishing point.

Maureen is full of energy and questions and I can't make the transition. I insist on going into the unicorn room for a nap. Really, I set up the laptop and import the footage from the camera. I want to see it again. Be there again. The fish, the glittering water, the big bird—it was a Bald Eagle! I edit and add Lyle's music and when Maureen taps on the door for lunch, I come out and put it on her big TV.

Maureen cries, "You did it. You caught him and let him go."

It's a few hours before I've got the flight back to LA. I spend the rest of the afternoon with Maureen. She pays me five hundred in cash and I say I've gotten a lot out of this adventure, but she insists. We play cards—she has to teach me—on her screened-in porch and eat blackberries from her yard. As much as I'm trying to be here, I don't know when I've been this exhausted.

Maureen puts a wrinkled palm on my hand. "Afore you go, promise me something. I'm gonna put your number in my phone book— *In case of death, call Prestonia.* Do for me what you done for my Lyle."

"I don't actually do this regularly. This was just—"

"I won't take no for an answer. Promise me."

"Okay. But don't need me too soon. You want the same as Lyle? Fishing?"

She points to the colorful garden beyond the porch. "I want to be among my roses."

It's the perfect place for her.

On the plane back to Los Angeles, my eyes are leaking constantly. What's going on? The window view is a blur of tears. At least I'm not sobbing, although that feels close. If anyone talks to me, I'm liable to dissolve into a puddle.

Outside the airplane window, tiny little trucks on tiny little strings of gray traverse the infinite expanse of ever-changing terrain. People down there drive tiny little cars and live in tiny little homes. And every one is doing tiny little somethings. Driving a kid to school, working, watching television, arguing, tending babies or parents, crying, laughing, waiting. Some are even fishing. Cooking around a campfire. Honoring a lost friend. How do they do it? I don't think I can manage.

TIME TO PEE

"WHY ARE YOU always bothering me!? Leave me in peace!!!"

Tango's eyes swirl back and forth under his lids. Heavy dreaming. He's back in New Orleans and Mama is drunk and the tax man is pounding on the door. Young Leon Thibodeaux shakes his mother's cold, squishy arm again. "Fuck you!" the woman yells.

Leon knows he shouldn't, but he does. He opens Mama's purse and scrounges inside. At the bottom, crumbs, ripped tissues, pills of some kind, and quarters, dimes, nickels, and pennies making a dollar-sixteen. Wallet open. There's a picture of Leon at five. Messed-up look even then. Picture of Dad looking tough. But it ain't the picture he saw years ago. That man was Black, this man is white. Who is this man? Did he exist? Don't know if that's even a real photo. Maybe it's a man clipped from a magazine. A figment.

Any cash? Seven dollars.

This won't satisfy the taxman, Leon thinks. *Gotta get into Ninja.*

The boy's been feeding the ceramic Ninja bank it ever since Papaw gave it to him.

CRACK! The coins tumble and roll across dirty carpet with the smash.

The taxman's pounding increases.

Gotta gather this. Say she's sick, say she's hurt, say she's trying.

The coins and dollar bills gathered in his t-shirt held up over his thin brown belly. Don't slip now.

Open the door to the pounding and the man looks down at the boy. "What you got?"

"Cash. She sick. She hurt. We trying. Honest."

It being New Orleans, the man takes off his top hat and scoops the coins and papers out of Leon's t-shirt. Gives the boy a tickle finger to his belly at the end. Leon doesn't laugh.

The man doesn't like the lack of response and scowls. "Subsequent funds comin' by Monday or you and yr' mama're out."

The boy nods, knowing that to do anything else is to risk chaos.

Mr. Taxman leaves and, on cue, Mama hollers, "I'm dying! Where is anyone!?"

Captain growls.

Tango jerks awake. Taxman and Mama vanish. No money due. No horrors. No panic. Peace. Peace now under the bridge. All is well.

Captain barks. Tango whispers, "What is it? Cops? Teenagers?" He looks around but sees nothing. Time to pee.

He and Captain pick their spots. No matter how often Tango tells him, Captain doesn't understand that we want to pee *down the hill,* not above our camp.

Tango steps out from behind the footing and skids near the bottom. He unzips and lets go and watches the little trickle edge around the scrub and brush to the stream beneath the bridge.

The traffic overhead is just starting. Soon it will be a constant swish of tires. Someone going somewhere for some reason. Don't know why. Wonder if they do.

There's a pat-pat sound.

"Oh!"

Tango turns, still sending out the long yellow arc of pee.

A pink-suited jogger stares at him from the path, wide-eyed.

Tango shifts, showing her his back, shaking off and zipping up as Captain barrels down the slope toward the stranger.

The woman screams.

"CAPTAIN, STAY!" Tango yells, and the dog freezes. Tango thinks this is a perfect time to practice his Buddhism. He turns to face the woman with a smile to imply he's no danger. "Sorry, miss. Didn't mean to startle you."

"Stay away. I have pepper spray."

Tango holds up his hands to look friendly and unthreatening.

The woman's face is red. She backs up, fumbling with her pockets. "You can't be here. It's a public park. And—INDECENCY! This is absolutely unacceptable! INDECENCY!" Pulling the pink canister of pepper spray from her sweatpants, she holds it, arm outstretched, toward the man and dog. "You stay away or I'll get you. Both of you."

Tango and Captain don't move. They watch the woman back up along the trail and then spin, running away.

"We gotta be more careful."

BACK TO CALIFORNIA

I DRIVE HOME from the airport. Pull up to the wide parking lot gate. I can't find the clicker to open the underground garage. Oh. I'm in Studio City, trying to get into the Avalon apartment. Damn it. I wish I could just go in. I need to rest. That trip was new and exciting but HARD. I'm exhausted. No wonder I don't travel. Everything is so unpredictable and strange.

I drive to Eagle Rock and, before I get to the house, I can hear it. The quinceañera music. That same song. Park and drag myself into my home. Unpack. Carefully remove the huge pinecone from its t-shirt protection. Put it on the formica table. It looks good there. I'm tired. Maybe I can sleep. Lie down. The quinceañera music stops and starts, stops and starts...

Morning light. Birds sing and chirp on the wisteria-enclosed balcony. I pretend that I'm in Rooster's tent listening to Wyoming birds. My alarm goes off. Time to get back to real life.

Dress in business attire. Blow-dry my hair. Do the makeup, covering the freckles. Cram feet into heels. Dad used to say, "If you want to move around the millions, you got to look like a million." Maybe, but he didn't have to wear heels.

Set my coffee down on the table and the pinecone wobbles. I pick it up and smell. It smells like the forest. Pine scent and earth and smoke. I know what I'll do. I'll invent Take-Your-Pinecone-to-Work day. I switch my purse to a larger one and place the massive pinecone in. Time to go. Drive across town. I picture a person in a plane looking out the window, down on this view. All these tiny little cars full of tiny little people inching along the tiny little thread of highway. What would that person think of me? They'd never suspect I'd have a pinecone in my purse. I bet no one on this highway has a pinecone in their purse.

Enter the underground garage. It's nice to know where to turn and what lane to take. It's nice not to be bewildered by new stuff. Park in front of the sign: RESERVED—PRESTONIA CHESWICK. My own parking space. I earned that.

Parking elevator up to the marble-floored lobby, nod to the stern security guy, push UP on the elevator button. The door opens with a tasteful PING that researchers must have spent years perfecting. Swish closed and take the silent transport up to the 20th floor. Another PING and there's the plush carpet and tawny sofas and indirect lighting on gold silk walls and bronze backlit letters heralding the firm founders' names and I nod to the receptionist as I silently pad in my high-heels through the wide doors into the massive room filled with the matching desks for the lower echelon. The smell is comforting. A mix of every high-end perfume and cologne combined with carpet cleaner and Windex. I skirt along the windowed offices lining the edges. Past Mr. Gromley's office. He nods. Past the nameless workers who don't look up from their computers. Around to my office. My very own designated space. Wow. It's only been a few days, but it feels so good to be back. Everything is comfortably familiar. Brent, in his office across the buzzing room, ignores me. He's handsome. Muscular. Why did we break up? Didn't we get along? We talked about high finance, analytical modeling, and structuring mergers. Is it too late to get him back?

I take the pinecone from my purse and set it on the glass desktop. It's very different from everything in the room. Different from everything in the entire building. This might be the only thing that doesn't have right angles. The only thing not manufactured. The only thing not bought and sold.

Turn on the computer and the numbers come up. Numbers that instantly make sense. Numbers that mean money. There are graphs and columns and pie charts and scrolling updates and I understand it all. It's so comforting.

My phone rings. One of my best clients. I pull up his file and we do small talk about his kids for a few minutes before I field his questions. I tell him about the media merger on my radar. My suggestions make him happy. He'll net five-figures today and be set for rapid growth when the merger happens. Hang up and do the trade. It feels good to use my expertise. I can't light a fire with one match but I *can* do this. Well, I probably *could* light a fire with one match if I practiced.

The morning progresses and I make several clients several thousands and the firm several hefty commissions. Mr. Gromley strolls by and taps on my open door.

"Your family emergency resolved?"

"Yes, thank you. It was a bit scary but turned out okay."

He nods then stops, peering intently at my desk. "What is that?"

I follow his glare. "A pinecone. The family emergency took place in what you might call wilderness."

Mr. Gromley winces. "Not workplace compliant. Remove that *thing* from view."

I quickly scoop up the offending item and deposit it in my purse on the floor.

My boss coughs his displeasure and leaves.

The phone rings and I pick up to another client. She's interested in liquidating several low-risk stocks and moving into more high-risk ventures. I do my best but it's hard to focus. *What the hell is wrong with having a pinecone on my desk? Is it carrying hidden creatures? Does it have germs that might infect the firm? What makes it "not workplace compliant?"*

I've been at this job for a few years and I know I'm valued because I've been financial-analyst-of-the-month three times. I've been told I'm doing stellar work, and I've been told my analysis is second-to-none, but I've *not* been told that I can't have a pinecone on my desk.

As I speak with the client I notice that there's a little bit of dirt on the glass where the pinecone sat. *Residue.* Take that, Mr. Gromley. You can't get rid of Nature so easily. I wonder if the pine/earth/smoke smell still clings to the pinecone. I wonder if it would overpower the cologne/carpet cleaner/Windex smell. I need to know. I excuse myself from the client, hang up, and bend to open the purse at my feet.

The pinecone looks like a trapped wild animal. I should set it free. As I lift it from its designer cage, smells and images waft up. The forest. The river. The swirling eagle. Glistening trout skin. Rooster with his "Embrace it" advice. That was such a magical, wondrous place.

A muffled giggle breaks the spell. Turn to my right. Through the glass wall, Sylvia is staring at me with manicured fingertips at her lips, not hiding her condescending smile. Turn to my left. In his office, Josh is frozen, eyes pinned on the pinecone on my lap like it really is a dangerous beast. I wish it was. I wish it could leap up and wreak havoc across the firm. I wish *I* could leap up and wreak havoc across the firm.

I stand, set the pinecone on my desk, walk out of my office, and tap on Mr. Gromley's door. He waves me in but holds up a finger to wait, as he's grunting on the phone.

I wait. My heart is racing. *What am I doing? I should just forget the pinecone. What could I say is my reason for coming in?*

Still grunting on the phone, Mr. Gromley gestures for me to sit. I do. His office is just like mine. Floor-to-ceiling window behind the glass desk. Computer. Phone. Chair for client. That's it. No family pictures. No clay figure made by a kid. No diploma. No citation. No pinecone. I stare at him. He's got the fancy suit and through the desk I can see his fancy shoes. Got the expensive haircut. Got the man-style manicure. Everything is as it should be but his pursed lips and knotted brow, jerking knee and dead eyes. He's been doing this for over thirty years. I'm him in thirty years.

Mr. Gromley hangs up and blinks at me.

I need to ask him why the pinecone isn't workplace compliant but the words aren't coming. He continues to blink at me.

"I'm leaving," I say. "I can't give you two-weeks-notice. I'm leaving. Quitting. Now."

His pursed mouth slits open. I thank him, return to my office, put the pinecone in my purse, and head for the lobby door.

Brent intercepts me. "What the hell are you doing? Gromley says you quit!"

I nod, trying to get around him, but he darts like a goalie to block me.

"You can't quit! Where are you going? Another firm recruit you? Who was it? Gromley will match them—"

"Excuse me."

But Brent doesn't. He grabs my wrist. "Quitting this fuckin' perfect job? Moving into a stranger's house that was given to you for no fuckin' reason? Shit is not right. And what the fuck is up with putting the IKEA plant in the bed? You're deranged."

And for some reason, I'm not afraid. For some reason, I smile and say, "Do not take my wrist unless you are prepared for the consequences." I feel calm, but are my snakes rising? Who's Medusa now, asshole?

Brent's eyes widen and he drops my wrist and backs up, instinctively cupping his hands to protect his tender spot. He sputters, "You quit? What the fuck are you going to do?"

I whisper slowly, "I don't know, but it won't have to do with money."

Brent screams, "That's insane!" way too loud for an investment firm setting. The lowly desk workers stay glued to their computers, pretending they didn't hear.

I wait for Brent's horror to dissipate.

It doesn't dissipate. "You're going to waste all the years, all the training, the fuckin' double major in Math and Econometrics, studying to pass the CFA, everything you've accomplished, everything you've worked towards, and you're gonna traipse into the wild blue without a clue?"

"You got it. Bye, Brent."

I slide around my ex, step through the lobby, smile sympathetically at the receptionist, glide down the elevator, wave at security, ride down to Parking, pirouette to my car, zoom out to Wilshire Boulevard, and just like that, I'm free.

ERIKA'S IDEA

I'M SHAKING WITH ADRENALINE, driving away for the last time. Last time? Wait! What have I done? It felt right in the moment, but FUCK! Can I go back? Mr. Gromley is gonna be pissed off. Can I exploit his ignorance and misogyny and explain this away as PMS hormonal psychosis? Not likely.

A splat of something hits the windshield. And another. Fuck, it's raining! Why now? This is the last thing I need! As I drive through an increasing storm to Eagle Rock, I give myself a good, familiar tongue-lashing. *What the hell are you up to, young lady!? Another impulse? Time and time again, you throw your life away on impulse! Damn it, you don't think ahead!!*

I know the words by heart. My parents always said I didn't think ahead. "Look before you leap," they'd intone with perennial parental perturbation. How they hated my changing majors each semester. How they hated that everything I was interested in was frivolous and would never result in a career.

After two and a half years at UCLA doing everything *but*, I was given the ultimatum talk. They told me I was rebelling against my upbringing and sabotaging myself. "You know finance. You know investing, stocks, bonds—the ways to make money off of money. You grew up getting it through osmosis at the dinner table. Don't turn your back on what comes easy. This is meant to be." After elucidating the parameters and explaining that any other course would lead to a distinct lack of funds, they convinced me.

I transferred to the business school, got my degree, started at the investment firm, and they were finally proud of me. I'd settled down with a classy job and a steady income, doing what I was meant to do.

Arriving at my inherited home, I jam on the brakes, ram the car into park, and stomp through the pouring rain to my house. Slam the front door hard enough to rattle the old 1920's windows. Mail is scattered on the floor from the slot.

Your house needs water line insurance! Call Home Warranty

now! SCAM!

You are pre-approved for an exclusive credit line. No hidden fees. Call now! SCAM!

Letter with law office return address says *a petition has been filed with the court by plaintiffs in case #57-C-7798. You must respond immediately or forfeit your right to appeal. Call now!* Bullshit SCAM!

Rip them to hell and toss them in the recycling. Now what?! I had a life! I had a job! I had underground parking! What the hell am I going to do now? Now that I've thrown my ENTIRE LIFE AWAY?

A call comes in. Run to my purse and there's that damn pinecone! It's all that thing's fault! I yank open the back door and fling the huge thing out past the balcony. A dull thud in the yard. The phone keeps ringing. Look at it—it's Erika. I answer the phone and launch right in—"Erika, because of YOUR advice I did that strange, pointless, off-track thing and it SCREWED ME! I quit my job at the investment firm and now I'M FUCKED. And it's YOUR FAULT!"

"Right. What's your address, luv?"

Half an hour later, a white cargo van pulls up to the curb. Erika darts through the rain to Agnes's house. Inside, she moves about, taking in everything. "Blimey! Look at this place. Ye got yeself a feckin' home 'ere! I'zat an ass?"

"What?"

"Nae, t'is a burro, innit? Can neer tell twixt the two. Them an' donkeys. Lookit the walls! What colors! This lady 'ad taste! I wish I couldda met 'er!"

"Yeah, well, I'm in a crisis. I quit my job. REMEMBER?!" I yell, stomping to the kitchen because I'm not interested in hearing compliments about Agnes's too crazy, too retro, too full of personality home.

Erika joins me to sit at the formica table and I know I don't know her, but she's so damn comforting and I don't have anyone else to talk to and I'm freaking out so I can't help but express my fears and doubts about leaving the firm.

"It was a good job. I knew how to do it. I excelled! Fuckin' financial-analyst-of-the-month three times, damn it! I made money, had benefits. Now it's all gone. What am I gonna to do?!"

"Calm y'rself, luv. Nothin' t's some'in ye cannae rectify. There'll always be 'tother money-place that'll want ye."

"But I'll need references and Mr. Gromley isn't about to give me one. That's a burned fuckin' bridge! Flamin'. Over. You can't cross it!"

"Right. But, I still don't know—tell me aboot the strange, pointless, off-track thing ye did."

"I did it because of YOUR prompting! You sent me to fuckin' Wyoming!"

"And what happened there, luv?"

To make her understand, I tell her about scattering Agnes Sloan's ashes at the carousel in Griffith Park and the wild improvisation with the security guard. I tell her about posting the film on social media and that leading to the second request and the adventure in Wyoming. I tell her about cooking pot roast, picking beans, playing cards with Maureen and fishing and filming ashes and building a fire and camping with Rooster and the memorial film.

Erika slaps the table with her palm. "Bloody 'ell, lemme see this!"

I pull up the film made for Lyle on my laptop and push play. She has tears in her eyes as she watches.

"Gimme a glance o' t'other one. The one for Agnes."

I show that film. Again, she's got tears. When it's over, she shakes her head.

"Jesus, Mary, and Joseph!"

I don't know what that's supposed to mean. Is it good or bad?

Erika pounds the table, shaking the little chicken and rooster salt and pepper figures. "It's *right there* in beautiful color."

"What is?" I ask.

"Yer feckin' new job, lass. And I bet, from the way ye spoke, ye had more fun doing these scatterings than sittin' at that shite job movin' money."

She's crazy.

"This was a fluke. Two flukes. Not a profession."

"Feck all! D'y'know how many folks have urns and boxes of the dead stuffed away in closets? Auld Lang Syne relatives they dinnae wanta deal with? Guess what 'appens? The closet owners pass away and some poor bloke 'as to clear the flat and what d' ye think they find? Ashes of some stinkin' sod they dinnea ken! Believe me, t'is nae rare. You'll be doing a grand service and I know it'll ge' ye a living and help t'others wi' dying."

She's serious. Scattering ashes for a living. That would send my parents over the edge.

"Ge us a pen an paper," she orders.

I don't use pen and paper but I know Agnes's journal is in the top drawer of the bedside table. The journal she wrote to me in. There were lots of pages left. I bring it to Erika.

"You need a brochure," she says. "Put a flier, brochure thing in places where the dead people congregate. Funeral homes, cemeteries, churches, and the like."

She writes down *brochure*.

I put my hand on the paper to stop her writing. "This isn't a job for me. Do you know how scared I was of that Rooster guy? The Security man? I'm not a people person, I'm an investment person. Pie charts and money flow is what I know."

Erika pulls the journal out from under my hand. "Bull shite. Ye managed, dincha? What pay did that Wyoming lady ge' ye?"

"She paid the expenses, travel, food, and added five hundred dollars."

Erika writes *expenses plus five hundred*.

"That's a grand start. Ye can always raise it if ye cannae cover your life and have a bit o' pin money on the side."

"I'm not scattering dead stranger's ashes for a living. It's absolutely absurd."

Erika's face widens like it's found Nirvana. "Ahh! Perfect! Embrace the absurd!"

Rooster's words come back to me. *Embrace it.* But he didn't mean something like this.

Erika sees I'll need convincing. "Tell you what. Ye drop doon tae Trader Joe's and ge' us some cheese, kippers, crackers, and whatever Scotch they have. I'll start brainstorming your brochure, which we can also use to figure the website. We'll 'ave it set, website up, and brochure printable by nightfall. Deal?"

It's clear she won't stop, so I trudge to my car, drive through the deluge to Trader Joe's. I buy all she suggests, but it doesn't mean I'm going to actually do this crazy scheme. We'll just have a fun night playing.

We take screenshots from the two scattering ashes films I made and concoct a nice description. As she's typing it out on my laptop, she keeps saying, "Shite!"

"Erika, you say shite a lot. Where are you from? England?"

"Ye cannae tell from me accent?"

I shake my head.

"Born 'ere in the States, tae Jamaican mum and Orkney pah, who moved us tae Ayrshire, Scotland when I was a tiny-tot. Moved tae London when I was nae but twelve, got a big feckin' lesson right off cause I talked like a Scot. Feckin' changed my dialect right quick, but feckin' lessons kept up on account me skin t'was 'alf a shade darker than the ferntickled lot. Sorry, freckled. Moved te Paris when I was o' age and wantin' tae see the world. Merci and all 'at. Ten years 'ere. Lots of encounters in the city o' lights if ye get my drift. Next two years in Algiers, handsome lads all aboot, then Galway, Ireland. They say shite alot. Workin' on scenery for the theater, y'know. Likes o' *Waitin for Godot* an' all the rest. Grand times. Pick up words and ways o' talkin' along the journey. I can say *fucking* instead of feckin' but it jes disnnae fit w' me. I n'er say where I'm from since it took an amalgam o' places t' make me. What 'bout ye? Where' ye from?"

I pour her another scotch and upload my financial-analyst-of-the-month photo for my CEO picture on the brochure to get off answering about my FECKIN' lack o' travel.

The rain is never-ending, and that, with us drinking, has Erika suggesting she spend the night. As the deluge pours down, we keep pouring and downing and the brochure takes shape. It takes a whole lot of laughing to figure on a name. We discard *Ashes R Us* and also *Got Ashes?* I tell Erika of how I pretended to be making a film *Ashes-to-Ashes* in Griffith Park and she likes the name and we finish the fliers and half the bottle of scotch and Erika spends the night on Agnes's couch with the burro lamp glowing by her head. I lie in bed in my flannel cowboy pajamas thinking that this was the craziest thing I've done since my wasted semesters, and it won't last more than the night, but it was really fun.

WATER RISING

THE RAIN CRASHES DOWN from the Colorado Bridge. Waterfalls curl off the pavement and splatter hundreds of feet below into the Arroyo. Around the cement footing, puddles gather and grow. Captain whines beside Tango, shaking from the surround-sound cacophony.

Tango wakes in a panic. He may be miles and years from that place, but he's instantly transported back.

Leon Thibodeaux is eight years old in the little house that used to be his Mawmaw and Papaw's. Mama is snoring from her nightly bottle of cheap wine. The wind has kept him awake. It slams unknown things against the siding. He pictures ninja stars embedding into the wood. Samurai swords skewering the walls. He stares at the glowing lamp by his bedside. The one Mama bought him at a yard sale when she won fifty dollars in the lottery. A little glowing scene of a snowy cabin in the woods. He's never been anywhere like that. The smoke from the chimney somehow moves with the flickering firelight in the windows. Leon stares and stares, wishing he was there, cozy and warm. The light goes out.

The young boy swivels out from under the sheet, his feet hit the floor and jerk back. The floor is cold and wet. In underwear and a t-shirt, he steps to the light switch by the door. Click. Click. No power. Into the hall. The carpet is soggy under his bare feet.

The dirty shag squishes as he steps into Mama's room. He shakes her shoulder.

"Water's coming in," young Leon says.

"Leave me be!" she grumbles.

He leaves her and sits in the kitchen. The noise of the storm grows louder. He searches the junk drawer and finds a box of eight used birthday candles, a Zippo lighter, and a dim flashlight. Melts the bottoms of the little candles to set them upright in the ashtray on the kitchen table and lights them. He watches their orange flames wobble as they burn down, down, down, and one-by-one, go out. Should have made a wish.

Back to his bedroom to slip into wet sneakers. The water is ankle-deep.

Better try his mother again. "Mama. The water's risin'."

Mama hisses, "Don't wake me."

He keeps trying and finally splashes her with water from the floor. "Wake up!"

And she does. He points the dim circle from the flashlight at the flood surrounding them.

"What have you done, you fuckup!?"

"Mama, it's a storm. We got to leave."

Somehow her brain sparks and she sits up.

"Check outside, Leo."

Leon sloshes to the front room. The flashlight beam moves over the thigh-high water. The whole room is floating, magazines, fake flowers, the lightbulb Mama wanted him to put in on the front stoop. Leon wades to the front door, turns the deadbolt, and pulls at the handle. "It won't open."

"Don't worry. It's gonna go down, Leo. You'll see," Mama says, but the boy's not so sure.

"If it don't, we got to get higher."

He moves the wax-filled ashtray to the kitchen sink, drags the formica kitchen table into the hall, climbs onto it to stand and push open the attic hatch. The hatch opening is only a few feet square. Not sure Mama can fit through.

Mama can't get on the table, so Leon pulls around the folding step stool she uses for the top dishes, and she climbs up. The table's center creaks. It isn't meant to be wearing a heavy woman. Lift the step stool onto the table and she climbs it, holding onto her young son's arm. The boy shines the dim flashlight to illuminate the opening.

"I ain't goin' in that dark hole."

"You are, Mama, and I'm gonna shove you in if you don't start movin'."

Mama stands on the top step and she can get her arms through but can't pull herself into that small square. Leon has her move aside, and climbs in. They don't have a stand-up attic. Just a small sloping space. He has her try again as he pulls.

Takes a lot of trying and cursing and begging, but she gets into the attic as the water covers the kitchen table.

"Where's my wine? I need a drink," Mama says.

"Drink's underwater," Leon answers.

Sounds of the world crashing into their little home. Sounds of floating objects, inside and out, bouncing against the walls.

There is a house-shaking CRASH below. Bright light coming from somewhere. The boy peeks down out of the attic opening, beyond the hall, into the living room. The picture window has broken and car headlights tilt and rock in the open space. Muffled screams from that direction. The water swirls and the headlights drop underwater and spin away from the house.

Darkness again. Leon shines the flashlight beam around the room. High water sloshes against the mantle. The urns holding Mawmaw and Papaw are getting their feet wet.

Should he swim over to get them? Haul them across the room and lift them into the attic? Mama will be angry if they get soggy.

"Mama, I'll be right back."

"You stay here! I'm not sitting here alone!"

The boy obeys but keeps his eyes down below, watching the flood rise. The flashlight beam follows the water's progress. It inches up to the middle of the two grandparent's urns. They wobble and then, as if invited to dance, they rise and bobble free, floating across the living room. Leon watches their progress as they journey, bumping into each other, drifting apart, coming together, tipping and righting in the churning soup. They follow the flood, rocking back and forth, out the broken window, into the expanse of blackness, drifting off until the flashlight beam no longer can find them.

Water is higher now. Four feet below the attic. Three feet. Two feet.

"This attic is gonna flood, Mama. We have no way out."

"The water be goin' down soon. You wait."

But Leon has seen enough movies and TV shows to know that the flood always comes and kills those who are not movie stars. And he knows they aren't stars.

"I'm gonna bust open the roof. Gotta get something. You stay here."

He says that last bit as if she would somehow rise to the occasion and make a plan for their survival. She doesn't.

What can break open the roof? They don't have a hatchet or ax or saw or drill. Got to dive down to get the hammer in the junk drawer. Leon turns off the flashlight to save its battery, sets it at the attic edge, and slowly lowers himself into the cold—feet dancing—*where's the step stool?*—feet dancing—*Where's the table?*—they must have floated off.

Leon takes a deep breath and drops. Neck stretched up, he swims through the freezing black toward what should be the kitchen. Feeling, feeling—*are those the dish cabinets?*—dive—reaching down—*there's the faucet*—up for another breath and dive again—hand glides along counter and down—grip the edge—should be the drawer—*where is it?*—should be a handle—*where is it?*—*YES!*—pull the drawer and things rush upwards, knocking into his face, on their way to the surface. Fingers fumble through objects in the drawer. Tape. Pens. Keys. A wooden handle—could it be a handle of—*damn*—a screwdriver. Box of matches. No good now. Tangle of something—Mardi Gras beads—tangling another wooden handle—metal at the end—*YES!*

Grab it and push off the floor and the ceiling is higher than expected and finally up to GASP in breaths. Now swim—*which way?*—feeling walls, that's the clock—he's in the living room—push off the wall—*where's the hallway?*—water in his mouth—head hitting the ceiling—there are only a few inches of air! Find the hole to the attic!

"MAMA! Call out so I can find you!"

A distant "LEO" beneath the clatter of the storm.

"CALL AGAIN!"

Another and another and Leon swims to the sound and something's in his way—the formica table—wedged in the doorway—got to dive under—something smooth and very big slinks across his chest—*are there sharks?!*—rise and where is he?—"CALL, MAMA!"—and "LEO!"—she's nearby—feel along the ceiling—feel along the ceiling—there's the hole—feel edge—lay the hammer there and something tips—something hits his arm—moves past him—the flashlight!—too late—he pushes the hammer farther back and pulls himself into the attic.

Leon wants to rest but knows that has to wait. He yells over the storm, "I'm gonna bust a hole in the roof, so we can get out!"

"Don't, Leo. The water will come in!"

"Water's rising from below. We'll drown in this attic if we can't get onto the roof."

"What about Mawmaw and Papaw? You can't leave them on the mantle, Leo."

"They're gone, Mama. They washed away."

"NOOOO!! Go down and get them! NOW, boy!"

"Mama, I can't. They went out to sea."

Leon's mother feels around in the darkness and finds his thin shoulder and moves her hand up to find his face and—SLAP!

"Go get them, loser! Don't come back until you find them!"

Leon crawls away from his mother and touches the attic roof and SLAMS the hammer up. It knocks hard and sends pain down his thin arm to his elbow.

His mother screams, "You little fuckup, get down there!"

WHAM! Leon hits again. Another jar to his arm.

"Get your ass moving and find your grandparents!!!"

WHAM! The pain angers him and he smashes repeatedly against the unyielding roof.

Mama wails in the darkness, "Mawmaw, Papaw. I'm so sorry the boy doesn't care! He let you die! Forgive me for my worthless failure of a son."

WHAM! WHAM!

FUCK! FUCK! He's just a kid. He doesn't have man muscles. Even with man muscles, would he be able to break this roof? It was built to be strong. There's no way he can do this. They're trapped. People pray at times like these, but he never learned how.

He drops onto his back, staring open-eyed into blackness as his mother sobs. The water below rises. He feels it licking his back. It's here and won't give up until they're dead.

A drip splashes his face. And another. A drip means a leak and a leak means softer wood and—SMASH! Again and again, he slams the hammer into what might be where the dripping is. SMASH! Hammer sinks in and is stuck.

"AHHH!" Leon screams and pulls at the hammer. "It's not moving!"

"I don't care!" Mama moans. "I want to die!"

The boy yanks on the embedded tool. It doesn't cooperate. He lies down to kick at it with his boy feet. Wood screeches, kick again, another screech and cracking. He kicks and the hammer and a chunk of wood drop on his bare thigh. Feel up into the space—something flopping—shingles!—push and wind catches the edge, it rips away, and outside air and rain rush in. The sky is filled with flashes of light, explosions in the distance. Sparks from far-off catastrophes.

Pry and wrench and hammer and torque and the hammer-hole becomes a head-hole and a boy-hole and finally a mom-hole. Leon pulls his mother out. Both are pummeled by the storm, clinging to venting pipes. Around them are screams and moans and smashes of objects and wind and rain and howls of unknown creatures in a terrifying hell.

They don't sleep, clinging to the life-raft of their roof, skin scraped by the rough asphalt shingles. Dawn inches its way through the storm. The water sloshes against the roof, already up over the edges. If it rises farther, they'll have to swim. The rain and wind slash at them and Leon curls his small, shaking body around his mother to protect her from the lashing.

A thing slides against his calf. He looks down in the growing gray light to see a water-moccasin snake searching for a place to land. FUCK! A wild fling of his leg sends the creature flying.

As the light continues to grow, Leon watches the floating parade. Tables, cars, garbage cans, bloated bodies.

A dog swims around the horrors and claws its way onto their roof. It pants like it's been in the water for hours. Leon knows not to approach unknown dogs but this is a strange time. He whistles and gestures for the dog to come and it does. It shakes and curls itself against the boy's legs, whining softly. Having the dog feel safe, makes Leon feel good. Maybe he can keep this dog. It would be good to have a friend.

As morning arrives slowly, the rain lessens and stops and the sun scorches down. Hours pass. The dog cocks his head listening, yelps at something, leaps from the roof into the water, and paddles off. Leon calls for it, but it ignores him.

"Get help, Leo," Mama pleads. "I'm thirsty. The sun is burning me. I can't go on!"

Leon takes off his t-shirt and drapes it over his mother's head. She moans as he listens to the screams and pleas for help coming from all directions. He scans the flood for any sign of Mawmaw and Papaw. Did the two urns bob along together, bumping into the swollen, floating dead? Did they ride the current and gently drift out to sea? Will they remain floating in the gulf forever?

Helicopters arrive. They circle and pick up folks from the rooftops. Leon swirls his t-shirt at the rescuers and screams to be next. Finally, he and Mama are pulled up by orange-suited commando types and choppered away. In the swirling machine, high above the flood, Leon pats his mother's hand. She jerks away and glares at her son. "You left them to die. I'll never forgive you."

The rush of water continues surging down the Arroyo's embankment, swirling past Tango and his dog. "Gotta get to higher ground, Captain."

He grabs the duffle bag of supplies and sleeping bag and Pema's book and Clayton's urn, dragging everything up to the very top of where the highway meets the arroyo.

Clutching Clayton's cold metal to his chest, Tango whispers again and again, "I got you, buddy. You're safe. You're safe."

BUSINESS AFLOAT

IT'S STILL RAINING when we wake up bleary and hungover. Erika doesn't say much, just kisses both my cheeks, "More fairy touches for the ferntickles," pats me on the butt, and with, "Later, luv," steps out into the storm.

It's after eleven o'clock and I'm not at work. I'm not in my business suit and heels. I'm not styled and made up. I'm not staring at numbers.

This is not okay.

I need to find a new position ASAP.

Time to start brainstorming. Set up the laptop on the table. Find my old résumé. It's been years since I've had to update it. I won't be able to get a reference from Mr. Gromley, but I have all the credentials any firm could want. I delete my old statement and start fresh. My years of experience have taught me what an employer would want to hear: *strategic insights, qualitative inquiry balanced with quantitative analysis, longitudinal cross-functioning leadership, and synthesizing future-forward implementation* is a good start. This will be today's mission.

But I need to eat something first.

Cereal and milk is all I can manage. That and tea.

After experiencing my first "cuppa" in Erika's apartment at the Avalon, I searched for and found Agnes did have a tea set. Teapot, cream pitcher, sugar bowl, cups and saucers, little tiny spoons, and silver tongs for something. Inside the teapot was a note in Agnes's neat script. *Grandma Eulailie's tea set from Kalamazoo. Don't chip it!*

OKAY, AGNES!

Now, here I am, sitting on the balcony of my new home, watching the pouring rain, with a whole tea setup on the wicker table beside me. I should have made tea for Erika when she was here! She'd like that I have the whole setup. I snap a picture and text it with: *Fancy a cuppa?* She'll be glad to see me following her lead.

I stare at the rain. Before moving to Agnes's house, I didn't much think about rain. Of course it affected traffic and that was a drag, but since my car at the Avalon Apartments was in an underground lot, and parking at the investment firm was in an underground lot, and I shopped at Whole Foods on Olive with the underground lot, I wasn't really exposed to rain. It was more of an idea than an experience.

Wow! This rain is really serious. It doesn't normally rain this hard in August. I can't see the usually visible hills of Griffith Park. I can hardly see the end of the backyard. The clatter of the zillions of drops on the balcony's corrugated metal roof is like applause at a rock concert. And the world smells very different from the usual dry mix of car exhaust and dust. Now I smell wet earth, wet asphalt, and wet plants—a mix that's both acrid and yummy. Agnes Sloan's backyard fruit trees must be happy soaking up the water. I should learn how much they need so I don't kill them from neglect before I sell this place.

My phone rings. Screen says it is from Kansas. I don't know anyone in Kansas. Probably a car warranty or some other scam. Swipe to decline.

Is this the start of El Niño? That security guard at the carousel in Griffith Park said the ashes would be washed in with the next El Niño. I picture Agnes' ashes swirling and mingling with those of her lover, Tracy. That was a good thing I did. I'm kinda proud of that.

A gust of wind hits hard. The trees in the yard below do different dances. Some have stiff branches that don't sway and their leaves only slightly quiver. Some are sagging, waterlogged and depressed-looking. Some are tossing their limbs this way and that like an improv student pretending to be a tree. I bet I looked like one of those when I did that exercise in acting class. I should have tried for the older, more mature tree and just wriggled my fingers. I felt really stupid in that class, but it was fun. I guess I felt really stupid in most of the classes I took during those pointless semesters. I never felt stupid with the economics or math classes. Guess 'cause I already knew everything from growing up with my financial-expert parents.

Knock, knock. Someone's at the front door. I creep close. Knock, knock. Fuck! Is it Brent? He *would* show up, especially after I quit the firm. Maybe he convinced Mr. Gromley to give me another chance. I could get my old job back. Save me making a new résumé!

"Hello?" I whisper to the door.

"Oy, 'tis I. 'Ere fer the cuppa."

I don't know if I'm relieved or disappointed, but I open the door and welcome Erika in. She gives me another hug and kiss on each cheek. It's so foreign to me to have this greeting every time, both coming and going. I never hugged anyone except family I hadn't seen in months. This's nice.

I get Erika set with her cuppa and we watch the rain together. She doesn't say anything, so I don't either. It's uncomfortable and I try to think of a mutual-interest topic, but after a while it's okay, and after a while longer, I actually enjoy it.

We listen to the rain turn from sounding like the rock-concert-applause, to bacon sizzling, to someone's fingers tapping out an unknown, broken melody, to finally, nothing.

"Right-o. Now that the weather broke, let's get to it."

I didn't know we had an agenda. Erika has me print fifty copies of the brochure for *Ashes-to-Ashes* that we made last night.

I shouldn't be wasting time on this. I've got a résumé to prepare.

"I haven't really decided on this—uh—career path, Erika."

"Ye dinnae need 't decide. Just do." And she hustles me out. The sun is shining and everything is sparkling after the torrential downpour.

As I climb into her van, I see the back is a huge empty cargo space. "Why do you have such a big vehicle, Erika? Isn't it hard to get around?"

"'Twould be a mite hard to transport me paintings and sculptures in a Mini Cooper."

"Where do you transport them?"

"Tae collectors and galleries."

Oh, I guess she's a real artist.

We drive around to distribute brochures in the surrounding towns: Eagle Rock, Highland Park, Mount Washington, Glendale, Atwater, Silverlake, Pasadena, South Pas, and Altadena. Funeral homes accept them. Churches also. A few hospices. There's only one cemetery in the immediate area and it doesn't accept the brochures, I guess because scattering ashes is competition for burials.

It's fun hanging out with Erika. She's so different from my peers and the analysts. Her van has a CD player built in and we listen to an ancient band called The Clash and they're good.

It's several hours later when we finally run out of the fliers. She drives me back to Eagle Rock but pulls into the Trader Joe's lot. "Just poppin' in for a sec."

While she's gone, I try to remember all the places we put the fliers so I can go collect them. Then, when no one calls wanting to get ashes scattered, I'll tell her it just wasn't meant to be.

Erika returns with shopping bags, drives the few blocks to my home, and invites herself in. She carries the Trader Joe's bags to the back balcony and then has me contact Maureen in Wyoming for a testimonial and tells me to have Rooster write one as well. While I do this, she collects a metal roasting pan and removes one of the grates from the oven and disappears down to the backyard.

I don't want to perpetuate this absurd mission, but I'm kind of curious what Maureen and Rooster might say, so I do as I'm told.

After I'm done, Erika returns from the yard, bringing with her the smells of smoke and food.

"Grab plates, cutlery, a towel, and yer filmin' camera."

This is mystery enough to make me obey.

Down among the fruit trees, the yard is squishy and saturated. Erika flips roasting chicken thighs and mixed veggies on her makeshift charcoal grill. I immediately see the need for the towel. The glass-top patio table carries a small lake. Wipe it dry, set the plates and silverware, and hurry upstairs for the salt and pepper poultry figures, napkins, and to turn the last of our "cuppa" into iced tea.

After our wonderful chicken and veggies, Erika picks a pear, a fig, and a peach and lays them "butterflied" on the grill. They come out blackened and soft and sweetly delicious! I can't figure out which is best!

The quinceañera music starts next door. Erika squeals and starts dancing in the mud. This time the music plays straight through. When it ends, cheers and applause burst from the teens next door. I know that must mean they've finally done the choreography right, but Erika curtsies like it's for her.

With the music over, the afternoon sun lowers, and Erika crushes the still-smoking charcoal briquettes with a rock. When they're mashed to a fine grey powder, she has me set up my camera to start filming. She walks directly to the large patch of white calla lilies.

"Let's start 'ere. Tell me when yer rollin'."

I turn on the camera and Erika gently scatters grey ashes among the lilies. In a surprisingly great Southern accent, she says, "We gathah heah to honah, and remembah the life of beautiful Miss Lilly as we set huh remains to eternal reast among the flowahs she loved so well. May the Lord bleass huh soul."

She nods, I cut, and she moves on, searching, searching. We stop at the foot of the ancient walnut tree. "Ye might start at the top and pan doon tae the ground."

I start filming at the top and TILT down to the ground, where she scatters more ashes sounding a bit like a newscaster. "Fred was a strong, wise elder just as this tree is. His father planted a walnut in 1935 when Fred was born. It grew as he grew, both becoming striking fixtures in our community. It's fitting that his ashes reside here."

I push in toward the craggy bark, then tilt again to see the entire canopy. Hold on that. One, two, three...Cut.

"I got a spot," I say and point to a little structure of balanced rocks in an open area in the yard.

"Ach, the cairn. Perfect."

Once I'm set, I nod to Erika and she scatters ashes around the rocks as I say, "When Samantha lost her beloved dog Charger, she told everyone she wanted her ashes to be scattered over his grave. Today, with love and sorrow, we mingle these dynamic souls together. Rest in peace, Samantha."

I cut the camera and Erika gives me a big thumbs up.

"Got a smaller bit o' ashes, luv. Maybe not enough for a person."

I look around. There's a muddy puddle where the gutter lets out. "Got a weird idea."

"Weird 'tis good," Erika says.

"You'll have to do the filming. Here's the button to start. Tell me when you're rolling."

I look at the sun and suggest she move so the view is backlit. When she's filming, I gently pour the last of the ashes, put my hands in the goo, and mix them with the mud. "Darling Emma knew what she liked and she liked mud. If she had lived, she might have become a famous sculptor." I mold the gritty ash and earth, creating a central form. "She made mud-pies first, but quickly graduated to mud horses and mud people. We know she would have loved to be made into a little mud girl." I add a head and limbs. "She'll dry and maybe remain as a little mud girl for a while, and then crumble and dissolve into the ground like us all." I set the little figure standing on the grass. The sunlight glistens over her form. "We miss you, Emma. Rest in mud."

I glance at Erika. She's got tears in her eyes and gracefully moves in to get a closer shot of the little mud-child, waits a beat, then pushes the button to cut. "Jesus, Mary, and Joseph! Ye've got quite the imagination! And you can sculpt!"

"I don't think I'll ever see this yard the same way again. Let's take a look at the footage!"

As Erika cleans the dishes and roasting pan, I input what we shot into the laptop. We sit together at the kitchen table to create the *Ashes-to-Ashes* website. We use graphics from the brochure. We upload the films of Lyle's scattering, Agnes' scattering, and the fake ones of Lily, Fred, Samantha, and Emma. I'm shocked at how great these look. With a little color-correction I make them seem like they were filmed in entirely different times, weather conditions, and locations.

That done, right on cue, the two testimonies come in. Maureen's is so over-the-top with praise it makes me teary. Rooster's is more measured, but that's 'cause he's a man. We make these five-star ratings. Erika writes a very moving one pretending to be Agnes's relative and other fake ones for the make-believe ceremonies we just filmed. Just like she did with the voiceover, she makes each of them sound like they're from completely different people. And they are all five-star ratings! We pick colors and fonts and organize the pictures and quotes and it's professional, and personal, and super fantastic!

When we get it done, she has me push PUBLISH and the *Ashes-to-Ashes* website goes live. We cheer and high-five each other and it feels great.

"I'm proud o' thee, luv. T'is a grand thing yer doin'."

And she gives me a hug, kisses on each cheek, a pat on the butt, and trots out the door.

After she leaves, I stand on the balcony looking at the sunset glow on the hills of Griffith Park. I feel discombobulated. That felt so fun and creative and—it was a ridiculous waste of time!

I spent the whole damn day on this pointless, absurd scheme.

I should delete the *Ashes-to-Ashes* website right now, but that would be a further waste of time and I need to get down to my real-life business. Work on my résumé. I'll reach out to my best clients to ask for testimonials. Would it be unprofessional to use five-star ratings in a résumé?

I step back to the laptop on the kitchen table, open the résumé template, and burst into tears.

WHAT TO DO WITH CLAYTON?

TODAY, TANGO'S GOTTA FIGURE OUT what to do with Clayton. He stuffs his belongings into the sleeping bag and tucks it far up behind the bridge footing, slips Clayton into the duffle-bag, drapes it over one shoulder and leashes Captain. The man and dog scramble up the Arroyo Seco embankment and onto the Colorado bridge. He still keeps an eye out for that ragtop jeep, even though he knows his benefactress Agnes Sloan is dead. No sign of it.

It's a hot walk but not far. He makes it to the small library between Pasadena and Eagle Rock and ties Captain under a shady jacaranda tree. Tango doesn't like going into libraries. He knows they're a common refuge for his kind. He hates seeing the filthy bundles on the floor. Hates seeing the ragged people pulling out any old book and pretending to read, but really just getting out of the rain or heat. He doesn't want to be associated with them, even if he knows they're the same.

The woman at the information desk looks up. Her glance takes in all of him and he sees the judgement, and the frustration that she can't legally turn him out.

Tango approaches her, trying to calm his insides to make his words sound gentle, but the familiar fury at her disgust makes his voice shake. "Excuse me, Ma'am, I need to use a computer for a spell."

He can see she resents being asked and wants him to be invisible so she can ignore him. "You have to leave an I.D. or license to use one. Do you have that?"

He takes the military dog tag from around his neck and sets it down on the counter along with his I.D.

She pushes the dog tag back with a long fingernail. "You know how to use the computer?"

"I do."

"You have one hour."

Tango thanks her and steps to the computer farthest from the front and any eyes. He pulls Clayton's urn from his duffle bag.

Google search: *Clayton Robert Linley. 1957-1979.*

Nothing.

Search for: *Clay Linley.*

Nothing.

The guy died before Facebook and social media, so he won't have a past there. Try *Clayton Linley image search*. Nothing.

Punches the keys with dirty fingers. *Where to take ashes with no relatives.*

Finds several sites. People actually do this. Actually take care of the ashes of other people. What a strange business to be in. Lots of expensive places. Nothing he could afford.

Maybe cemeteries or funeral homes would know what to do. He goes to Google Maps and searches nearby. Funeral home right on Colorado Blvd. Easy. They might give him advice.

The librarian stands in front of him. "Time's up. Here's your I.D."

Tango puts his I.D. in his wallet and Clayton back in the duffle bag as the woman waits. She makes no effort to hide the clean white cloth in one hand and bottle of spray disinfectant in the other. Gotta erase all trace that he was there. He tries to give her a genuine smile to throw her off guard, but it comes out as a grimace.

Step out into the glare. Unleash Captain and head home.

His mama used to say, "I can only do two things in a day, and one of them is lunch." That's how Tango feels right now. The library visit is enough for one day. Funeral home can happen later.

A JOB

AT EIGHT-THIRTY IN THE MORNING, I dress in my business pantsuit, do my hair and makeup and put on heels. At eight-fifty-five, I email my new résumé and cover letter to six investment firms downtown. That's done! They'll see these when they get to work at nine and I should get a call at nine-o-five.

My reward will be a fruit breakfast from the backyard. I step down the stairs and glance to the gutter area. The little mud-figure of Emma is still standing. Wonder how long she'll last.

Exactly at nine-o-five my phone rings. YES! I answer, trying to sound friendly but also talented and competent. "Hello, Prestonia Cheswick here."

"I'm calling about ashes to be scattered?"

Fuck. Should I hang up? My pause gives the woman time to continue. She says she's super impressed with the films on my website and wants a special ceremony for her father. She's a speed talker and I can't get a word in.

"Where can we meet? Can you meet now? I'm free right now. I'm in LA. You're in LA, right? Tell me where you are and I'll be in the car in one minute."

I don't want anyone to know where I live, so I suggest we meet at Cindy's Diner. It's just around the corner.

"I'll GPS it and be there ASAP. Name's Janet. I'll recognize you from your website photo. See y—"

And she cuts herself off.

Fuck. Fuck, fuck, fuck, fuck.

Change out of the heels into flats and walk to Cindy's. The big sign with geometric elements is the space-age, mid-century-modern Googie style like the Astro Diner, but its building architecture isn't. The building is an unimaginative stucco box with a grey double-pitch roof. However, the interior is just what you'd want for a retro coffee shop. Bright orange booths and counter stools. Orb lights over each table. Formica and chrome everywhere. I'd have never known about this cool place if not for Agnes Sloan giving me her house. It's only a block and a half away.

I order a coffee and sit in a booth facing the door. A short wait and the woman, Janet, enters waving energetically. She looks to be in her thirties and as she sits, she sets a cardboard box on the table. "I didn't know if you wanted Dad here now or not, so I brought him. This is Ed, my father. Ed, meet Prestonia. Prestonia, Ed."

Do I say *Nice to meet you*?

Before I can figure that out, Janet launches into a story about how Ed always wanted to learn to fly and how he finally did so in his sixties and he wanted his ashes scattered from a plane. The waitress comes by and Janet points to my coffee and nods, not breaking stride with her narrative. She tells me she knows the pilot of a small Cessna plane who was her dad's instructor and she can hire him to perform the ceremony but he can't fly and scatter and film at the same time and she's afraid of flying, so, "No can do."

Her coffee comes and Janet pushes it aside to lean across the table, eyes wide. "I don't know if there is a word for it, but it's a real phobia. Like if I even *sat* in a plane, I would die. I mean really D-I-E. It's as bad as people have with spiders or ladders. Who knows what caused it. I've never been in a plane, but it's there, so why risk it? What if I did go up and it crashed? I can't even think about it. Not for me. Not even for dear old Dad. But what am I to do? His last wish and I can't fulfill it. I cried. I tell you, I cried real tears. So you can imagine my absolute relief when my friend showed me your website. YAY! I said. Really. I said it right then. YAY! I can't tell you the weight you've taken off my mind."

Fuck. I'll lie and tell her that I'm way too booked—

Her eyes widen even farther like we're co-conspirators and she whispers, "When I found *Ashes-to-Ashes* I got so excited that I contacted Dad's flying instructor and he can do this tomorrow morning at eight. I already PayPaled him his fee. Expenses taken care of! I'll meet you at Van Nuys Airport, give you the five hundred cash and wait there 'til you fly back. It won't be like a super-long flight."

Fuck.

She puts a small hard drive on the table. "Here are all the extras you can edit in. I saw your other movies and figured I'd bring everything I could think of. This has photos of Dad from when he was a kid and up to his last day. Home movies, videos of his plane taking off and landing. And music he liked. Anything else you need?"

I don't even have time to respond when—

"Oh, I almost forgot!" She hands me a piece of paper. "This is what I want you to say when you do the scattering." She grins, looks around the diner with, "We're all set then!" and leans over the cardboard box on the table. "Dad, Prestonia'll take good care of you. Bye. Love you!"

And she shakes my hand with a precise up and down, puts a ten-dollar bill on the table whispering, "Expenses," and leaves. I stare at the untouched coffee across the table.

Fuck.

Walk from the diner carrying Ed and the hard drive. Back home, I connect the drive and look through the material. There's so much. It would make a twenty-part documentary to include it all. An incredibly boring twenty-part documentary. I'm going for something between ten and fifteen minutes.

I scan quickly, pull some of the best bits, photos, and videos. Make sure to get everyone in the family. The home. All the stuff that'll make people weep. Footage of him looking proud, stepping into the plane. I enlarge it for a close-up and pause on the smile he held for a brief millisecond. Freeze-frame to keep that smile going.

That and the footage of scattering should do it! This will be easy. I've already been in a plane so that won't be hard.

BOB'S REQUEST

TANGO GOES TO THE DOG PARK to drop Captain off with Bob

before getting his weekly shower and clothes cleaned at All Saints Church. As Captain and Daisy race off to play, Tango asks his friend to keep Clayton's urn safe while he's gone, in case of another meeting with teenage boys. He's in a rush, and Bob has something he wants to discuss, but says it'll keep.

The Church clean-up is the usual and no teens molest him on the way back. He purposely passes the gas station where that Middle Eastern mechanic helped collect Clayton's ashes. The man is there again. Tango waves. The man waves back. That feels good.

At the dog park, Tango splits the church sandwich with Bob. After a few minutes in silence, Bob says he has a favor to ask.

Tango turns to him with a smile. Bob is thinner than ever. His skin looks slightly yellow. Breath is labored. Tango winces, realizing he's not been here for his friend. *Shit. Why was I focused on myself?*

"Shoot, brother."

"I've got an appointment scheduled. For surgery."

"Anything bad?" Tango asks.

"Not good. Stents in my heart."

"What are stents? Can you get rid of them?"

"Stents are like little straws they're gonna put in to make the blood flow better."

Tango takes a bite of his sandwich to look away. The bread, or something, clogs his throat. An unexplained anger rises in him. *This anger ain't real,* he thinks. *It's cause you're scared and don't know how to react. Take your time.* He chews and forces himself to swallow. *Speak now. Be there for the man.*

"Shit, Bob. You gotta be scared."

"I am. Got a favor to ask."

"Answer's yes."

"Good. I need you to take care of Daisy while I'm gone. She will be in good hands with you and Captain. You know her and I know you care for your friends."

"It won't be cozy for Daisy."

"You could stay at my house. It's under contract but the

closing isn't until the end of the month."

"Closing?"

"When it's actually sold. There's a whole process but it's mine until then. Stay there."

Tango looks up at the sky. "Well, see—I'm the outdoors type."

Bob smiles. "I understand. I expect to be out of the hospital in three days—hopefully. Can I bring you by the house now and give you the bag of her dog food? I'll drop you three at the arroyo after."

At his house, Bob insists on Tango taking two tote bags with him. They're filled with cans of tuna, beans, cookies, dried salami, crackers, cheese, bottled water, and bread. Loaded with supplies, he drives Tango and the dogs back to the hideaway camp. Daisy and Captain are overjoyed to be together.

Bob laughs at the ecstatic friends. "I expect Daisy'll never want to return." He shakes Tango's hand. "I'll leave you to it. See you on the other side."

"Good luck, friend. Rest easy that Daisy'll be well cared for."

UP IN THE AIR

THE NEXT MORNING. I'm up and dressed in my black outfit and the camera is charged and I've got backup batteries and load everything, including Ed, into the backpack. Still early, so I trot downstairs to the backyard for a fruit breakfast. So yummy. Okay, off to this last crazy adventure.

I've never been to the Van Nuys Airport. It's small compared to LAX. Janet spots me as I park and runs to meet me. "I'm soooooo glad this is happening! Thank you!"

She hands me five crisp hundred-dollar bills and leads me to a small hangar where we meet her dead father's flying instructor, Maclellan. He's got a jaw trying to destroy a piece of gum, a khaki cap with the letters USMC—University something I guess—and the requisite mirrored aviator sunglasses. I can't see his eyes, but I can tell he's glaring at me. All business. "You got everything? We can't turn around and come back if you forget something. If you have to pee, do it now."

I tell him I'm fine and he marches me to a plane. A tiny plane. A plane hardly bigger than my car. A two-seater.

Wait. Just him and me? No co-pilot? No group of tourists waiting to board?

"You ready?" The pilot asks as he reaches up and opens the passenger door.

I mumble, "sure," and he walks around and climbs in on the driver's side. I don't see how I'm supposed to get in. The seat is high up and there's no step or handle or anything to help.

"Station your foot on the landing gear and climb aboard."

Below the door there's a slanted axle thing holding a tire. It has a thin bracket halfway up. I get my foot up there and grab onto the edge of the door frame and lift enough to get a knee onto the floorboard and from there I very in-delicately haul myself into the plane.

"Buckle up," Mr. Pilot says as he does things with the levers and switches and in a second, the propeller, only a few feet away at the nose of the plane, swirls. I really hope it's attached well and can't come through the windshield. We start vibrating. The noise needs to be turned down. Over the motor, there's a lot of rattling, like screws undoing. How old is this plane?

Maclellan tilts the controls toward the runway, puts on his headset, says some numbers and letters into the mic, and there's no waiting or all those things my previous flying experience had like "put your seat backs up" and "store your tray tables" and suddenly we're moving way too fast on this short road, heading for disaster, and he pulls back on the steering thing, and we lift into groundlessness, smashed hard against the back of our seats and I'm not sure breakfast was a good idea. Higher and higher, now turned sideways and I'd be spooning with the pilot if not for my seatbelt.

We level off and the city is much closer than that Wyoming flight. I can see cars and trucks and people and dumpsters and we push higher and swing left away from the morning sun and the San Fernando Valley is suddenly visible as a valley. Mountains skirt it. We follow the notch of the highways passing through the gap and stay over the widest one. Is this the 5 north? We keep following it. I've only been as far north as—Hey! There it is! Magic Mountain Amusement Park!

"Did you know the deceased?" Maclellan asks.

"No."

"I taught him to fly. It was hell. Man never shut up."

His daughter inherited that gene, I guess.

The pilot continues. "I don't know how he ever took a breath with his constant yammering. Couldn't get a word in. He's quieter now."

I smile like that might be a joke but he's not smiling, so I switch to nodding.

Farther, farther, desert suburbs, scrubby forests, a big lake, and now really tall mountains. Who knew there was such a crazy mix of lands! Probably a lot of people, including lumberjack Garrett, but I didn't!

We fly over the mountains and start circling.

"Here's the spot. Mount Pinos. Scatter him here."

I look at Maclellan. "How do I scatter him? Is there a slot or bomb-port type of thing?"

"Open the door and dump him out."

I stare at him. He's not smiling.

"Seriously," I say, "How do I do this?"

"Open the door and dump him out."

I point to the ground below. "We're in the air. I'm not opening the door."

"Give him to me. I'll open dump him out my door. You can film it and we'll be done."

If he opens the door and dumps Ed out, I'm guessing he will not be holding the controls. If he falls out, I can't fly, so maybe I'd better do the dumping. We probably shouldn't call it dumping.

"The seatbelt holds?" I ask.

"So far."

I check it and check it and check it again and check it one

more time.

Open the box with Ed. He's in a plastic bag with a twist tie. I undo the twist tie and turn on the go-pro camera on my lapel. I lift the paper of what I'm supposed to read and click open the latch of my door.

Whoa! The wind is strong! I'm not sure I can open this!

I lean forward and push and push and the door opens and the ground below is like a dare, and wind and engine are crazy loud, and I shout the first line against the roar, "Dear Dad, we are sending you off by way of your favorite—" and pour the bag— and the ashes all swirl INTO THE PLANE! We gasp and cough in a cloud of Ed! Slam the door. What the hell! I've got him in my eyes, in my mouth, up my nose!

Maclellan makes a choking sound.

Don't fucking die on me!

He opens his door and yells over the roaring wind, "Open yours!"

I do and the cloud of Ed tornadoes in the middle of the cockpit, splits, and jettisons out the two doors. Simultaneous SLAMS!

I start shaking. Seriously shaking. Like people who almost experienced death supposedly shake. With my tremors, the speckles of grey dust covering my black clothes dance.

Maclellan tilts us in a wide curve back toward civilization.

Fuck. The film of this will be a mess. Probably not useable. I can't show that to Janet. This is the last one, but I'm not going to present a piece of shit. Ed and his family deserve more.

"Could you please circle over the mountain one more time?" I ask.

"You dumped the man and made a mess of my plane. I'm done."

"I promised I would say the words Janet wanted."

"Not gonna happen, girlie."

I can't believe he won't do this. The film will be shitty and I'll let down Janet and Ed. There's got to be something I can do. Try acting? But who? I remember my Introduction to Cinema class.

That teacher taught only old films, never current ones. Most modern he ever got was the 1980s. One old movie had Robert Mitchum in the original *Cape Fear*. That guy was scary! I'll do him.

"Well, pardon me all over the place. Mister, you were hired for a mission and the mission isn't done until I say. My reputation is on the line. I've got a crisp C-note in my pocket with your name on it if you turn this heap around and let me do my job."

Maclellan looks at me like he's trying to place the actor. "Let me see the hundred."

I pull a bill from my pocket and hand it to him.

He takes it and the plane tilts back toward the mountains.

Check the go-pro camera. It's still on. Point it out my window and shout over the roar of the engine in a non-Robert-Mitchum voice, "Dear Dad, we are sending you off by way of your favorite activity. Up on high. We miss you and love you. Up here you have a head start to heaven. Fly high, Dad."

I slip back to Mitchum for, "Gonna open the door to get an unobstructed shot." Check my seatbelt again and open the door, tilting the lens out of the crack to get the mountain landscape below.

SLAM!

"I'm done."

Our trip back is silent except for the throbbing motor and our occasional coughing. Gradually, the view of the San Fernando Valley below gets closer. Buildings enlarge. Cars become distinguishable. People sprout limbs. Maclellan says some numbers and letters into the mic and the airport runway comes into view and grows larger. But we're heading in fast. Way too fast. I grip for the armrest but there isn't one and my hand squeezes the door handle and I can't let go cause we're aiming at the ground! This man wants to scatter us! The man touches a control and the propeller in front of us slows and STOPS! He IS trying to kill us! I gulp back a scream as we drop down and the runway lines whip under us and he switches something and the propeller starts up again but in the opposite direction, making us lurch back while moving forward and he drops us down and I feel the tires cushion us as if we're a baby being set on a pillow. We slow and glide along the runway like it's completely normal and he curves us around to the hangars and the propeller circles to a stop. The noise is gone except in my ears. The man turns to me. In his sunglasses, I see the reflection of a terrified wide-eyed girl.

I can tell he has a lot to say. His clenching jaw is pulverizing his gum. He gnarls, "Get the hell out."

He doesn't need to ask twice. I somehow jump down and as I hit the pavement, a cloud of Ed puffs from me. I'm very grateful to be in touch with the Earth again. I brush off and shake my hair hoping to look normal before I see Janet. Lots more of Ed gets scattered. I turn to thank Mr. Pilot, but he's already at work spraying the plane controls with Dust-Off. Or should I call it Ash-Off?

Janet is running across the airport pavement toward me. I'm not really anxious to relay the experience to her. I hurry to the parking area. She catches up with me and is breathless but that doesn't stop her mouth. "How was it? Was it wonderful? I'm sure he loved it. I wish I could have been there! I can't wait to see the film. Hey! How about we watch it now! Can you show me now? We could sit in my car. Oh, yes, yes, yes! I'm so excited!—"

I mumble something about professionalism and being committed to crafting the film and not wanting to give "spoilers," as I trot away, trying not to leave a wake of dust.

In the parking lot, I dump my gear in the trunk and hop in the car. It's nine o'clock. Only an hour has passed. Feels like a lifetime.

Drive past Griffith Park. Grit in my teeth. Across my skin. Black clothes powdered. Back to Eagle Rock, I park and walk up to the door, slip off my shoes and empty the grey sand onto the Birds of Paradise plants framing the walkway. Inside, strip completely. Empty my pockets of the four hundred-dollar bills, wondering for a second if I should launder the money. Decide not to and put the dusty clothes in the washing machine. Shower the bits of Ed clinging to me down the drain. Brush teeth, gargle, and spit. I will never, ever, ever scatter another ash!

FUNERAL HOME

CAPTAIN, DAISY, AND TANGO walk on the shady side of the street into Pasadena. The funeral home has a typical California look—stucco and Spanish terracotta curved roof tiles. Tango ties Captain and Daisy to a hose spigot in the shade and opens the wide wooden door. The building must have tight seals on the windows and doors because as the door closes, all sound from outside vanishes. The air is cool and carries a faint perfume. Barely audible hypnotic music plays. Across the room, there's a vase of flowers and several brochures on a marble tabletop, glowing under soft recessed lighting. The walls are a soothing grey-green. As Tango slowly steps across the thick, soft carpet, he imagines lying on it.

"Can I help you?"

Tango turns to the compassionate voice. A large man in a tasteful suit, who obviously works out at an expensive gym. When the guy takes in Tango's visage, his eyes drop the faux compassion.

"We don't have work or any handouts."

"I'm not looking for either," Tango says, feeling anger rise. "I'm inquiring about how to go about dealing with ashes from an unknown—"

"We don't do that. Leave."

"Man, I'm just asking a question. I found an urn—"

The dude steps close and puts his palm on Tango's chest, pushing. It's instinct or anger that causes Tango to snatch the man's thick wrist and instantly slide his other hand between the man's fingers, grab the index, and bend it backwards. The man's knees buckle. Tango gives him a hard shove and the guy crashes into the wall.

Mister Funeral Home rebounds and slams Tango backward, bashing him into the marble-topped table. The brochures scatter, and the vase falls, spilling water and flowers over the papers, and Tango slips on the clutter and drops to the plush carpet, glad its thick pile saves his knees.

An arm reaches around his neck and the guy's got Tango in a headlock. Damn! The man yanks Tango up and pushes him, still in the headlock, to the door.

"Open it, fucker."

Tango does, as the arm tightens around his throat. Bright sun and the rumbling of traffic floods over them as Tango is steered out by the neck. Captain and Daisy bark wildly and struggle against their leashes. The bright sun is dimming for Tango as he chokes out, "I can't breathe!" The man tightens the headlock. Tango's knees buckle and he's hanging by his neck in the man's elbow, hands clawing desperately to relieve the grasp. Captain rears and bucks furiously against his collar. The man presses Tango's windpipe further so no air gets in. Black clouds Tango's eyes and his face swells. Captain wriggles his head free and barrels across the parking lot toward the two men—a blur of anger. Tango feels the guy tense as Captain races toward them. The man lets go, Tango drops, Captain leaps, and the dude is back in the building, feeling the hot breath of the dog on his wrist just as he slams the door. Captain scratches and barks, digging great masterful scratches into the wood. Good dog!

Tango, struggling to catch his breath, gives the finger to the building in case someone's watching. It takes him several minutes to stop coughing and to have his eyes adjust to the world again. Finally, he struggles to his feet, steading himself with a hand on Captain's anger-raised back. As he limps toward Daisy and Captain's empty collar and leash, he wonders about himself. *I thought I was over this shit. Shit that got me kicked out of the army. That shouldn't have been an altercation. He put his hand on me, but I didn't need to react. I'm not sure any of that Buddhism shit is getting in.*

Something is stuck to his sneaker, dragging on the pavement. He kicks and it flies off and lands wet, face up. A brochure. *Ashes-to-Ashes.* The big font says: *Let me help you honor your loved one's remains.*

Tango picks it up. There's a picture of a young woman: Prestonia Cheswick - *Ashes-to-Ashes* CEO.

"Damn. I recognize you, Prestonia. You're that chick I met by Trader Joe's who inherited Agnes Sloan's house and her ragtop jeep."

As Tango walks with the dogs back toward the Colorado Bridge, he reads the *Ashes-to-Ashes* brochure. The whole thing strikes him as strange. The benefactress Agnes Sloan gives him cash and when he follows the ragtop jeep to thank her, he meets this young Prestonia woman who just happens to be someone who scatters ashes and that's what he needs for Clayton.

"What do you think, Captain? Is it fate or coincidence or too good to be true?"

Captain barks.

"Not sure what that means, Captain. I guess I'll call this Prestonia tomorrow. At least she may have an idea of how to get Clayton a home."

He folds the brochure and slips it in his wallet beside the last twenty from his disability check, and they scramble down the embankment to his Arroyo home.

LAST EDIT

I CAN'T BELIEVE it's only ten. If I was at the firm I'd have been staring at numbers for the last hour. I'm still stunned by the flight over mountains and coughing up bits of a dead man. But it's over. The clothes are swishing with the last of Ed's ashes, the four hundreds have been sponge-wiped and put in my purse and I'm scrubbed clean. Only a slight itching in my eyes.

I make myself tea with the whole tea set which makes me think of Erika. I feel angry at her for causing all this, but at the same time, I almost want to call her and tell her about the crazy adventure. My phone rings—maybe it's her or maybe it's for another *Ashes-to-Ashes* job. No way. I'm done. The phone says the number is from Kansas again. Not falling for a fucking scam. I block the number.

Arrange the camera and laptop on the kitchen table. Start

importing the footage into the computer.

Since this is my last time doing this shit, I'm gonna do it right. I isolate a clean sample of the plane sound so I can have the sound program lower it behind the words I had to say. It comes out distorted so I record the words again as a voiceover and add the plane sound low behind it. Now it's perfect. Something to remember. No. Never doing this again, so nothing to remember.

The footage of the sprinkling of Ed's ashes is a complete mess. A sandstorm in a cockpit. No one will want to see their father's remains like this.

Start with what works. The moment before the ashes hit the fan. Have the footage of the ash-box opening, move frame by frame until the instant the ashes begin to fall and enter the plane. Zoom in on the footage to remove the box from the frame and dissolve to ultra slow motion. Long, long dissolve between those ashes and the shot I took of the mountains below. End with that mountain shot.

Download stock footage of glitter falling and incorporate hints of that within the ashes. Just enough you get a feeling of wonder but not enough to have it conscious. Color-correct the footage to give a bit of Magic Hour golden-sheen to everything. Lay in voiceover. Add music. I choose Albinoni's *Adagio in G Minor* which I first heard in Peter Weir's movie *Gallipoli* during my film semester. It's a tearjerker.

Here's what I learn: you slow down footage enough, keep the incremental dissolves moving, add sweeping classical music, and you can make even a disaster look beautiful. Not that I'll EVER use this lesson again. Anyway, incorporating the home-movie and the family photos shit, it makes a very moving video. Even gets a tear in my eye. I send Janet a link to download the film and—I'm DONE with this absurd pointless adventure! Just gotta delete the website and shut this fiasco down! Go to the website editing page. Where is the button to delete it?

A notification comes in. Janet. She's extremely happy and insists I include her father on the *Ashes-to-Ashes* website. Fuck!

I upload Ed's scattering to the site and she quickly sends her testimonial review and five-star rating. I'll have to wait to deactivate the website. Maybe in a week she'll forget about it. Maybe in a week, I can put a "down for maintenance" notice up and have *Ashes-to-Ashes* slowly disappear.

TAKEN

CAPTAIN AND DAISY ARE SLEEPING off their meal beside Tango as he munches a cheese sandwich on rye from the bounty that Bob gave him and reads Pema. If he can find the right passage in the book, maybe he can find an antidote for why he fought that guy at the funeral home. What he finds is: *The future is completely open, and we are writing it moment to moment.*

The words stun him. The future is open? And can he really write his own future?

Captain growls and lifts his nose in the air. Daisy immediately wakes, ears up.

"What is it? A coyote?"

There are rustling sounds coming from many directions. Tango and the two dogs tense.

"Attention!" A megaphone voice. "Illegal encampments will be dismantled and cleared. Collect your belongings."

Tango stands up and hurriedly grabs his things. Clayton's urn, sleeping bag, clothes, Bob's supplies, Pema—

Daisy and Captain bark furiously as police step out of the brush, palms on their gun holsters.

"We got a complaint about you and your dog. Public indecency. Put your hands on your head."

Indecency. The jogger lady in pink.

Tango shakes his head. "I'm going. I'm packed and going. Let me get the dogs and I'll be gone."

"We got a complaint. Gotta follow through."

Two animal control officers move forward with long poles dangling looped wires at the ends, circling Daisy and Captain.

"Stop!" Tango screams. "You can't take them! I'm caring for

one of the dogs. He's not mine."

The cop inches closer. "Get on your fuckin' knees with your hands on your head!"

Tango thinks of leaping and smashing the man in the nose, but remembers Pema and that fighting has never brought him anything good. He lets go of all he's carrying, drops to his knees, and puts his hands on the back of his head.

Cuffs ratchet around his wrists, his hand is twisted and he's pulled to his feet.

Two female officers wearing green rubber gloves, shove the duffle bag, Clayton's urn, Pema's book, the sleeping bag, and food from Bob into a large clear plastic bag.

"You can't take my stuff! It's my property. There are important things in there!"

One of them peels off the back of a bright red sticker, sticks half of it on the bag and hands the other half to the officer holding Tango. "You can pick up your stuff at the warehouse. Here's the receipt. Don't lose it."

One of the animal control guys snares his wire loop around Daisy's neck and pulls it tight. The dog leaps and twists at the end of the pole.

The other dogcatcher tries to snag Captain, but the dog darts around, snarling and barking.

The cop holding Tango un-holsters his gun, raising it toward the furious dog. "Get out of the way, man, I'll take care of this."

"NO! NO!" screams Tango.

The officer clasps his gun with both hands and takes aim at the seething, whirling dog.

BAM!

The bullet misses and Captain continues darting back and forth, snarling.

Tango leaps in front of the officer, blocking his aim. "Stop!"

"Get back, asshole, This dog's vicious!"

Tango keeps moving to stay between the cop and Captain. "Don't shoot him! I'll make him stop!"

"Get out of the way, or you're next!" the officer yells, shifting the gun to point at Tango's forehead.

"CAPTAIN, SIT!" Tango yells.

Captain sits. Silent and panting.

The cop turns to aim at the still target.

"Please!" Tango screams.

"I got him," says the animal control officer, stepping in to slip the loop over Captain's head. The cop lowers his gun, glaring at Tango. "Guess what, asshole. The county will put that fucker down when you don't show to bail him out."

As Tango is shoved toward the path, the two dogs are dragged on ahead.

"Where are you taking them!?" Tango screams at the dog-catchers.

"Lacy Street Shelter."

Tango is driven downtown to the LA County Jail. He's booked and has his wallet, pocket knife, military dog tag, and shoelaces removed.

"Can I get my call?"

The intake officer stares at him, not blinking. That must require a lot of effort. After way too long, the man asks, "What call?"

"The one we get. The call we can make."

"That's only in the movies. It's not real life. No calls."

"You're shitting me."

The non-blinking man cracks a smile. "Yeah, I'm shitting you. You can't dial. We dial. What's the number?"

Tango doesn't have anyone to call but Bob and that old man's probably in the middle of surgery. Fucking shit time to have a heart problem. "In my wallet. Call that number."

The man pulls everything from Tango's wallet, looks through the contents, unfolds the brochure, and holds it up to Tango. Tango nods and the officer dials. After a moment, he speaks, "This is Officer Szitanyi from the Los Angeles County Jail. We've got a Leon Thibodeaux in our facility here who wants to speak with you."

Tango watches the man frown. It's clear that this call isn't going well.

Tango yells at the thick bulletproof barrier. "Tell her Agnes Sloan sent me!"

Five seconds later he's on the phone. The woman's voice says, "I don't know you, but I know Agnes Sloan, so if you have something to say, say it now."

Tango takes a breath. "Prestonia, Agnes Sloan helped me, as she helped you. She gave to us both. I'm not asking for anything but what she might do—help someone. I'm Tango. We met when I talked to you about Agnes Sloan outside of Trader Joe's. I recognized the ragtop jeep. I've got a dog and I'm also taking care of a dog for a friend who is undergoing open-heart surgery. The two dogs were picked up and taken to Lacy Street Shelter when I was—evicted from my home under the Colorado Bridge. Please, please, please, Prestonia, check if the dogs are safe and, if you can, get them out. Captain's a reddish pit bull/border collie/something mix. Matted fir. He has one of my military dog tags on his collar. It will say Leon Thibodeaux."

"What?"

"Thi—bo—deaux. Tango, hotel—I mean—T, H, I—" and he spells out his name.

"Got it," Prestonia says.

"Other dog is Daisy. She's a Dalmatian. Collar has a tag with Bob I-don't-know-his-last-name and a Sierra Madre address. Both Daisy and Captain are in danger of getting *put down*, 'cause they were captured on the wrong side of the tracks."

There is a moment of silence.

"Please, Prestonia. Please. You're honestly the only person I have to call. The only one who can save these dogs."

The silence continues. Enough silence that Tango can hear behind him the screams and clanging doors of his future.

"Okay," Prestonia says. "And where are you?"

Tango asks the officer where he is and relays the info.

"Okay," she repeats and hangs up.

And Tango is escorted to the cell. First time he's been forced indoors in so long. Three other men are in the small room. Tango has had enough of men's methods to know not to acknowledge any of them, but he spits on the floor to show he's a fucker. It seems to work. He climbs onto the top tier of a bunk and lies shaking.

Chill, man. Breathe. You remember Pema. What you think and feel isn't real. You can control it. You can do this, son. And Tango turns to the wall so the trickling from his eyes can't be seen. *Son?* No one ever called him that.

WHAT'S NEXT?

I STARE at my phone. How the hell did this homeless guy get my number? Is he stalking me? Did he follow me from Trader Joe's?

I'm not going to check on those dogs. I wouldn't know where to start. Who does he think I am? I don't even like dogs.

Besides, I don't have time for this. There's a reason I'm sitting at my computer, right now—there are things to do! People to contact. I haven't heard anything from my first round of résumé distribution, so I've got to research more firms.

A large truck or something goes by, rattling the old house windows, jiggling the cabinet doors, and the little ceramic dog toothpick holder on the kitchen table beside my laptop tips over.

You're kidding.

It's a fucking truck. It's not a sign.

It's fucking vibration from the street. It's not Agnes Sloan. Still, she did what he said—help us both. Maybe...

An online search gives me the animal shelter on Lacy Street. Not my neighborhood. Change into jeans because dogs are dirty and, if I manage to get them, they might get their paws on me. Drive there in Agnes's ragtop jeep because dogs are dirty and, if I manage to get them, they'll fill that car with mangy dog hair. I lock the doors as I pass homeless tents, railroad tracks in the middle of the street, and abandoned buildings. I skirt deep road divots as I make my way to the shelter's parking lot.

Inside, overwhelming smells of urine. Walk past cage after cage of desperate, pleading, terrified, vicious dogs. There's a Dalmatian and a matted red mutt together in a cell. "Captain? Daisy?" The two start jumping and twirling and yipping with glee. Guess these are them.

I go to the front desk and tell the receptionist that I'm here to pick up "Daisy and Captain. Daisy had a collar from her owner Bob from Sierra Madre and Captain had a dog tag, like real military dog tag with the name—" I look at my phone memo and decide I can't pronounce the long string of letters so show the name to the receptionist.

And surprisingly, that is enough to get them free. That and a fifty-dollar fee. Minimum twenty-five dollars per day, per animal.

I don't know how to get these dogs to the jeep. The staff gives me ropes to tie to the collars but how do I walk them? I step out and try, "Come with me, dogs." The dogs stick by my side. So far, so good.

Open the jeep's tiny back door. "Get in." And they do. Shut the door. Deep breath.

I slide into the driver's seat. The dogs seem quite happy in the back. They're wagging their tails but keep sniffing around my driver's seat. Shit, are there still bits of Ed's ashes there?

The matted one barks at me. What does he want? I don't know about dogs. What am I supposed to do? I should call Erika. I expect she knows how to handle everything.

The dogs are in the back of the jeep, staring at me as I sit on my stoop waiting for Erika. When her van finally drives up, she immediately lets the dogs out and they pee for a long time on the Bird of Paradise plants. She then takes them into the house and out the back door onto the balcony and sets down a big bowl of water, which they seem very glad to have. She squats down and rubs their ears and looks them in the eyes and whispers to each one. Returning inside, she asks me a lot of questions about the phone call from the man. I show her the long string of letters that makes up his name.

"Leon Thibodeaux. Fella's prob'ly from N'orlinz."

I don't know how she knows these things. Maybe I'll get like that when I'm older.

"Let's go see this Thibodeaux, let 'im know the pups are well."

"Um. He's in jail. Not a good idea."

"Ach, jail's no indication of cherecter. Ye've naer been?"

I give her a look that should suggest NO!

"Never bashed a bloke we' yer brow on a New Year's Eve, then?"

"Not yet," I answer.

"Load up the dogs. They'll want to see their daddy."

I don't know what it is about Erika that makes me unable to say no.

We return the dogs to the jeep and half an hour later we're walking into the County Jail. Why do I feel like they'll arrest me just for being here? At the front, we talk to an officer behind bulletproof glass. I'm about to show him my phone memo with the long stretch of letters, but Erika says, "We're inquirin' to visit wi' yer guest Leon Thibodeaux. We're no bringin' any cakes wi' metal rasps."

The officer tries not to smile, but gives up. We hand over our I.D.s and go through the metal detectors and are pointed to the visiting room. In a few minutes, the man I met at Trader Joe's enters. He's wearing the same cargo pants, the same green t-shirt and bulky army jacket. Same scraggly beard, but with a surprisingly tidy haircut.

When he sees me, his face shows all his worry. "Prestonia! Did you find the dogs?"

"They're in my car."

He covers his mouth and puts his head down like he's trying not to cry. After a moment, he collects himself and whispers, "Thank you, thank you, thank you."

Erika points for him to sit. He does. Everyone does what Erika suggests.

She leans close to scrutinize the man. "Lad, I'm Erika. Yer Leon Thibodeaux?"

"Call me Tango."

"Why Tango? Ye fancy the dance?"

"Was in the military. They'd ask my name and I'd say, 'Leon Thibodeaux' and they'd say, 'Leon what?' so I'd spell it out with military alphabet. Tango, Hotel, India, Bravo, on-and-on and they'd say, 'Fuck it, I'll call you Tango'."

A smile dances around Erika's lips. "Ye want to do that alphabet name—double time?"

"Ma'am." He takes a deep breath and, "Tango-Hotel-India-Bravo-Oscar-Delta-Echo-Alpha-Uniform-Xray, Ma'am!"

Erika squints at him like she's investigating his soul. "What'd ye do, lad, tae get in this predicament?"

"Live under a bridge. Peed at the wrong time."

"You resist the coppers?"

Tango shakes his head.

"Ever violent?"

I see a movement in his eyes—like he's thinking of how to answer. He winces and tries, "I grew up male."

Erika isn't having that answer. "E'er in prison fer violence?"

He gives an embarrassed shrug. "Got thrown in the brig and got my OTH."

"What's 'at?"

"Other-than-honorable discharge from the army."

"What'd ye do?"

"Threw chairs at my C.O."

"What stopped ye?"

"Ran out of chairs."

"Still violent?" Erika asks.

The man exhales slowly. "I'm studying Buddhism. Trying a new way to be. Trying to understand that what I feel and think isn't reality. Trying to see that the chip on my shoulder isn't reality."

"If it's a new way, how d'ye know it'll take."

"I don't. All I can do is work at it."

Yeah, great, I can just imagine the last thing his victim will hear, *Guess that didn't work.* I look at Erika. She's nodding at this guy and she gestures to the guard that we're done and the man is taken away and I'm glad to be through with this adventure, but Erika starts a whole procedure for getting this previously-violent, possibly-still-violent man out of jail! I try to suggest he isn't our problem but she shushes me and after way too many bureaucratic questions and forms, she puts up his bail, and he's let into our care and we're crossing the lot and this so-called-Tango squints and says, "There it is. Agnes's ragtop jeep,"—undoubtedly saying that so I'll think we have this great connection, but we don't—and the jeep across the way is jerking and jiggling from two dogs barking and bounding against the windows. The man joins the two dogs in the back and they're all wagging their tails.

Erika's beaming. Me, I'm fucking furious.

As I drive, Erika leans over the back seat to eye the homeless violent criminal and Captain licks her face. Wiping the slobber away, she asks, "Yer livin' under what bridge, Tango?"

"Colorado Street Bridge in the Arroyo Seco in Pasadena."

"Yer stuff still there?"

"Taken. They gave me a receipt. You're from the UK?"

Erika gives me a sly glance like—*Should I go through the whole story?* I'm too mad to react.

"The world, by way o' Scotland. An ye?"

"Hell, by way o' N'Oleans."

As I drive, I wonder where I'm driving to? The Arroyo? Erika's apartment at the Avalon? Not my house.

As if he's reading my mind, the man says. "Drop me and the dogs anywhere around here. We'll make our way."

"Feckin' not in the cards, Tango," says Erika. "We know ye ain't got but the shirt on yer back. Ye could stay wi' me in the 'partments, but dogs ain't permitted, and I'd imagine yer more the outdoors type."

The guy bows his head as if he's grateful for her understanding.

Erika turns to me. "So, Prestonia? Ye have a grand fruiting

back lot. Can ye give Tango a spot under a tree and maybe a blanket?"

Why is this suddenly my problem!? I'm not a homeless shelter. The guy admitted he's violent! And what about his dogs? Do they attack on command? Maybe all three are killers.

The man speaks before I have to, turning to Erika. "Ma'am, you're imposing your kind assumptions onto this young lady. She doesn't need to be involved. Y'all did enough already."

We slow to a stop at a red light. He opens the door and whispers to the dogs, "C'mon."

They hop out, he shuts the door, and I yell, "Wait!"

Everyone waits, even the people in the cars next to us.

I don't know why I yelled, "wait." So I wait. It comes to me. "Why did you call me? How did you get my number?"

The man opens his wallet and holds up the *Ashes-to-Ashes* brochure.

"Blimey," Erika whispers.

"I've got a buddy—an urn of a buddy's ashes. He needs to have a home found for him. I got your brochure and was going to call you about him, but it felt strange 'cause of the coincidence with Agnes Sloan. When they arrested me, this brochure of yours was the only number I had."

Agnes Sloan again. I don't know what her agenda was, but she is really fucking with my life. What does she want? I look at the man and dogs standing beside the car. Erika looks at me. The drivers in the other cars look at me. I'm overruled.

"Agnes Sloan says *get in.*"

The man points and the dogs hop back in the jeep. He slips beside them and gently closes the door.

I take a deep breath, but I can't speak. Everything is beyond my control. I'm so worn out.

Erika must sense this 'cause she says, "Prestonia 'as a back lot with bonnie fruit trees, and a covered balcony wi' a dry, safe spot below. You and the pups 'ill be stayin' ootside. Nae mess, nae noise, nae bother. Right, Tango?"

Why does she use his name like they're friends! It isn't even his real name!

"Yes, ma'am," the man answers. "We'll stay out of sight and be gone in the morning."

Erika laughs, saying, "We'll see about that, luv,"

I pull up to my small house. Erika commandeers the rest. Maybe I'm acting like a pouty kid, but I don't want any part of this. Still, I can't exactly go into my bedroom and slam the door. I sit silently as Erika gets this Tango man water and leads the dogs to the balcony and finds the closet with blankets and an extra pillow and even gets a clean towel, which I don't know where he'll use, because he's not going to be in MY BATHROOM.

The man takes these from Erika and nods gratefully. He's got the look of sweet submission down. Bullshit.

He turns to me. "Thank you so much, Prestonia. I know this is not what you want. I won't stay but the night."

I shrug like a thirteen-year-old.

"Can you show me where you'd like me to stay?"

I lead him out the balcony door and walk down. Erika stays behind. At the bottom of the stairs, I point to the little mud figure of Emma. "Can you keep away from that? Keep the dogs from knocking her over."

Tango looks at the figure then turns to me, concerned. "Is that —is it—made with ashes?"

I like how worried he looks. "Yes. A little girl. Emma."

He covers his mouth and then, "Can I—can I put the chairs around her so the dogs can't accidentally—I wouldn't be able to bear it."

He seems really distraught. I nod and he moves the two vintage metal chairs carefully to enclose the little mud figure.

"This is a really unique idea," he says. "Creating a sculpture *made* of the ashes, not just a container holding them. Quite a concept."

What's he trying to do, butter me up so I'll drop my guard and he can do whatever? I point to the area under the balcony. "It's covered here. Dry if it rains again. Down there, you can sleep under trees, but the birds will be noisy and they drop a lot under the mulberry tree. Your choice." I turn to go back up.

"Thank you. I don't need anything else, but—"

Here it comes.

"—I should get the dogs some dog food. Mine was confiscated."

I sigh wearily. "There's the Trader Joe's where you first spoke to me, two blocks up. I suppose you need money."

"No, Miss. I've got enough. I'll go out this side gate. Thank you, and I'll say goodnight." He turns to the dogs and puts a palm up. "Stay." And steps out.

I return upstairs and find Erika waiting with her hands on her hips. "What bug is up yer ass? Yer treatin' the fella like 'es a disgustin' pariah. I thought ye were above such nasty judgments."

"We don't know him."

"You dinnae need to be friends, but 'e's a person and should be treated with kindness and respect."

"He admitted to being violent."

"Aye, he admitted as much, rather than lie. And who wouldn't throw chairs if they're in the military? I would! And did ye naer ken a fella who grabbed ye hard or forced his will upon ye?"

I see Brent's Medusa-snake-neck-veins writhing and his hand squeezing my wrist and his fist punching out the porch light. Brent would never consider himself violent. I don't see him that way either. Maybe because Brent isn't homeless. Brent has an apartment and a job and money—and so what if I'm judgmental, if I'm right!

"That man was thrown out of the military for violence! THE MILITARY! FOR VIOLENCE! And he was in jail!"

"Many o' the best people in th' world 'ave been in jail."

"And I don't want to take them home either! I don't want him here!"

Erika looks at me and sighs. "Ok, luv. I hear ye. I'll take 'im to me 'partment at th' Avalon. But ye know I cannae take the dogs."

"Don't you get it!? He's not our problem!"

Erika looks at me like she is pained at what I'm saying.

"Prestonia, don't be an arse."

"I'm sorry, we can't all save the world. If you care so much, take him back to the Arroyo where he was living."

"The lad has no belongings. No bed, no blanket, no clothes, no food. You can't—"

"I can! This is my house. Agnes Sloan gave it to me."

Erika leans close and lowers her voice like she is moving in for a checkmate. "Agnes Sloan gave ye this house. And she gave that man money. She asked ye to scatter her ashes. Ye did and started the business o' *Ashes-to-Ashes*. That man found your brochure for that business and called ye when he needed help. If that tis nae Fate, gimme another word for it."

I can't think of any rebuttal except *Fuck you* and that doesn't seem like a good idea, so I start making dinner in hopes it will stop the discussion. Pasta's easy, so I start a pot of water and open a jar of sauce. I feel Erika watching and judging, but I don't need to be who she wants me to be.

"Can ye nae find a bit o' Agnes Sloan's generosity in ye? Just take the dogs, lass."

"Oh fuck, Erika," I say. "You know he's not going to accept being away from them.

Sauce in a pan. Light the flame. Water isn't even starting to boil. Sprinkle in salt from the ceramic chicken shaker. Pour in olive oil. Watch for the bubbles. I'm facing the stove and not watching her, but behind me the vintage vinyl chair sighs, telling me that Erika's sitting.

"You'll stay for dinner?" I ask.

"Please make enough for two."

I turn with a plastered-on smile, get out two bowls and silverware, and set the formica table. I hope we're not going to be silent and sullen throughout our meal.

The back gate squeaks and shuts quietly. No sounds beyond that. Good. Keep it that way!

Water's finally boiling. Spaghetti in. Set the timer. Erika gets a glass of water as I hover over the stove, occupying myself with stirring the sauce and pasta. The timer finally dings and I drain the pasta, divide it up between the bowls, and pour on the sauce.

Sounds of footsteps moving up the stairs. A knock on the back door. Damn!

I open it and Tango holds up two dog food cans. "I'm sorry, miss. I forgot that my can opener was with my confiscated stuff. Can I borrow one?"

I don't use cans very often, so have no idea where Agnes would keep an opener. It isn't on the counter where I'd expect it. As I search the cabinets, Erika moves past me and opens a drawer by the sink and pulls out a small hand-style opener. Oh. I was looking for an electric unit. She hands it to Tango.

Tango smiles, "Thank you. If it's all right with you, I'd like to pick a piece of fruit or two from your trees. If that's okay."

"Of course. Pick anything you want," I say, glancing at Erika so she'll know I'm making an effort.

Erika lifts her bowl of pasta and the glass of water. "Prestonia means ye can 'ave the fruit fer desert. First ye 'ave this."

What the hell?

Tango shakes his head. "I don't want to take your meal."

"Ach, 'twas always intended for ye. I'm off o' the carbs."

Tango tries to fit the big cans of dog food in his pockets but struggles.

Erika waves him off. "Ye ge doon an gi' the pups their supper. Prestonia 'ill follow wi yer's direc'ly."

The man nods and shuffles down the stairs, as Erika looks through the cabinets.

I'm furious at her. Why is she trying to control my life?

"Erika! First you tell him he can spend the night and it's NOT YOUR HOUSE! Now you give away MY FOOD. All without asking. It's not okay!"

She loads a tray with the dinner and adds a pitcher of water. "Luv, yer nay in practice wi' this sort o' interactin'. It's new t' ye. Ye didnae ken how tae say it yerself, so I gave ye a hand."

She's right that I'm not used to this. For good reason. I don't want it in my life! But—she's defeated me.

"One night. That's all. I'll lock the doors and windows but if I'm murdered, I'm blaming you."

"Right-o." She hands me the tray. "I'll be off then, luv."
"You're leaving?"
"Ye can manage, can't ye?"

I am not sure I can, but I don't want Erika thinking she has to take care of me. "Sure. No problem."

And she gives me a kiss on each cheek saying, "Gi' me a ring if you need anythin', an' wish Tango a bonnie night." She pats me on the butt and leaves whistling what must be an old Scottish jig.

I don't want to, but I can't very well pretend I forgot, so I carry down the tray.

At the bottom of the stairs, I hear Tango whispering to the dogs. What is he saying? Is it code to attack?

I set the meal on the patio table, relaying that Erika wishes him a bonnie night. I don't mention that she's left. Tango thanks me and wishes me goodnight, so I go up to eat my dinner and lock the doors. When it gets dark, I check the doors three times, and go to bed, where I stare at the ceiling, and listen for sounds of that man trying to break in, and worry about him being a murderer and me being an arse.

BUS TRIP

TANGO WAKES EARLY. Prestonia's backyard is starting to glow. He can see the care put into this place. The fruit trees flourishing. The mulch around the plants. Flowers beaming. It's a sanctuary for sure.

Tango flips the covers off his body, causing the dogs to jump, ears and noses at attention. "Shhh. It's cool. I'm going out for a bit. You be good."

And after filling the pasta dinner bowl for the dogs and triple checking his pocket for the red receipt, he wants to leave a note, but doesn't have a pen or pencil, so scrapes an arrow in the dirt by the back gate and tells Daisy and Captain to STAY. When he exits, they immediately jump to watch him leave and mess up the arrow. Returning, he wanders the yard, selects a few rocks and sticks and a huge pinecone and arranges them on the patio table pointing to the gate, then slips out and up the driveway, toward the ragtop jeep of his benefactress. As he scootches past, he lays a hand on the hood. *Thank you.*

Now to find a way to Downey and this warehouse that has his belongings. At the bus stop outside of Cindy's Diner, he checks the posted times, finds one heading in the right direction, and waits. The bus driver is helpful and suggests the best route. He thanks the woman and settles in for the first leg. The bus is full of tired-looking folks. Maybe they're on the way to be cleaners or nannies. Or they're students. Or actors new to town and anxious to make that first audition. Everyone in the bus looks somewhat ashamed for not driving a car to their destination.

The next bus carries him on the long ride through downtown and beyond. It takes almost two hours, and he stops counting after the first fifty stops. At Rosa Parks Station, he gets out and waits for the eastern bus to Lakewood.

Descending from the bus, he still has to find the warehouse. A mail carrier gives him directions, and he sets off. It's already hot and sure to get more so. Please let his belongings be there.

An hour and a half later, he's slogging through an industrial area. No pedestrians. A large windowless building looks to be the one. March across the pavement. Up to the door. No signs. Nothing but the number. He checks the red receipt. Right address.

Rings the bell and waits.
Rings the bell and waits.
Knocks on the door and waits.
Rings the bell and waits.
Nothing.

This is the place. It's way past opening. They have to let him in.

A distant horn plays "La Cucaracha" over and over, growing closer. A taco truck moving down the street. Tango hurries to it, waving.

The truck slows and stops.

A Latino man with a wide mustache slides the passenger door open. "Hola, que pasa?"

Tango gestures to the warehouse. "They open? When? A que tiempo?"

The man shakes his head. "Sorry, hommes, they're fuckers. No regular hours. No way to know. Complete pendejos!"

Tango slumps. "Gracias."

The dude slides the door shut, and the truck starts off, stops, backs up—the man steps out and hands Tango something wrapped in foil and a Coke. "Keep the faith, hommes."

The burrito is the best Tango's ever had. The Coke, too.

He waits another two hours. No one shows up. Another long series of buses brings him back to Eagle Rock. He hears Daisy and Captain greeting him before he even gets to the house.

Prestonia whips open the front door as he's about to slide past the ragtop jeep in the driveway. He freezes.

"What do you mean, leaving me alone with these dogs? Am I a dog person? No! This isn't right. No note, no call, no text."

"I don't have a phone," Tango explains. "And I didn't have paper or pen. All I could think of was an arrow of rocks and sticks on the table by the back gate."

"What the fuck!"

Prestonia slams the door and Tango hears her crossing the house, bashing open the back door, marching downstairs and—

"Fuck! And with the pinecone!"

Clomps back up. She reopens the front door. "I don't how I was supposed to find that message or know what it meant."

"Sorry," Tango says.

"Well, thank you for the sign. You'd better go down before anyone—" She gestures to the neighborhood street. "I mean, go down and see those dogs."

He slips around the jeep and to the back gate. The dogs yip happily and cover him with love. He gives them all his attention and soaks up theirs. It helps so much.

After that warm greeting, Tango moves to the water spigot

and kneels, setting it on a dribble and filling cupped hands over and over until he's swallowed enough. Pours more handfuls over his head and face and looks up to see Prestonia stepping down the stairs with a glass of water.

"Oh. Guess I'm too late—"

His beard and hair dripping, Tango stands and bows, takes the glass from her with a "thank you," and drinks again.

Prestonia looks at the dogs awkwardly. "They're happy now."

"They feel best when they know where their person is."

"You were gone a while. Where were you?"

"I tried to get my belongings back."

"Can you live without them. Is it worth it?"

"I can live without my sleeping bag that Agnes Sloan bought me. I can live without my supplies and toiletries. I can even live without my Pema book. But I can't live without seeing Clayton respected."

"Who's Clayton?"

"The man whose ashes I was hoping you'd help me find a home for."

DOWN TO DOWNEY

TANGO TELLS ME about the trip to Downey. I can't believe he went down there on a bus. I've never even been on a city bus. If he has to take another bus tomorrow then he'll have to stay here again. If I help him get his stuff, he can move back to the Arroyo.

"I'll drive you down and we can get your stuff now."

"I'll go by bus tomorrow. I don't want to impose on your further."

"Nonsense. I'm free now. Let's go."

I suspect he knows it's not entirely altruistic of me, but I don't care.

We leave the dogs in the backyard and slip into my Audi. His ripe smell immediately fills the closed space. I won't be able to stand it. "Second thought, let's take Agnes's ragtop jeep."

The jeep is airy and Tango's scent is easier to bear. Still, I'm going to have to put some sort of air freshener in here after he's gone. I turn on the radio so he won't talk. It works.

Traffic isn't bad and in an hour we're pulling up to the warehouse. There's one car out front. As we approach the building, a woman exits the door, locking it.

"Hello, ma'am, we're here to collect my belongings," Tango says.

The woman has had enough. Enough of life and every part of it. "Not today. Tomorrow."

I try my corporate voice. "My friend was here this morning. He was waiting and no one was here. He needs his belongings."

"Did I not say tomorrow?"

Suddenly I see that there is a world I don't know at all. A world where people are not accepted, not helped, and always disregarded. A world where you will NEVER get by. Where you will NEVER be enough. Where you are totally FUCKED. I've never encountered it. Well, I guess I have since meeting Tango. He's totally fucked. And this woman is in that world. She's both fucker and fuckee.

"Ma'am, can I give you something for your time? I'm sure they're not paying you enough."

She's interested.

Tango shifts uncomfortably. He doesn't want this approach. But it's what I can do.

I never carry cash. Or not small cash. I don't carry ones, or five, or tens, or twenties. But because of scattering Ed's ashes, I have those four hundred-dollar bills tucked in my purse. I pull one out.

"Can you stay a little while longer? Give us time to find his things?"

The hundred is accepted with a curt, "I don't have all day. Half an hour, tops."

And we're let in. To darkness. She clicks on lights. Bang, bang, bang. One section after another.

The warehouse is immense. The size of a football-field. It's filled with rows and rows of wide metal shelves, four-tiers high, all overflowing with stuffed clear bags. Each shelf is four feet above the one below, the tallest being about twelve feet high. We can't see the bagged items on the third or fourth shelf.

"Is there an area for recent acquisitions?" Tango asks.

The woman spreads her arms in answer.

Tango twitches his neck and moves his head in such a way that it looks like he's trying to tip a wasp out of his ear. He looks so angry. He may act gentle, but those eyes are holding so much fury, he looks ready to snap and bash someone's head in.

Trying to block that possibility I ask, "Tango, what am I looking for? What colors? What objects?"

"Purple sleeping bag. Battered black backpack. Green army duffle bag. Pema Chödrön book with her smiling face. Silver urn."

We get to walking. I take one aisle and Tango takes another. Scanning. Eyes moving up and down, high and low. Left and right. Stuffed in the large bags I see cooking utensils, bundled letters, newspaper clippings, clocks, baby clothes, toys, framed portraits, artificial flowers, china figurines, engineering books, canned food, worn sneakers, half-knitted sweater.

The cement floor is cold. My feet are hurting. Endless bags. Plaid, paisley, jeans, sweats, t-shirts, jackets, dresses, flowered prints, stripes. Finally get to the end of the long row. That took twenty minutes. We'll never get this done in half an hour.

Start the next row. Tango's not even finished with his first one.

Get looking! Don't pay attention to what he's doing!

Scan past girlie-magazine, flashlight, sunglasses, football, baby carriage, spices, ukulele, fishing rods, dartboard, underwear, children's books.

"Your time is up. I've got a life. You can come back tomorrow."

I pull another hundred from my purse. "Another half hour?"

She's okay with that.

Resume the search. What if they fling the most recent ones all the way to the top and we can't see them?

"How do you put things on the top shelf?" I ask.

"Cherry picker."
"Can we use it?"
"No."

I've only got the two hundreds left. Is it worth losing time to see higher?

I pull out one of the bills. "Can you take us up?"

She takes the money and points at Tango. "Not him. Only you."

I follow her to a bright red vehicle on squishy black wheels with the closed zigzag lifting part. She unlatches a small gate and climbs up onto the little enclosed platform. "Get in."

After my experience with getting into the plane, I know enough to watch her. It's awkward, but I manage.

She closes the gate, turns on the motor and tilts a stick and we start rising. I grab the metal rail as the platform sways and jiggles, moving us higher until we're fully extended on the scissor part and I look down—*it's so far!*—but we can see what's on the top shelf.

"Where to?"

I can't let go of the rail to point, so use my chin to indicate *anywhere.*

We jerk forward and I swear we'll tip and crash but we don't. Yet.

We inch along very slowly. We'll come to the end of the half hour in no time.

Tupperware containers, prescription bottles, cell phone, binoculars, bird feeder...

I glance down at Tango. He's so small and moves like he knows he's lost everything. But it seems he always looks that way.

Forks, canned food, cowboy boots, jockstrap, chess set...

We round the edge of an aisle and start down another.

Watering can, jar of buttons, high heels, watercolor kit...and a smiling woman.

I call down. "You said a smiling woman?"

Tango rushes below us. "Short hair?"

"Yes."

"That's Pema. That's my bag."

The woman un-velcros a pole with a hook from the side of the cherry picker, snags the bag and pulls it closer to the platform, yelling down, "Receipt number?"

He reads off the number and she pulls the bag onto the platform and we scissor down. When we get to the lowest point, she snarls, "Receipt." She double-checks the number, has him sign a paper, and he gets the bag. "Thank you!"

She grunts and opens the gate for me. "I've got to get the cherry picker secured, so you both have to leave now."

We don't need a second more. I drop down to the cold cement and we're outta there.

Crossing the parking lot, Tango keeps thanking me and promising he'll figure out a way to repay the money I gave the woman. I tell him not to worry about it, and *don't tell him* it's a small price to pay to get him out of my life.

When we get to the ragtop jeep he opens the sack and then paws through the items until he gets to the urn. Holds it up for me to see. "Prestonia, this is Clayton. Clayton, this is Prestonia. She's a person who deals with ashes. She's gonna help you get Home."

Hopefully that will be easier than finding him was.

I drive Tango back to my house. The two dogs are thrilled to see us both and greet me like a long-lost friend.

"They're always this way?"

"Dogs can sense good people," Tango answers.

As he carries his retrieved belongings down the back stairs to the fruit tree yard, I wonder if he's saying I'm a good person. I never considered that as a possibility. There are so many mean thoughts, so many judgements, so much doubt and fear and anxiety and whatever society smashed into me, I'm sure the distillation is on the negative side. Could I be wrong?

But it's a homeless man saying I'm a good person. Not exactly reliable.

Erika pops into my head with *Prestonia, don't be an arse.*

There's a knock at the back door. I open it to Tango and the dogs.

"I feel I should give a call to Bob, who asked me to take care of his dog while he's in surgery. Can I use your phone?"

For a second I wonder what mischief he can get into with my phone, then I hand it to him, closing the back door a bit to pretend to give him privacy, but really to make sure he stays outside.

He bends to look at the phone number on Daisy's tag as he dials, then after a moment, says, "Hey, Tango here. Daisy is fine. Relocated for a moment but all is good. No worries. Hope you're on the mend. Take care, friend."

He opens the door and hands me the phone and we split off to our respective spaces. Tango under the mulberry tree at the far side of the backyard, and me at my kitchen table. This spot has become the hub of this home. Maybe it's the view across to Griffith Park. Maybe it's the birds darting around the wisteria vines framing the balcony. Maybe it's the chicken and rooster salt and pepper shakers and dog toothpick holder. Maybe it's Agnes Sloan's spirit.

The sun ambles toward the Griffith Park Observatory, thinking of heading to bed. Where did the day go? My stomach growls. I should eat something. Could have fruit from the yard, but I'm not sure I have the energy to see Tango again. He makes me uncomfortable, like I'm supposed to take care of him because he's homeless. I'm still learning how to take care of myself—

Sound of steps coming up the stairs. Tango waves at me through the window as he steps onto the balcony.

I open the back door. "Can I help you?" I say, sounding way too much like a saleswoman in a fancy boutique confronting a homeless man.

"Occurred to me you might be hungry. I've got plenty to share. Bob set me up. If you want. No worries if you don't."

Shit. How come he's more considerate than I am?

I should say no. I should decline. He needs to keep what he has. But I am hungry.

"I'd be grateful, thanks. I'll clear space," I say, closing my laptop on the formica kitchen table. *Hold on, this man smells rank. Don't invite him inside.*

"How 'bout we eat in the yard so the dogs don't get lonesome?" I suggest. "I'll gather plates and everything."

He agrees and steps back below. I keep the door open so I can carry everything, gather glasses, plates, silverware—*Does he use silverware?*—*Maybe he only eats with his thick, dirty hands*—and put them on a tray. Then pick up one of Agnes's bottles of red wine—*Is it dangerous to invite him to drink?*—and put it back—*Maybe he'd be fine*—pick it up again—*But what if he isn't?*—and put it back.

"Figured you might need help carrying things," Tango says at the door.

My hand is on the bottle. Did he see that whole back-and-forth thing?

The man picks up the tray saying, "I don't drink, but it won't bother me if you do." And he steps down the stairs.

I collect the vintage napkin dispenser and the chicken and rooster salt and pepper shakers. Did this ceramic rooster always look so amused? He looks like Rooster from Wyoming. Amused at the scared, naïve, un-worldly chick. His words rumble again in my head—*Embrace it.*

Add the bottle of wine and trot downstairs.

Daisy and Captain greet me again like I've not seen them in decades and Tango stands beside the patio table. He's wet his hair down but it doesn't change his raggedy caveman look.

The patio table has an assortment of food spread across it. Bread, cheese, crackers, salami, and tuna fish. The centerpiece is the huge pinecone. Seeing it makes me smile. We squeeze the plates and silverware and salt and pepper figures and napkin dispenser within the mix. Setting the wine down, I feel the blood rise to my face. Why is that? It's my house, I can have a glass of wine. I sit and—shit. It's not a screw-top. I hop up—"Forgot the corkscrew."

But Tango says, "No worries," and pulls a pocket knife from his pants. My heart jolts—*I knew he was a killer!*—and he hinges out the corkscrew, opens the bottle, and pours me a glass.

I glance at that little rooster, imagining that it's *really* chuckling now.

Tango cuts a slice of cheese. "Reminds me of how I ate with my Mama. We lived in N'Orlins and didn't have much—'cept always enough for Mama's cheap wine—that's why I don't drink—and she'd always say, 'Let's piece-on things tonight.' That meant mostly oyster crackers, cereal maybe, ketchup packets, day-ol' po-boy bread from the shop down the way."

Is he telling me this so I'll feel sorry for his poverty-stricken childhood?

He continues with a smile. "The way Mama'd say it, it sounded special. 'Let's piece-on things tonight.' Felt like we were rebels somehow."

Wow. It's a good memory for him.

"Well, it's new to me," I say.

The rooster almost glares at me, so I add, "Thank you for sharing all these pieces."

TAKING IN PRESTONIA

PRESTONIA AND TANGO piece-on-things. For the moment, as they eat, Tango actually feels relaxed. The police are not going to grab him here. The pink jogger won't show up. Thanks to this young woman, he's got his dogs and his belongings back, including Clayton's urn. He's sitting with her. On a chair. At a table. With dishes and napkins and forks and fancy salt and pepper novelty shakers. Someone might see this scene and think —two people are eating dinner together. Like it's normal. Of course, they'd see one is a mess and the other is perfect, but still it feels bizarrely ordinary. Like a make-believe moment and right now, Tango sees that this woman's not glaring at him for being who he is and that feels good.

He needs her *Ashes-to-Ashes* help for Clayton but she seems so ill-suited for such a job. When he first saw her in the Trader Joe's parking lot, she had dismissed him abruptly, judging him with a single glance. He had seen her makeup and expensive clothes and had judged her as being a part-of-the-establishment, television-weather-woman square. Her driving Agnes's ragtop jeep was an incongruous juxtaposition.

But now, he questions those assumptions. He lets himself take a good look at her while she pours another glass of wine for herself.

She's pretty, with dark reddish hair just below her neckline. Eyebrows dark and angled like an old time movie star. Freckles dot the top of her cheeks. All the bits are where they should be, but there is something rigid and closed about her. Like she's guarded against the world. A pretty fortress with a closed drawbridge and moat that probably has alligators. Tango knows why *he's* that way, but can't imagine why someone with every privilege would be so defended.

But it's not like he can ask. They're from different worlds. This evening is an anomaly and whatever issues she has are no concern to him. He'll get help for Clayton and then be out of her pretty red hair.

AFTER PIECING

THE MEAL IS UNIQUE. We mix and match tidbits of things. I've never eaten this way and it's fun in a goofy, kid-like way. Brent would hate it.

Tango suddenly jumps up—jolting my heart again—and yells, "CAPTAIN, STAY!"

The dog is sniffing that little mud figure by the gate.

"I'm so sorry," he says, pulling the dog away. "I moved the barrier of chairs so we could sit."

"No harm done."

Tango sits again. "If it's okay to ask, what happened to that little girl?"

I know he wants the *Ashes-to-Ashes* business to be legitimate for his friend in the urn. I can't tell him I scattered a girl in the yard. "This *Ashes-to-Ashes* business, it kinda just started and it's real and everything, but I only had two—I guess you'd call them clients—and two isn't enough for a website, so me and Erika—we filmed scattering charcoal briquette ashes as if they were people ashes and in various places of this yard we kinda made up several memorial films. That's the made-up little dead girl who liked to make mud pies."

I can't read Tango's face. Is he thinking I'm immoral or—

He bursts out laughing. "Oooo! That's wicked! Damn! I see you now. You aren't who you pretend to be!"

I don't exactly know why, but this pisses me off. I'm not a pretend person. I'm serious and determined and—

"Can I see the films? The real and fake?" he asks.

I guess it couldn't hurt to show him. Not like he's going to go online and expose my lies. I go upstairs, bring down my laptop, and show him everything. He gets tears in his eyes just like Erika did. I tell him about the pilot who wouldn't turn around and my strange improvisation being Robert Mitchum. When it's done, I close the laptop, and we find ourselves in darkness. When did the sun set? I can see only his outline but I like not being able to see him and him not being able to see me. Makes things easier. Plus, I've had enough of his Neanderthal-caveman looks.

One of the dogs starts snoring beneath us. Tango *shhhs* it and asks, "You just started this business?"

"Right after Agnes Sloan had me scatter her ashes."

There's silence. He's thinking he'd better not have a nascent business scatter the ashes of his friend in the urn. He thinks I'm not experienced enough. Fuck him. I'm not an Ash Scatterer anyway!

A big sigh comes from Tango. "You starting a new business gives me hope that things can change completely. I might have to figure out my own next move."

Okay, so he wasn't thinking that about my business. Or he's changing the subject so I won't try to sell him my services. He couldn't afford me anyway.

Tango continues, "That book with the woman with the smiling face, Pema Chödrön, is helping me imagine change. Just before I was arrested, I read her line—*The future is completely open, and we are writing it moment to moment.*"

Why is he telling me this? Is he trying to give me advice? I don't need advice from a homeless man. I begin stacking the dishes in the dark.

Tango continues, "So you're creating an entirely new future with the *Ashes-to-Ashes* business. What did you do before?"

Something makes me not want to tell him. Is it because he's homeless and I worked with millions? I don't have to justify myself to him. A bit defensively I say, "Financial analyst at an important investment firm."

"Fuck me!—oh, sorry—but no wonder you stopped. It's so—wrong for you. A dead-end-job for a person who has a big dose of creativity." He chuckles—"Actually, *Ashes-to-Ashes* is really the *Dead-End-Job.*"

Is that a pun or is he putting me down? Before I can decide, he adds, "You may act establishment, but what I've learned tonight tells me you're someone who likes to make mud figures, likes to have adventures, likes to piece-on things, and is way more of a rebel artist than a money-manager."

This irks me. He doesn't know who I am. "Actually, I excelled," I say. "Multiple times, financial-analyst-of-the-month. I had, *and will continue to have,* a stellar career—"

"Yeah, but these films—you're a great filmmaker and—"

"So I studied film, doesn't mean it was a calling. I also studied Acting, Art, and Architecture. Am I an architect now? Should I be?"

I can feel Tango peering at me in the darkness, like Erika did with him, as if trying to see into my soul. Why does he think he can peer into my soul!?

"Prestonia, I'm not saying what you should be an architect—"

"Good, because I don't want to be."

There's a sound of a deep inhale and slow exhale, then—" Why do you think you studied those things?"

"I rebelled against my financial advisor parents for several semesters"

"I don't think you were rebelling—"

"I was rebelling."

"—I think you were following your interests."

"Those were wasted semesters!"

"No learning is wasted," Tango says.

"Oh, and where did you go to college, Mister know-it-all? What did you study?" The minute I say this, I know it's mean and nasty and I should apologize but I'm too mad to do that.

Silence.

What if he's angry? Will he hit me? In this darkness, I won't be able to see it coming.

"I didn't go to college," Tango says quietly. "Didn't finish high school, but I see things. I see a person torn between what they think they should do and what they want to do."

Why does everyone think they know me better than I know myself? I stand and grab my laptop. "Yeah, well, you're wrong. I know what I want. I just sent out new résumés for another BIG MONEY JOB. As soon as I can, I'm shutting down the *Ashes-to-Ashes* website."

"But you can help with Clayton? His urn—"

"No. I'm not doing that ever again."

"But you're so good at—"

"I SAID NO! And—you—Tango or Leon whatever—you might think you do, but you don't fucking know me! Good night!"

I turn away, then look back to his dark figure. "I don't expect I'll see you again, so have a good life."

Stomp up the stairs, slam the door, click the lock, turn off the lights, and flop on the bed fuming. *Asshole thinks he knows me? Fuck him.*

TIME TO GO

TANGO LISTENS as the birds start their song. These are the early ones that get the worms. It's not yet light. Just an inkling of an idea of light. Perfect time.

It's been a good sleep. Surprising how much less stress there is here in a backyard compared to the arroyo. But this isn't home. This is a young woman's house. And she wants him gone. She made that very clear last night.

He rises and packs his belongings. It's going to be a little hard to carry it all, but doable. Especially if he gets going before the world is up.

The dogs seem to understand the need for discretion, and they both sit attentively while he writes *Thank U* in pebbles on the patio table. That's the best he can do.

Out the side gate, dog on each side, Bob's food sacks, sleeping bag, duffle bag, Clayton's urn, Pema—all bundled and riding with him. It's a slog along Colorado Blvd but just as the eastern sun blasts across the sky, they're crossing their bridge, and soon the man and dogs will slip from the road down the path to the familiar refuge under the footing. Then it will be time to rest and try to make sense of the days. Make sense of being *Grateful* and at the same time, *Hurt*.

COFFEE OR TEA

I WAKE FEELING defensive. Was I a jerk last night? Was Tango a jerk? He seems to think I'm something that I'm not.

I should go down and get that tray. Maybe he's already absconded with it and the dishes—I'll be really upset if he took the rooster and hen salt and pepper shakers!—and what about the silverware—maybe those were really silver and he's selling them on the homeless black market.

You're being an arse. He's probably still down there, cold and wishing he had a hot drink. Why not be kind?

I could bring him something hot. Coffee or tea? No one drinks tea except Erika so I'll bring coffee. I'll go down as if I'm collecting the tray from last night. If he's friendly, I'll give him the coffee. If not, I'll ask him to find a home elsewhere and take that tray up.

I pour a coffee and step down the back stairs. The dogs aren't barking at me. I guess they really do like me.

At the bottom, no dogs. The blankets, pillow, and towel are folded neatly by the mulberry tree. Good. He got the message.

I march to the patio table to check the silverware on the tray. Everything is clean and stacked and it appears that nothing is missing. There's a mess of pebbles, but from one angle it could read—*Thank U.*

Damn. I was defensive and mean, and he didn't deserve it, but I'm glad he's gone. It's for the best. At least, my best.

My phone rings—maybe it's another ash scattering. Better not be. I'm done with that. "Good morning. Prestonia Cheswick here."

"Ms. Cheswick, this is Natalie Tillis from Goldman Sachs. We got your résumé and Ms. Sharon Bloom asked me to call to see if we could set up an appointment for you to come in for an interview. Are you free this morning?"

BACK HOME

TANGO WALKS DOWN the steep embankment with Daisy and Captain. He's worn out from the hike and the emotions of the last few days. As the trio approaches the footing of the bridge, the dogs growl.

"What is it, Captain?"

"It's me, motherfucker," an angry voice yells. "Get lost or you're dead."

A man rises from behind Tango's cement home holding a heavy tree branch. He's got scraggly hair and a ragged beard, and wears clothes that might have had colors once, but have long since become a greasy grey.

The ridge of hair on Captain's back stiffens. Tango feels the same. This is an invasion. A violation. This can only lead to bad shit.

"Listen, man, I've been here for a long time. Cops busted me here a few days ago but this is home for me.

"Fucking leave, man. This ain't yours now. It's mine."

What would Pema do? Certainly not violence, but would she condone giving up?

Dropping Bob's bags of supplies and the duffle bag, Tango takes a few steps toward the man while holding the leashes of the two dogs. "Man, I had a rough time and I just want to rest. There's folk that can help find you shelter at All Saints Church—"

"I got my fuckin' shelter, dude. Get lost!"

And the man stomps down the slope toward Tango, swirling the tree branch over his head like a medieval weapon. Tango thinks, *There is no way that these dogs won't hurt this man if I let them go. And no way that this man won't hurt the dogs or me if I don't.*

Daisy and Captain bark and snarl and pull at their leashes.

"STOP!" Tango yells. "These dogs will tear you to pieces if I let them go. I don't want them responsible for your death, and I don't want to take the fall for what they do to you."

"Fuck you," is the man's answer, and he continues down. Daisy and Captain roar furiously.

Tango suddenly remembers Prestonia and her pretending to be like Robert Mitchum for the Cessna pilot. Could he do something like that? Pretend?

"One more step and I'll let the dogs loose!"

The man stops.

Tango bends, lifts Clayton's urn out of the bag and holds it high. In a low, slow voice he says, "I summon the spirit of this man, this warrior, this great chief, and—Arise now! Ashes of this hero, arise and scourge this interloper! Surround and haunt this heinous trespasser into the territory of the dead." Tango flashes back to that time on the roof during Hurricane Katrina. "YOU, dead, who've been washed away. YOU, snakes and bloated bodies.

YOU, AVENGING SOULS, occupy and surround this man and drag him into the black fetid abyss forever!"

The man stares at Tango with confusion.

Sliding the leash loops up his wrist, Tango peels off the gaffer's tape sealing the urn and puts his hand on the lid, ready to lift. "Are you prepared for this wrath?" he asks the man.

The man looks around in every direction, worried.

Remembering the Cajun-French he knows from Mardi-gras, Tango intones with a deep ominous voice, "MON CHÉRI, LAISSEZ LES BONS TEMPS ROULER!!

The man scrambles up the bridge footing, grabs a sack and takes off running as Tango shouts after him, "LAISSEZ LES BONS TEMPS ROULER!!!"

After the man disappears, the dogs quickly settle down and Tango leads them to their home, but he's throbbing with adrenaline. Pretending worked! Prestonia would love this!

No, stop. She hates you, he thinks. *Forget that.*

But, still, he didn't fight the man. He pretended and it worked. Was it good, what he did? Would it be acceptable to Pema?

He rolls out his sleeping bag but even as he sets it up he wonders—knowing some other man lay here and peed here and did whatever here—will this place ever feel like home again?

INTERVIEW

BACK IN MY GREY BUSINESS PANTSUIT and heels again. Ouch! Haven't worn heels in—how long? I think it might be just a week but it feels like months. Got my fancy briefcase. Got my makeup applied. Got all trace of freckles covered. Got my serious, competent, financial advisor face on. Still, I feel out of touch.

You're nervous. It's been years since you interviewed.

That's right. Rooster said to embrace it.

I don't think he meant—

Hush.

I smile at the face in the mirror and straighten my shoulders.

Step out my front door and—why do I feel like driving to Century City in Agnes's ragtop jeep?
Don't do it. It probably still smells like than man.
I unlock my Audi.
"Looking ready for business, Prestonia," Alberto yells from his yard.
"Yeah. Interview. Gotta play the part."
"I hear ya. Good luck."
Drive across the city to the offices of Goldman Sachs. I'm nervous about the meeting. But they wouldn't call me if they didn't like my résumé. If I can explain why I left my last job, I should be fine. Just gotta ace this interview. Goldman Sachs! Sky's the limit!

Elevator up to the gleaming offices. Same interior design as all these places. Modern, sleek, understated good taste with hints of old money and tradition. I'm right on time and the receptionist calls Ms. Bloom to let her know I've arrived. Seven minutes pass. Not long enough that I'll be perturbed, but long enough to show I'm less important than she. I usually tried for six.
A young man in an Armani suit strides across the lobby. His eyes flick over me and find something wanting. Have I screwed up already?
"Ms. Cheswick, Ms. Bloom will see you now."
Intern to fetch me. Nice touch. Too important to leave her desk.
I follow the intern and am led to a large windowed office. Staying behind her desk, Ms. Bloom stands to shake my hand. That same nanosecond of taking in my visage. Evaluation is: *Fair-Needing improvement.* Shit.
We go through the usual fake small talk. The view. I laugh, casually pointing out the building from the first *Die Hard* movie. She says she hopes the bad guys don't come here. We laugh. Then talk of UCLA and my background. Look through the résumé, remarking on the CFA and accolades. I feel her judgement dissolving. Finally, she gets to the point.

"Why'd you leave your previous position?"

"I was dissatisfied with the advancement possibilities. If I may, seeing you behind this desk, gives me hope."

"Glass ceiling?"

"Yep. Guys riding the escalator up were much less qualified."

"Been there. Our situation is better. Not perfect, but you know the score."

We talk about expectations and possible scenarios of employment and she offers a salary significantly higher than my previous one. I can read the signs that she wants me and I'd be valued as an expert. It feels really good.

I know the game of feigning disinterest, so I say, "Let me think about it overnight."

She knows the game and says, "Of course. I look forward to hearing from you."

We shake hands and the intern is suddenly there to escort me back to the lobby, give me parking validation, and wish me "Good day."

Back on Santa Monica Boulevard, passing the palm trees and gleaming high-rises, my heart is beating with the possibilities. As I head north and east, the high-powered, important-people structures give way to corner mini-malls and these give way to Thai Town, and keep going, past Mexican restaurants, laundromats, and check-cashing joints to Glendale's Little Armenia.

Entering Eagle Rock, red and yellow stripes catch my eye. The same two shades as Agnes Sloan's ragtop jeep. I pull over to the side of the road by the striped umbrella shading a cart where a woman is selling mango slices.

I gesture for one. She expertly peels the fruit's rind in a long circular strand and slices thick chunks of juicy orange flesh from the pit. As these are arranged in a cup, I realize I have no cash except for the last hundred-dollar bill from scattering Ed through the air. Good. Time to get rid of all trace of that *Ashes-to-Ashes* fiasco. I hand the bill to her, wave that it's hers, and I'm on my way. The mango is sweet and drips down my chin and onto the tasteful silk blouse. Those stains won't come out but who cares. I've got money coming in. I'll call Goldman Sachs tomorrow and accept the job and move to the West Side. Leave this riffraff neighborhood.

On my street, I park and stroll into my house, finishing the last of my fruit cup. Wipe my mouth with the sleeve of my business jacket, change out of the clothes, and toss everything in the garbage, crowning the pile with my high heels. It's all old. I need a fresh start for my life at Goldman Sachs.

WHAT FUTURE?

OKAY, SO HOW DO YOU START the future, Tango wonders. So far, he's had a traumatic boyhood in New Orleans, a stint in the military that ended badly, and an escape to surviving outside of everything. Is there another way?

"How does anyone get anywhere? I'm not good at anything, Tango says aloud to Captain. "What can you do?"

Captain tilts his head. *Smell and track real good. Love you. Defend you. Defend home. Roll in dirt. Scratch and stretch. Enjoy good strangers. Enjoy Daisy. Be open to the next thing.*

"Okay, Captain. I hear you. If you're so smart, tell me what can I do?"

Staring intently at Tango, Captain continues, *You saved your Mama from that flood, so you're a hero. You lifted that hammer and busted through that roof. Military taught you that you ain't good at discipline or standing at attention or suffering mean people. You've got heart and kindness for most folks and self-awareness that's getting stronger with the Smiling Buddhist Lady. You care for us dogs and your friend Bob and that confused girl Prestonia. You don't know what you want to do and think maybe it's about time you figured something out.*

Tango puts his hand on Captain's head. "Thank you, friend. You're wise. Do you want the rest of Bob's salami?"

Captain and Daisy both tilt their heads and lift their ears, ready for the treat.

Tango slices of the meat and tosses a chunk to each dog. "You two are good teachers. That'll be the plan. To start my new future, I'll follow your lead and be open to whatever good things are tossed my way."

He looks to them for validation but they're busy chewing.

MAKING HOME PERSONAL

I'M NOT BACK FROM THE INTERVIEW fifteen minutes when knocking brings me to the front door. I open onto a large painting filling the doorway. It's bold and vibrant with swirling strokes of yellow and lilac amid great swaths of blue and green. There's what could be a colorful horse or something and what might be a sparkling sky. There're hints of landscape to the abstraction, like a Diebenkorn mashup with Turner.

Erika peeks around the side. "For ye," she says.

I'm shocked. I've never had real art before. My forays into art making were nothing to display. Museum posters were as close as I got to putting art on the wall.

"Erika, this is stunning! But—I couldn't possibly take it."

"Ye shall. It were done with ye in mind. See, that's the stripe o' flying to Wyoming, the mountain, there's a fish, this is a flash of a carousel, see that green quilt with the sparkles, 'tis yer plane-ash scatterin'. This paintin's for none but ye and I shall help ye hang it."

This is overwhelming. Tears flood my eyes. Erika must see this 'cause she edges by me with the painting, through the living room and into the bright kitchen. Beside the formica table, there's one yellow wall that has no cabinets or appliances. It's covered with small framed pictures of Agnes's life, postcards, a cowboy calendar, a cluttered bulletin board made of wine corks, a list of her important numbers, and a crinkled, dried bouquet of ancient flowers.

"I reckon' it's time ye took down this lot o' Agnes's world and begin puttin' up yer own world. Me paintin' can be yer start."

I don't tell her that I'll probably be moving to the West Side soon. Will I see her again after I move? Will I see her after I'm part of the Goldman Sach's elite? She's a sweet, kind person, but not really West Side material.

We remove the old items on the wall but because I feel a bizarre, irrational loyalty to Agnes, I don't throw them out, but put them in her closet. Someone else can deal with these when I sell this place.

Erika, being who she is, has brought everything to hang the painting. She drills a small hole in the wall, holds up a little device with a bubble to mark a spot for a second hole.

"What is that?" I ask.

"A level. Unless yer in a tsunami, water is always gonna give ye the correct level. Ye want the bubble in the middle."

"I think my bubble is always in the middle."

Erika laughs. "Aye, Lass. 'Tis grand for hangin' art, but ney se much for livin'. Ye might want tae tilt yerself a bit and be off-kilter now 'n then."

I doubt that will happen, especially now that I'm going to work for Goldman Sachs.

She drills again, pops little plastic things into the holes, and powers in long screws, leaving the tips out a bit.

We lift the painting's wire over the screws and it's up! Wow!

"This really looks great here!"

"Let's have a cuppa and gaze a' spell."

I make our tea and we both sit facing the wall and enjoying the new vibrant view. Erika's the tea expert, so when she thinks it's steeped enough, she lifts the strainer out of the pot and dumps the wet loose tea in the garbage. She lingers there. "'Tis a curious lot in the bin."

I join her and see my high heels topping the professional clothes covered with wet cuppa leaves.

"I—felt that I was done with them."

"Good for you, lass! That's feckin' brilliant!"

She thinks I'm dumping finance and giving this *Ashes-to-*

Ashes a try, but she's wrong. I'm moving up in the world.

"Ye have enough to live on?"

"No worries. Especially now—"

"Oh?"

I flounder and add, "Especially now since I've no rent or mortgage."

"Good. Neys the time when ye get te figure a bit aboot yourself. Relax. Notice the world. Gaze. Make this house more t'yer likin'."

"Suggestions?"

"Let's go 'round an excise the super-personal things o' Agnes's and the things that ye dinnae like or care fer."

We step to the living room and look around. "I don't really like these runners and cloths on everything."

She lifts a runner off of a wooden table. Below is a Post-it note. Erika reads, "This white ring was scorched into the wood from Tracy's hot cup of coffee. She wasn't careful with her liquids and I got mad. But when she died, I couldn't bear to fix it."

"Okay," I say. "Let's leave Tracy's ring."

Erika turns the Post-it over in her hands. "'Tis odd leavin' this note 'ere."

"Not the first one. One even had my name."

"Ha! Wish I'da met this woman."

Get back to looking around. "I like the mid-century modern lamps and furniture, but not so much the figurines scattered everywhere. Except, the kitchen's rooster pepper shaker means the Wyoming man Rooster and the dog toothpick holder reminds me of the only two dogs I know, so I'll keep those for the memories."

"That's why they have a hold o're us. Memory and all that shite. Knickknacks can be cluttering, but if ye set 'em in one spot, 'tis one statement rather than many. Like putting a frame around them. Gives structure."

I nod, saying, "The artist Cy Twombly might not work so well without a frame."

"Steady on, I thought ye studied film and actin' afore the

blasted money career."

"And architecture and art."

"No wonder ye know of these myriad o'concepts. Ye're a poly-creative."

I don't know what that means, but it feels good. I might have to put that on my business card. Prestonia Cheswick: Poly-creative. Oh, I forgot. I'll be Prestonia Cheswick, Goldman Sachs financial advisor.

"Ye bein' a poly-creative lass, are nae a run-o-tha-mill person. What is run-o-tha-mill is a financial analyst. Ye were a cog in that machine, easily replaced by t'other cog. Sure ye can afford all the latest top-o'-the-line goods, but what fills yer soul? Ne'er would be fulfilled workin' such a toil as that."

I don't want to hear her dissing my new plans, so I steer us back to the subject of removing some of Agnes's things.

It takes a while but we remove most of the tchotchkes and runners and cloth mats and little rugs, then carry the exorcized items down to the backyard and the tiny Model-T-sized garage. As we are packing them in, Erika looks around the space.

"What?" I ask.

"Nothing. I was just thinking it's a nice little space for—a studio or—something."

"I may be a poly-creative, but I don't need a studio yet."

"Right-o. I better be off then."

My phone rings. Erika pauses, eyes wide and hopeful—"Maybe *Ashes-to-Ashes*."

I answer and a gravely voice asks, "Hello, is Tango there?"

"No," I say, shaking my head to Erika. She blows me a kiss and leaves as I say, "But I know him."

"This is Bob. Tango left a message for me using this phone. I had heart surgery and I'm recovering but I need to talk with him. He has my dog, Daisy. Any chance you know where he is?"

Damn it, I thought I was done with that man.

INTO THE ARROYO

I'VE NEVER BEEN to the Arroyo. It's just a little past Eagle Rock, at the edge of Pasadena. Among the big mansions from the robber baron days, there's a sloping drive down to a parking lot and public toilet building. The Colorado Bridge glows big in the distance.

I walk on the dirt path toward the bridge. I'm surrounded by trees and grasses and brush of different kinds. A little river trickles in a cement canal beside the path. People pass walking dogs, talking on their phones, doing power-walking. It's not exactly the isolated location I'd imagined.

As I near it, the bridge soars high overhead. I didn't realize it was such a serious drop from up there.

The manufactured canal gives way to a wide natural creek below the bridge. A place that's clearly home to lots of wildlife. A family of ducks swims in swirling water. Birds flit from berry bushes. It's quite magical. The bridge itself is a wondrous concrete structure of looping arches that curve across this ravine. I stop and look for any sign of Tango. Nothing but brush and scrub. No encampment. I wait until everyone else is out of sight and call—"Tango?"

There's a slight sound way up in the dark junction where the footing of the bridge and the hillside meet.

I try again. "Hello, Tango?"

Two dogs appear from behind the footing and start racing down the embankment.

A voice yells, "Brace yourself!" and the dogs bound down and splash through the expanse of water, sending the ducks quacking, and leap up at me, paws wet and tails wagging, and I barely stay standing as Tango emerges from the darkness way up high. "Prestonia!" he yells as if he's happy to see me.

The two dogs swirl and yip like I'm a long-lost friend. It feels good even though my arms get scratched and my shirt is covered with muddy paw prints.

Tango slides/trots down. "You found me." He puts out a dirty hand and I can't let it just hang there, so I shake it. It's really rough.

"This is it? This is your home? I mean, it's nice but—it's like in the middle of a public place. People are everywhere!"

"I can deal with it. Just got rid of an interloper this morning. I used your pretending method and it worked. I wasn't Mitchum, but I was scary."

I can't help but smile. "Your friend Bob called. He needs to talk to you." I hand him my phone pointing to the Bob call so he can return it.

He does. Listens to whatever Bob is saying and answers, "I can't do that. Doesn't want to be involved. She's a civilian."

"A civilian? What's going on?" I hold out my hand for my phone. Tango resists.

"Phone, Tango."

He hands it over and I put it to my ear. "Bob, this is Prestonia. What involvement?"

I listen and nod and nod and say "uh-huh" and "where?" and hang up.

Tango looks at me expectantly.

"We're going to Bob's house. We're bringing Daisy to see him, then we're returning to my house/Agnes's house where you will leave Daisy with me."

Tango smiles, saying, "You must know that I don't follow orders."

There's a gasp on the trail behind us. A woman in a pink sweat suit stares at Tango.

"YOU AGAIN! YOU CAN'T BE HERE! I'M CALLING THE POLICE!"

She pulls out her phone and I don't even think but step to her. "Put the phone down," I say.

She doesn't. I lift mine and hold it up to film her. Need someone tough—Meryl Streep in Jonathan Demme's remake of *The Manchurian Candidate*. I start slow. "You have no idea of the horror you're about to unleash upon yourself. I work for an influencer with over 1.2 million followers and they are going to make your pink life an unmitigated hell."

She pauses.

"You work for—"

"Yeah, you think these influencers film their own content? Are you a complete idiot? I'm one of seventy-three content providers who daily find things our client might use. We're paid to dig up dirt and, lady, you're dirt."

I hear her phone ringing.

"Once your deeds are broadcast across every platform, you will be hounded. You'll be ostracized, lose your job, your friends, and every bit of anonymity you took for granted. Poof, all gone."

The speaker on her phone says, "9-1-1. What's your emergency?"

I move closer, pushing my cell toward the woman's face and whispering. "You mistakenly reported what you thought was a crime and you want to withdraw that complaint."

The woman sputters. "But he—"

"You were mistaken."

The woman's hand shakes as she holds the phone close. "I made a complaint a while ago. I want to report that it was a mistake."

Tango and I watch as she states her name and describes the complaint and says she doesn't want to press charges.

Her speaker-phone asks, "Are you being coerced to say this?"

The pink jogger looks at us with wide eyes and shakes her head. "No, no, I just realize my error."

"Okay then. The records show that the man is out on bail. We'll close the case and release the bail funds."

"Thank you," she says and hangs up.

"Well done," I say. "Remember, I have you on video and I will release it should you backtrack. Now get the fuck outta here."

Pink lady sprints away. I'm completely shocked at myself and turn to Tango.

He doesn't look as shocked as I am. "Like I said, you aren't who you pretend to be."

Good lord, I'm shaking and want to burst out laughing except she may still be close.

FUCK ME! *Who was that person I was just now!?*

"You were great!" Tango says. "I've never seen a Mitchum movie but that didn't seem like what I'd imagined."

"This time I was Meryl Streep," I answer. "Who knows who I'll be next time."

Tango nods. "I'm trying to be a new me, too. Trying to imagine a new future. Guess it better be somewhere else though."

Daisy and Captain look at us both and cock their heads, waiting for what comes next.

I'm flushed with adrenaline, and maybe that's why, or maybe it's because I know that I won't have that backyard long, but for whatever the reason, I say, "Collect your things. You've got a nice spot under the mulberry tree out of reach of joggers. Your future starts now."

Tango's face flushes and he turns away blinking. "Thank you."

I don't know what to say, so I say, "You're welcome."

He turns back to me, looking serious. "Prestonia, your future starts now too. What are you going to do?"

I see the West Side apartment and I see the Century City gleaming corner office at Goldman Sachs and I smile at my secret and call to Captain and Daisy and pretend to get sidetracked by their gleeful greetings.

VISITING BOB

TANGO AND PRESTONIA collect the belongings from behind the bridge footing. As Tango puts leashes on the dogs, he looks around his home. "I'm gonna miss this place."

"It'll always be here. You can visit."

"Or come back if my self-written future doesn't work out."

Prestonia can see he's having a hard time leaving, so she switches subjects. "I'll take these bags of supplies and one dog. You take the rest."

Tango slips the duffle bag over his shoulder and takes

Captain's leash. "Onward."

They lead the dogs along the arroyo path out to the parking lot.

"Agnes Sloan returns!" Tango says, seeing the ragtop jeep.

They load the back of the car with the bundles and urge the dogs to lie on them, then climb in and head off. Tango squints out the passenger window trying to keep tears from forming.

They drive up into the Sierra Madre foothills with Prestonia's phone giving directions and park in front of a modernist home surrounded by trees.

"Holy shit, this looks like it was designed by the architect Richard Neutra. He built a lot in Los Angeles and, during my architecture semester, we got to visit several."

"Probably more interesting than visiting banks and investment firms during your finance semesters," says Tango.

Prestonia looks away, knowing he would judge her for going back to that life. She'll keep it a secret. He doesn't need to know.

Tango hustles the dogs out of the jeep. Daisy breaks free and races to the wide orange door, barking and twirling ecstatically.

Prestonia's phone rings. She answers, and in a moment, hangs up. "Bob wants us to let ourselves in. He's sitting so he won't get knocked over by Daisy."

They open the door and Daisy tears in, toenails clattering on the shiny red linoleum—across the bright space to Bob, sitting on a mid-century chair. A floor-to-ceiling wall of glass behind him shows a view of a beautifully landscaped courtyard. The furniture is perfect for the modernist design. *This* is a house for *Architectural Digest*.

As Bob is smothered with licks and happy whines, Tango leads Prestonia to the man. "Bob, this is Prestonia. When we have a moment, I'll tell you of all she did for me."

Bob wiggles a hand beneath Daisy's squirming belly.

Prestonia reaches through to shake it. "Good to meet you, Bob. You have to tell me who's the architect of this incredible house, and I'm afraid I'm going to have to see all of it."

"I'll have to look up the name. I never remember it but he

worked with Rudolf Schindler, Richard Neutra, and Frank Loyd Wright."

"Didn't I just say Neutra, Tango?"

Tango nods and Bob waves for her to explore. "Feel free to look around. Come sit, Tango. Tell me what's been going on."

And as Prestonia wanders, marveling at the architecture, Tango tells his old friend about being arrested, the dogs being rescued, staying with Prestonia at Agnes's house, and her new job of scattering ashes.

LEARNING MORE OF TANGO AND BOB

AFTER CHECKING out the entire house and the incredible grounds, I return to the living room. Bob is alone and tells me Tango's showering and doing his laundry. Daisy, the Dalmatian, circles and curls onto a black and white, spot-spattered, cowhide rug. Her spots blend seamlessly with the rug and it's a wonderful joke of design.

"What the fuck." I can't help but say.

"Hmm?" Bob wonders.

"Daisy—a Dalmatian on the cowhide of the same pattern. That *must* be on purpose! It's perfect! Who thinks of that?"

"My wife. A set decorator for the movies for years, and when we got this house and the dog, she had to make Daisy part of the mise en scène."

"Unbelievable! Your wife is brilliant!"

Bob points to a metal-fish-shaped-sculpture on the mantle. "Was brilliant."

"Oh, I'm sorry. She made that sculpture?"

"She made that urn."

I step to it. It has some sort of iridescent material within the metal that changes the color of the scales as I move back and forth. Mouth open, the fish is curved as if it's leaping out of water, and one long splash is all that holds it to the base.

"Wow. It's beautiful. She's—inside?"

Bob grunts and gestures for me to sit on what looks like a real Eames lounge chair with ottoman. I tentatively sit on the edge of the ottoman.

I'm not sure what to say. Or if I should. What does someone say to a person this old? Maybe he'll start reminiscing about the good ol' days or—

"You want to know about Tango," Bob says. "Usually we meet once a week at the dog park so I can watch Captain while he goes to All Saints Church for a haircut and shower and getting his clothes washed. I guess he missed this Monday."

I feel the blood flushing my face. I thought he smelled and I wasn't going to let him in my house to shower and I never thought he might want to clean his clothes. I'm really an inconsiderate person.

Bob must read my thoughts. "We're not always thinking of what we take for granted."

"You know Tango well?"

"He's a friend."

"Seems like you two'd run in different circles."

"Seems like you're judging us both."

Damn. This isn't going well. I should just shut up.

"You have more questions," Bob says. "Go ahead and ask."

"Is he dangerous?"

"No more than most of us. But I know what you're asking. I've seen how he treats me and animals and people who are kind and that's enough for me."

"How'd you meet him?"

"At the dog park. I tripped on a root and fell and although the park was full of people who love animals and may be liberal-minded, only one person cared. He ran across the entire field and knelt and asked if I was okay, helped me up, cleaned my shin at the water fountain, and escorted me and Daisy to my car. I see him every Monday and he shares his package lunch from the church even though he knows I'm not homeless."

"You're certainly not homeless."

"You can't know a person's life by looking at their home or

lack of it."

"Sorry." *I'm really screwing up this conversation.*

"I'm guessing you're new to a lot of the world."

There is something in this that hits me in my gut. Makes me want to cry. I'm so new to everything except my tiny, insular bubble. "You might say that."

"Anyway," Bob continues. "I'm not homeless, but I've lost all that meant home to me, so might as well be."

I probably shouldn't ask what he lost. Again, he guesses what I'm thinking.

"I lost my job, in that I they forced me to retire. Worked down the hill at JPL."

"The Jet Propulsion Laboratory?"

"You got it."

Oh, my god. A scientist. Now I *know* there's nothing we can talk about.

"I worked on the NASA rovers and other space developments. You want to know about how to reverse the thrusters on rotorcraft on Mars, ask me. It was a dream job." Bob tilts his head to the mantle. "Lost my wife to emphysema a year ago. My grown daughter Luna was kind enough to come be with me."

His face swells red with grief and he coughs and whispers, "Two weeks later Luna was hit by a speeding ambulance and killed. So I've nothing. Except a home."

We sit in silence. I don't know what to say about death. Am I supposed to be an expert now that I've scattered a few ashes? Dealing with death, scattering ashes, is not a gig for me.

A man steps into the room wearing a terrycloth robe. I don't recognize him. Wait, is that Tango? The beard and mustache are gone. He isn't the same man at all! He's like—hot!

"Hope you don't mind, Bob. I borrowed a razor."

Bob laughs, stroking his whiskers. "Weren't mine, musta been my daughter's."

I can't get over how Tango looks. "You're—so young! How old are you?"

"Twenty eight."

I thought he was past forty. He's only three years older than I am!

"Vast change, Tango. Good for you," Bob says.

"Yeah, well, I'm working on my new future."

Bob slowly stands, keeping an eye on Daisy in case of any tackles. "Hope that future involves dinner, because I had some delivered. You like Chinese?"

As Tango sets the table, Bob gives me directions about warming things. We sit at the sleek teak table under an exquisite paper orb lamp and eat. Tango tells Bob of the way I handled the pink-suited jogger that was calling the police.

"She's really good at channeling scary people. First was Robert Mitchum, and that one was Meryl Streep."

"Good choices," Bob says. "Mitchum is the perfect blend of scary and mesmerizing. Streep can annihilate you with a glance."

I'm surprised a scientist would know anything about movies, let alone specific actors.

Bob adds, "I'm surprised a young person would know anything about Mitchum."

Luckily, he isn't privy to my previous thought, so I say, "Seems like you're judging me because of my age, Bob."

Bob points a gnarled finger at me and says, "Touché."

"I studied film, but really it was my granddad that introduced me to Mitchum and lots of others of that time. Granddad William Cheswick. He died just before I was born but I've seen him a lot. He was a Hollywood bit player—a character actor in black and white old-timey movies and early TV shows. I've seen him driving Humphrey Bogart down a dark street, applauding Fred and Ginger in a nightclub, glaring at Peter Lorre, shot by a Dragnet bad guy, riding on a horse beside John Wayne, and getting punched by Mitchum."

"You'll have to point him out to me sometime," Bob says. "The three of us could have a movie night."

Movie night with an ancient scientist and a homeless man? I don't think so. To get out of answering I ask, "You ever see *Sullivan's Travels?*"

"Many times. Preston Sturges directed that one."

"Preston Sturges was my grandfather's best friend. Granddad was one of the prisoners laughing at the end of that movie."

Tango eyes me. "This Preston Sturges have anything to do with your name, Prestonia?"

I smile at Tango and tap the side of my head. "Story goes, my granddad laid his hand on my mother's pregnant belly and insisted the child be named for his venerable friend. When they got me, and I was of the female persuasion, they adulterated the name to Prestonia."

Dinner over, and Tango's clothes washed and dried, Bob suggests we be on our way. "Thank you for taking Daisy with you. I can't manage her until I'm more mended."

We say our goodbyes and I drive the dogs and Tango back to the house in Eagle Rock. I keep glancing at Tango. He doesn't look even slightly homeless cleaned up with his beard gone. "Tango, I'm sorry I didn't let you shower and wash your clothes at my place."

"I didn't expect it."

"Please know you're welcome to."

I lead the dogs as Tango carries his belongings down the driveway to the backyard. As I pass the garage, I remember what Erika said about it being a good studio—*or something*. Now I know what she meant. "Tango, you're welcome to stay in the backyard under the mulberry tree or balcony, or, if you'd like a private space out of the elements, you can stay in the garage. It's cozy—in a garage kind of way."

"Thanks, but I'm the outdoors type."

"Just take a look. If there is anything you want to use from there, feel free."

Tango opens the side door. The space really is cozy. For a garage. Boxes are piled high, but the furniture stored there is laid out in such a way as to be inviting.

He stares at it as if tempted, then turns to me. "I can't do the indoor thing but let's pretend. I'm gonna give you money for rent until I find a place of my own. I get a check monthly, so don't think it's from panhandling, which I've never done. I'm renting this garage and that includes access to the yard. Sometimes this renter will stay out in the yard, enjoying the out-of-doors, sleeping there. I gotta have that. But you have access to the same out-of-doors. You gotta have that. I will pay you weekly. We don't have to talk, or eat together, or be involved any more than any tenant and landlord. That work for you, Prestonia?"

For some reason, this spears my heart, but I nod.

"I, um, we'll talk about that later. Now, about staying here—what about, what about—when you need to use the bathroom."

Tango pulls several small green bags from his pockets. "Dog cleanup bags. The parks all have them. I use them for the dogs and myself. Pop it in the garbage can and done."

Before I can respond in whatever way I would have, the Quinceañera music starts next door.

"You may want to rethink staying here." I say. "This can be incredibly annoying."

Tango and the two dogs cock their heads. "Someone's at the front door."

I ask Tango to join me, as I'm still leery of Brent. We go up and it's Alberto.

"Hola, Prestonia. Today is the last rehearsal before the Quinceañera. We're having a party in the backyard." He puts his hand out to Tango. "Oye, compa, I'm Alberto."

Tango shakes the offered hand. "I'm Tango. But don't ask me to dance a tango."

"Well, come by anyway. You're both very welcome." And Alberto heads back to his house.

I turn to Tango and whisper, "He looks scary, like a shaved-head, gang-banger type, but he's quite nice."

There's a flash of something in Tango's eyes and he looks about to speak, but then takes a really long, deep breath and lets it out slowly, finally saying, "Yeah, I thought he was nice."

I start back into my house when Tango says, "I don't know what a Quinceañera is but I haven't been to a party in a really long time. You game, Prestonia?"

I'm really surprised. I'm sick of this music and am not really great with strangers, but I shrug and we walk next door.

The backyard party is full of teenagers and their parents. Alberto introduces us and everyone is polite but no one is speaking English except to us. By the big grill, they make sure we're loaded up with tacos and a red Jamica drink I learn is from Hibiscus flowers.

The teens perform their choreographed dance, and it's really quite good. I feel bad I had such negative thoughts about their practicing. Everyone cheers when it's over. Other music starts. It's like polka music but Spanish style and the entire crowd starts dancing. I watch as Tango scans the people. Out of the blue, he walks away from me, edging around the dancing kids and parents. At the far side of the yard, he approaches an old woman sitting alone and bends to speak to her. He holds out a hand and she takes it and he slowly dances with her.

Why is he doing that? Now I'm left alone, damn it! Alberto sidles up to me and offers his hand. Shit, shit, shit. I don't know how to do this kind of dancing. I take his hand and he steers me to the center of the group and I try to follow his lead, leaning in for two beats, leaning out for two beats, now he's got me spinning, twirling, and I feel like I'm the swirling end of a cowboy's lariat. As the music stops, he bows and nods for me to look as Tango walks the old woman back to her seat. Alberto leans close to me, whispering, "This Tango is much nicer than that last hombre. Muy bien, chica."

I look at my neighbor. He's not seeing Tango as a homeless man. He's seeing Tango as a good man. Maybe I should try that.

A DIFFERENT FUTURE?

THE SUN IS LONG GONE when Tango and Prestonia return from the neighbor's party.

Captain and Daisy are happy to see them and get dinner. As

they eat, Prestonia brings water down for them and for Tango. She goes back up and brings down a towel and a flashlight and a candle with matches. Another trip brings extra blankets and a pillow.

She whispers, "Sleep well," and disappears upstairs, ending the night with the click of the door deadbolt.

Tango sets up his sleeping bag under the balcony. He puts the book with Pema's smiling face beside the pillow. Puts Clayton's urn on the other side. He spreads the extra blankets beside his sleeping bag for Captain and Daisy. He opens Pema's book randomly. A passage about breathing. Why would she write about breathing? Don't we do it all the time? She writes about focus and slowing down. Tango takes in a long slow breath and exhales even slower. Again. This feels different. If you change your breathing, can you change your life?

Tango sets the book down. Maybe this is not that place below the bridge in the Arroyo but with the Pema's book and Clayton's urn and the dogs—it feels like home. Tango wonders if home is what you carry with you, rather than where you are.

MORNING WITH TANGO AND THE DOGS

AGNES SLOAN DOESN'T HAVE A KEURIG coffee machine. I've been using the old-fashioned stovetop kettle and a French press, and it's not always easy to get the right amount of grounds. Lately though, I've enjoyed the loose tea more. My cuppa. I wonder what Tango would like.

I load a tray with an electric kettle I found in the back of one of Agnes's cabinets, ground coffee, loose tea, and a mug. Take the tray downstairs. Tango is lying in his sleeping bag reading his smiling woman Buddhism book. The two dogs give me a tapping tail greeting.

"Agnes had an electric kettle I'm not using. The garage has electricity. I brought both tea and coffee."

"I really don't need all this. I've had a lot of time without."

"That was the old future," I remind him. "The new future includes hot drinks."

I set everything on the patio table.

Tango thanks me and adds, "I like that we're both starting new futures and leaving the old futures behind. Here's to hot drinks and mud figures."

I glance over at my little mud figure. A pretend-dead girl. That's me. I'm pretending to be one thing and I'm really another.

My phone rings. I look at the caller I.D.—Goldman Sachs. My heart starts pounding, and I wave to excuse myself, trot up the stairs to my kitchen and answer.

The receptionist says that Ms. Bloom is calling. I thank the young woman, and there's my new boss with her capable, confident voice. "Ms. Cheswick, good morning. I trust you had time to think about our offer. We'd love to have you. I'll just reiterate the terms we spoke of."

As she recites the salary and perks and benefits and expectations, I feel the pull of the slick furniture and the marble tiles and the lingo I'm so comfortable with. I see my new apartment on the West Side. I see the Keurig coffee maker and white walls. This future will be entirely known and lucrative and an undeniable success. I'll be making an entirely—familiar—future.

Erika's swirling colorful painting fills my view. The painting she did of my *Ashes-to-Ashes* life. She won't understand. She sees something in me that I don't see. She called me a poly-creative.

Down in the yard, there's the faint whistle of the electric kettle. Tango won't understand. He sees me as a filmmaker, improvisational actor-channeler, and mud-sculptor.

Agnes Sloan's little ceramic dog toothpick holder looks up at me. I never knew any dogs before Agnes. I'd never been to the Griffith Park Carousel or driven a jeep or had that Hibiscus-Jamica drink or been to a Quinceañera party or flown on a plane or traveled to another state or been camping or visited a jail or met a homeless person or had a piece of art painted specifically for me or made extraordinarily wonderful mud sculpture with the fake ashes of a fake dead girl. If I can do all this, I can do anything.

"Ms. Bloom," I say. "I appreciate your generous offer but I've come to the conclusion that my future lies elsewhere. Thank you." And I hang up and point triumphantly at Erika's painting.

FUCK!

I run down the stairs. Tango is slipping on his sweatshirt, his chest is visible for a flash. *Nice!*

"I did it!" I scream. "I turned down that high-powered finance job and wrote my brand new future!"

My hands go up for high-fives and Tango grabs them, shaking them in celebration of my triumph. "Good for you! Did you bring in Mitchum or Streep?"

"I did it as myself! It was fuckin' the best!"

"Well done!"

"Let's celebrate. I gotta call Erika. Her painting tipped the scales."

I call my Scottish-by-way-of-the-world friend. Is she my friend? I've never had a friend that wasn't my age. She's the first!

"Erika, I know I said I wasn't going to, but I sent out financial advisor resumes and Goldman Sachs called and I had an interview yesterday and it went great and they made an incredible offer and I said I'd think about it and I did and was going to take it and then when they called your painting was there and I remembered I'm a poly-creative and mud figure sculptor and suddenly—by saying no to them—I wrote an entirely new future!"

A Scottish scream blasts through my phone, causing Tango and me to crack up.

"We're celebrating today. You want to join us?"

"Who's we?" Erika asks.

"Me, Tango, and the dogs."

Erika tells me she will be here in two shakes of a lamb's tail and hangs up. I don't know about lamb's tails but I expect that means fast.

Only it's not. After a few minutes, I go back upstairs and after forty-five minutes, I start to worry. Did Erika get in an accident? After an hour, there's a honk outside. Tango rushes up the driveway, and I hurry to the door, and we meet out front as Erika pops her trunk and bends low, lifting something. "'Ope ye don't mind the wait. 'Ad te pick up a spot o' lunch. Gee us a hand 'ere, loves." and she carefully holds up a foil-covered container, then screams. "Jesus-Mary-n-Feckin'-Joseph! Is that clean-shaven lad me friend Tango?!"

Tango grins and shyly ambles to her. She sets down the container and holds him at arm's length, surveying him with relish. "Blimey, yer a stunner. Enough to make an old lass curl 'er toes jest lookin' acha. 'Ere, take this in. It's hot, so mind yer digits." He lifts the container and carries it into the house. "Yer next, lass."

I move beside her.

"Why'd ye nae tell me the lad 'ad transformed hisself? Ye'l ne'er gee me a thought if that bloke's aboot we 'is undeniable face tae dream o'r."

She gets me stuttering, "I—I—"

"Ne'er mind, luv. Grab both these bags an keep 'em upright or 'ey'll spill."

I take the bags inside and Tango has already pulled the table out from against the window, found another chair, and is setting out plates. He raises his nose to sniff the air. "Erika's brought a spread, and from the smells, I've got an idea of what."

As I open my bags, Erika enters with two more foil-covered containers.

"Tango, luv, when's the last time ye 'ad a meal from yer 'ome town?"

He smiles. "I thought I recognized the scent of N'Olins."

She uncovers containers and opens cartons. "Barbecue ribs, fried chicken, crawfish étouffée, shrimp 'n' grits, catfish fritters, cornbread, mac 'n' cheese, fried okra, mashed 'taters wi' gravy, and gumbo. Did I leave anythin' oot?"

Tango smiles. "I hate to say it but—"

"'Old yer 'orses." And she lifts a grease-stained bag. "Can't forget the—"

"—Beignets."

And the two of them laugh and seem to know all about this food that I've never had except for fried chicken and mac n cheese. But I'm game for everything 'cause I'm writing an entirely new future that has an entirely new menu.

After a lunch full of unknown dishes, dishes I'm unconvinced of, and dishes I'm converted to, we sit quietly, listening to the birds and watching the light change on Erika's painting.

A call comes in on my phone. Is it Ms. Bloom trying to convince me to reconsider? The I.D. doesn't say so, but who knows what she might do for subterfuge.

"Hello?"

A gravely voice says, "I'm calling for *Ashes-to-Ashes*."

"This is *Ashes-to-Ashes*, Prestonia Cheswick here. How can I help you?"

Tango, Erika, and I do a silent scream to each other.

After a few seconds, I realize the call is from Daisy's owner, Bob. I hand the phone to Tango. He listens and nods and says, "I'll talk to her about it," and hangs up, handing the phone back to me.

"He wants to hire *Ashes-to-Ashes* to scatter his daughter's ashes, and he wants me to be part of it. He hopes you'll find a person to take care of Daisy and Captain while we're on the job."

"Done," Erika chimes. "I'll stay 'ere. 'Tis better to be with them at yer house than trying to hide 'em at The Avalon."

BOB'S PLAN FOR HIS DAUGHTER

THAT AFTERNOON, Tango and Prestonia drive to Bob's house with the dogs. Daisy and Bob are overjoyed to see each other again, but the old man looks very weak.

As Daisy cuddles with her owner, Bob tells them of his hope. "My daughter Luna has a place in New Mexico. I've not seen it but I know it's something like sixty acres. I'll pay for your flights, rental car, motel—unless you want to stay at her place, which is fine—and five hundred for each of you. Probably three days, two nights. Or more if you're having fun. Sound okay?"

Prestonia had imagined that the job would be somewhere around Los Angeles, not a place she and Tango would have to stay overnight.

Bob points to a unique, home-made-ceramic-cookie-jar looking thing. "Here's Luna," he says, getting weepy. It's clear he's reluctant to let her go, but Tango sits with him, listening and occasionally, quietly speaking.

Prestonia steps away to give them space and plays with the dogs in the courtyard. In a while, Tango taps on the window to call her in.

"Bob wants me to go through his things and pick some clothes for the trip. We're about the same size, even if he's a bit taller, but I've been wearing the same batch of clothes for so long, I don't know what to choose. Can you help?"

They look through the closet and bureau. Bob has a lot of white shirts and suit jackets for his JPL work, but Prestonia picks the most casual clothes available: a blue farmer shirt, lightweight checked shirt, blue jeans, black jeans, a leather belt, two T-shirts, several pairs of socks, and a straw fedora.

Prestonia holds up a pair of boxer shorts. Tango shakes his head. She wonders if that means he doesn't want someone else's underwear or that he doesn't wear underwear.

Bob calls from the living room, "Suitcase is in the back of the closet. Pack whatever you want. I ain't gonna use it."

Suitcase packed, they return to Bob. He hands Tango Luna's ceramic urn and gives Prestonia an address, a significant bundle of keys, and an envelope of cash.

Tango shakes the old man's wrinkled hand and takes the urn and dogs to the car as Prestonia promises Bob that he'll feel like he's there when she shows him the film of scattering Luna's ashes. He puts his palm to her cheek. No one in her life ever touched her cheek in this gentle cupping gesture, and now both Bob and Rooster have done it. Part of Prestonia bristles, and the rest wants to cry.

Back home, Prestonia books a flight for the next afternoon and arranges a car rental. She puts it in her name because she doesn't know if Tango drives and doesn't want to find out at the wrong end of the steering wheel.

Packing her filming equipment, she decides that since scattering ashes is her new job, she should have something better than her lapel Go-Pro or her phone. A quick trip to Sammy's Camera in Pasadena gets her a great quality digital camera for filming. Now she's all set!

The next morning, Tango, wearing blue jeans and a farmer shirt, carries Bob's suitcase to the front door.

"Oh!" Prestonia gasps at seeing him.

"Not good?"

"I just, you look so—normal—I mean *different*. I've only seen you in the baggy army jacket and cargo pants. It's good. You look good."

"Okay. Thanks."

When Erika comes over for the house keys and to learn what to do with Daisy and Captain, she gasps—seeing Tango dressed so differently. "Jesus, Mary, and Joseph, look at the fella! Can ye not stay 'ere wi yer pal Erika and let the lass go alone?"

Tango tries to hide his smile but gives up. As he carries their luggage to the ragtop jeep, Erika gives Prestonia a clear *Fuck this one!* look. Prestonia gives her an *Are you mad?* look, and hustles out the door.

After parking at LAX's longterm parking, they head to their terminal and start for the TSA security line. Tango hesitates. Prestonia turns back. "You okay?"

"You think they'll let me through?"

"Why wouldn't they?" she asks. "Do you have something on you they'll find?"

"No, but I feel guilty. They can see guilty. If they try to stop me, I'll have to pull up my best Buddhist learning, but it might not work."

Prestonia waves him to sit on a bench. "Why are you feeling guilty?"

"Because I *am* guilty. I've screwed things up my whole life. I've been guilty since day one."

Prestonia stares at the floor. Beside her, Tango's leg jitters up and down. "Listen," she says. "I feel guilty, too. I think it's normal around police or these people. Like they'll find something out about me. Something I don't even know. I think if we were happy and smiley, they would probably suspect us of something. They won't suspect someone who looks like they feel guilty because that's normal!"

Tango smiles. "You really feel guilty?"

"Everyone does!"

Tango stands and starts toward the security line. "Thank you. I'm okay now."

Prestonia joins him with, "Don't look so relieved, they'll suspect you of hiding your guilt!"

They get through the TSA security easily, wait at the gate, board the plane, and finally rise into the air. Prestonia looks like she is getting used to flying. She thinks to herself, *I've never been to New Mexico, but it's probably not that different from Wyoming.*

Tango, beside her, grips the armrest. His arm isn't resting. No part of him is resting. The sound and speed and pressure in his ears are sending him back. He begs his mind and body to stay cool. *Don't lose it now, man. Things are good.*

Turbulence jolts them and Prestonia gives him a look like *I'm kinda scared, are you?*

As he slides helplessly into his own internal hell, Tango can't reassure her so gives a twisted grimace and turns away as the memories envelope him.

ARRIVING FROM THE DESERT

TANGO WAS ON MILITARY TRANSPORT AIRCRAFT returning

from the desert across the sea. He was in his combat fatigues and feeling a mix of trepidation and elation as they approached California. What would he do when he got there? He could get a taxi, but to where? He could walk, but to where?

One of the flight crew must have thought he looked green around the gills 'cause she brought him a handful of packets of Saltines "to settle the stomach." He stuffed them in his pocket.

When they landed, there was a large boisterous reception in the hangar, and *everyone* was there. Yet, no one in that *everyone* was there for him. Not with him getting out with an OTH—Other Than Honorable discharge. The band played and women and kids ran to hug his comrades and the flags waved and a senator or congressman or someone of importance said welcoming words about their sacrifice—and at that moment, he realized, there was no place in this world for him. The army didn't want him. His mother hadn't wanted him. No one on earth wanted him. He was, and would always be, alone.

He dropped from his at-ease position and sat on the tarmac. Beside him, a soldier hugging a young wife turned and asked, "You sick?"

"Guess so," Tango replied and started screaming.

The baffled soldier signaled for help and several men loaded the screaming Tango into a Humvee and drove him away.

Tango's not sure what happened next.

Not sure how many days or weeks or months he was in that chilly white space. There, people screamed incessantly—or was it just him? There, there was nothing but being locked inside, never out in the air. There, he was controlled by the pills and finally, after the pills numbed him into submission, they let him out. They dressed him in the fatigues he'd traveled in, complete with discharge papers, cash, I.D., his duffel bag, and the pocketful of Saltines. He was dropped in Pasadena at the corner of Orange Grove and Colorado Boulevards. He'd never been there but saw the beautiful bridge, and when he got close, heard the trickling stream far below, and skidded butt-to-rocks all the way down the ravine.

An emaciated red dog growled at him. Tango bent low to meet the creature's eye, widened his stance, and growled back. The dog lifted its lips to show gums and teeth. Tango tried to do the same, gave up, pulled from his pocket the airplane Saltines, tore open the wrapper and tossed the small squares to the dog. An instant chomp and swallow and wag. That was the beginning.

"You remind me of Captain Weaver. A complete sonofabitch but righteous. Have I gleaned your essence?"

The dog barked in the affirmative.

"Captain it is then. Where's the bunkhouse?"

And the dog seemed to understand, for he trotted up the bank to a spot behind the huge cement footing supporting the bridge and welcomed Tango in.

NEW MEXICO

TANGO HAS NOT SAID A WORD the entire flight and whenever his elbow touches mine on the armrest, I feel him shaking.

We land in a tiny airport in Santa Fe. It's much smaller than the one in Casper, Wyoming and the one in Van Nuys. A rental car is waiting for us and we load up and strap in. I tap the address of Bob's daughter's place into my phone, and we're off.

Tango is unreadable. Is he upset or angry or content? He's just looking out the window.

Keep driving.

New Mexico's not like Wyoming. It's deserty, like LA, but also has mountains on all sides and a quick search tells me that we're at the bottom of the Rockies, which is very cool, since I've been to Colorado, so I know the Rockies! The houses look like they were built of mud many centuries ago. And from my architecture semester, I know these are *adobe* houses made of mud and straw, and some *were* built centuries ago.

We drive north and after an hour of turns, the little civilization we saw becomes NO civilization. No fast-food joints. No mini-malls. No sky-scrapers. No NOTHING! What the hell is this place?

"This is my kind of place," Tango says—his first words since leaving LA.

I look again at the phone which keeps saying *lost cellular service*. "We're not connected to GPS anymore so maybe we're *lost* in your kind of place."

"Let's ask him," Tango says, pointing to a boy riding a burro by the side of the road (I know burros now from Agnes's lamp!).

"Hello there. Can you tell us where Ojo Caliente might be?" I say, sounding more like a financial advisor than I'd like.

The boy points. "Go on until the road stops in a T. Turn right. Follow that and you'll get there."

"How long?"

"Three, four hours."

What!

The kid grins. "If you're on a mule," he says.

Damn! It's a mule, not a burro!

"What if someone was in a car?" I ask a little snarkily.

"Twenty minutes."

We thank him and continue on.

It's evening, and the sun sends dramatic shadows across the land. Big black birds circle and caw overhead. We're on a dirt road and I'm thinking we're fucked.

"That's it," Tango says, pointing to a ceramic mailbox held up by a bizarre structure made from what look like bicycle parts.

Get out and find the gate across the driveway locked with a thick chain.

"Got the keys Bob gave you?" Tango asks.

This Tango guy is on top of things. I pull out the large bundle of keys. Try the smaller ones first. One of these opens the padlock. We push the gate wide and drive in.

Bump over rutted road and past scrubby brush and there's a large fallen tree blocking our way. We leave the car and climb over the trunk and walk to what we hope will be some sort of dwelling. Walking is really hard. Like, bizarrely hard. I'm incredibly out of breath. Am I dying?

The sun's gone behind purple mountains, and stars are popping up across the wide sky. I stop and point at a familiar constellation of three dots which meant something that I forgot and pretend to look at them so I can catch my breath.

"It's the altitude. Much less oxygen up here. Take it slow," Tango says.

How does he know this and I don't? He's from New Orleans, which must be the lowest altitude anywhere.

I stomp down the road ignoring his advice. I think we might be passing fruit trees but it's too dark to really see them. Finally, we curve around to a low adobe house.

I pass Tango my phone with the flashlight on so he can light the front door as I try keys. Why are there so many keys? We finally get the door unlocked and peek in. Musty smells. A scurrying sound.

BLAM!

A gun blast behind us.

"Fuckin' hands up and turn slow or you're dead!" a woman's voice adds.

We turn, hands up.

A super bright high-beam covers us. No view of the person behind it.

"You're trespassing. Gimme one reason not to shoot you."

I can't think of a reason. Why is that?

Tango speaks. "We're here at the request of Luna's father. Luna died in Los Angeles and we're here to bring her ashes to the place she called home."

Fuck, I'm glad he's here.

The high-beam clicks off and we hear a person step forward in the darkness. Soft coughs. A catch in the throat, then the voice adds, "Sorry. Gotta be careful. Don't want no vandals on my watch. I'm Luna's neighbor over that side. No 'lectricy here at her place. Gimme a sec." There is a long pause in the darkness. After another cough, the woman says, "I wondered why she didn't pay utilities from afar. She's—was—a great woman and—I'll miss her."

Tango quietly says, "I'm Tango and this is Prestonia. Can we get your name?"

The woman turns the flashlight back on and points it at her face. She's seventy or more. Long white hair adorned with several feathers. Deep-set, wild dark eyes, a scar or tattoo of something on her cheekbone. She's wearing a bathrobe with bears and moose and fish on it. "Call me Ello."

"Ello?" I ask.

"The letters L and O."

Tango, probably from knowing that letters can mean something else, asks, "L. O. stands for—?"

"Last One."

Tango nods like that makes sense. "Thank you for keeping a vigilant eye on Luna's place, Ello," Tango says. "Didn't mean to cause you alarm and sorry to bring sad news."

"Stay put. I'll bring water and lanterns. Don't go in the house until I get back. Liable to be critters, snakes, scorpions, and black widows."

Ello disappears in the darkness. In a minute we hear a motor start and we watch her headlights move out of the drive and turn at the dirt road. They get farther away until they're tiny specs, then turn and continue parallel to Luna's drive, and finally stop and disappear. There are no other lights anywhere. Nothing but the glow of the stars.

A bunch of coyotes start a racket of howls and yips that sounds like an orgy or massacre. I've never heard it in real life, only in movies. Tango seems quite at ease here. I'm freaking out. If there are coyotes, there may be bears and cougars and murderers and—what about *inside* Luna's house? We should drive back to Santa Fe for a hotel. No way I'm sleeping with snakes and spiders.

In the distance, headlights turn on again. They complete the same circuit in reverse and end up curving up to us. Somehow she got around that fallen tree.

Ello steps out of her ancient pickup truck and hands us two

lanterns and a box of matches and bids us follow her inside. Her high-beam flashlight illuminates the kitchen. It's got an old iron wood stove and a little electric one. A retro fridge. White country-style sink. Shelves full of all sorts of homemade ceramics and dead plants.

"Damn. The jade and cacti might make it. I'll give them some of the water I brought for you and bring more tomorrow. Let's look in the cupboards for mice and spiders."

She shines the light in the spaces. A few scampering shadows run, but no spiders.

We move into a large living room that's full of sculptures of welded junk, mobiles, and pottery. It has mismatched furniture, a clay-like curvy fireplace in the corner, and a glass-wall, floor-to-ceiling window black with the night.

We move through an archway to a wide hall and peer in the bathroom.

She inspects the toilet and cabinets and tub. The tub has two dead mice and several insect carcasses. "Got trapped by the sides." She holds the wastebasket in the tub and flicks them in with her flashlight. "Don't use the toilet. No water to flush. Luna's on a well, but you need power to pull the water up."

We move to a bedroom. The bed is high off the ground, which gives me some relief. Ello pulls back the sheets and checks beneath the pillows and across the ceiling. She moves one blanket at a time and, finding nothing, says, "Next room. This used to be a big family home, so there are beds in each room. Luna never changed that."

"'s okay. We've seen enough," Tango says.

I wonder if he thinks he's going to sleep in the same bed with me. Not gonna happen, dude.

Ello interrupts my thoughts. "We'll check all the rooms. Don't want surprises."

We check three more rooms. Each has a different look and style. Some ceilings are covered with planks, some with round logs. Some rooms have little niches built into the walls. One has a day bed, the next has a twin bed, and the last room has an old-fashioned, wrought-iron double bed surrounded on three sides with mismatched windows. A recycled conglomeration that must bring in a lot of light. I ask Ello about the architectural differences in the rooms.

"Lots of old houses are like this one. Have another kid and add a room. Have a grandparent move in and add a room. Like people, houses change over time."

I wonder if I'm changing over time.

We head back to the kitchen. The old woman grabs Tango's hand and pulls him outside. They return with him carrying four gallon-jugs of water. She waters the wrinkled jade and cactus pants as we watch.

"Why is your name Last One, Ello?" Tango asks.

He seems okay with people more than I am. Like asking questions. I never do that.

"I'm a medicine woman. Healer. Learned from my mother, who learned from hers—way back to the beginning of time. I have three children. All grown. Grandchildren, too. None had the spark to learn these ways, so I'm the Last One. My first name was Tadawi. Wind Woman."

"So your knowledge of healing dies with you?" I ask, attempting to contribute to the conversation.

"Only if I die," she says seriously, then cackles. "I'll teach anyone. You want to learn?"

I shake my head and she slaps my arm, then turns to the door. "You passed Luna's fruit trees on the way in. Apples are ripe, if you want breakfast. And don't let that downed tree stop you. It's only there for show. Veer to the left and skirt around the piñon trees and you'll be back on the drive through the orchard. I'll check on you in the A.M. Don't start a fire in the wood stove or the kiva until we check for bats or other critters. Fire pit outside is okay."

And she's gone. Again we watch her headlights. She must live miles away. Maybe in the past, people didn't live right next to each other all the time. They didn't always hear someone watching porn in the apartment above or sobbing to Billie Eilish in the studio next door. I wonder if it's better not to be on top of each other. Maybe miles apart is a good idea.

After a long moment of watching until Ello's headlights go out, Tango suggests we get the car. "I can do it but I haven't driven in many years."

I kinda want him to anyway. It's not like he'll drive off a cliff. But if he went, I'd be alone with bats and spiders. And what if he doesn't come back? What if he takes the car and disappears? "Let's go together," I suggest.

And we huff and puff with our lanterns all the way through the orchard to the car behind the tree barrier. We get in and drive around the Piñon pines and back to the house. From there it's unloading the luggage.

"I'll grab a blanket and sleep outside," Tango says.

"What about coyotes?"

"Had them under the bridge in the arroyo in Pasadena."

"Sleep in the rental car. It's safer."

"I'm used to the wide open."

I see he's adamant. We go inside and he grabs a blanket. I find an extra pillow and say, "I'll leave the door unlocked. Please come in if there is anything hungry and carnivorous out there."

Tango smiles, tips an imaginary hat, takes a gallon of water, and steps out into the darkness.

Great. I'm alone in this strange house that's probably full of creatures that hid when Ello shined her flashlight.

I strip the bed again and move the lantern over every inch of every cover. Check the ceilings like Ello did. Check the closets and corners. Check the path to the toilet. Oh, I can't use the toilet. I hurry to the front door and step out.

"Tango?"

"Hmm?" comes a voice in the darkness.

"Where should I—um—pee?"

"Hold on." And he emerges and takes my lantern and leads me around to the side of the house. Holds up the light and moves it around. "No spiders. No snakes. No underground nests. This should be okay."

I peed outside when I was camping with Rooster, but it was nice under the pines and on soft pine needles. This place is rough and thorny and scary.

"Or, you could look for a jar in the kitchen and pee in that," Tango adds.

I'm flooded with relief. "Yes, I'll do that. Thank you. Goodnight!"

And I hurry inside. There are several empty jars in a bottom cabinet. I pee over the toilet just in case. It works out perfectly.

I've packed Agnes's flannel cowboy pajamas that I've come to see as mine, but they seem too open to sleep in if there are hidden snakes and spiders and mice in the bed. I tuck my pant legs into my socks and button my shirt up to the neck. Finally, I slip under the hopefully-safe covers and blow out the lantern.

Probably won't be able to sleep at all.

UNDER THE BIG SKY

THE COYOTES KEEP THEIR CACOPHONY going but Tango feels comforted by it. The sky is dark and the air may be thin but it's clean and smells of plants and dreams. He curls deep in the blanket and looks at the vast night above. There are so many stars. *This is freedom. This is safety. This is where I could be okay*, he thinks. Then he adds, *This is my future.*

Ravens cluck above Tango. He wakes to them cocking their heads at him in the apple tree overhead. "Sorry. I'm in your spot," he says, quickly rising and slipping into his jeans.

The sun isn't yet over the mountains to the east but the sky is light and the air is brisk. He jogs down the dirt road, trying to warm up and collects several apples from the trees. There's an absence he's not used to. He glances down to where he'd expect Captain to be trotting by his side, but the dog isn't there. So strange to be without his friend. *Hope the dog is okay,* he thinks.

A separate inner-voice answers. *Captain is more able to adapt to changes than you. You need to learn from him. He's probably very content right now, asleep in Agnes Sloan's house on a soft bed with Erika and Daisy.*

Tango wonders if sleeping in a soft bed in a house could ever be a possibility for him again.

A lizard runs across the road as the sunlight hits the top of the apple trees. There are mountains visible in all directions far, far away. With the vast distances so evident, he feels an expansiveness inside. For the first time in years, Tango takes a long, deep breath, pulls in more—and exhales out a little of the anger and fear and terror and shame.

Time for breakfast. He's got apples and he's sure he saw cans in the cupboards as that Ello woman searched for spiders. In the wide expanse of dirt in front of the house is a fire pit surrounded by large rocks and what looks like charred pottery bits. Some of the rocks are flat-topped so you could sit or place pans on them. Under the porch is a bounty of stacked wood and kindling.

Creep into the house and peruse the cans. Cans of red beans and rice. That'll do. Open them into a frying pan that looks like it's seen a flame before. Countertop has Ello's matches. There's a blackened pot he can use for heating water. Maybe he'll be able to find coffee or tea after the fire gets going.

Back out to the lightening sky. Fire catches the twigs, then branches and logs. Flame crackles. Ravens, crows, and lots of birds Tango doesn't know bloom over the sky. Pink clouds. A hummingbird zooms to his face, hovers, and zooms off. *That was on purpose,* he thinks. *What if I believe in coincidence and messages? This would be: WELCOME!*

BREAKFAST IN NEW MEXICO

I WAKE UP to an odd sound. Can't place it. Under the bit of birdsong and wind there's—nothing. No cars. No horns. No phone. No evidence of civilization. How can anyone live like this? Eagle Rock was hard enough, being a block away from a busy street. This is SILENCE. Even with the sound of rustling twigs and birds and air, it's real silence. Like before humans were invented. Like *rock* silence.

I slide out of the bed looking for spiders or whatever. Pull my pant cuffs from being tucked into the socks and unbutton the top of my shirt. Guess at least nothing crawled in my clothes.

Open my makeup kit.

Don't do it! my brain yells. *You're not putting on makeup for a homeless man!*

I never go without makeup if I'm going to be seen. It makes me feel very awkward but I follow orders and just brush my hair.

Out of the bedroom and down the hall to the living room. The floor-to-ceiling window now shows a courtyard with sculptures and pottery and cacti under the canopy of a large shade tree. It's nothing like Bob's mid-century landscaped courtyard, but beautiful in a Georgia O'Keeffe-desert-landscape-way. There's even a large white cow skull! Across the courtyard is a room with many windows. I can see straight through it to a beautiful, blooming tree drooping pink ribbons of flowers. It takes me a minute to realize this is the last bedroom with the mismatched windows.

I pass into the kitchen and, through the open door, see smoke. Standing behind the smoke is Tango. He's hunched as always, like he's got the weight of the world on his shoulders, but he doesn't look homeless. Looks more like a guy camping. Like a normal guy camping—

My brain kicks in. *He's not a normal guy camping. He's homeless. Meaning no home, No job. No aspirations. Couldn't even last in the military where they WANT people to stay. Stop thinking that he's normal!*

Tango looks up and catches me watching him. I yell, "Good morning!" as if I just got to the door.

"Good morning!" Tango yells back. "It's wonderful, but I'm missing my dog."

Oh my, I don't know what to say to that. I never had pets growing up. Both parents thought pets were dirty and inconvenient. But I like how Captain and Daisy greet me. "I understand. Kinda. I never had a pet but I'd love to get to know one."

Tango smiles and waves me over to the fire pit. I stand beside him as he pokes the burning logs with a stick.

"They're just like us. Some are wise, some are silly, some are dominant, some are cowering, some try to be invisible, some want to be on top. Dogs are as varied as humans."

"Which dog are you?"

Tango looks at me like I'm asking a crucial question. I want to backtrack, but I don't know how.

He gets back to poking the fire. "I was gonna say I try to be invisible but, somehow, out here, I feel big. I don't know why."

"Maybe you *are* big," I say before I can stop myself.

Tango looks at me, and maybe it's the fire reflected in his eyes, but—gosh, he is handsome in a weird way, but of course we could never—

"You didn't cover up your freckles," Tango says.

Now I'm mortified! I should have put on makeup! I feel those freckles turning bright red.

"I'm glad," he adds. "They're sweet."

Fuck! What am I supposed to do with that!?

Thankfully, Ello's voice interrupts my panic. "Saw the fire and brought you more water, coffee, and Indian fry bread."

Tango takes a tray from her.

"Indian fry bread," I say. "What is that?"

"Indian fry bread," she answers.

We sit on the porch around the rough wood table and have a fabulous breakfast of Indian fry bread, red beans and rice, fire-roasted apples, and Piñon Pine coffee. For a moment I think of Brent and his foodie mentality and how he'd dismiss all this. Inside my jean pocket, I give him the finger.

Ello watches Tango eat and after a moment declares, "You've got Indigenous Peoples in you. Native blood, yes?"

Tango shrugs. "I don't really know. Creole white-looking mother. Father was someone she met during Mardi Gras. She said he was Black, but I never knew him. I'm a jumble."

I stare at Tango and I can see the mix in him. His features are of all sorts of ethnicities, and it's an alluring conglomeration. *Get a grip, Prestonia! Remember where he's from. He's homeless! Don't forget that!*

Ello points a boney finger at Tango. "I see lots of peoples in you and some are Native American. And *some* in you, it be high time you got rid of."

"Okay," Tango says with a question-mark tone.

"You want to let some go," the old woman orders. "But be proud of every one of your ancestors. All of them culminated in the magnificence of you."

Tango coughs dismissively.

Ello leans toward him fiercely. "You stop lying. Stop pretending. That golden bird you buried inside isn't dead or gone. Uncover it and soar!"

Tango and I freeze, not knowing how to react.

Ello laughs. "Hey, you never heard a medicine woman talk before? Where's Dragon?"

Tango and I look at each other. "Dragon?" we both ask.

"Hope he's not far. Luna's got sixty acres and I've got three hundred. Could be anywhere."

Ello stands, turning away from the fire, puts two fingers in her mouth and—WHEEEEE!

A sharp whistle.

Okay. Even something far away could hear that.

Ello puts up a finger.

We wait.

The birds cackle.

The fire crackles.

The wind—

Is that the wind?

Something—

is galloping—

cascading—

—toward us!

We look to the sound but see only brush and scrub and desert and—

A small grey terrier leaps!—lands in Ello's lap and snarls and snaps at us.

"Meet Dragon," Ello says as the small beast plants his paws on her thighs and asserts his magnificence.

She tells us about how Luna found the dog abandoned. She tells about Luna asking if Ello would take care of him just until she got back from Los Angeles. She tells of not knowing Luna was dead. "I took in Dragon, but I didn't know it would be for so long. You take him now."

I'm about to disagree when Tango says, "Of course, Bob will want Luna's dog."

"Gonna scatter Luna's ashes today?" Ello asks.

"Yes, but our first mission will be to scout for the best location and lighting conditions," I say, trying to sound professional.

"Might think to watch a video before anything. Give you insight into her," Ello suggests.

And we convene around my laptop in the kitchen. Pull up local Wi-Fi networks and choose *MedicineWoman*. It takes a moment for Ello to remember her password but we get in and start the video. A tall, beautiful woman stands in front of what is clearly this New Mexico house and she's smashing ceramic pottery in the fire pit. Vase after cup after plate. With each crash she screams in furious anger. After a particularly horrifying scream she looks at the camera, gives it the finger, then marches to the lens and the video ends.

"Wow. That's really disturbing. Do you know when this was?" I ask Ello.

"When her mother died. Before she went back to take care of her father."

"She must have been upset about her mother dying," I say, trying to be compassionate.

"She was upset about having to take care of her father," Ello says.

Tango looks at me and with the minutest head movement indicates: *Don't tell any of this to Bob.* His head movement makes me focus on his neck and the top of his sternum. What would it feel like to touch that?

What is wrong with you!? Yeah, you haven't had sex in a while, but are you that desperate? He is not for you! Get that through your head!

SCATTERING LUNA

PRESTONIA'S LOOKING AT ME *like she wants me to do something,* Tango thinks. *I'm not sure what to do. I've never been sure. Can I abdicate?*

Ello looks to Tango. "What do you think? How do we honor Luna?"

Prestonia's eyes widen. *Why's this old lady asking Tango and not me? Doesn't she know this is my business? It's my job to answer. What was the question?*

Tango gestures to the fire pit outside. "We could do it like her. We could smash everything."

Ello smiles. "I wanted to take one or two of her pieces, but I respect smashing. Destruction is as positive an action as construction."

Tango turns to her with surprise. "Destruction is as positive an action as construction?" he asks.

"It is, always was, and always will be," says Ello.

Tango looks to Prestonia for corroboration. She's got a confused smile that makes him think she's more clueless than he is. But it's her glowing freckles that really capture his attention.

Ello pushes Dragon off her lap and stands. "Let's go to her pottery shed. Tango, kick that fire out."

As he does, Ello turns to Prestonia and skewers her with those dark eyes. "*Never* leave a fire unattended."

Prestonia understands the metaphorical message, and

blushes deeply.

They leave the fire pit in front of the house and walk toward three other distant buildings. Closest is a greenhouse, about one hundred yards away. As they pass it, Ello says, "Luna grew a lot of her own food here."

"She sounds quite self-sufficient," says Tango.

Prestonia wonders to herself what the big deal is about being self-sufficient.

They continue on. Another fifty yards brings them to the pottery shed. The big room has a wall of windows, several wheels for clay work, two kilns of different sizes, and two walls of wooden shelves filled with beautiful pottery. Vases, cups, plates, animal figures, boxes, sculptures... all with a wide array of glazes and markings.

"Luna was a real artist," Ello says.

"Prestonia studied art," says Tango.

Prestonia scoffs. "That and a batch of other pointless classes."

Ello slaps Prestonia's arm. "Just because you can't see a point doesn't mean something's pointless."

Prestonia turns away, looking at all the pottery and trying to soothe her hurt feelings.

"We can't smash these," Prestonia says angrily. "What if Bob wants some of Luna's art? What if she saved exactly these ones as her favorite work? As CEO of *Ashes-to-Ashes*, I'm responsible for the scattering and the video and how it's perceived by loved ones. Bob would not want to see us smashing his daughter's work."

"That's true," Tango says. "He's the one who'll be watching. What do you want to do?"

Ello and Tango stare at Prestonia, which makes her feel belligerently determined to assert her position as *Ashes-to-Ashes* CEO. "We need to circle the area until we find a suitable spot."

Ello cackles. "You mean *spiral* the area. You place rocks to mark the spiral and scatter her along the path, culminating at the fire pit."

Tango glances to Prestonia and he can see she doesn't like

having someone else make the plans, but he can also see she respects the idea.

"It's your call, Prestonia. You're the boss," he says.

"Let's scout the spot."

They step out of the pottery shed and Tango looks toward the dark barn in the distance. "What's in there?"

"The barn has Luna's tools, rusty metal, bicycle parts, broken furniture. Basically a massive pile of junk to build stuff with."

They walk back to the house and stand around the fire pit.

Prestonia tilts her head this way and that, as if imagining the design. "We lay down rocks to delineate a spiral that ends at the fire pit. After we've built that, we can walk along the path scattering her ashes."

"I would like to be here when you scatter Luna," Ello says. "She was a good neighbor and friend. I'll be back after you finish the spiral." She bends to Dragon and tells him something in another language and walks to her truck. The dog stays put, eyeing Tango and Prestonia warily.

As Ello drives off, Prestonia picks up a rock. "Shall we?"

It's a lot harder than they imagined, collecting enough rocks and spiraling them from in front of the house into tighter and tighter circles as they try to converge at the fire pit. The lanes they make are wide and thin and oblong and too close and too far, and it makes them both frustrated, plus the sun is high. They retreat into Luna's house for water and bit of shade. Dragon follows them but growls and snaps if they try to get near him.

In the kitchen, Tango pours a bowl of water for Dragon and two glasses for them as Prestonia twists her red hair into a knot and gets it up off her neck using a spoon as a hairpin.

They sit at the porch table, drink, and stare out at the desert.

Prestonia sighs. "We're making a mess. It's not a spiral."

Tango nods at her. There is a little wisp of hair sticking to the back of her neck. He has to turn away. "We need to make it uniform. Each lane, the same width."

"How do we do that?"

"How wide do you want each pathway?"

Prestonia holds out her hands for the measurement.

Tango looks at those hands now covered with a mixture of dirt and sweat and has an impulse to grab them. He wants to feel that skin.

Stop it! he thinks. *She'll yank away and slap you. Don't mess up! Forget that now and forever, man!*

Prestonia watches Tango thinking. There's a twitching of his mouth and a squinting of his eyes. He seems in pain. "Tango?"

"Yeah, sorry, just calculating. Looks about two feet."

He walks off the porch and paces around the fire pit as he talks. "A long rope. Every quarter circle is six inches more and a complete circle is two feet from the center. We expand the rope from the fire pit like a clock. One quarter—six-inches, a half—one-foot, three-quarters—foot-and-a-half, back to Noon—two-feet. One expansion spiral done. From there we use a two-foot template."

Prestonia has no idea what he's talking about. Tango says, "I'll be back," and heads for the barn. Prestonia watches him go. He seems angry, marching heavily. Did she do something wrong?

As Tango stomps past the greenhouse and pottery shed to the barn, he berates himself under his breath. "This is a good thing you got now. This is working, asshole. You have a purpose and can do it and she's being nice. DO NOT THINK THAT NICE MEANS ANYTHING! If you screw this up, you will be back under that bridge and it'll be only a matter of time before you're in jail. You will lose Captain and he'll be killed. Consider the consequences, man! She's not for you!"

He reaches the barn with its dark weathered wood and massive sliding door. Pulls the handle and the track must be littered with leaves or debris because it's very hard to move, but his frustration helps and he slides it open enough to slip sideways through the gap. A quick look around yields what he needs and, after the long walk back past the other buildings, he returns to Prestonia with a thick rope, metal pipe, sledgehammer, and new attitude. As he pounds the pipe into the center of the fire pit, he tells her about the barn and the tools and welding tanks and rusty junk. "If we were staying longer, I'd try welding something."

Prestonia is secretly glad they won't be around for him to blow up the place.

With the rope tied to the pipe, Prestonia walks the first bit, expanding out six-inches for the first quarter turn as Tango sets down a small line of rocks to where she stands. Halfway—another six-inches out, and he follows with the rocks. Another six-inches at three-quarters, and another at the first position. Now they're two-feet out.

"And we keep expanding with the six-inches?" Prestonia asks.

"No. Now we use a two-foot stick and the path will spiral out at the correct width."

He breaks a stick into a two foot length and hands it to her, instructing her to keep it touching the first line of rocks and moving as he sets more down. As the spiral grows, he uses larger and larger rocks, and it becomes quite beautiful. At the end of their rope, they figure it's large enough and Tango wrenches out the pipe at the center. The path forms ten rings to the fire pit center and is about forty feet across.

Either Ello is watching them with a telescope or she has a sixth sense. At any rate, she arrives as soon as they're done, with more water, corn-nuts, and muted praise for their spiral labyrinth.

Prestonia says, "We can film the scattering now. Ello, you knew Luna, so it would be great if you would scatter her."

"I'll have to say words as I go. They won't be in English. Get the fire going again. Helps pull the spirit up."

They light the fire and with the camera ready, Ello holding the ceramic jar of ashes at the entrance to the spiral, Tango and Dragon under the porch, Prestonia pushes *Record* and says, "Action." There is a long pause, then a high yipping scream slides into a song of lament. Ello steps in rhythm to her song, stomping and shuffling, bowing and bobbing, a hand moving back and forth from the jar of ashes, keeping a gentle stream of the grey powder sprinkling from her fingers. Prestonia moves with Ello, the camera following her hands, her feet, her keening voice, circling in to the center where the old woman flings the last of the ashes into the fire. A FLASH of something ignites and sends a cloud of blue flame bursting skyward. Ello whispers several phrases and bows, then turns to Prestonia and says, "Cut."

Prestonia turns off the camera and wipes her eyes as she glances at Tango—who's also brushing away tears.

FILMING FROM ABOVE

HAVING FILMED ELLO from the side and behind, I know the spiral isn't visible unless you shoot it from above. There's a homemade wooden ladder made of tree branches propped against the side of Luna's adobe house, and I ask Tango to move it closer to the spiral. When it's in place, I pull myself up two steps and stop. It feels really rickety. "I can't go higher and this isn't high enough. Could you film from up on the roof, Tango?"

I give him my camera, he climbs easily up to the roof, and I duck out of sight of the lens. When Tango says he's rolling, I direct Ello to recreate the sprinkling. I hope Tango gets it. I don't want to climb up there. Maybe someday I'll buy a drone.

When Ello reaches the center fire pit again, she yells, "Cut." and Tango climbs down.

"I have to go," Ello says, spiraling out of the labyrinth.

"Let me check the footage first," I say. "We might need pickups."

"You've got everything you need and I have a pregnant goat due at any moment. Want to be there for her."

Tango always seems to think ahead because he asks, "Ello, could you give us directions to the nearest market so we can get something for dinner?"

Ello steps into Luna's house, comes out with a sketchbook and charcoal pencil, and makes a map that looks easy to follow.

After she leaves, I set up my computer in the kitchen where

it's cool and dark. Tango asks if he can watch me work.

"It'll be pretty boring," I warn.

"I doubt that," he replies.

I get started and he pulls up a chair behind me so he can see the computer. I feel him close, and it gets me jumpy and fidgety. Is he looking at the screen or at the back of my neck? Do I have freckles back there? Damn, I should have let my hair down!

The footage I shot all works, and the rooftop shots are perfect. "Well done, Tango!" I turn around to face him—*he's super close*—and I feel a jolt in my chest. I quickly turn back and unhook the camera from the computer. "I'm going to get some B-roll—shots of other things around the place, the orchard, pottery shed, greenhouse, barn... Could you look through the house to see if she has any photographs of family or her as a kid?"

Tango doesn't say anything, so I have to face him again. He's shaking his head, looking at the worn planks of the floor. "Feels like an invasion of Luna's privacy."

"I understand," I say. "It took me a long time to look around in drawers and closets at Agnes Sloan's house. But she was dead, and Luna is dead, and we're trying to make a memorial film that will be moving and honor her. We need pictures."

Tango agrees and starts the search.

I go out and hurry to the orchard. As I film close-ups of apples and a lizard sunning on a rock and swirling ravens, I try to calm myself. *Listen, you and Tango are worlds apart. Just because he's clean shaven and out of the homeless clothes doesn't mean he's suddenly a catch!*

I focus on the work and move on to get beautiful shots in the pottery shed, sunlight streaming in the wavy glass windows, hitting the glazed works and making them shine. The barn has a whole lot of rusty bits of machinery turned into sculptures. Everything looks very good through the lens, even the spiderwebs. The greenhouse is good from the outside, but the plants inside are all dead, so it's not so pleasant for this video. I circle around the back side of the house and get the courtyard sculptures and the little room with the windows on three sides and that tree with the drooping strands of flowers. It looks like a pink waterfall. It's so beautiful I have to google it. Tamarisk tree. I film that. Get back to the house and film sketches in the drawing pad, go to the kitchen and film her cups and inside all the drawers. One has wooden utensils that look hand carved. One has fix-it materials: super-glue, twine, rubber bands, paper stapler. One is filled with shards of broken pottery.

Step down the hall and find Tango on the bed with a box of photos. As I enter, he quickly wipes his eyes.

"Good pictures here," he says. "Birthdays, vacation trips, lots of warmth. She was well-loved."

"Let's shoot them in the kitchen. There's more light."

Tango collects the photos and carries them in. I set my tripod over the kitchen table and film the pictures as Tango moves them, one after another, in and out of frame. He's right. She was well-loved. I don't have any pictures like this of me with my parents. And I bet, for sure Tango doesn't.

"That's good for now. I have to save my battery in case we see something else to shoot. Better get to the market before it gets any later."

Tango suggests that he stay behind to sweep out what he can of the house while it's light and to see if he can make friends with Dragon. "Don't forget to get him some chow."

The roads are empty. The scenery keeps changing. First, it seems like a dry desert scrub but then there's a deep canal-like wash that has cattails and green trees and trickling water. I see two deer and several huge swirling birds. The road curves and ends in a T, and I look at Ello's map and try to memorize the stop sign by a dead tree so I can turn at this road on the way back. With no cell service GPS, I hope I can find my way. I guess people used to do it in the old days. Maybe I can manage. Make a left and a few more feet there's a white cross with plastic flowers by the gravel edge of the asphalt. Someone died here. I'm grateful for the sign to show me where to turn.

Whenever the trees are low, the view goes on forever.

Mountains. Reddish rocks and cliffs. It's unlike anything I've seen except in Westerns.

A little adobe building up ahead. The sign out front is weather-worn and I can only make out the second word: Market.

Park and walk in. The bell rings over the door. It's dark and cool inside. Flies circle.

"Hello?" A voice from somewhere.

"I'm here for groceries," I say, hoping I haven't just walked into someone's front room.

"Hold on." There's a shuffling on the wooden floor and several clicks get overhead fluorescent tubes blinking on. It is indeed a store. Wooden shelves of cans and a bank of old-fashioned refrigerators.

"Lookin' for anything special?" says a squat woman waddling out from behind an aisle of candy bars, beef jerky, and fishing lures. She's got long black hair that looks like it should be grey considering all the wrinkles that appear as she smiles warmly.

I don't imagine there'll be much here I could eat. "We were thinking of cooking over a fire."

She waddles to a refrigerator and holds it open for me. Points out—"Elk, pheasant, beef, trout, or chicken. Salmon, too, but that's not local."

The meal Rooster made of the fish comes to mind. "I'll take the trout. Do you have butter and white wine?"

"'Course. You'll want lemons. Some folks do onion too and capers."

"Please."

"Corn on the cob goes good in the fire. Keep it in the husk, soak it in water and put the whole thing in the fire. Keep turnin' and it gets nice black spots. Add squash, tomatoes, and garlic for Calabacitas."

This is great! Tango is going to be amazed.

"Yes, and what about for breakfast?"

"Eggs, tortillas, cheese, green chili, beans."

She sets me up with everything. I add two gallons of water, two cans of dog food, a small milk, and a box of teabags—so I can feel Erika is nearby.

I pay and the woman says, "Vaya con Dios."

I've lived in LA long enough to know that one, so I wave and say, "You, too."

The meal will be exciting. It's fun to make something that's delicious and elaborate. I bet Tango will be impressed.

Stop thinking of impressing him!

The memorial cross by the side of the road signals me and I make my turn. Another beautiful drive in this exotic land and I recognize the ceramic mailbox and turn in the driveway, angle around the tree barrier, through the Piñon pines, and up to the edge of Luna's spiral. The little dog Dragon comes running up, barking and lifting his small body off the ground with every ferocious roar.

I don't see Tango anywhere. Did he walk off? I doubt he'd be inside, with the way he hates being confined.

I step out of the car and there's a whistle from somewhere. Dragon stops barking and looks up, so I follow his gaze. Tango stands on the roof waving. "This land is amazing. Everything is wide and open. Saw you from miles away."

He was watching me. That gives me a jolt of something.

Is it a good thing or a bad thing?

Dragon trots up to me with his little nub of a tail bobbing back and forth.

"He thinks you have food," Tango says, climbing down the crazy, wobbly ladder.

"I do. And lots. Let's get that fire going again. Can you light it with one match?"

DINNER BY THE LABYRINTH

PRESTONIA DOESN'T REMEMBER everything that Rooster did to make his fish so delicious, but theirs turns out pretty good. The Calabacitas mix of corn, tomatoes, squash, onions, and garlic works as well.

They sit on the porch eating their dinner at the rough wood table. As the sun sets, silhouetting bruise-blue clouds with a vibrant orange, Prestonia lights the lantern Ello brought over but keeps it in the kitchen so they can watch the stars arrive. The little dog Dragon curls up on a braided rug Tango brings outside.

Prestonia and Tango don't speak. The evening sounds are perfect without anything they could add. Owls 'whoo' each other. Crickets sing. Distant coyotes yip. And way off in the far mountains, thunder rumbles.

When all traces of light have left the sky, Tango stands. For an infinitesimal moment, he imagines going in the house with her. The thought hurts and he roughly shakes his head like Captain would to banish it. *Remember what could happen. You'd lose everything. Remember your place in the world. You are meant to be invisible.* In the darkness, he puts out his hand to Prestonia but realizes that would only lead to more painful thinking so slides the hand up to scratch his cheek. They wish each other goodnight.

Dragon watches the man head for his rolled blanket below the nearest apple tree and watches the woman head into the house. As she slowly closes the front door, the dog makes his decision and slips inside.

KATRINA IN NEW MEXICO

BOOM!

Tango wakes in a panic. The thunder, lightning and pouring rain mean only one thing. Get to higher ground or you're dead.

He whistles for Captain but when there is no response he remembers that he's away from the dog for the first time. How is Captain? Is he alright?

BOOM!

Another roar of thunder. Got to find a safe space. High. The water is coming.

BOOM!

WHERE IS HE?

BOOM!

I wake up in a panic. What's happening? It's a storm but something else. There's moaning somewhere behind the clattering of rain on the roof and the thunder. What is it coming from?

A movement beside me. What is that!? I reach for my phone and turn on the flashlight app and there's the little dog Dragon looking up at me. He seems to think I'm going to be of use as comfort. I put my fingers on his tiny skull and give it a swish back and forth like I'm cleaning a dirty spot on the counter. "There, now. Everything's okay," I say. This sounds like a person about to find out about the second-act reversal. Uh-oh.

Listening, all I hear is rain. I probably dreamed that moaning sound. I'm not going to get out of bed to check. I'm cozy here in my cowboy pajamas. Close my eyes and BOOM!

A distinct moan follows.

Shit. I should check what that is.

Pull a blanket around my shoulders and slink to the front door. No delay between the lightning flashes and the thunder. It's right over me. Over us. Us? Where is the other part of us?

Open the door and look across the yard to the apple tree. Lightning flashes over the crumpled, soaking wet blanket.

"Tango!" I yell. It feels like Brando yelling "Stella!" in *A Streetcar Named Desire*, but during a thunderstorm. I doubt Stella or Tango could hear above this pounding storm.

"Tango!"

There's a sound—that moaning I heard earlier. Where's it coming from?

Dragon trots beside me as I hurry back inside for the high-powered flashlight Ello gave us and point the beam around the muddy yard. The spiral labyrinth—Luna's ashes are getting washed in by the rain. The orchard. The rickety ladder.

Another moan.

Dragon barks and looks up to the roof.

Fuck.

"Call 911 if I'm not back in five minutes," I tell Dragon. He cocks his head, not quite clear on the concept.

I flip the blanket over my head, duck through the torrent to the ladder, and take a grip. One foot on the branch beam. It held Tango, so should hold me. Pull up and test the next. So far so good, but this is not an OSHA ladder and it's already swaying with each step. Another rung. Pull up. The blanket is slipping but I can't spare a hand to grab it. It slips off and drops. Shit. Now I'm soaked. Another rung. I'm high enough that I'll be hurt if I fall. Why am I doing this? No one goes on a roof in a thunderstorm!

Another moan. It's coming from above me.

Fuck, fuck, fuck.

Okay, is this what Rooster talked about? Embrace it! Embrace what?! Embrace the fucking ladder!

I take another step, and the thing sways and creaks, and there is no part of this that's safe, and pull up and I'm peeking over the roof. There's a lump there. A moaning lump.

"Tango!"

The lump moves and turns to me.

"Tango, you need to get down. It's dangerous up here in the thunderstorm."

"We'll die! Flood's coming. Got to stay up here!"

"No. No flood. We're safe on the ground. Come down."

"Come up. We'll drown below!"

BOOM!

We both scrunch down.

"TANGO! GET YOUR ASS DOWN HERE! JUST BECAUSE I DEAL WITH ASHES DOESN'T MEAN I CAN DEAL WITH A DEAD BODY! ESPECIALLY ON THE ROOF!"

The lump doesn't move. Fuck. I can't go onto the roof and drag him.

"PLEASE, TANGO!"

And the lump rises a bit and does a military elbow-crawl towards me. Thank god. Keep going. He's almost here. Keep going. And now, his face is dripping and close. *Fuck me.* Like kissable close.

"You slide down and I'll be behind you," Tango says.

It takes longer than it should, but I'm able to descend the ladder and he comes down right after me.

BOOM!

He steers me inside. He steers me! I'm the one saving him! With his hand on my waist, I can feel the side of his body against me. Both our clothes are soaked through and we're shivering.

"We need to get you warm, Tango," I say, shutting the front door.

"Where's the pup?"

I open the door. On the porch, Dragon looks up at me like he's offended that I left him behind and trots in.

Depositing Tango on the couch, I rush to the other rooms, collecting blankets. Cover him with one, wrap myself in another, light a lantern, and sit in a side-chair. We shiver in silence, trying to get warm.

BOOM!

"Why'd you get on the roof, Tango?"

"Katrina hurricane. We flooded. Lost Mawmaw and Papaw's —my grandparents—ashes in the storm. Climbed up into the attic, but the water kept rising. Had to bust a hole in the roof to escape drowning. Pulled Mama up and we spent the storm on that roof."

"How old were you?"

"Eight."

Fuck. I was making mud pies while he was saving his mother from drowning.

"You survived," I say. "And that time is over. We're not in New Orleans. It isn't going to flood here. The storm isn't trying to kill you. We're safe here. Inside, with it all happening outside, it feels kinda cozy. Don't you think?"

Tango looks at me for longer than normal. Is it the lantern light or are his eyes really golden amber?

He blinks and turns away. "I don't know how to deal with kindness. It's a new thing. I would like to—to accept it."

"Embrace it!" I say emphatically, without meaning to.

"Okay," he says. "I'll sleep inside tonight. Here on the couch."

Dragon flies onto the couch at this declaration and I'm suddenly jealous that Dragon's not going to sleep with me. Am I becoming a dog lover?

Tango looks at me and smiles slightly.

"What?" I ask a bit defensively.

"Those pajamas. Cowboys roping steers?"

"Yes," I say, wrapping the blanket tighter to cover the rodeo scenes.

"I like 'em. They suit you."

I don't know whether to admit they're Agnes's or pretend they're mine, so I avoid the issue with another question. "What did you and your mother do after Katrina?"

"Moved from place to place. Got into a shelter for a while but I got beat up and—treated bad—so I skipped out. Slept in abandoned buildings, under bridges. Survived."

"Why'd you join the military?"

He looks at me like I have no clue how the other half lives. I guess I don't.

"No other options," he says.

"Why the army?"

"That was the recruiting office nearest me. In a mall. They asked if I had an affinity to any special training and I saw the poster with sparks flying and a guy wearing a thick face shield and said, 'Welding.' They sent me to boot camp and then thirteen weeks in Virginia to learn welding. That's most of what I did overseas. Armor repair, protection structures. It was good as a way to stay apart from the others. Something I need."

"I remember you told Erica you got kicked out for throwing chairs. What made you throw chairs?"

"Bad day. Just got back from putting in a CDS—Culvert Denial System that I'd welded."

"What's that?"

"If you have tunnels or waterways under a road, the insurgents can put in IEDs—Improvised Explosive Devices—and blow everything to shit. We would install these big welded grates on each end so nothing could be hidden there."

"Thanks. Go on."

"So we'd put in the CDS and there was a tense screaming match between our unit and the locals and I was jacked up with adrenaline when I got word the chaplain wanted to see me. That's never good. He has me out in the tent chapel and tells me to sit down. I don't. He tells me my mother passed and he wants me to pray with him. We weren't praying people. Didn't have any religion. Said I'd skip the prayers. He started praying on his own. All about Mama going to a better place but maybe she was a sinner and I gotta pray or she might be doomed.

"I got mad and told him to shove it. C.O. came in at that moment and commanded me to apologize to the chaplain. I told him to shove it. He ordered me out as that chaplain kept yammering, 'God forgive her sinful ways,' and I picked up the folding chair in front of me and flung it at the chaplain. Good aim, too. He had to knock it away with his arms, and you could tell it hurt. C.O. yells, 'Don't disgrace your mama's memory,' and a chair flies at him. Chaplain darts out while he can. Chair after chair off to the C.O. and he's cornered. Screams at me, 'Your mother died a lowlife drunk. Fell in the street and never got up.' That gets all the chairs flying, and when they're all thrown, I lunge through the mess with plans to give a beating to that C.O. when the MPs take me down. Put me in the brig."

Tango takes a deep breath. "I sent cash to the funeral-home to pay for Mama's cremation. There was no funeral. No funeral band. No mourners. No family. Place was supposed to keep her ashes 'til I got home but I called when I was dropped out onto the streets of Los Angeles. Funeral home told me they had no record of her. Another forgotten person lost. That's why I want—MUST —find a home for Clayton. People can't just be lost."

He looks so despairing. I should talk about something else. Something to make him feel better. Maybe say something nice to him.

"Tango, you did really great today filming and finding the

photographs."

He nods, staring at the floor.

Think of something nicer. "I could use someone like you working at *Ashes-to-Ashes*."

My brain flips out. *What the hell did you just suggest?*

But before I can backtrack, waves of emotion pass over Tango's face. Shock and relief and pride and gratitude and he smiles so gently, "I would be honored, Prestonia."

Shit. What the fuck have I done!?

FLYING BACK TO LA

MORNING BRINGS SUNSHINE, so Tango and Prestonia string a rope between two apple trees and hang the soaked blankets to dry. Ello comes by with a soft pet-carrier bag and a concoction she says will help Dragon with the flight. After packing their wet clothes and having a little breakfast, it's time to leave. When Ello wishes them a good flight, Prestonia puts out her hand to shake and Ello slaps it hard, then pulls her into a boney hug and whispers, "Time you figured yourself out."

Ello grabs Tango and gives him a long, tight hug and whispers something to him. He nods, smiling.

During the long drive down to the airport they're mostly silent. But Prestonia is fidgeting. Finally she asks, "What did Ello whisper to you?"

"Stay off roofs. What did she say to you?"

Prestonia doesn't want to share hers because it feels like a flaw or insult. "Just good luck."

Tango looks at Prestonia, wondering why she has to lie so much.

In the plane, Tango tucks the carrier bag holding the drugged terrier under his seat. He wonders if the little dog will do okay with Captain and Daisy.

Prestonia, remembering how tense Tango seemed on the

flight out, tries to distract him. "What do you want to call your position at *Ashes-to-Ashes*?"

"I'll do whatever you need. Carry equipment, climb ladders, film in high places—"

"For the website, we need a title."

"If you're the CEO," says Tango, "I should be administrative assistant."

"You need to be head of a department, not an assistant."

"What department?"

"Logistics. You can be a Logistics technician, no, Logistics Administrator," she augments. "No, *Chief* Logistics Administrator,"

"I don't know anything about the logistics of scattering ashes."

"Neither do I. We'll take a picture of you when we get back and put it on the website."

Tango looks uncomfortable with the idea. "I don't really like pictures taken. I don't look good in them."

"You're crazy. You looked a bit ragged before with the beard and the army jacket and all that, but you look great now."

"Cleaned up, but still a motley mess."

Prestonia shakes her head vehemently. "No. Tango, you're—unique. You don't look like everyone else, and that's a wonderful thing."

Tango stares at the magazines in the seat pocket in front of him. "Thank you," he whispers.

They say nothing for the rest of the flight. Tango shifts his elbow on the armrest between them and it just barely touches Prestonia's arm. The two of them focus all their attention on that tiny half-inch of contact. Both of them hope it isn't accidental, but both suspect the other doesn't even notice. Prestonia keeps her face turned to the view below and Tango keeps his head low but occasionally pretends to look out the window, while studying the contours of Prestonia's face.

After they land, Prestonia takes her phone out of airplane mode. Calls are waiting. As Tango gets their luggage down from the overhead bins and pulls Dragon's soft carrier out from under the seat, she listens to voice mails. As they leave the plane, she relays what she heard.

"Erika says Captain and Daisy are doing fine. Bob wants to know how it went and would like to see us and get Daisy back. Goldman Sachs says they understand hardball and have increased their offer—but you know I'm not going to accept. And we have another *Ashes-to-Ashes* client."

It's late afternoon when they get back in the Eagle Rock. Captain and Daisy and Erika smother Tango and Prestonia with love until the dogs both notice the strange-smelling soft carrier.

"Easy, Captain. Dragon's a friend and he's drugged up, so be kind."

"Ach, I ken the travel takes it out of ye, so I'll be vanishin'. Gi' us a ring when ye have time for a cuppa so I can hear o' yer adventures." She kisses Tango on both cheeks and pats him on the butt, does the same to Prestonia and leaves.

Tango unzips the carrier and gently pulls the floppy dog out. Dragon opens his eyes and growls his greeting to the larger dogs. Lots of sniffing and side looks. Tango carries the little terrier out to the backyard where the newcomer finds a good spot to pee. Captain and Daisy sniff the new scent and both take a turn drowning it with their pee.

As Tango unpacks in his backyard spot, Prestonia starts editing. She cuts together the scattering and the homestead shots and remembers that Ello showed them a YouTube of Luna smashing her work so she looks for that site but instead finds several videos of Luna singing and playing banjo. She adds Luna's music and starts incorporating the photos. As she cuts in the photos, she keeps pausing to stare at the strong, calloused hand that moves the pictures in and out of frame. Tango's hand.

A tap on the back door has her quickly flipping down the screen of her laptop as if she'd been caught watching pornography.

"Hate to disturb you but, could I get a little of that cash Bob gave you? I need to scrounge up some dinner."

Prestonia leaps up from the table. "I'm so sorry, Tango. I'm unbelievably dense." She rushes to grab the envelope and hands him five hundred-dollar bills.

"That's too much."

"That was the deal we made with Bob."

After a long moment, he says, "Okay," and turns to leave, but pauses at the door. "Do you need anything from Trader Joe's?"

"No, thanks. I'm just going to—what did you call it?—*piece on things*. Is Dragon okay?"

And the little terrier must be listening because he bounds in the door and leaps onto Prestonia's lap.

She's startled by the sudden move. "He—is this okay? Should I let him do this?"

"You're lucky. Captain's too big to sit on my lap. Consider it a blessing."

Tango steps close to rub that little grey head. Prestonia looks down at the hand scratching behind Dragon's ears, wondering what would happen if she touched it. Tango stares at his hand on the dog. If he just shifted it a few inches, it could be at her cheek and those sweet freckles. He could touch them gently and she might look up. He could bend close and—

Tango bends close—

"He wants to stay with you," he whispers.

Prestonia flushes. "Wh-what?"

Tango straightens quickly and steps to the door. "Dragon wants to stay with you. They've all been fed, so I'll say goodnight."

"Goodnight. Thanks for your work. I'll leave the back unlocked if you need—or want anything."

Tango nods and steps down the stairs and Prestonia pulls the terrier close 'cause she desperately needs and wants so much.

LUNA'S VIDEO

I WAKE UP to movement beside me and my heart somersaults.

Did Tango sneak into my bed last night? I flip around and face the scruffy snout of Dragon. A mix of relief and disappointment. *So, you have a crush on this man. You've had crushes before and they pass. This will pass.*

I get out of bed, start the kettle, and open the back door for Dragon to pee. He takes off down the stairs and there are yips and happy-sounding barks from below.

Dress in jeans and a t-shirt and put a bit of makeup on but not over the freckles!

In a while, Dragon races back up, leaps onto my lap, places his front paws on my chest, and after a long stare at me, licks the tip of my nose. Is that a kiss? He really likes me! Oh, damn. We're giving Dragon to Bob. Bob'll want his daughter's dog.

After a nice slow morning, Tango taps on the door. "I wondered if you could help me get Daisy and Dragon over to Bob. Maybe show him the scattering video if you're done editing."

"Can I show it to you first?"

I open my laptop, cue it up, motion Tango to sit in front of it, and push play. The video starts, but I'm watching the back of his neck. Is this what he was doing when he was behind me in Luna's home?

When the video ends, he grunts and sniffs, and his hands reach up to wipe tears away.

"Beautiful. Bob will love it." He turns around to face me. "That was such a magical place. I'm so glad to have experienced it with you."

All I can do is nod. If he keeps talking like that, with those eyes that really *are* amber, I'll never get over this crush.

We load Daisy, Captain, and Dragon in Agnes's ragtop and drive over to Bob's. He's overjoyed to see Daisy again and is glad to meet Dragon, "But I can't take another dog on. Would you keep him?"

Tango and I both answer yes.

"Prestonia will take good care of him," Tango adds.

I'm so happy not to have to give Dragon up. "He's my first

dog," I whisper, and Tango squeezes my arm.

Bob can't stop watching the video and can't stop crying. He hugs us both and chokes out that he'll call when he can, and we leave him to his mourning.

Back home, I upload Luna's scattering video to the website and ask Tango if I can take a picture of the Chief Logistics Administrator. He wants to be under the mulberry tree in the backyard with Captain and Dragon by his side. I'm reluctant to do that, saying it would be inappropriate for an employee portrait.

Tango shakes his head. "I'm not the kind of person to have a portrait-type picture like yours."

He's referring to the financial-analyst-of-the-month picture I uploaded for my *Ashes-to-Ashes* portrait. "What's wrong with that picture?" I ask, already defensive.

"You look like a person who gives the weather report on TV."

"I do not!"

"You do. All styled hair and makeup and fake smile."

"I DO NOT look like that!"

Tango puts his hand up to calm me. "No, you don't. You look alive and vibrant and—that picture isn't you. You should have one that looks like you."

Oh. Okay. "I guess I don't really think outside-of-the-box I've been in for so long."

"Let's try this," Tango says, sitting under the mulberry tree with the dogs.

The photo comes out beautiful and warm and makes you want to know this person.

I sit where he was. "Take one of me so I can get rid of the TV-weather-reporter-one"

"No," he says. "Different personalities, different backgrounds." And he has me follow him upstairs.

"Stand there," he says, pointing to Erika's painting. Click, click.

The photo makes me look wild and eccentric and like a person who is a—what did Erica call me?—a poly-creative! YES!

Upload them both to the website. There is a sound by the

front door and Dragon barks furiously and races to it as the mailman drops junk through the slot. The little dog tears at the invading papers.

"Dragon, stop!" Tango yells.

I step to the shredding terrier. Pick up pieces of a scam Home Warranty offer. A torn envelope of a scam letter from a fake law firm stamped with: *Last Notification*. Scam water line insurance. "It's okay, Tango. Dragon can tell they're all scams."

"But *Last Notification*—it looks important."

"That's how they get you. Make it seem important and crucial that you respond. Dire consequences if you don't do this or that by the deadline. It's bullshit. You probably aren't used to it as you don't get much mail under the bridge. Rip 'em to shreds, Dragon."

Tango turns away as the dog does just that and my phone rings. It's Bob.

He asks to talk with Tango if he's available. I find Tango in the backyard and hand him the phone and return upstairs. I play around a bit with the website until Tango returns to tell me that Bob has decided to spend some time at his daughter's place in New Mexico. "The video was so vivid and wonderful, he wants to experience her place in person. He's going with Daisy and doesn't know how long he'll be gone."

I immediately call the old man back.

"Bob, Prestonia here. You need to get the electricity at your daughter's place turned on. It's not only for having lights but the well pump. So power and water. Do it before you leave. I'm sure you can do it online."

He thanks me and hangs up. Suddenly I feel like I didn't do that right. I gave a logistical suggestion but didn't acknowledge that he might be feeling a whole lot more than logistics. I don't know if I'll ever get this living thing down.

SILVERLAKE APPOINTMENT

TO MEET THE NEW *Ashes-to-Ashes* client, Tango and I drive from

Eagle Rock to Silverlake, passing trendy boutiques and expensive restaurants and the occasional family establishment that hasn't been forced out yet. On Silverlake Boulevard we pass the eclectic mix of Southern California homes, most built in the 1920s. I imagine the aspiring actors hurriedly leaving these bungalows, catching a streetcar into Hollywoodland, trying to get a part in a Chaplin or Keaton film. I pull over to show Tango the steep steps rising between houses.

"The Music Box steps. These were the ones Laurel and Hardy dragged the piano up in that movie from 1932. They looked so young and excited to be in such a crazy film. Breaking the fourth wall with their weary glances at the camera."

"You'll have to show me that film sometime," Tango says.

I wonder if he's just being polite or if he really wants to see that film. He said *you'll have to* rather than *I'd like to*. Does that mean he wants to see it *with me*? It means—I'm thinking too much.

We park up the hill on a side street. Step past hot-pink bougainvillea vining up stucco, someone singing opera from the open window, over purple litter of jacaranda trees, and wafts of jasmine. Check the address and step through the iron gate to the Spanish-style carved wooden door framed by stocky jade plants that must have been planted by those aspiring actors a hundred years ago. Who knew jade could get so large!

Ring the bell and straighten my shoulders. There's a peephole. No doubt we're under review. What do they see? A young woman and man. A couple? Do we read as a couple? I don't think so.

The locks click and the door swings open revealing a bald, boney middle-aged man in shorts and a t-shirt. Barefoot. He is so white as to almost be transparent. Blue veins are visible under his skin. He must never see the sun. A ghostly hand is out, "I'm Stanley."

The hand is cold and clammy. "Prestonia. And this is Tango."

The space beyond him is dark. He gestures us in and shuts the door behind us. The Venetian blinds are closed and in the dim light I can see the room is full of boxes and stacks of magazines, a rack full of clothes, shopping carts loaded with newspapers. The smell of cat pee permeates the place.

"Let's go through to the breakfast nook. It's got the best light."

We follow Stanley, winding the narrow alleyway through the morass of THINGS into the equally-cluttered dining room, which may or may not have a dining room table, take a fork in the maze to enter a small kitchen, and Stanley clicks on a fluorescent which lights up an octagonal breakfast nook completely full of STUFF. There's a tiny uncluttered spot on the table and one empty stool. Must be where he has his meals.

"Just a sec," Stanley says, moving a heap of clothes to reveal a chair, and picking up an antique gum-ball machine to reveal another. "Sit."

Tango and I sit and I open my satchel for the contract, feeling Tango tense beside me. He's fidgeting in a way I've never seen. I hope he doesn't freak out and start throwing chairs or something. He'd never run out of stuff to throw here. To get out of here quickly, I get down to business, explaining our fees and process, and ask about his deceased.

Stanley groans. "I would love to do this on my own. I want to respect my mother's wishes and it horrifies me to admit I'm not capable at this time. I've had her for the last twelve years. Each year I thought—this is the one, I'll go out. But it hasn't happened and I don't think it will. I haven't been out since I don't know when. I'm sixty-two. It won't get easier."

"There is no shame in having *Ashes-to-Ashes* take care of your mother. On the contrary. Her wishes will be honored and you will be privy to the whole ceremony."

"I say I'd love to do it myself but—I can't. It's not fear, it's just —I feel comfortable here."

Tango gestures around the space. "You have your things."

"Yes! I have my things."

I try to sound comforting. "Let me assure you that you'll feel a sense of closure and accomplishment."

Stanley shakes his head. "I feel so guilty. I'm a bad son."

Tango immediately counters him with, "No, no. You're doing this *for* your mother. It's not a failure."

Is Tango talking to Stanley or himself?

Stanley continues to express his shame until he feels he's been sufficiently guilty and then he signs our contract. I get the coordinates of the location for the scattering and the words he wants to be read, swipe his credit card on my phone, and he stands.

"I'll get mother."

He winds his way through the dining room and disappears. Tango immediately stands, glancing at me with the same thought —*will the guy be able to find his mother?*

There's no room to pace or move, so Tango rocks back and forth, stomping one foot and then the other.

A HUGE CAT leaps on the table and YOWLS at Tango.

The distant voice of Stanley calls from the next room. "That's Mortimer. He's a Pisces."

"Okay, good to know," I yell toward the dark interior. "Sorry to say, I'm allergic to cats."

Arriving with a two-foot tall Smokey-the-Bear figure, Stanley says, "This is Mrs. Ada Rudinski. She loved bears."

He hands me the bear. It's hard plastic, has a hat, shovel, and yellow cloth bandana around its neck.

"Your mother's inside Smokey?"

Stanley nods. "I had to saw the head off and tape it back after I put her in. Bandana hides the tape."

"Pardon me for asking, but is she loose in here?"

"Ziplock bag."

"Perfect. Thank you. We'll take good care of her."

I stand and hand the bear to Tango. Stanley starts crying. and waves us on, sputtering, "Sorry, sorry."

Tango and I move into the next room's darkness, navigate the maze, pass stacks of magazines, now each topped with hissing cats, reach the door, and escape into bright fresh air.

We hustle up the hill and dive into the jeep. Slam the gear into *Drive* and take off.

"AHHHHH! I'm really glad you're allergic to cats!" Tango yells over the roaring engine.

"I lied. I had to get outta there!"

"It was worse than prison!"

"I thought Agnes's house was cluttered. She was a minimalist compared to him!"

"Now you know what I feel like when I'm stuck inside."

Slowing down for the red light, I turn to Tango, "Really? It's that bad?"

"Not *that* bad, but I need to feel free, like I can escape, and I need to see far. Not have the view end at six feet or less."

I nod as the light changes. "I get it. Since moving to Agnes's house, I spend my time either on the balcony looking out at the long view to Griffith Park or at the kitchen table staring at that same view through the window. Expanse somehow makes you feel free inside!"

"Exactly."

DRIVE TO BISHOP

I LOOK UP the latitude and longitude coordinates for the job. It's not even in LA. It's up north in the Eastern Sierra mountains. Maybe we'll be near where Bogart did the movie *High Sierra*. It'll take most of a day to drive there, a day to get into the mountains to scatter the ashes, and another day to drive back, so we'll have to stay overnight. Am I happy or nervous? Yes.

I ask Erika if she'll watch Captain and Dragon.

"Feckin' o' course! Ye get yer ass up there tae the mountains with that bonnie lad."

I need to make a motel reservation for two nights and ask Tango what kind of bed he wants for his room.

"Won't need a bed or a room."

"I don't know that there'll be a bridge for you to sleep under."

"I'll stay in the car. Closer to being outside."

After several minutes of prodding and assurances, I reserve a single room at The Village Motel in Bishop.

Tango packs Bob's suitcase with Bob's clothes and I pack my retro suitcase with my clothes and the film equipment. We load up Tango's sleeping bag and pillow, Mrs. Rudinski in her Smokey-the-Bear urn, sparkling water and snacks, and start off. The beginning is pretty boring, but after Palmdale and Lancaster it gets more interesting. We swerve the curves through ragged Red Rock Canyon, pass black volcanic-rock plains, get hints of the beginnings of the Sierras, come to a vast straight road that goes on forever, then the little town of Lone Pine. The mountain range looms over us to the left and somewhere is Mount Whitney, the tallest mountain in the lower 48—except I can't tell which one it is in the mess of peaks.

We drive by a building with what looks like a film mural. I slow as we pass. The sign says *The Museum of Western Film History.*

"Don't you want to stop?" Tango asks.

"We can't. We've got a job to do."

"Hold on. Pull over."

I angle us to the road's shoulder.

Tango looks at me with a serious expression. "I'm Chief Logistics Administrator and I think it's important to visit this museum."

"We've got to keep going."

"Says who? And if you want a reason, you're a filmmaker and I'm sure this will help you with your art, which will help *Ashes-to-Ashes*, which means it is a business excursion."

I make a wide U-turn and park in the museum lot.

Inside, we see a short video about the history of film in the area. So many westerns were shot in the local Alabama Hills. From Fatty Arbuckle in the silent movie era to Tarantino's *Django*. Everyone was here. John Wayne, Randolph Scott, Barbara Stanwyck, and of course, Mitchum.

As we're looking at a poster of Mitchum in Zane Grey's *Nevada*, an old woman steps beside us.

"I was a girl when Robert Mitchum rode his horse into the Winnedumah Hotel up the road in Independence. When he was arrested for marijuana, my parents forbade me to watch his movies, but I always snuck in because he was so cool."

"He's very cool," I say.

"Your fella has that in him as well," she adds, nodding toward Tango. And she walks off.

Tango shakes his head at her back and leans to me laughing, "Bullshit."

"She's not wrong," I say. "You have a cool, slow, laconic way of moving and talking. And a twinkle in your eye, like life amuses you."

"So wrong. Life scares the hell out of me."

I can't believe he admitted that out loud.

I stare at the poster. "Life scares me, too. That's why I did the financial advisor thing. It was predictable and I wouldn't have to deal with unknowns."

"I get you," Tango says. "That's why I lived hidden under a bridge. It was predictable and I wouldn't have to deal with unknowns."

After the museum, we drive on to the next town—Independence. Thunderclouds drop their cargo as we crawl at the town speed limit of twenty-five, windshield wipers not making a dent in the deluge. Streaked view of the big, old-fashioned Winnedumah Hotel.

"Wish I'd known about Mitchum staying here. I would have made reservations for this place."

"Next time," Tango says.

What does he mean by that? Next time we scatter ashes up here? Or next time, like we're coming up just to stay at this hotel?

We continue on and it's dark by the time we reach Bishop.

The rain has stopped as we pull up to Las Palmas restaurant for a quick meal. We must both be tired, 'cause we hardly speak.

Drive on to The Village Motel. It has retro-neon glowing orange and green against the clear night sky. *Heated Pools,*

Kitchens. Open the car door to the smell of wet sage and something wild. I check in at the office and carry Mrs. Rudinski in her Smokey-the-Bear urn into my room with my suitcase. I step out again to give Tango the car keys. He takes them and asks, "Could I use the bathroom for a wash up before I retire to my sleeping carriage?"

"Of course."

I step aside, and he slips into the bathroom, closing the door. The shower starts. I creep closer to listen.

Don't imagine it. Don't imagine him dropping those clothes. Don't think about him stepping into the hot shower. Damn it!

I grab the room key and stomp outside.

Look at the motel's cool neon. What year do you think that was made?

—*Suds, and steam, and skin*—

Hey, do you know any of the star constellations?

—*Those hands moving over his chest, his belly, his*—

What do we have to set up for tomorrow? Is the camera battery charged? What's the to-do list? Think! Name what you're bringing. Laptop, camera, extra battery—

—*his neck, shoulders*—

The charging cord, Mrs. Rudinski's bear urn—

—*arms, wrists*—

Memorial words to read, longitude/latitude—

—*small of the back*—

The room door opens behind me. "I hope I didn't drive you out."

"No, no, just needed some fresh air."

"Watch out, you'll end up like me. Thanks for sharing your bathroom. I'll see you in the morning."

"Okay. Goodnight." I go back in my room as Tango heads for the car. Close the door and move to the bathroom. Steam fills the little space. A wet towel is folded neatly on the rack. *Don't.* But I do. It smells of soap or shampoo, not him.

I turn on the TV. Flip around and find a classic. Sterling Hayden in Kubrick's *The Killers*. I know my granddad isn't in this one, but I need to watch something. Anything to keep from thinking.

BLUE LAKE

MORNING LIGHT wakes Prestonia.

The bedside clock reads 10:30. That can't be right. She checks her phone. How did she sleep so long!? Dress quickly and step out to the car. Sleeping bag is rolled up neatly. No sign of anyone. Where is Tango?

The office door dings down the row of rooms and Tango exits, holding two coffees. He hands one to Prestonia. The cup is a paper cone fit into a brown plastic holder. What era are they in?

They sit at one of the picnic tables and gaze at the mountains. The coffee is terrible but somehow fits the ambiance.

"Sorry I slept so late," Prestonia says. "I don't know what happened."

"You must have needed it. It's not a problem for the scattering, is it?"

"Not at all, but we should get going soon. Hopefully we can find a spot for some breakfast on the way."

Prestonia changes into her black outfit and loads her backpack with the video camera, extra battery, extra capture chip, the words to say, and water. She tucks Mrs. Rudinski's bear urn inside a cloth bag and programs the latitude and longitude of the scattering site into her phone. It's somewhere in the mountains by a lake.

They drive up Line Street and soon are climbing the steep road into the mountains. The desert scrub changes to aspens and pines, and they're up at 9,000 feet and even the car seems like it can't get enough oxygen. Up and up and they're at Lake Sabrina. As they park, they watch a man and woman unload two goats from their truck, strap saddlebags on the animals, gather hats and walking sticks, and start off on an adventure.

Prestonia nods to the one building at the far side of the

parking lot. They walk over to it, now suddenly able to see the huge lake surrounded by snow-covered mountain peaks. It's stunning.

In the shop/boat-rental/cafe they get burgers, bags of potato chips, and water. Sitting on the balcony overlooking the boat landing, the wind is brisk and cold. The view makes everything taste wonderful.

Back at the car, Prestonia lifts her backpack, about to slip it on when Tango stops her. "Not so fast. I gotta be here for something. I'll be your goat." He takes the backpack over one shoulder and the cloth bag with the urn over the other and says, "Point the way."

With the GPS on, they start along a dusty trail beside the lake. There are pine trees and huge boulders and flitting birds, and they both pause—out of breath.

"Elevation again," Tango says.

Prestonia looks at her phone. "And it looks like we'll be going over ten thousand feet on this hike."

Tango leans close to see the screen. "What's the destination?"

They both feel the proximity and try not to move. Prestonia points at the map, edging a little closer to show him. "Place called Blue Lake. Six-mile round trip. I wonder how long that will take."

"In Basic Training, Quick Time was 120 steps per minute, so came to about 3.4 miles an hour. At that pace we'd make six miles in under two hours."

Prestonia stares at him like she's amazed he could know such things but really imagining if they could shift even closer.

Tango smiles at her, trying to distract from his pounding heart. "With this terrain and altitude, I don't think we'll be marching Quick Time."

They move away from each other to continue on, definitely slower than military Quick Time. A quarter of the way around the lake Prestonia pauses. "I need to get the camera."

Tango hands her the backpack and she retrieves the digital camera. Takes a slow pan of the lake. "Got to incorporate this incredible scenery. But really, I need to catch my breath. This is really hard. You want to go first?"

"No, the goat doesn't set the pace. Go at any speed you want. Stop and shoot video. We're not in a rush, are we?"

"Let's not hike, let's saunter."

"After you."

And Prestonia hands him the backpack, keeping the camera, and starts off at a saunter. Tango lets her get a few yards ahead and follows, keeping his eyes on all the different parts of her.

They continue to the end of the lake where the trail takes off beside a rushing waterfall. Now it's climbing, not sauntering. The noise is quite loud and Prestonia stops often to film and catch her breath.

Clouds gather overhead and block out the little sunlight that made it through the trees, dropping the temperature several degrees.

They climb and pause and climb and pause and look back to see Lake Sabrina getting smaller each time. A long, blue mirror lying in a valley of rocky mountains.

After reaching an apex, they turn and follow the ragged trail into a treeless section. All around them, massive boulders fell at some point. All around them, massive boulders look like they *may* fall at any point.

The GPS says they're half a mile from the destination and at an altitude of over ten thousand feet.

"I wish," Prestonia pants, "I was—the type of—person who—would—just scatter—Mrs. Rudin—ski's ashes—here."

"But you're—not," pants Tango.

"No."

One of the things I like about you, Tango thinks.

March on. Another long slog over boulders with no path visible. And they come around a bend, and a vibrant turquoise lake shimmers and gleams.

"We made it!" Prestonia yells. The words bounce across the mountains and repeat back to her. Her eyes widen.

"HELLO!" Tango calls out to the snow-covered peaks. They call back to him. "My first echo!"

Prestonia yells "HELLO!" and Tango joins in with his own "HELLO" and they continue screaming the word again and again, overlapping the echos, trying different rhythms and speeds, until the two can't speak for laughing.

After they catch their breaths, they sit on a flat boulder by the lakeside and unpack the equipment and Smokey-the-Bear urn. Tango removes the tape around Smokey's head and pulls out the ziplock bag of ashes and asks, "Should we scatter from the ziplock or—"

"Smokey," they say in unison.

Tango pours the ashes from the bag into the plastic bear and sets the head back on.

Prestonia looks around the area. There's a spot with several wildflowers, overlooking the lake with mountains in the background. She sets up her camera on a tripod low to the ground and asks Tango to stand with the Bear urn ready. "When I say action, scatter some—not all—of the ashes around those flowers."

"Got it."

"Can you call for some sun to back-light the ashes?"

"SUN NOW!" Tango yells. The words bounce across the mountains and, for some strange reason, there is a gap in the growing clouds and, as the words echo back, the rays blast down.

"Action, Tango!"

Tango gently lifts the head off of the bear and sprinkles ashes. They swirl and glitter in the sunlight.

"Yes! Cut! I'll change my angle."

She hurries to a spot behind Tango and leans over his shoulder, focusing on the bear-urn. "Action!"

He scatters more and she slowly moves the camera so it lowers with the ashes.

"Cut! Great! I'll get closer—and action!"

She lies on the ground and films the ashes falling among the wildflowers. Prestonia gradually tilts the camera up to frame the mountains lit by the sun.

"Cut! So great, Tango! I'll take some more shots around the area and we'll head back."

The sun, no longer vital to the production, sulks off behind the towering clouds.

Tango watches Prestonia work. It's clear she has a very good idea of what she might need. And it's clear she knows how different angles and views will augment the final piece.

"I wish I could film you right now, Prestonia. You look so alive. So in-your-element."

Prestonia smiles. "I feel that. Thank you."

After a few more shots, she puts the camera back in the backpack. "Let's get outta here. I'm freezing!"

And they start down as thunder rolls in the distance.

It's not easier going down. The trail is steep and rocky and, in several places, Prestonia and Tango have to slide on their butts to keep from tumbling. At the turn toward the waterfall trail, the clouds darken and ZING! Something hits Prestonia on the head. "Ow!"

And another hits Tango on the arm. "What the—?"

PING, ZING, PANG—a deluge of hail smashes around them. They dive below a pine tree, but the needles are no protection. Tango holds the backpack over Prestonia's head and slips the cloth bag over his. Marble-sized hail bounces on the rocks, ricocheting up to pummel their legs.

The crash of thunder.

"We gotta get away from this tree!" Tango yells. "Under that —" and he huddles over Prestonia as he leads her to a boulder resting over two smaller ones.

They scramble up the loose shale hillside to the tiny shelter and huddle in next to each other. The hail continues, zinging the parts of them not covered. Feet, shins, knees. Prestonia is tucked into Tango's armpit. Warm there. It feels good to them both.

Another BOOM and the hail tapers off.

"Let's go while we can," Tango says, squinching out of the shelter.

They slide down to the trail. The ground is littered with icy balls. Tango lifts several, wipes them off on his shirt and pops them in his mouth. "Good."

Prestonia does the same. "Mmmm. Very good."

They trot when they can and scoot on their butts when they need to. They both notice the clouds darken over them, but neither speaks of it.

As they reach the top of the waterfall trail, the clouds open up, and rain pours down. They might as well be under the waterfall. Freezing rain saturates them, but they keep going on the now swampy trail.

Lightning and BOOM! Very close. Very dangerous.

The sky is dark and a crackle of light tangles the air right down the path! Way too close!

"In there!" Tango yells.

They hurry to an overhanging rock in the mountain wall. Almost a cave. This allows them to be several feet back from the entrance. Water drips in rivulets from the jagged roof rock. Tango and Prestonia huddle together, shivering from the cold and adrenaline. Water trickles along the ground and down into their sanctuary, soaking their pants.

"This is bad. This is real bad," Tango whispers. "We've got to get to higher ground."

"We're at ten thousand feet. That's high enough."

"But water's coming in."

"We may get electrocuted, Tango, but we're not gonna drown."

Prestonia activates the flashlight mode on her phone and moves the beam over the ground in front of them and behind.

Tango nods repeatedly, breathing fast and shallowly. "You're right. You're right. The water goes out behind us. It's okay. It's okay."

BOOM!

Prestonia clicks off her phone. "But we can't leave until the lightning stops."

The storm continues and day turns to night. Tango and Prestonia shiver continuously.

"It's r-r-really cold. Will we fr-fr-freeze to death?" Prestonia asks. "I've seen t-t-too many movies of what happens. *Th-th-the Shining, D-d-day After Tomorrow*. If we get hyp-p-p-pothermia we'll get drowsy and f-f-fall asleep and d-die."

"Come s-s-sit between my legs and lean ag-g-gainst me. We'll k-k-keep each other warm."

She can't see his face in the darkness, and wonders if he's thinking the same thing she is. *Trying to stay warm is a good excuse to touch.* She turns and moves between his legs, her back against his chest.

He continues. "P-p-pull your knees in t-t-to keep the cold air out. Here's the b-b-back pack and cloth bag. If it's ok-k-kay, I'll put my arms around you."

"That's ok-k-kay," Prestonia says through trembling lips.

He wraps his arms around her and they form a tight circle of at least a concept of warmth. Both are in their own thoughts and hyper-aware of where their bodies are touching.

Tango moves his head over Prestonia's shoulder and lays his cheek against her neck. He feels her flinch but he doesn't move back. He takes a long, deep breath and lets out an incredibly slow exhale of the warm air down her chest. Pema's book taught him about breathing, but this isn't about meditation. Take in a long deep breath again and slow down the exhale. Over and over. With his chest rising behind her and slowly deflating, Prestonia's breathing begins to match his measured pace. It calms them both.

The storm rains down beyond their shelter. Flashes of lightning and booms of thunder. Prestonia has stopped shaking, and her head slowly tilts back against Tango's shoulder. He feels her heartbeat against his cheek. He relishes the sweet sourness of sweat and adrenaline rising from her skin. His legs are cramping, and his left arm is asleep, and there's a sharp rock jutting into his back, but this is the most wonderful he's felt in his whole life.

AFTER THE STORM

I WAKE TO A SOFT TOUCH on my cheek. Eyes open onto a strange vista. Orange pine trees in a pink sky framed by black?

The soft touch again. "Prestonia?"

I'm aware of someone curled against me. Spooning position. My head on a backpack? Turn to see Tango, barely lit by dawn.

"It's light out. We should go," he says.

"I don't want to get up. It's warm here. I've been cold for too long."

"Come on. We'll get you warm again."

He rises behind me, steps out of our shelter, and disappears from view. Sounds of peeing. I need to do that.

I get up, hurry outside, and slip behind a house-sized boulder to pee. My phone says it's 5:39 in the morning.

We gather everything in silence, check twice, and head down the trail. The path is wet and slippery with broken tree branches littering the way. Dawn isn't yet breaching the mountains and it's terribly cold, but the world is infused with a glorious pink glow. Or is that me? Tango was so kind, exhaling down my neck to warm me. That was the first time I've slept with a new man without sex. This is a new feeling—the jittery, jumpy tangle of nerves.

But he didn't try anything. I know we were both in survival mode, but you would think he might have, if he was interested. Is he waiting for *me* to make the first move? Or is he drawing this out so we'll actually *know* each other before anything happens? Whatever the case, it's exciting.

Down to Lake Sabrina. Along the shore trail. Past the docked boats, the closed shop/cafe, to the one car in the parking lot. I start it up and turn the heat on high. Tango spreads his sleeping bag across our laps and we drive down the long road to Bishop.

Tango and I enter my room at The Village Motel at 8 in the morning.

I dump my backpack on the bed with, "I'm taking a shower first, okay?"

Tango nods and I grab my suitcase and disappear into the bathroom. Water on HOT, step in and let it penetrate. I'm bruised all over my shins and thighs. Blisters on my feet. Scraped hands. Yet nothing matters but warmth right now. I can't even lift my arms to wash. Just let me stay under this hot stream.

I don't know how long I'm in the shower, but I finally get out, and slowly and painfully dress in clean clothes from my suitcase. It hurts to raise my arms or lift my legs. I should add hazard pay to this job. As I'm closing the suitcase I notice a little elastic pocket in the top of the case. Pull it open. Inside is an ancient sewing kit, a package of tissues, and a folded note.

Enjoy the Adventure!

Agnes again.

How long has this been in there? Is she stalking me? How many more notes will I find?

When I come out of the bathroom, Tango is asleep on the bed. He looks so sweet, breathing softly. He's got a wonderful nose. His hair is a mix of tight and loose curls. I gently get on the bed beside him, staring at his profile. How could I ever have been scared of him?

BISHOP MORNING

TANGO WALKS two blocks to a small western-style bakery and buys a hot coffee, hot tea, and a variety of pastries. The street is full of people. Some are in shorts, pastel shirts, fanny packs, and sandals. Those people talk loudly and point and don't make eye contact or room for him on the sidewalk. Others are in worn jeans, scuffed boots, sweat-stained shirts, and battered cowboy hats. Those, men and woman both, meet his eyes and nod to him as they pass, as if he's a regular person or even one of them. It makes him feel normal. Like there's the possibility of change.

As he walks, he replays the time on the mountain. Especially the feeling of that night. She was tucked against him and he was keeping her warm and safe, and she trusted him, leaning back to sleep with her head on his shoulder. It felt so good and right. Could he ever become a man someone could trust and count on?

He turns the motel key and quietly unlocks Prestonia's room. She's asleep, curled under the quilt like she's still trying to get warm. He wants to lie beside her but doesn't dare, so he sits at the little round table and waits. There's a microwave in the room if the coffee and tea get cold. He's happy just to watch her breathe. When he first met her, she looked pretty in a rigid, square way, but now, red hair a mess, relaxed in sleep, he finds her beautiful.

Her eyes move behind the lids and lashes. She's dreaming.

Is she dreaming of me? Tango wonders. *No. No one dreams of me, unless it's Captain.*

She makes a squeaky little moan that's the sweetest sound he's ever heard. Worried that she'll wake and find him staring at her, he goes to the bathroom, turns on the water, flushes the toilet and makes whatever noise he can.

LEAVING BISHOP

NEXT THING I KNOW, I'm waking to noises in the bathroom. Tango enters and offers me hot tea and coffee. He must have gone somewhere other than the motel office because the tea is good! And he's got pastries.

"I'll wait outside," he says. "We can have breakfast out there when you're ready."

Gee, he's considerate.

It takes me a while to get dressed because I can hardly move. All my muscles are so sore! Finally ready, I go out and we eat at the picnic table, then checkout and start back.

"Remember those little one-street towns—Big Pine,

Independence, Lone Pine and that really long stretch of straight road?" Tango asks.

"Yep."

"Well, if you want driving relief, those might be good places for me to practice. You can always say no, or change your mind if you don't feel I'm good enough."

"That sounds wonderful." I pull over to the side of the road and we hop out of the running car and circle around the hood to switch seats. He grins at me like a little kid as we pass in the middle. I love his joy.

Wait a minute, you're using the word love—

Shut up, I tell myself, and snuggle under Tango's sleeping bag in the passenger seat.

WHO'S THAT?

TANGO HELPS ME CARRY the equipment and luggage into my Eagle Rock home. As I drop my suitcase on the floor, Captain and Dragon race to greet us. It's almost like they love us both! The house smells like home. I'm so glad to be here. Erika gives us big hugs and relays how the pups were good and there were no issues. Then she stares at my bare arms. "Ye've got bruises and scrapes and I see yer standing on yer last legs. Something I should know?"

She glances at Tango and I can see she's hoping for a juicy story.

"Only adventure."

"Right. That's enough. I'll be goin'. Have a grand rest and ye can tell me aboot it later."

She leaves and Tango takes the dogs down to the backyard. I should get to editing, but I'm so exhausted from the day and the drive. Even though Tango did half of it, I had to focus to make sure he was okay—which he was. Very attentive and careful.

There's a knock on the door. I open it to four unknown adults. They don't look like they are from around here. Dressed really square, like Mormons out to convert me.

I shake my head. "I'm sorry, I'm not interested."

"Are you Prestonia Cheswick?" the middle-aged man asks. With his very neatly cropped hair and thick neck and green-mint-ice-cream polo shirt, he looks like he could be a manager at a tire store.

When I don't answer, he continues.

"You're a hard girl to contact. We've tried many times—visiting, by mail, phone, but you've not responded."

"Responded to what?" I ask.

"We understand you recently took occupancy of this house," the man continues.

"Yes. I inherited it."

They all look at each other as if they expected this absurd statement. "Well, the judge will decide. We've made every effort to apprise you of the progress, the filing of the petition with probate court, you have ignored all requests for discovery, depositions, and mediation. We came to this house earlier in hopes of talking with you but never found you home. We researched and saw your employee-of-the-month photo online and visited that financial firm hoping to talk with you, but we learned from your colleague that you no longer work there. We did all we could to do the responsible thing but you've missed the many appointments, been non-compliant in all discovery requests, and our lawyer suggests you are unreasonably intransigent. Monday is the hearing. We hope you'll find the time to attend."

"Who are you people?"

"I'm Roger Wright. This is my wife Sandi Wright. My father, Gus Wright, and his wife Doris. Doris Wright, maiden-name Sloan."

My stomach drops. Inside the house, Captain and Dragon bark through the window at the strangers.

The older woman steps forward. She's got a grey bowl-haircut, a shapeless orange dress, and cruel, bird-like eyes. "This house belonged to my sister, Agnes."

My heart is banging against my chest like it wants to escape. I have to cough to get a word past it. "I was given this house by Agnes Sloan. She wrote my name as sole beneficiary in her will."

"We'll let the court decide. This Monday. Nine AM. Los Angeles Superior Court, Room 457. Here is our lawyer's number if you wish to negotiate a settlement and avoid this mess."

She hands me a business card.

"Why are you doing this?" I ask. "You people don't look like the type that would appreciate living here."

"Oh, we wouldn't set foot in this hedonistic hovel of depravity. But even dumps like this sell for over a million in the land of fornication and sodomy. That will be enough to buy us mansions in the Kansas heartland."

The background of dogs barking gets louder and then softer.

"You're not getting my home, so fuck off to the heartland."

They jerk back like I really scared them. Wow. I wasn't even doing Mitchum or Streep—

"His eyes are crazy," Roger hisses and I turn and Tango's behind me with his fists raised and his jaw clenched and he takes several heavy steps toward them—

"The man's a lunatic!" Roger screams, scrambling the relatives backward.

Tango yells, "Get the fuck off Prestonia's lawn!"

As she hustles into the car, Doris squeaks, "We'll see you in court!"

They screech off down the street and Tango drops his threatening look. "What did those jokers want?"

"To take my home," I say, and burst into tears. I can't see, sobbing against his chest, but he manages to steer me inside and sit me at the kitchen table. He calls Erika and as she races over, he makes the tea.

When Erika arrives, I explain the situation through tears. Erika curses enough to make me feel a little better.

"Feckin' wankers. Do ye ken a lawyer type?"

"No. Maybe the guy from GitRDone.com who first told me of Agnes's will could help."

"Better call 'im. It's Thursday afternoon. Ye want to find someone afore the weekend when they'll all be oot golfin'."

I find the number and call Joseph at GitRDone. He gives me the name of an estate litigation attorney, and I call that man, Mr. Morganstern. He seems very perturbed that I didn't respond to any of what he calls "the discovery requests." I have to tell him that I don't know what discovery requests are and that all the calls and letters I got seemed like scams to me.

It's clear that he's frustrated by me. "You may end up with a default judgement since you were noncompliant."

"What does that mean?"

"You lose."

I'm stunned into silence.

The man growls a sigh of exasperation and says he'll take the case for a retainer of three thousand up front. I send the money to his account and sign in to a video conference call with him. He's got a wide face with a tight-trimmed, salt-n-pepper beard and thick trendy glasses. Probably in his forties. He has me show the papers I have, copies of what I signed at the Astro diner, and the journal with Agnes's note written directly to me.

When he sees the copy of the will, he says, "California does recognize holographic wills, but they're easier to contest."

"Holographic?"

"Hand written. The plaintiff is related to the testator?"

"What's a testator?"

"The deceased who made the will."

"What's the plaintiff?"

Another exasperated sigh. "The party that is contesting the will. Your enemy, so to speak."

"Okay, what was the question?"

"Is the plaintiff—your enemy—related to the dead person?"

"Yes, her sister."

"That's a bonus. Siblings don't automatically have judgments in their favor."

"Good."

"Unless the deceased has no spouse, children, or parents."

Shit.

"Courier me the will and all other documentary evidence. Give me the contact information for anyone from whom I can get helpful depositions. Doctors, neighbors, banking personnel, witnesses to the will. I'll see if I can meet with the plaintiffs' lawyer and do a rush discovery. Maybe we can negotiate a settlement and avoid a trial in court."

"I don't want a settlement. Agnes Sloan gave me this house and I'm going to keep it."

"Fine. Your cash, your call. Dress nicely but conservative. No cleavage. Cover any tattoos. No piercings. Definitely wear makeup, but not trampy. Heels but no spikes. Zero perfume. Unless you hear otherwise, I'll see you in court on Monday."

I gather all the papers and journal and GitRDone.com contracts and contacts and even the little notes Agnes left for me around the house. Erika sets up a courier, they arrive, and the package is whisked off to Mr. Morganstern.

For the rest of the day, and all of Friday and Saturday, Erika and Tango are with me whenever I want to curse and yell and cry, but mostly I go online and try to figure out what the case will be like. I don't learn a lot except that I was stupid to think that just because I got a will and keys, I didn't need to file papers with the county and I should have paid attention to the letter from the lawyer that WASN'T A SCAM! and the Kansas phone calls. The weekend passes very slowly and I have lots of time to decide on my court wardrobe. It isn't until now, Sunday afternoon, that I get a text from Stanley about Mrs. Rudinski's ash scattering and I realize I've not even started editing. Fuck. How can I concentrate on that!?

Only, when I start, it's a welcome respite from my courtroom worries. I import the footage and edit the angles and add sound effects and music and do a voiceover of what Stanley wanted me to say but seeing it makes me remember being with Tango and him breathing on me to keep me warm and his chest rising and lowering against my back and his face—

Get to work!

When I finally finish, I show the film to Erika and Tango and they love it and cheer, but I'm too distracted to notice. I'm petrified about tomorrow.

PREPARE FOR COURT

ALL I KNOW OF COURT IS from the movies or TV. I wake early and Dragon watches me slip into the last of the damn clothes I thought I'd never wear again. Business suit with skirt. Stockings. Conservative heels. Pastel blouse open at the top but not open all the way. Everything is a message, isn't it? I pack the will papers and Agnes' journal and suddenly remember the notes she left. At least one had my name. I collect all I found and add them to my briefcase, then stand for inspection. Dragon doesn't look impressed. I wish I could take him to court with me. Or some ally. I can't do this alone. Should I ask Tango to go with me? Should I call Erika?

Tango taps on the balcony door and gestures to his outfit of Bob's blue farmer shirt and jeans. "I don't have a suit or anything businesslike to wear. Should I stay away, or maybe sit in the back?"

I get teary and then wave so the tears don't mess up my just-the-right-amount makeup. "I'm so grateful to you for coming with me. But you'll probably have to sit in the audience part."

I'm sure they don't call it the audience part.

Erika lets herself in without knocking. Captain and Dragon swirl around her. She's wearing a bright summer dress with abstract flowers and vines decorating it. The fabric looks like Matisse painted it. Closer, I can see that she painted it.

"What e're the outcome, ye 'ave huevos confrontin' these bastards."

"Huevos is what Agnes had," Tango adds.

"Well then, I'll take my huevos and go to court with my two friends and win this case."

LOS ANGELES SUPERIOR COURT

THEY ENTER THE MASSIVE LOBBY of the Los Angeles Superior Court building. The building is old and has the patina of seriousness. The tall doors and shiny floors and guards and echoes make everyone who enters feel small. There is a discrepancy between human size and JUSTICE size. Humans are less-than.

Tango follows Prestonia and Erika feeling not the normal less-than, but an extreme less-than. He wants to leave. There's a metal detector to go through that will catch something, even though he has nothing to hide. They will catch that he is someone who doesn't belong and they will expel him.

"Come 'ere, Tango. Best we get caught t'gether," Erika says, gently tucking her arm around his waist and pulling him to the metal detectors.

They go through without any embarrassing beeps or alarms or searches.

Tango keeps his eyes on the patterned floor as he follows Erika and Prestonia. They stop at a vendor of candies and snacks and coffee. "Anything, Tango?" Erika asks.

He shakes his head. Couldn't eat if he wanted to.

"I'll have a coffee and an energy bar," Prestonia says. "Got to keep my hands and mouth occupied so my brain will stop spiraling."

She buys the items and they head to the directory. There are a lot of names and departments but nothing that seems to relate to them so they decide to go to room 457. Fourth floor.

Head for the elevator and push the old style elevator button. Several people join them as they wait. Lawyers in their impressive suits. Plaintiffs in sweatshirts and jeans. A mix of the ones who are living in pain and those who are oblivious to it. The crowd grows larger.

The ding sounds like it's from the nineteen-fifties and the door opens. The elevator already has several people in it, but the new crowd surges in. Doors close and everyone shifts to maintain an acceptable distance from the others.

The elevator shudders up slowly. Incrementally. It's too crowded for Tango and he's sweating, trying to practice Buddhist breathing but it isn't working.

I need to focus on the micro so I can exist in this macro, Tango thinks. *That might be something I learned of Buddhism, or something I made up. Either way, I've got to get a grip.*

He stares at the shoes of a man rocking back and forth beside him. The laces are ragged and hardly holding.

DING! They stop at the second floor. Doors open and more people push in.

Keep it together, man. Micro. Micro. The elevator travels up, shimmying and groaning. He turns to watch the dark brown fingers of a woman twist her wedding ring around and around. DING! Third floor. The woman squeezes out and the doors close.

As they travel higher, Tango hears a sharp hiccup sound and sees a bald man with tattoos on his face trying to hold back sobs.

This isn't a human space but it is full of humanity. And I'm just another of them, Tango thinks.

The thought gives him a moment of peace, and then the doors open on four.

MORNING TESTIMONY

WE STEP OUT OF THE ELEVATOR and down the hall to room 457. Erika pulls me to sit with her on an old wooden bench beside our courtroom. She holds my hand. Tango drops on my other side. This is the last place he wants to be. I should tell him to leave but I don't want to. Instead, I take his hand. He looks startled but gives me a little squeeze to let me know it's okay. His hand is strong and rough. Shockingly rough. Brent worked out but his hands weren't rough. People that live in the wild probably have rough hands. I like it.

Benches for the plaintiffs and witnesses line the wide hall.

Most everyone looks like they are from the wrong side of the tracks. No one from the West Side. Lots of whispers and silent crying.

The benches have shiny dark arms. Shiny and dark from the tension rubbed into them. Several doors along the hall have standing signs: *Quiet please. Court in session.*

Across from us there is a bank of three old fashioned phone enclosures. Booths I guess they called them. I remember scenes in old black and white movies of reporters. Maybe Gary Cooper in *Meet John Doe.* These booths have wooden accordion doors and half circle seats, but no pay phones anymore. Only empty spaces where those once hung. Guess they're no longer relevant. Just as I think that, a lawyer type slips into one, slides the door closed and talks on his cell phone. Guess they're somewhat relevant after all.

The elevator dings again and the four relatives of Agnes Sloan exit. They see me and sit on the bench across the wide hall. Whispering and glancing and giving us the once-over—more than once.

The sound of men laughing heartily makes us turn. One is my lawyer Mr. Morganstern. He sees me and nods, shakes the hand of the other man and steps my way. The other laugher, a young man with short brown hair and a muscular build tightly packed into a sharp suit, looks like he could be Brent's brother. He walks to the seated relatives of Agnes Sloan and shakes their hands as Morganstern puts his out for me. Hey! These two lawyers better not be friends!

Mr. Morganstern leans close to me. "There is still time for a settlement. I've seen the plaintive's discovery and—"

"I'm not settling!" I hiss.

A court person comes out and says, "The court is open for Sloan versus Cheswick." I enter the courtroom with my friends. I'm so glad they're here! These are the best people I've known in years or maybe my whole life.

That thought lasts a second before the enormity of the COURT hits me. This room is just like every court movie. *The Verdict, A Time to Kill, To Kill a Mockingbird.* I'm ushered to the front as Tango and Erika take seats in the pews or whatever they're called. Mr. Morganstern motions me to the defendant's table. This is so intimidating. Next to me is the table of Agnes Sloan's relatives and the Brent-lookalike attorney. He's got a smug smile as he nods at me. He thinks he's already won. Evil, fucker. I hate him.

The judge enters, a grey-haired man in a black robe, and we all rise at the bailiff's suggestion. He sits and we sit. He puts on reading glasses and pushes around his papers.

"When's the jury get here?" I whisper to my lawyer.

"No jury. Just the judge."

Shit. I hope he likes how I dressed. I fasten one more button on my blouse.

There is a bit of mumbo jumbo talk and things get underway. The relatives testify one after another and insist that Agnes was not in her right mind in giving her property away to a stranger. Agnes's sister Doris Sloan is invited to the stand and sworn in. She tells where she's from and her relationship to the deceased. The evil attorney asks if she was surprised to find that I'd been named in a will.

"Totally. First of all, none of us know this Prestonia Cheswick. You have to look her up on a genealogy site to see that we're even slightly related. And more surprising is that I was listed as the sole beneficiary in a previous will."

What?!

The lawyer asks to present exhibit 1. He lifts a stapled document and gives it to Doris.

My lawyer flips to a copy of that document in his binder. This will is typed and has witness signatures and notarization. Looks a lot more official than the handwritten one with my name as beneficiary.

The evil lawyer asks Doris, "When did you first know you were in Agnes Sloan's will?"

"We talked together, we were close, back maybe five years ago. She had no children, no husband, no one else she wanted to leave her home and assets to. She asked me if she could make me her beneficiary. I agreed but hoped—" she wriggles her chin tearfully and gets a catch in her throat, "—that wouldn't be for decades."

I want to kill her.

"Can you think of any reason that she would suddenly change her mind?"

Another tearful chin-wiggle. "None. We loved each other."

My lawyer cross-examines. "I understand that when your sister Agnes married another woman, Tracy, you were not supportive of the marriage."

"I was happy for her."

"Didn't you let it be known that you thought that same-sex marriage was 'an abomination'?"

"I never said anything like that to my sister."

"You're aware that if Tracy hadn't died, she would have inherited Agnes Sloan's estate immediately as the legally married spouse?"

"But she died first."

"Yes. No further questions."

Next, the opposition brings in an expert witness, a doctor who spends too much time adjusting his comb-over and with elegant elocution describes "chemo brain" as a form of psychosis.

"Do you believe that Agnes Sloan was in her right mind when she created this will to give her home to a stranger?"

"No, from my knowledge of the progression of her disease, she was a very sick woman. I do not believe she was of sound mind."

My lawyer brings in Agnes Sloan's actual doctor, a tall woman in her fifties with a ponytail and twinkling eyes. She describes her patient as quick-witted, intelligent, not "losing her marbles," sad about her terminal diagnosis but resolved to live and die as she wished. "She was of sound mind when I was with her one week before she passed."

The other lawyer asks if "a sudden—even over a few days—a

sudden cognitive decline in one who has such serious health issues was possible."

"I don't think that happened," Agnes's doctor replies.

"But it is possible?"

"Yes. It's possible."

The doctor is dismissed and it's suddenly my turn to the stand. I do the right hand up thing and swear to tell the truth. My heart is pounding. I'm not used to this kind of attention. Everyone is staring at me. At the back of the room Tango gives me a strong nod and Erika makes a fist salute in front of her chest.

My lawyer, Mr. Morganstern asks questions about my background and the call from GitRDone.com and how I got the will and the box of ashes and the keys to Agnes's house in Eagle Rock. I explain that it was a surprise but that I saw my name in her will. Mr. Morganstern asks to present Exhibit A and we all see Agnes's sweet cursive writing declaring me the sole beneficiary in her will.

Mr. Morganstern asks, "Was there anything else besides the will that made you understand that Agnes chose you to inherit her house?"

"Yes. Her journal. I found what she wrote to me."

My lawyer asks to present Exhibit B to the court. "Ms. Cheswick, can you please read the portion of the writing Agnes wrote specifically to you?"

I'm given the journal and go to the marked page. I've not looked at this since I first read it.

"Hello! If you're reading this, I'm dead," I read aloud. "I'm going to take a wild guess—ha, ha—and assume you're Prestonia. I know you're wondering why you, but all I can say is, there were no kids in my life, nor relatives I wanted anything to do with (they hated my so-called 'lifestyle,' ergo fuck them)—"

I glance at the table of relatives. They stare at me with vitriolic glares. I turn back to the careful cursive writing.

"—so I went to Ancestry.com and found you. My brother was your grandfather. So I'm your first cousin, twice removed. I think!

I didn't google you as I thought I might find out something about you that would make me second-guess this and I'm tired. All I know is you're young and probably could use an inheritance of this sort."

"Thank you. No further questions."

I start to stand but the judge tells me to remain.

The relative's lawyer steps up to me. "You say you found this purported journal in Agnes Sloan's house?"

"Yes, in a drawer of her bedside table."

"And you know that she wrote it?"

"I assumed she did, as it was in her house."

"But you don't know for sure."

"No."

The lawyer gives me that little smirk again. "Could someone else have written it?"

My lawyer objects, "Asking the witness to speculate."

"Sustained," the judge says.

The evil lawyer asks, "Could you have written it?"

"I didn't."

"That's not my question. *Could* you have written it?"

"I didn't."

"Objection, asked and answered," Mr. Morganstern interjects.

The lawyer grins. Clearly he's got more evil up his sleeve. "Are you aware of a nurse or aide or friend attending to Ms. Sloan in her final days?"

"I don't know if she had anyone."

"She may or may not have, but you're not aware in either case, correct?"

"Yes."

"May I have a look at the journal?"

I pass it to him.

He flips through the pages and hands it back to me.

"Please look at the first page and the pages that purportedly are her final thoughts to you."

I do.

"What do you notice? Would you say the handwriting is the

same?"

My lawyer stands. "Objection. The witness is not here as a handwriting expert."

"Overruled. Please answer the question."

My neck is getting a workout looking back and forth between the two lawyers and the judge. Oh, I see it's my turn. "The handwriting's different, but that's because she was ill. You can see the handwriting gets more wobbly and the letters larger. She was very sick at the end."

"Are you a doctor?"

"No."

"So you are not an expert in her medical condition?"

"No."

"Objection."

"Sustained."

"Ms. Cheswick, remembering that you have stated that you are unaware of whether or not an aide or nurse or friend might have been helping her, is it possible that the differences in the handwriting from the beginning to that last entry, could be due to another person writing it. Someone she might have been dictating it to?"

"Yes, it's possible."

"Another person could have written it, or yourself."

"Objection!"

"I didn't write that."

The lawyer glances back at evil Doris Sloan. She smiles and nods, so he continues. "I understand that the court has *exhibit C*, several—," the man tries to contain his smile. "*—post-its* that you say the deceased left for you to find after she died."

I'm handed Agnes's notes. He's making these seem like they're silly and childish and inconsequential. They're not! I lift one.

"They're not all post-its. Some are on a piece of paper. This one was pinned to clothes in the closet. It says: *Are you snooping?* and then you open it and it says: *Ha ha, just my silly sense of humor. Have at it, Prestonia! It's all yours.* See, she wrote it specifically to me."

"And as per my previous line of inquiry, could a person other than Agnes Sloan have written that? "

"Objection, leading the witness."

"A neighbor? A caretaker?"

"Objection."

"*You*, perhaps?"

"Objection!"

"I didn't!" I yell.

The lawyer smiles sympathetically. "No further questions."

I look at the judge and he nods for me to step down. I'm shaking and can hardly walk across the tile floor to my seat at the table. The judge says we're recessing for lunch and pounds his desk and we all rise as he exits.

That was horrible! I've destroyed my own case!

LUNCH BREAK

TANGO, PRESTONIA, AND ERIKA walk a few blocks from the courthouse to Little Tokyo. The talk centers around that manipulative lawyer and his pompous grilling. They slip into a Japanese restaurant and take a booth. Peaceful plucked-stringed music plays. The place seems full of tourists or lawyers.

Prestonia sits beside Erika and they both face Tango.

Prestonia asks Tango, "Have you had sushi before?"

Tango leans in so the glow of the overhead paper lantern hits his face. "Mostly not on purpose. Had raw fish as a hazard in N'Orleans, not a luxury. Mama didn't have the green or the knowledge to do otherwise. Still, in my days with the military, we had a few celebration drops of fresh fish right into the desert that were wonderful. They imported in chefs and we had it all. Wasabi was the least fresh bit."

Embarrassed by her assumption of Tango's ignorance, Prestonia blushes and focuses intently on her menu.

They order several rolls, tempura shrimp, seaweed salad, and miso soups. While they wait, Tango opens their chopstick packages and folds the paper wrappers in an origami style for them to rest the sticks on.

As they eat, Prestonia can't help but watch Tango to make sure he knows that he should add wasabi to his little dipping bowl of soy sauce, and not to dunk the tempura shrimp in that sauce. He doesn't need any coaching or correcting.

When the waitress asks if there is anything else, Erika says, "I'll be takin' the check, lass. Dinnae gee it to naught but I."

Prestonia objects. "No, you won't. You're here because of me, I'll take it."

"Shant, and say nae mer aboot it," the older woman says with a tone that stops any further discussion.

Prestonia notices that Tango has his head down for this exchange. She realizes that Erika was trying to save him embarrassment, and wonders, *Why is she always considerate and I never am?*

They rise from the booth and Tango pockets his little paper origami chopstick-rest.

SURPRISE WITNESS

WE WALK BACK TO THE COURTHOUSE and wait in the hallway outside of our room. Tango asks to borrow a pen. I don't carry those 'cause I have a phone, but Erika passes him one from her purse. He carefully opens the folded origami chopstick rest, writes several things, refolds it, and returns the pen.

The court door finally opens and we take our places.

I'm wondering who is next when my lawyer calls my neighbor Alberto Velazquez to the stand. He is in a suit and tie and looks very respectable. As he passes he glances at me and gives a twitch of a smile.

"How do you know the deceased?" Mr. Morganstern asks.

"I was her next-door neighbor."

"Did you know her well?"

"I did fix-it jobs for her for over twenty years. We invited her over for parties. We watched out for each other and the neighborhood."

"And how did you find out about her death?"

"I knew she was sick. Cancer. She had enough of the pain and wanted to end it. She asked me in one day to witness her make a will. I watched her write it and signed as a witness. Then she asked if I still had a key to her house. I did and she told me to come back on Sunday morning, let myself in, and if she was dead, to call the number on a card she'd leave on the kitchen table. She handed me five thousand dollars in cash. I declined it, but she insisted."

"Then what happened?"

"I came back on Sunday morning and let myself in and she was on the bed, dead. She looked very peaceful. There was a card for a place—GitRDone—and I called. They did the rest. Came with a doctor for the death certificate, took her body, had her cremated, handled the will and everything. She was smart. She made sure it all got done."

The other lawyer stands and asks if Alberto knew me ahead of Agnes's death, if he could have colluded with me to make this handwritten will. My lawyer objects and Alberto denies knowing or colluding with me. The lawyer suggests that maybe Alberto came in after Agnes was dead and found the five thousand and took it and decided to write a will so he could then work with the new beneficiary for more money. There is a lot of objection even as Alberto insists that didn't happen.

"One further question, Mr. Velazquez. Are you aware of the laws in the state of California as to the requirements of legally binding last will and testament documents?"

"No."

"So without this knowledge you didn't suggest to Ms. Sloan that one witness is not enough? You didn't relay that the legal requirement is for *two* witnesses otherwise the holographic will, the handwritten will, is invalid? You didn't offer to get your wife or another neighbor to be a second witness?"

"No. I didn't know."

And Alberto is allowed to step down.

I wonder if there will be any more witnesses or do they now do the summation thing. The relatives have spoken and I don't see who could be left.

The opposing lawyer announces, "We call the next witness, Brent Cooper."

My stomach revolts and bile burps into my mouth. Turn around to see Brent smiling and striding to the witness stand. What is this bastard doing here? He's on their side? The traitor!!! My lawyer leans to me, whispers a few questions and I give him a fast summary of the jerk.

"Do you vow to tell the truth, the whole truth, and nothing but the truth, so help you God?"

Brent looks directly at me. "I do."

He explains how we know each other. He says that we were a couple for two years and shared the Avalon apartment for nearly that many.

I glance to Tango in the back of the courtroom. *Why am I glancing at him? Am I worried he'll judge me for having Brent as a boyfriend?* He turns away from my look immediately. *Why is he turning away? Please don't turn away!*

Brent goes on to describe how we worked in finance together. How I was a star of the firm. "Financial-advisor-of-the-month three times! I was so proud of her!" He describes his shock at my departure, and my moving out to "live in a sketchy neighborhood with no interaction with friends or colleagues."

"And as far as you were aware, how did Prestonia Cheswick and Agnes Sloan know each other?"

"She never mentioned that woman and when I asked who she supposedly inherited the house from, she said *a stranger who she didn't know.*"

There is a murmuring in the courtroom. We all feel it. Things are tipping the wrong way again.

Brent is questioned about what he knows of what I've done

since leaving the firm. He describes being concerned about me and googling me and finding out about *Ashes-to-Ashes*. "She goes from being one of the best financial minds to throwing that away and starts a business of dumping unknown people's mortal remains. It's a bizarre, morbid, possibly illegal enterprise. It scares me to see how far she's fallen."

The opposition lawyer concludes his questioning and my lawyer steps up to the witness. "Mr. Cooper, as I understand it, you were furious when Ms. Cheswick broke up with you. Are you trying to get revenge for her hurting you?"

Brent looks surprised by the question and shakes his head earnestly. "I can only guess where you're getting this supposition. I loved Prestonia. I still do. We were together for a long time, but her self-sabotaging was becoming a problem. I suggested we take time away from each other and she moved out, sullen and—I don't know, you might say—deranged. Now I regret that I didn't see some of her behaviors as cries for help."

"That's not true!" I yell.

BANG, BANG, BANG—the gavel pounds and the judge warns me to keep silent.

ME keep silent! What about Brent?! He's fucking lying!

My lawyer turns to me shaking his head to keep me quiet, then turns back to Brent. "What was this self-sabotaging or deranged behavior you saw in Prestonia?"

"Well, no one throws away a successful career that came from hard work, securing licensees, certificates, and years of experience. She had the instincts, knew the thrill of the hunt, displayed a keen take-no-prisoners attitude, and accrued serious financial renumeration. Give that up?—that alone is bizarre. But when I suggested we take time apart, she snuck into my apartment, broke my artisan glasses, and tucked a plastic plant on her side of the bed like it was supposed to be her. Who does that?"

My lawyer turns away. "No further questions, your honor."

Brent's excused, he steps away from the stand, and pausing at my table, looks at me in a most caring and sympathetic way. "So good to see you again, Prestonia. Good luck with everything."

I want to bash him in the nose with my forehead like Erika got thrown in jail for, but I don't think that would help my case.

The two lawyers step up to the judge. They talk for a moment and then the judge says he will return after his deliberation. We all stand and then sit.

There's very little time from when the judge exits and when he returns. He asks me to rise and says, "Ms. Cheswick, this court has looked at all sides of this and it is the court's decision that not only was Ms. Agnes Sloan not in her right mind when she willed you her house, but under California probate law her holographic will is not valid without *two* disinterested witness signatures. Therefore, this court finds for the plaintiff. You have one month to vacate said home. If you have accrued any repairs or renovations, the plaintiff shall reimburse you once you provide receipts."

He pounds the gavel and that's it.

That home-stealer Doris steps to my table and leans over me. "You can keep any of Agnes's belongings and furniture. Take what you want, we'll have a junk man dump the rest. You can keep that crappy jeep as well. My sister had no taste."

I'm shaking with disbelief and rage.

Tango hurries to me and holds down my shaking fist. "Breathe," he suggests as he puts an arm around me on one side and Erika does the same on the other. They lead me out of the marble halls.

"Fuck them," Tango says.

"Abso-feckin'-lutely," adds Erika.

And all I can think is—

I'm homeless.

HOMELESS

ERIKA AND TANGO BRING ME to the house I no longer own. The dogs surround us, but give me more attention than the others, like they understand I'm hurting.

Together the two make dinner with leftovers. I watch them in a daze as they work in a kind of silence reserved for people who have nothing hopeful to say. When Erika sets out bowls she asks, "Tango, luv, what'd ye scribble on the little folded paper? If ye don't mind me askin'?"

He hands it to Erika. She unfolds it and reads, "Just because you're here, doesn't mean you did anything wrong. Or are guilty. Or less than."

Erika nods. "You write it for Prestonia, or yerself?"

Tango shrugs. "I was going to slip it in between the cracks of the benches for someone else to find, but I got so riled up listening to that ex-man talk about Prestonia that I forgot."

"That bloke was a stunning wanker. Never saw what our lass would have 'im for."

Tango nods looking at Prestonia. "He has nothing for *our lass*. She's way too good for him."

"Feckin' true, lad."

I'm sure they mean well, but I feel like shit anyhow.

After dinner, Tango does the dishes and Erika gives me a hug and kisses on each cheek and says, "Somethin's ahead, luv. Believe it." And she leaves.

I slump lower in that vintage chair by the formica kitchen table. What am I supposed to do now? I can't let all of Agnes Sloan's furniture and items get dumped. What should I take? Where do I take it?

Tango fills a glass of water from the faucet and passes it to me as he slides into the other vintage chair.

"Should I get rid of everything, Tango?"

"No. You should sleep. You still have a home. You have a roof and furniture and a bed. Rest now. Everything else can wait."

"How'd you get so wise?"

"Practice. No. I'm kidding. It's that Buddhism book by the woman with the smiling face, Pema. That book made me see things different. Like, everything is impermanent."

I stare at the little dog toothpick holder. I'm never gonna let that go.

"But, I don't want to lose everything, Tango."

Reaching across the table, that man's rough palm lays gently over mine. He nods and shakes his head at the same time. "I understand. I loved my home."

I look at him and see he's not kidding. The spot under the bridge.

"I loved the curve of the creek. The ducks. The whir of people going to work high up on the bridge overhead. I loved the seasons declaring their existence. Blossoming, fruiting, bearing, … it was all my home. The concerts on the wind from the Rose Bowl. The concerts of the crickets. The coyotes making themselves known—living in the middle of this major city! The soft dirt I made behind the pylons. The comfort of that structure. It was home and I loved it and, now like you, I'm homeless."

My phone rings. Whoever it is, I can't deal with it. Unless it's Brent. I'll fuckin' answer that call.

I check the caller ID. It's Bob. I hand the phone to Tango. "Bob."

Tango nods and steps out the balcony door. I scratch Dragon behind the ears. He's happy to be with me. I guess I'm a dog person now. Tango reenters and hands me my phone.

"Bob wants me to join him in New Mexico. He's trying to fix up Luna's place and says he's too old and frail to do the work alone. I'd like to help him."

"That's fine."

"Yeah, but I committed to working for *Ashes-to-Ashes*. I'm Chief Logistics Administrator."

"Not gonna need that position anymore. Go help Bob."

Tango shakes his head. "I don't like the idea of backing out on my commitment. Especially now when you're—"

"I'm okay!" I yell too aggressively. "I've got ideas for my new future."

"Tell me," he says, almost as if he doesn't believe me.

"You go help Bob, and if you're comfortable driving, take

Agnes's ragtop jeep. I know she'd like you to have it."

Tango blinks back tears. "She drove that jeep that early morning on the Colorado Bridge. She pulled over and because of what she did—stopped me."

"Stopped you?"

"I was gonna jump."

"What!"

"There was no future at that time. No purpose. No reason for anything."

He relays the whole incident to me. The jeep, her calling him *sir*, him marching away, her speeding backwards and confronting him, the envelope, her gratefulness.

I lift Dragon off my lap and rush into the bedroom, grab a photo album and show Tango the great picture of Agnes by her ragtop jeep, arm on it, wild grin.

"You should have this picture, Tango."

"If I keep the jeep, you keep the picture. Put it in your wallet to remember her huevos. I thought she had huevos when I saw her on the bridge. She gave me something besides the money that morning. She treated me with respect. That meant everything to me."

He's saying that about respect because I've not always shown him that. Sorry. I'm not as holy as Agnes. I pull the ragtop jeep key off of my keyring and Dragon hops back onto my lap and looks in my eyes. I rub his ears. "Yeah, Dragon, and finding a place that allows *you* will make my rental search harder. Nothing will be affordable without a good job."

"*Ashes-to-Ashes* is a good job."

"If you're living without a mortgage in a house you thought you inherited, yes it is. Not otherwise. I only know one job that makes the kind of money I'd need and I don't see any way to avoid going back to that."

"There will be a way. You're writing your future—"

"No, Tango. I tried that and it didn't work! There is reality. Reality about needing money and facing the truth. *Ashes-to-Ashes* was as frivolous as those semesters of film, architecture, acting, and art. You can't make money from any of that shit!"

"Money isn't the most important—"

"I'm not interested in sleeping in the arroyo or in Agnes's ragtop jeep! I'm not like you! I like walls and a roof and doors and refrigerators and showers and electricity and hot drinks! I'm going to call Goldman Sachs. They wanted me. I'll beg them to let me join. It's my only choice."

Tango plays with the little dog toothpick holder on the table. "Maybe—maybe, I could get a job. I could get a regular job and we could split the rent. Then you could still do *Ashes-to-Ashes*."

Oh my god. Is he suggesting this because he wants to help, or doesn't want me to do finance, or wants to be with me? Him get a job? This man lives for being outside. This man hates being told what to do or having a schedule. This man would change his life so I don't have work for Goldman Sachs?

"Tango, I appreciate the offer, but I can't let you do something that would stifle and smother your soul."

"Prestonia, that's exactly how I feel. I can't let *you* do something that would stifle and smother your soul."

I stare at Tango, my anger rising. "Wait. Who are you to talk about my soul? You don't know me."

"Didn't you just talk about my soul?"

"Oh please."

Tango stands and paces the kitchen. I look at his neck, worried that Medusa veins might be rising, but see none. He stops and takes a deep breath. "I can shave, wash, change clothes, learn Buddhism but there ain't nothing I can do that can scrub away those heavy-duty labels you stuck on me. I will always be the ragged man in the Trader Joe's parking lot. '*Sorry, I don't have any change,*' you said, before I even spoke a word. You assumed you knew my story, stuck a label on me, and because you can't release that label, I'm gonna keep the one I have of you."

"What's my fuckin' label? Let me guess. Rich bitch. Entitled, clueless jerk. Unkind, privileged, upperclass, snob asshole."

Tango stomps to the table and I jerk back. He slowly reaches down and takes the ragtop jeep key. "You and I are different."

"That's for sure."

He looks at me like it's for the last time and a not good last time. "What is it you people say? *All the best.* Because—why not? Why shouldn't you people have all the best? Leave the crumbs to the rest of us."

"Ah! The true colors. Class warfare? Fuck you. Get out of my home!"

"Willingly."

And Tango puts two fingers up to salute Dragon and steps out to the balcony and closes the door with a slight click and not the slam I was expecting, which means he's a more refined person than I am. *Fuck him.*

ALONE

MORNING BRINGS TANGO and Captain gone in Agnes's jeep. The loss of them stuns me. I'm on my own now.

Dragon seems to feel the loss of them as well. He tries to get me to pet him but it's annoying. I can't take his neediness now. *I'm* the one who needs comforting.

The house feels so empty. And it will be more empty when I'm forced out. I look around the place. The walls aren't mine, the door, the floors, the backyard with the fruit trees, the balcony, this fucking formica table and its stupid fucking tchotchke figures! Nothing is mine. I used to have things. Why did Agnes Sloan give me this house if it wasn't legal? Did she know it was going to be taken away from me? Did she do it only to get me to scatter her ashes with Tracy? No, that's not true, but FUCK! I'm so fucking angry! I had a wonderful, predictable life before Agnes Sloan and since her interference, I've had nothing but chaos and mayhem!

My arm swipes across the kitchen table—"FUCK YOU, AGNES!"—and the rooster and hen salt-and-pepper shakers and the little dog toothpick-holder go flying. Flying and crashing to the ground.

Dragon ducks behind the table and crouches with his ears flat and tail low.

"Fuck! I'm sorry, Dragon, but you don't know what I've been through. I've been fucked over!"

Pick up the rooster's head, the toothpick-dog's legs, the hen's tail. *I could glue these together to make a new creature.*

Stop it! This is old people junk! And you are DONE making shit! Toss it all!

I sweep up the pieces and dump them in the trash.

I turn on the kettle. Why am I using a kettle? I'm not a fucking tea drinker. I drink coffee! I need a fucking coffee maker!

I gotta get a Keurig coffee maker NOW!

Okay. You need to chill out. So you lost the house. So Tango left. So what. They weren't for you anyway. Agnes's house and the ashes scattering shit and nutty people—they're a BLIP. A BLIP in your life. This blip has only been a few weeks. And it's over. You still have everything you need. This is a moment for re-calibration, analytics, and optimizing. You know how to do this. You're a fucking professional. Put your fucking game-face on and get to work!

I straighten my shoulders, take a deep breath, and dial.

Ms. Bloom at Goldman Sachs, takes my call. I explain that I had a family crisis and wasn't sure if I'd be able to commit to the job so I thought it best to decline.

"Did the family crisis get resolved?"

"Yes. Very resolved."

Ms. Bloom wastes no time with pleasantries. She suggests that we need to agree on new terms. I'm offered less but it's a decent salary. My heart starts pounding. *I'll be able to get my life back!* Because I'm not sure how shaky the ground is, I don't make a counter offer.

Hoping she can't hear my heart, I say, "That sounds good, Ms. Bloom."

There's silence on the line.

Oh, no. Is she backing out? Please, please, please. I need this. I've never needed anything more in my life!

She asks if I can start tomorrow.

I have to cover my mouth to keep from crying. *Take a breath and speak!* "Of course. I'd be happy to."

"Then I'll see you at nine."

I thank her and hang up.

Sobs of relief burst out. *I'm getting my life back! Tomorrow I'll be the Prestonia I've always known!*

I open my laptop on the formica table and look up rental apartments on the West Side. I'll set up some viewings for the weekend so I can move quickly. No sense hanging around here.

A few rentals within my budget don't allow dogs, but some of those are really great looking. I set up several appointments for Saturday. It's exciting to see the pictures of white walls, clean matching furniture, and balcony views over the city. This is going to be great.

But time to kick into gear. Today I need to buy a new set of clothes.

You gotta look good to get good service in the high-end stores so I dress in my best business attire and put on makeup, including covering the freckles, Dragon watches with concern. Last time I dressed this way was for court and I came home crying. Is he making that connection? When I start the blow-dryer's roar he squeals and races away. I yell after him, "Get used to it!"

Erika calls but I don't pick up. I can't have her questioning my actions now. Can't lose my resolve.

I grab my purse and step out. As I lock the front door, Alberto trots over.

"Miss, I'm so sorry. I feel so bad, I didn't know about the two signatures. Mi esposa, I could have asked her to sign—Lo siento mucho, mucho."

"It's okay, Alberto, but I'm really late for—a meeting. Gotta go." And I hurry into my Audi and race off, tears fucking up my makeup. I've cried more since getting Agnes's house than in all the previous years. It's fucking sick!

This is why I have GOT to get back to my real life. I can't have these interactions. People expect me to be a certain way—that THEY want me to be—and I'm NOT INTERESTED! The interaction—or NON-interaction—at the Avalon Apartments was bliss. No one talked to anyone there. We knew not to. Fucking how it's supposed to be!

Drive across town to Beverly Hills and the exclusive fashion shops and spend a lot of money on clothes. That figure in the dressing room mirror is so familiar. This is how I'm supposed to look. Confident. Competent. In-control. These outfits are exactly right for the world I'm returning to.

On the way back, I pass a vintage shop with clothes hanging outside in the wind. Something about the multiple colors and patterns flapping and twirling makes me pull over. I park and as I'm about to enter the shop the breeze sweeps a cool, silky shirt across my face. It's a button-down with small yellow polka dots scattered haphazardly across the light blue cloth. It's funny. Almost a clown shirt. Not sure when or where I'd wear something like this, but I buy it. Maybe it's something I lounge in as I lie in bed on a Sunday morning, reading the New York Times Review of Books.

When I get home, Dragon seems desperate. I guess he was alone all day. He'll have to get used to this. It's the way life is going to be from now on.

WORKING AT GOLDMAN SACHS

WAKE TO AN ALARM. Dress in painful clothes. Spend half an hour hair styling and doing makeup. Speed and stop and speed and stop across town with everyone else. We are all on the move and part of what makes this city.

Park in the underground lot, then it's the slick elevator, the tasteful lobby, the wait of ten minutes, and the intern to collect me. Ms. Bloom is more aloof than our first meeting and I act contrite and we review the new terms and shake hands and I'm shown to my little cubicle and given a folder of my clients and I'm left alone and a man comes by to greet me. Chet has got the requisite impeccable haircut and gym-build and perfect clothes and I can see we'll be an item in two weeks and sex will be good and he'll invite me to move in one month later and it'll be a condo on the West Side and we'll have cappuccinos from the machine in the kitchen and croissants and bagels on Sunday morning reading the New York Times Review of Books in white Egyptian cotton sheets and Dragon will have to be given away but it's all perfect and the money will keep coming, and coming, and coming.

I shake Chet's hand with a half-smile.

"Charmed I'm sure," he says, as if he invented the phrase. He leans close and whispers, "See you anon." With the closeness comes his scent. He smells of what I imagine is a combination of shampoo, deodorant, aftershave, moisturizer, and cologne. Like he took a GQ magazine and rubbed every sample fragrance over himself.

He's a no-brainer. Meaning just that, but also that it's a no-brainer that I'll end up with him. He'll flirt aggressively and I'll accept. It's Prestonia-101.

Intern Number Two suggests that I go down to accounting to fill out paperwork. I follow her and do the usual forms. W-9, home address—I won't know Chet's until later so I put down my nearly obsolete house in Eagle Rock—declaration of citizenship, pull out my license to have it copied. As the machine does its thing, my wallet sits open. The photo of Agnes stares at me with her wild grin, and arm on the ragtop jeep.

I close my wallet.

The day progresses as they do. Air conditioning too cold. Smells of carpet cleaner. Distant phone rings. Important chatter. Sore feet. Numbers on the screen. I do my job and it's easy. The clients are the usual and what they want is the usual. I satisfy them with my savvy expertise. In a blur of time, it's evening and people are leaving. I know I should be last so I can prove myself dedicated.

Chet steps to my desk. "Figured you need a treat for your first day. Sushi? It's close."

I don't have the strength to decline. He drives me in his new-smelling black sports-car to a high-end restaurant on Sawtell Boulevard.

Inside, he leans close and whispers, "They serve whale, but don't tell anyone. I tried. Too chewy." His GQ sample fragrances have diminished over the day and there's a musky humanness to him now.

We have an exquisite looking meal that I can't seem to taste and he doesn't use the little ceramic rest but lays his gooey chopsticks on the table instead. If only I'd kept that one Tango made for me from the paper. Chet tells me about himself and his plans and accomplishments. He brags about his scores on the CFA. Not even close to mine. He tells me about his condo on the West Side, then asks his first question of the evening. "Where do you live?"

"Got a few weeks left in a spot, but I'm gonna be looking soon."

Why did I say that? Because it's the script. Because this is the designated future.

Chet talks about his condo and his state-of-the-art appliances and silver-infused bed linens and then brings up a book he read about in the Sunday New York Times Review of Books.

"You read the book?" I ask.

"Not likely. You can get all you need from the reviews. Am I right?"

I pull the sides of my mouth up with effort. "I'm sorry, it's been a long day. Lots of newness."

"Gotcha," Chet says. "Stick with me and newness will be old hat in no time."

He pays because he won't let me contribute and drives me back to the Century City underground parking lot. Leans close for a kiss. I dodge the attempt. Hand behind my neck presses the issue. I pull away with effort and a smile as if it's all normal and slide out the door.

"Playing hard to get," he says. "I like that. Thrill of the chase."
I slam his door and the sports car races off.

It's late and the roads are pretty clear. My drive back brings me on an unexpected detour. I park on a side street and walk onto the Colorado bridge. It has beautiful antique lights all along the curved expanse. As I get to the center of the bridge I look down over the side. Darkness below. The faint trickling of water. Does anyone live down there now? Is this the view Tango had just before Agnes showed up? What would happen if I climbed this ledge and let myself drop? Where's Agnes Sloan to save me?

A car pulls up beside me. The passenger window descends and a man leans across to peer out. "Hey, babe, wanna get laid?"

I hurry along the walkway to my car, scramble in, lock the doors, and burst into tears.

Five minutes later, I'm at my soon-not-to-be-my-home. As I open the door, an envelope falls. I recognize the handwriting. Erika. I'll read it but I have a dog to greet first. I've never been so happy to see a dog as seeing Dragon tonight. He's overjoyed that I'm back. Maybe I can find an apartment that will allow dogs. But then again, I'm sure I won't have a yard and if I'm away all day, it's not a good life for him.

After letting him out to pee and giving him dinner and lots of attention, when he's calm on my lap, I open Erika's letter and can hear her accent in the writing.

Prestonia luv, tell me what's going on. I'm concerned for ye and want to know all. 'Twas a blow about the feckin' court case and yer sure te be in termoil. Let a friend help. All can be resolved. Your mate, Erika

This almost breaks my heart but I've got to be strong. I have decided on the future and she doesn't fit in it.

Dragon yelps.

I look down at him, rubbing those fuzzy ears. "I know it's hard, but sometimes we have to do hard things. It's for the best. You know you're not an apartment dog."

He puts a paw up, daring me to keep him, daring me to shake on it. I can't.

TANGO ON THE ROAD

CAPTAIN GROANS in the passenger seat. Tango has been driving since he left Eagle Rock yesterday at 5 am. He doesn't have GPS or a phone and no map. Just taking whatever roads seem to be heading in the direction of New Mexico. He'd have been there by now if he'd taken the interstate 40.

"I know, buddy. We're making progress. We'll get there somehow."

Captain sighs deeply and puts his nose between his paws.

The drive was hard at first, but because he practiced with Prestonia on the way back from Bishop, he isn't very nervous. He's only sad. Sad that Prestonia is out of his life. Sad that she could never see him as other than—other.

NEXT DAY, THE SAME.

BACK IN THE GLEAMING OFFICE that everyone wants to be part of. Back with the privileged people. Back with the ones in the know who can't help but show everyone they're the BEST.

I work with numbers. Numbers that mean nothing. Numbers that mean millions of dollars. Numbers that would make a big difference to the many people on the bottom and make no difference to the few on the top. But why do those who have so much, want more? I'm helping them. What does *more* do? Does *more* make them happy?

Does making *more* for those who aren't happy having *more*, make *me* happy?

If *no one's* happy, why is this a thing?

Erika keeps calling me but I can't bear to answer. She'll be hurt and angry and nothing I could say would make it alright. So I let the calls go to voice mail. And never listen to her messages.

I buy stocks and bonds for my clients and make a dozen of them several hundreds of thousands richer before lunch. Numbers are easy but they aren't sexy. They don't look at you tenderly or have beautiful callused hands or think about your feelings.

After lunch, which no one dares to take, Ms. Bloom checks on me and I relay the good news about my clients. I know what the fuck I'm doing and this is not rocket-science. It's not anywhere near as hard as something like SCATTERING ASHES! I don't tell her that. I look calm and confident and she nods with a mild affirmation and lets me get on with my day. She's coming 'round to believing in me again.

When Ms. Bloom's out of sight, Chet slides in beside me, arm around my neck in that possessive, somewhat-threatening gesture. "How's my girl?"

A head butt to the nose is what Erika suggests. Tango suggests a kick in the balls. Dragon is dangling—teeth clamped on the man's ear.

"Sorry, I'm kinda getting my sea legs here. Can't talk now."

"Later then. Dinner. I made reservations. You'll love it."

"I—I can't."

"Can't is a word we've outlawed at Goldman Sachs. You can and you will!"

Was Brent this much of an ass? I seem to remember the Alpha male domination. I've got to find a way to disengage.

"I have a boyfriend, Chet."

And suddenly I'm picturing Tango.

Chet hums a stupid melody that seems like a gameshow theme or something and then makes a BZZZ sound. "WRONG ANSWER! Try again."

"Can I get back to work?"

Chet salutes, hand to his chest then an upraised arm, says, "Anon!" and leaves.

'es a feckin' wanker.

What the hell! I don't need Erika in my head right now!

Go to the bathroom. Marble stalls. Marble floor. Marble sink counter. I feel like throwing up but it's too clean in here to imagine doing that.

Back to my temporary cubicle spot. I know this is just for a few days. My probation period. Next week I'll have the window office. I'll look out at the Nakatomi Plaza building from the *Die Hard* movie. I'll imagine the fun those crew members and actors had working on that film.

Maybe I could bring that pinecone in—
STOP! Those day's are over!

I'm called into a meeting. A batch of twenty and thirty-year-olds deciding what the middle aged and old investors should do. We have all the answers. Risk. Leverage. Profits for us. I feel sick again. Did I eat something bad? I try to breathe the sickness down and stare out the window. We're on the twenty-second floor and there is nothing but a view of buildings. No nature. No life.

BANG!

A bird hits the window right where I'm staring and there's an infinitesimal moment that it looks at me, then its outstretched wings crumple and the body descends. I imagine the drop. Twenty, nineteen, eighteen. Maybe it's tossed toward the street by an updraft and heads down to the Avenue of the Stars. An unnoticed impact on asphalt. It'll be run over by hundreds of cars in the next minute until no one could ever know it was a bird.

"Excuse me," I say.

Run and bust open the door and just make it. The bathroom doesn't want to be used for this. The high-end decor and fixtures object to my vomit. I let everything go. Everything.

Get out of the stall and spit and—the person in the mirror is a stranger. Styled hair, perfect makeup, designer clothes. I smile at her but she doesn't seem real. I give her my middle finger which makes her laugh and that face looks real. We peer at each other. What does she want from me? What do I want from her?

"You know," she says looking like some sort of sage.

"Fuck you," I say.

"Or you," she says.

I wave my hand under the towel dispenser and the machine spools out a section. Wave that under the faucet to get the water started. Rub that wet towel across my cheeks. There they are. The ferntickles.

Head out of the toilet and to my office and get my purse and step to the elevator and Chet is hurrying to me and I straighten my arm with my palm in front of his face and shake my head and I must look serious because he backs away and the sliding doors open with a ding and I push a button and drop to the underground parking and trot in heels to the car and start it up and put it in *Drive* and—put it back into *Park* and turn off the motor.

I step out of my car and walk to the green glowing exit sign. Push open that door and take the stairs one flight to blast into daylight. Sidewalk and tastefully landscaped medians where NO ONE ever walks. I look up to the building I've just come from. A glass monolith honoring a corporation. Walk the sidewalk, and I see it—one broken wing pointing skyward, tilting back and forth in the breeze as if waving to me. I lift the bird. It's still warm but has no life. Carry it down to my car, tuck it into a nest made of my designer jacket, and leave Century City for good.

At home, I carry the dead bird down to the backyard. Dragon is excited to see what I've brought.

I dig a hole by the stone cairn that Erika and I scattered fake ashes around and place the bird inside. Add some petals from the many flowers in the yard. Cover with soil. Dragon sniffs the grave and starts digging.

"No, Dragon." I move rocks from the cairn to cover the new grave. When it's safe from his digging I pull him into my arms. "I'm sorry if you were worried about me leaving you. I am not going to do that. Okay?"

Dragon blinks at me, not ready to believe.

"How 'bout we do something new and exciting and, though it

might be scary, we'll do it together."

Ears up and head cocked, Dragon wonders what that could be.

"You want to go for a drive?"

Dragon barks in the affirmative.

"It's two o'clock in the afternoon. Let's get packing."

PACKING

THIS HOUSE HOLDS much of Agnes's lifetime and Prestonia's two months. What to bring? Furniture and clothes and artworks and cowboy boots and glassware and doilies and photo albums and books and ceramic figures all call to her, but Prestonia can't bring everything. She does spend an hour opening cabinets, tilting back framed pictures, flipping through books to see if Agnes left her any more notes.

Behind the mirror in the medicine cabinet is *Here's looking at you, kid!* Under the bed is *No monsters allowed!* Tucked in the folded sheets is *Get Your Sh*t together!* In the Scrabble box is *Don't play the game if you don't like it!* In a sunglass case is *Open Vistas Ahead!*

With tears streaming over her freckles, Prestonia collects all the notes she can find. Time to load the car.

She lays the retro suitcase of her clothes and her film equipment in the passenger-foot-area and puts a blanket and sweater over it for Dragon's nest. She unscrews the legs from the formica kitchen table and manages to fit the top and legs in the trunk along with the two matching chairs. She slides Erika's painting, which barely fits, angled across the backseat. Fills in the space around it with Agnes's photos and hats, the electric kettle, and tea set. She paws through the garbage to retrieve the broken pieces of the rooster and hen salt-and-pepper shakers, and little toothpick-holder dog. She slips all she can find into a zip-lock and vows to repair them. Gotta bring the burro lamp and shade. She lifts it and a piece of paper flaps from the bottom. Agnes's writing again. *Bought on my trip escaping Kansas. A reminder to Giddy-Up!*

Prestonia laughs. "Thanks, Agnes. I needed that!"

She packs the lamp carefully behind the driver's headrest. Is that everything? No. Prestonia hurries downstairs for the mud figure of the pretend dead girl and the Wyoming pinecone.

"What do you think, Dragon?" She rubs the little dog's ears. "We're going into the great unknown. Wish us luck."

TANGO'S ARRIVAL

TANGO RECOGNIZES the ceramic mailbox and pulls into the driveway. The gate is open and he moves along to the log blocking the road, remembering Prestonia being out of breath as they climbed over it. He drives around it into the Piñon pines, back through the orchard and up alongside the spiral labyrinth he made with Prestonia. He can almost see her measuring the path as he set the stones. Can almost see the hair sticking to her neck. The freckles glowing—

Stop that thinking, man. She ain't here.

Before the jeep comes to a stop, Captain leaps out of the window and bounds toward Daisy who is charging from the barn. They collide in a leap of fur and yipping and tails swirling. Tango smiles to see Bob walking toward him. The old man seems less stooped and moves with a spring in his step. Tango hops from the car and gives his friend a big, but gentle, hug.

"I'm so glad to see you, Tango. And it's clear Daisy is glad to see Captain."

"Glad to see you, Bob," Tango adds. "Now, if you don't mind, I've got to let water out and then get water back in."

"I'll get you travelers cold drinks." And Bob steps inside as Tango goes around to the back of the adobe house. He pauses at the window for the room Prestonia stayed in.

She's not here, man. Keep moving.

When he returns, Bob is waiting with a tall glass of water. They sit at the porch table. The table where Tango had that fish dinner with Prestonia. This was her chair. Did she drink from this glass? Tango places his lips to the rim, hoping to find that spot—

Get a grip! She's gone!

Tango shakes his head to clear the thoughts and smiles at Bob. Something about the old man seems healthier, or happier. "You look good, my friend. New Mexico suits you."

Bob waves in the environment. "And being near Luna suits me. And that neighbor Ello woman has some powerful magic. She comes over every morning and stares at me and touches my skin and asks questions and listens and brings over herbal teas she makes to cure my ills. That tea is working."

"Doesn't hurt to have daily company either, I expect."

Bob laughs in agreement. "What about your daily company? I didn't imagine you'd be able to make it out here with all that Prestonia is doing. She could spare you?"

Tango looks off to the dogs playing. "Seems like she's not going to be doing that ashes gig anymore. She's giving up on a new future, going back to her old one. She lost the house she'd been given and that changed everything."

"Lost the house?"

Tango relays the story of the court case that took away Agnes Sloan's house. "Prestonia feels the *Ashes-to-Ashes* business can't make enough money to afford to rent in LA. She's going back to finance."

Bob shakes his head sadly. "Sticking with what she knows. What's comfortable. Some people just aren't good at risks."

"Hey now, Bob. You can't know what she's going through. Don't forget, I wasn't good at risks either."

A tiny smile wiggles under Bob's whiskers. "You really like her, don't you?"

Tango stands abruptly, gesturing in frustration but no words come out.

Bob puts his hands up to calm his friend. "I was just noticing you defending her. Didn't mean anything by it."

Leaning over Bob, Tango screams, "That ship has sailed! That idea came and went! It's over, OKAY!?" And he stomps off toward the back sixty acres.

"Sorry!" Bob calls after him. Tango raises an arm but doesn't turn around.

Tango marches in a straight line toward the dusk-lit mountains in the distance. Damn it! Why'd he have to yell. Why'd he have to be so touchy about her. She's living her chosen life in L.A. and they will never meet again. Ever. The fantasy fairy-tale he almost believed is over.

"IT WAS NEVER GOING TO BE!" he shouts to the desert and drops to his knees with a sob. He can change and he can learn Buddhism and practice being better and he can shave and clean up and help people but he will NEVER BE GOOD ENOUGH.

He knows deep down that all the changes he makes won't change the inner part that's worthless. If he'd only been quicker climbing up the arroyo hillside, he would have jumped off the bridge and never have met Agnes Sloan and none of this would have happened.

A familiar sound grows behind him. Galloping paws. The beat gets louder and Captain rushes at Tango, knocking him to the dusty ground, licking the sobbing man's face.

LEAVING EAGLE ROCK

PRESTONIA LOOKS AROUND the house one last time. "Thank you, Agnes. You changed my life."

She touches the wall and slowly closes the door and locks it and drops the keys through the mail slot.

"Ready, Dragon?"

Dragon pees on the Bird of Paradise plant and hops into the passenger seat. Prestonia looks at Alberto's house. It would be too hard to say goodbye. Prestonia covers her mouth to hold back the tears.

Alberto steps out of his front door. "Adios, chica. Lo siento."

"Take anything—everything in the house, Alberto. They're

going to haul it all away as junk."

"Si, gracias. Where are you headed?"

Prestonia shrugs, "Somewhere."

"Vaya con Dios."

Prestonia waves, gets in her car, and drives away. Who knows what will happen to that place. Maybe someone great will buy it and keep the oasis of fruit trees.

It's nearing seven pm. She doesn't quite know which way to go. Then, she does. She drives across Los Feliz to Griffith Park and swerves the roads until she gets to the carousel. It's empty of people. She parks and tells Dragon she'll be right back. Hops out and hurries to the spot where she scattered Agnes's ashes.

"Hi, Agnes. Sorry to tell you the house isn't mine anymore. But it did change my life. Completely. I'm really grateful. I hope you don't mind, Agnes, I'm gonna try to get a small amount of you. Take you on my next adventure. Probably get some of Tracy as well, which I'm sure you'll be okay with."

She scrapes at the earth and makes a little pile. Now what. Pulls off her shoe and sock and opens the sock to the pile and—

"Don't move!" orders a voice behind her. "Put your hands behind your head!"

"Officer, I'm not—"

"Hey, chill. I'm just kiddin' witchya." laughs the voice.

Prestonia turns to see the familiar face. "Shit! You scared me."

"Remember me? Claudio. What ever happened with the film I was in?"

"I'm sorry, Claudio. There was no film. I lied because I was actually scattering ashes of a person, not barbecue ashes."

"And now you're collecting the person?"

"Two people really. I'm leaving town and want to take a little of her—them—with me. The person I scattered changed my life."

"I know the feeling. You changed my life with your film—fake film. I got back into acting classes and booked a commercial that got me into SAG, and that landed me an agent. Security gig is now my day job."

"That's fantastic! I'm so happy for you!"

"Thanks. Wait—" Claudio trots a few yards away to a stand by the entrance of a trail, then hurries back with a dog poop bag.

"Perfect! This is much better than my sock." Prestonia takes the bag and scoops the dirt and hopefully some ashes into it. She puts her sock and shoe back on and stands. "Claudio, I hope to see you on the big and small screen!"

They shake hands and Prestonia carries the bag of Agnes-and-Tracy dirt to the car and, with a wave, drives off.

An hour later she's already in new territory. "I've never been here, Dragon. It's all new," Prestonia says with excitement.

Dragon looks at her, less than impressed.

They drive east and then north and hit Barstow and join the 40. It'll be smooth driving for a long while now. Boring but smooth. At ten pm, Prestonia pulls into a rest stop and takes Dragon out for a walk. He pees and drinks. "What do you think? A little longer?"

They drive on. Dragon sleeps on Prestonia's lap. She punches the dial for any station but all she finds are evangelical sermons. There are few cars on the road but many trucks. Do they mainly drive at night? She hits Needles and leaves California for Arizona. "Another state, Dragon. Want to try for all fifty?"

Dragon groans and stretches on her lap.

They pull over for gas and as it fills, she looks at her phone for where she could go on Interstate 40. "We can go to the Grand Canyon if we head north from Flagstaff. We could scatter Agnes in the canyon. We can go to Amarillo, Texas. Visit Oklahoma and see the places in *The Grapes of Wrath*. Next is Memphis, Tennessee to visit Elvis. In Nashville—we could see the locations for Robert Altman's movie of the same name! The Forty Interstate goes across the entire country to Wilmington, North Carolina. We could see the Atlantic Ocean!" She leans down to the scruffy dog on her lap. "You want to put your paws in the Atlantic, Dragon?"

Dragon seems to like the idea and Prestonia is thrilled. The world is open to her. Who would have thought she could ponder such an adventure?! The Atlantic Ocean! Could this be Prestonia? Could she be a new Prestonia?

Another hour and they pass Kingman and keep going. The highway is more desolate and there are absolutely no lights in the landscape. Maybe she should have found a motel in Kingman. Dragon whines and she tells him she'll pull over to the next place. Searching on her phone, Prestonia finds that she's in a wasteland except for a truck stop twenty miles farther. No lodging.

They drive those twenty miles and finally swerve in to the Truck Stop. Dragon's happy to pee and as he does, Prestonia collects a few dog-poop-bags from the dispenser, but warns herself not to get mixed up and toss the one with Agnes and Tracy's ashes.

There are several trucks parked along the lot edges, motors gurgling, parking lights glowing. Locking Dragon in the car, she hurries into the all-night convenience store, pops into the women's room for her own rest stop and a wash. The store has canned dog food and she gets one and a large water and package of cheese and a box of crackers and a stick of salami.

In the car, Prestonia gives Dragon his dinner and sets out the rest of the food on the dashboard. "I'll just piece-on-things tonight," she says, getting choked up with the words.

After her meal, she rolls up a sweater as a pillow to see what it's like to sleep in the car. After all, she's homeless and that's what homeless people do. She whispers to Dragon, "If Tango can do it, we can do it." Only her seat back can't recline because of all the items she packed behind it.

Dragon curls in her lap and gives her wrist a lick.

How could she have lived for so long without a dog?

AT LUNA'S PLACE

TANGO WAKES BELOW the apple trees. He should apologize to Bob for yelling and disappearing. He slides out of his sleeping bag and moves to pee on a tree. No pink lady joggers to catch him, no cops, but he misses the gurgling creek and the swish of the traffic on the bridge above. Could he go back?

Captain barks in the distance and Tango scans the wide expanse to find his dog running and leaping with Daisy. They clearly don't want to go back, but—could he?

The thought gives his heart a jolt. Could he go back and make it work? He misses that face—

It's still raw, man. Don't think. Forget her. It's past.

"Hot coffee and pancakes, Tango. Come 'n get it!"

Tango smiles at Bob's call to breakfast. If he can stay in the present, he can manage. He walks toward the house whispering, "Thoughts and feelings aren't real."

The porch table is set and a stack of pancakes towers on each plate. The same plates he ate from with her.

Stop it!

"Sleep okay?" Bob asks, pouring them both coffee.

Tango sits. "About yesterday—"

"Take a bite. See how you like them," Bob orders.

Tango obeys, forking a large multi-layered slice into his mouth.

"Now that you can't talk," Bob says, "I'm going to. Yesterday was my fault. I shouldn't have said a thing. I'm sorry."

Tango has trouble swallowing from his emotions. He finally washes the pancake down with hot coffee. "I'm sorry, too. I got wrapped up in make-believe. Let's just forget it."

"Done. Today we get to work. I want to fix up the whole place and make the buildings, outbuildings, barn, everything—ship-shape. Ready to sweat?"

Tango stabs another chunk of pancake. "After I fuel up."

They get to work, Tango out at the barn, replacing fallen, broken, and missing wood boards. He's working there while Bob's repairs the adobe on the shady side of the house. It's hot and dusty and as the hours pass, Bob keeps walking to the barn to bring Tango cool drinks. It's after four when he arrives with another round.

"Break time."

Tango sends a board through the table saw oblivious of Bob over the noise. Sawdust flies over him. When he clicks off the machine, Bob yells again, "Break time!"

Tango removes his safety goggles and pulls off his shirt, wiping the sawdust from his face with it. "We just took a break, Bob. You take one. I'll keep at it."

"No sir, mister." He hands an iced tea to Tango. "Desert work is dangerous cause your sweat evaporates so fast you don't notice how much you're losing, then you pass out."

"Yeah, I remember that from the desert overseas."

They sit together on an old straw bale, drinking in silence.

The barn has a lot of old rusty materials. Broken bikes, antique car parts, gears and pulleys. In the center is a very large battered wooden table. Surrounding it are shelves of items. Cubby holes full of junk. Tools arranged across home-made benches. Welding tanks strapped to a dolly by the table.

Bob stands and wanders through the workshop. "I'm so glad I came here. I see things I would never have known about Luna. It looks like junk, but see the shelves and cubbies? This has wires. Here are chains. This has hooks. Here are old bones, here ancient bottles. I did the same at JPL. I thought she wasn't anything like me, but she was. Organized, methodical, and creative as hell."

There's a bark at the entrance of the barn. Tango and Bob turn to see Dragon looking at them.

Tango stares at the dog.

"Dragon?"

Could this mean—

By the house, Prestonia is just exiting her car, pulling at the shirt stuck to her back. Far across the spiral labyrinth, past the pottery shed and the greenhouse, a distant figure is tearing toward her from the barn. He's shirtless and passes the greenhouse and the pottery shed and he's getting closer and she smiles, watching him leap across the spiraling paths of the labyrinth, and she replays his words from down in the arroyo those many weeks ago, *Brace yourself,* and she does, grinning as he reaches her, arms surrounding, lifting and spinning and she's held tightly with Tango's skin wonderfully everywhere.

It's a long moment of this reunion and they're both flustered by the intensity of it and separate awkwardly.

"You're here," Tango whispers, touching her arm as if to check that she's real. "Prestonia's here."

"I didn't know where else to go."

"Because this is where you are supposed to be!"

Bob slowly makes his way from the barn, while from somewhere in the landscape Captain and Daisy reunite with Dragon and happy barks bounce across the desert.

When he's near enough, Prestonia puts her hand out to Bob and he pulls her into a hug. "So glad you're here. We've missed you. This calls for a celebration. Work is suspended indefinitely."

They head into the house and Tango excuses himself to shower.

Prestonia exclaims, "You got the water going!"

Bob clicks a switch. "And electricity. It must have been difficult when you were here without either."

"More scary than difficult. We couldn't see if there were spiders or snakes. But it looks great now."

Bob pours two iced teas as the three dogs barrel into the room, panting and glassy-eyed with joy. They huddle around the water bowl drinking and drinking. Bob gestures for Prestonia to follow him to the living room. He sits on a mid-century chair. Prestonia squints at it, then her eyes move to the floor. A black and white spotted cowhide rug. As if on cue, Daisy trots in and drops onto the rug. Spots on spots.

"I recognize these from your home."

"Moved them here, 'cause I sold it."

"NO!" Prestonia screams. "I'm sorry—but it was so perfect!"

"Still is. I wanted to remember as it was, with the people I love in it. Not living there alone without them."

Prestonia nods. "I understand, but I loved that house."

Bob points her to sit in the Eames lounge chair. "I did too, but I'm loving Luna's house now."

Embarrassed, she looks around, "You've done a lot."

"Lot left to do. I want it completely fixed up."

Captain enters and drops on the cool cement floor. Dragon trots in behind him and hops onto Prestonia's lap, giving her a lick on the chin.

"Um, Bob, I know I barged in uninvited—"

"For as long as you want. Tango told me that you lost your home. He's very glad you're here."

Prestonia blushes and buries her face in Dragon's fur, trying to hide her smile.

ANOTHER CALL

MY PHONE RINGS as Tango steps out of the bathroom wearing only a towel. I'm torn between ogling his chest and needing to not do that. I smile awkwardly and hurry from the living room. Outside, I check the number. It's not Goldman Sachs, so I answer.

"Prestonia Cheswick here."

"I have a box of ashes. Can you help me?"

"Of course, I'm happy to."

A short conversation later I step back into the house. Sadly, Tango is dressed now. He and Bob and the three dogs seem to be waiting for my return.

"Our next *Ashes-to-Ashes* client, but with a twist."

I tell them that the woman bought a house and in the basement behind the jars of canned goods she found a disintegrating wooden box of ashes. She doesn't know whose they are and checked with the previous owners and she can't come up with any leads. I told her that I said we could take care of the ashes.

"That's like Clayton," says Tango. "We can't find any information as to who he was or where he might need to be. It's like these people are lost and forgotten."

"There are probably hundreds of people like that. No one knows or cares," I say.

Tango winces. "I don't know what happened to my mom. I

paid for her to be cremated but never could find out where she ended up. And, my Mawmaw and Papaw's ashes were washed off the mantle during Katrina. I should have gone after them. They're lost somewhere. Sunk in the Gulf or washed up on someone's yard. Did someone take them in? I'll never know."

We sit for a while. Bob looks up at the metal fish-shaped urn of his wife. Tango wrings his hands in what looks like self-flagellation over not saving those urns. I never knew a dead person of my own, so I don't know how this feels.

Bob says, "Maybe *Ashes-to-Ashes* doesn't only scatter ashes for those that request it, but honors ashes of those who are forgotten."

"How do we do that?" I ask.

"We have sixty acres here. There's space."

And the three of us sit up straighter, thinking of the possibilities. Then, I start imagining the disaster. "This is Luna's place, Bob. Her land. Did she have a will and was this place signed over to someone we don't know about?"

Bob taps his head to me, like I'm smart. "You're right to be on-guard after what happened to you. But way back when Luna wanted to buy this place she didn't have two cents to her name. I put up the money and signed the purchase papers, so, legally, it's mine. What's mine is yours, but to make it legal, you need to form an LLC—limited liability corporation for *Ashes-to-Ashes*. I'll do a quit-claim on the property and sign it over to the corporation. You have a business license in LA?"

"Um, no. I didn't think—"

"I've got JPL friends who can steer us in the right direction. We'll set the business up in New Mexico and sign the land over to that entity."

Tango and I look at each other. He starts, "Bob, that's very generous, but you may want to do something else with this place."

I join him. "Sell it. Travel. See the world—"

Bob holds up his hands to stop us. "My mind is made up. I don't want to ever sell this place and have it turned into a development or golf-course. I never want to leave Luna's home. I want to scatter my wife's ashes here. I want my ashes scattered here. I want it to remain wild and artistic and of use. I have more than enough from selling my home in Sierra Madre. Let me preserve this place."

Tango glances at me then turns to Bob. "I thought you wanted my help fixing this place up to sell it. So you're staying?"

"I'm staying, and hopefully you'll give me a good send-off whenever that time comes, 'cause I expect you two to stay on."

My eyes flick to Tango. What does he feel about Bob saying "you two" to stay on? Can he read my thoughts? What are my thoughts? Tango turns away to rub Captain at his feet. Is he turning away from me?

Bob clears his throat as if he's noticed the whole embarrassing thing. "So, it's good we're talking about expanding the *Ashes-to-Ashes* mission before creating the LLC. Prestonia, as CEO, you're okay with including the caring for lost ashes?"

"Absolutely and, gentlemen, I have an idea but need your permission."

They agree without even asking what it is.

I dial the phone and before she can say a word I say, "We're needing someone to handle a new aspect of *Ashes-to-Ashes*. You'll have to move to New Mexico. Are you in?"

There is a pause and then, "Feckin' right, I'm in. But no until ye 'pologize fer bein' t'world's biggest feckin' wanker."

"I'm so very sorry, Erika. It's really unexcu—"

"Right, luv, where d'I go?"

TIME FOR BED

AFTER DINNER and more talk of the future and Bob calling Erika to assure her she's welcome, the dogs and people are scattered around the living room. Daisy yawns which gets Captain yawning and Dragon picks up the cue and does a loud vocal yawn.

"It's late for this old man," Bob says. "I'm hitting the hay.

Prestonia, pick your room. There are sheets and blankets in each closet."

Bob blows kisses and exits. Daisy gives her canine pals a glance of *goodnight* and follows her man.

There's a long silence, finally broken when Dragon groans, hops onto Prestonia's lap, and paws at her. "He's tired. Long drive and too much adventure."

"You must be tired as well. You need help setting up the bed—I mean your bed—or anything."

"No, thanks."

They both stand.

"Which room are you taking?" Tango asks.

Prestonia wonders if his question means something. "The little one at the far end. The one with all the windows."

"That's my choice, too."

"Oh, sorry, you have that one—?"

"No, what I meant was, if I was going to choose, I'd chose that one. But I'm not choosing. I mean, I'm still outside under an apple tree. If it rains I'll go to the barn. I like the size and openness of it."

"Okay. I guess, goodnight then."

Tango wants so much to go back to that moment he held her. Prestonia wants so much to go back to that moment when he held her. Neither one knows how to get back to that, so they both nod and walk away, Prestonia into the hall and Tango out to the kitchen and beyond, where the door closes with a little click.

TERRIBLE BED THOUGHTS

I TURN ON THE OVERHEAD LIGHT in the last bedroom. It's a bare bulb and I'm so glad that I brought the burro lamp from Agnes's, but I'm not going out in the dark to get it now. I undo the bed and check for spiders or whatever the way that Ello did that first night we were here. The place is really quite clean. Much cleaner than before. No cobwebs or mouse droppings at all.

Dragon agrees with me that we can sleep as we are, so I turn off the light and we both climb in the bed. The wrought iron bedframe creaks and moans. The mattress sinks and I roll to an indentation in the middle. This may be more comfortable than sleeping in the car, but not much. Of course, Tango's probably on hard ground.

Tango.

I replay the way he ran toward me from the barn. He was so strong and lifted me and pressed me against his chest. And then let go. Why did he have to let go? Would we have kissed? I wish I could go back and relive that moment. It felt like I was in a movie, like *A Room With A View* when Julian Sands marches through the tall golden grasses to grab Helena Bonham Carter and kiss her—

I'm ridiculous. I want the fantasy. Opposites only fall in love in the movies. In *It Happened One Night* Clark Gable is a down-on-his-luck reporter and Claudette Colbert is a rich man's daughter. *Notting Hill* has Julia Roberts as a movie star and Hugh Grant as a book shop owner. Even Granddad Cheswick's film by Preston Sturges, *Sullivan's Travels*, has Joel McCrea as a famous movie director pretending to be a bum and Veronica Lake as a unsuccessful actress. Opposites fall in love in the movies, not real life. I know why they do that, because opposites create conflict and movies are all about conflict. Will they or won't they? No one wants to see a movie where they have perfect love and they're completely right for each other and have everything in common. But real life is different. I don't want conflict in real life. Tango and I sure had it that night when he left. I don't know that that can be repaired. I need to get a grip. He said it, 'You and I are different.' It's true. Tango and I could never work out.

But, as I lie in this terrible bed, just one more time I might as well think about that moment when he ran across the fields to grab me and lift me and spin me against his shirtless chest—

FIRST MORNING

PRESTONIA WAKES to un-filtered sun light. When you pick a room with windows on three sides and no curtains, you wake up early. If that beautiful pink Tamarisk tree was closer it might provide some shade for the windows, but it's several yards away. Prestonia pulls the pillow over her head and groans.

A dog whines in response. Dragon is at the bedroom door scratching to be let out. Prestonia lifts her pillow and watches. There's a disconnect with his movements and the scratching sound. Like the film is out-of-sync. Scratching sound but Dragon isn't scratching. Must be a scratcher on the other side. She squirms from the divot in the middle of the mattress, swirls herself out of bed, and opens the door. Captain greets Dragon and the two trot off. Still wearing the same clothes she traveled in, Prestonia wanders through the house to the kitchen. There's a French press half-full of coffee and she pours herself some in one of Luna's ceramic mugs.

Open the door. No one is around but from somewhere is the sound of distant, rhythmic clanging. Prestonia steps out with her coffee and slowly walks toward the sound, far off in the barn.

At the open sliding barn door she stops and watches Tango hammering on a piece of metal. His forearms are glistening with sweat, the muscles visible with each hammer swing. She wonders—if he looks up, will he march across the dirt floor to grab her again. She taps on the door frame. He looks up.

This is too painful, he thinks. *I can't manage it. She's there looking so beautiful and alive and it's scalding me.*

He smiles, says, "Good morning," and goes back to hammering.

Prestonia repeats his greeting and walks to the center of the room where Luna's workshop of welding, building, sawing, assembling is spread. "What are you working on?"

"Triangle," Tango answers and he holds up a triangle of bent metal.

"It doesn't meet," Prestonia says, pointing to the gap in the form.

"Not supposed to."

Prestonia nods and points at the dolly holding two large gas cylinders. "Those for welding?"

"Yep."

"You did that in the army."

"Yep."

"Seems like that could be fun. Making things with flames and sparks."

"I thought it was fun, but the army didn't think it should be fun. I got good at it but kept adding embellishments to the projects they gave me. They wanted everything fast and utilitarian and definitely not fun. Another mark against me."

Tango gets back to his banging and Prestonia assumes there will not be a repeat of the *A Room With A View* moment, so wanders out of the barn. When she returns to the house, Bob is making another pot of coffee.

"How'd you sleep, Prestonia?"

She winces. "Not so good. The mattress must be from the turn of the previous century. Great sinking middle."

"Good to know. I'll go to Santa Fe with Tango and pick up a new one for you and one for Erika. I'm sure the ones in the extra bedrooms are also bad."

"Bob, I love the light in that back bedroom, except at dawn. There are curtain rods up, so do you think I could poke around in Luna's things to see if she has any material I could use as curtains."

Bob gestures to the entire house. "Luna's casa is your casa."

Having such a response, Prestonia asks if he would mind if she hung the painting Erika did for her in a visible place. "I want her to know I love it."

"Can I see it before I decide?" he asks.

Prestonia hurries outside and, moving the burro lamp and boxed tea set and miscellaneous clothes stuffed around it, unwedges the painting from the back seat of her car and carries it into the house.

"Wow! That is seriously good art," Bob says. "I had no idea your friend would be so accomplished. I'll have to commission her to do a painting for me. Let's find a place in the living room."

They carry it in and Bob takes a small painting off a big wall and they lift the large painting onto that hook.

Both of them stand and gaze at it. Prestonia remembers how she thought that she'd never be able to talk to a someone so old let alone an old scientist. He's very easy to be around.

Meanwhile, across two states, Erika packs the last of her paintings into her van. She holds up her phone to take a selfie. Click!

In Luna's living room, Prestonia's phone dings. She lifts it saying, "It's the painting's painter," and shows Bob the picture—Erika smiling to the camera and holding her middle finger up to the Avalon Apartments behind her.

After Tango returns from the barn, he and Bob make plans to go to Santa Fe. They make a list of grocery items, miscellaneous hardware for repairs, etc., and ask Prestonia what she likes to eat.

"I, I think—it's kind of hard to have us eating each meal together. Are you expecting—"

"Oh, no. We'll probably just do that every once in a while. I think we're all, or at least *I'm,* used to a fair amount of solitude," Bob says.

"A lot of solitude," adds Tango.

Prestonia sighs with relief. "I'm glad. I've gotten used to living alone and want to have at least a good portion of the day to myself."

Agreed, they make their lists and Bob asks Prestonia to keep Daisy in her room with the other dogs until he and Tango are gone. "Since being separated when I had my operation, she doesn't want to leave my side."

Prestonia ushers the dogs into her room and they all watch as Bob and Tango drive to Ello's to borrow her pickup truck and then head to Santa Fe.

Once they're gone, Prestonia lets the dogs out and begins to unpack her car.

She transfers the dirt-ash mix of Agnes from the dog poop bag into a clean jar. "Better, Agnes?"

The burro lamp is placed beside the bed on an ancient side table. The closet is filled with her items and items from Agnes's life.

She looks through the drawers and closets and storage spots in the house. Finds a large tablecloth with prints of cactus. Perfect for curtains. She doesn't find any sewing materials, but remembers a paper stapler in the fix-it drawer. She grabs that and the super-glue, and makes a hem with glue and staples to hang the curtains on the rods.

Unloading the last items from her car, she carries the pieces of the formica kitchen table to her bedroom and after reassembling the legs, she opens the zip-lock with the pieces of the rooster and hen salt-and-pepper shakers and the little toothpick-holder dog, and sets the super-glue beside them.

Dragon hops onto the bed. Prestonia asks him, "What do you think? Do these figures want to be what they were, or something new?"

Dragon barks.

"Okay, we'll let them decide later."

On a short bookshelf under the window, she places the mud figure she made for the fake dead girl and the pinecone from Wyoming. Each brings back memories. Now it feels like home! Prestonia stares at them with wonder. *How strange to have objects that contain memories. I never had that in the Avalon apartment. Nothing there was personal. Am I getting a personality?*

LONG EVENING

IT'S LATE AFTERNOON when Bob and Tango return. After we unload the groceries and put them anywhere we can find space, the men carry the mattresses in. When mine is in place, I drop onto it. A smile spreads across my face as they watch. "Perfect!"

After setting up Erika's bed, Tango, Bob, and Daisy disappear to take the old mattresses to the barn, return Ello's pickup truck and borrow a chainsaw to cut the large tree blocking the road.

I do what I can to make Erika's room look welcoming, then sit around waiting for them to come back. As night falls, I don't know if I'm supposed to make everyone something to eat, or let everyone do their own thing. I decide on the later since that's what we talked about.

In the distance, the chainsaw's roaring finally stops. Bob, Tango, and Daisy come in covered with sawdust and dirt. The two men nod and excuse themselves, Bob to the shower and Tango to the hose outside. It's been a lonely day and I wait around in the living room, but no one joins me except Dragon. Finally, I step to my homey room and turn on the burro light and close my tablecloth curtains and lie in the new fresh bed with my dog beside me. But why aren't I happy?

ERIKA ARRIVES

THE NEXT MORNING dogs bark and bark and I step out to see what's going on and there's Erika's van and there she is getting out, getting mobbed by three dogs, and I run to her and grab her in a big hug and if I was stronger I might lift her and spin her like Tango did with me. Only this makes me realize that what he did didn't mean anything like a romantic *A Room With A View* moment but simply happy-to-see-you moment like I'm having with Erika.

Even with that sad thought, I'm so glad to see my friend. "I've missed you!" I say.

"And me, ye."

Tango trots up and gives Erika a big long hug that doesn't lift her off the ground but again makes me feel the one he gave me wasn't so special. *Boo-hoo.*

Erika is introduced to Bob and she immediately says, "So

sorry about yer lost loves," and Bob gives her a teary hug.

After we get her a cool drink I lead her toward her room, pausing in the living room.

"OH! Me paintin' 'tis grand there!" she says, admiring her work. She gives me another hug and I lead her down the hall to her room. She loves it and has me help her unpack belongings for her.

After a rest, I give her a tour of the place. Showing her the greenhouse, the pottery shed, the barn.

"Ye think I could use some of the pottery shed as me studio?"

"I'm sure of it."

"Will ye help me set it up?"

I'm overjoyed to have something important to do. She drives her van beside the shed and we carry out the paintings and supplies and sculptures. It's great to get to see each work as it's added to the studio. My friend really is a wonderful artist!

Oh, I should tell her that. "Erika, you really are a wonderful artist."

"Tanks, luv. That means a lot comin' from a poly-creative."

A FedEx truck drives up. Tango hurries from the barn to meet it as I exit the pottery shed. We converge as the driver unloads two packages. I pick up the smaller one and ask Tango to carry the larger one into the house for me.

"Not this one," he says.

"Please. It looks heavy."

He lifts it. "The package is for me. It's mine."

"Let me see." I move to look at the label. It's addressed to Leon Thibodeaux from Kelly Imports in Los Ang—

He pulls it from my view. "You couldn't take my word that it's mine?"

"What is it?"

"My package."

"Okay. So sorry. I just didn't expect you—that something would come for you."

Tango looks at me like I'm insulting him. "Is it so shocking that I could order something for myself? Just because I was homeless doesn't mean I'm an idiot."

"I didn't say that. I was just surprised. What'd you get?"

"That's my business, Prestonia."

"Oh, pardon me I'm sure! I'll mind MY business!" And I start back to the house.

"That'll be the day," Tango mumbles.

I spin to face him. "What did you say?"

"I said THAT'LL BE THE DAY. You *never* mind your own business."

"Well, I'm starting now. Have fun with your precious secret package."

He stomps to the barn as I stomp into the house.

Open my package. It's a cardboard box. Inside is a note that is from the woman who found this behind the canning jars in her basement. There's a clear plastic bag holding a disintegrating, rodent chewed, moldy wooden box and spills of greyish powder. A paper tag is nailed to the box but it has no clear writing anymore. I'm so flustered and angry at what happened with Tango I can't think of what to do with it. Was I condescending thinking he couldn't have gotten a package? But why was he so defensive?

Our ancient neighbor Ello walks in. She gives me a hug and says she wants to meet the new person.

"How'd you know there was a new person here?" I ask.

Ello looks at me like I'm daft, goes into the house, walks directly into the living room, and stands before Erika's painting.

I hurry to the pottery shed to fetch her.

Ello turns from the painting as we enter.

"Erika, this is Ello," I say.

"'ello, Ello."

"Hello back."

They stare at each other for a long time.

"You're a wise woman," declares Ello.

"Aye, 'n' a foolish one."

"Seen most of it."

"Done most o' it as well."
Ello squints. "I'm guessing you're fifty-two."
"Fifty-one."
"Fifty-two counting the time inside."
Erika nods.
"I'm seventy-eight," Ello says.
"And ye dinnae look a day younger."
They both laugh and Ello takes Erika's hand. "You've come a long way to learn."
"Always been doin' 'at."
"You found your teacher."
"And ye 'ave found yers."
The two crack up, laughing deep and long. I have no idea what is going on.

Ello stays for dinner and Bob makes a stir-fry chicken dish with rice. It's good and we're together, but I feel like I'm on the outside. Ello and Erika are chatting up a storm and laughing and Bob and Tango are talking of things that need building or fixing. And I can tell Tango's ignoring me. I'm watching it all but not part of any of it. Why did I come here? They never asked me. This may have been a big mistake. Maybe I can still get to the Atlantic Ocean.

I excuse myself early and lie in my bed and listen to laughter float across the courtyard from the other side of the house.

NOW WHAT?

I GET UP LATE. The mattress is soft and the curtains dark enough not to wake me at dawn. Besides, I don't want to show my face yet. I don't want to feel ignored or forgotten.

There are no sounds in the house. Maybe I can get up without having to talk to anyone. I sneak out and don't see anyone. Get myself some cereal and tea and hurry back to my room.

It's pretty in here. My room is all set up. The burro lamp. The formica table. My computer and film equipment. The pieces of those sweet objects from Agnes's place waiting to decide how to be put back together. The memory objects of my own adventures. I sit at my desk and eat my breakfast. Look at some YouTube videos. Check the weather in Los Angeles, not that it changes. Do street-view of Agnes's house. Do street-view of the Avalon. This is ridiculous. Stop it.

Close the laptop. Stare at the Tamarisk tree swaying its strands of flowers beyond the window. Birds hop from branch to branch.

What am I supposed to do now? There are no ashes to scatter, no film to shoot or edit, no mud-pie person to make. This is horrible!

I might as well see what everyone else is doing. Maybe we can waste time together.

Bob is in his room. The door's open and he's on the bed with a guitar and Daisy.

"I didn't know you played, Bob"

"Just now learning. Always wanted to play but my work got in the way. Now I've all the time in the world."

"That's cool," I say, hoping he'll invite me in.

He doesn't. Just fiddles with chords. I should say something. Get him talking about what he wants to talk about. Like being old or losing his wife and daughter.

"What is grief?" I ask.

Bob looks at me and his eyes water and he takes a deep breath. "It's like a hole that drops to infinity and you can't escape standing at that edge, looking down."

"Always?"

"Sometimes you look up and see the sun and people and it's okay and then a song comes on the radio or a leaf falls or a swish of fabric hits your ear and you're at the hole again."

"Does it get better?"

"I don't know. But I never want to forget them so I think it's gonna stay fresh for me."

I nod like I'm understanding him.

He strums the guitar like a Flamenco player and says, "Gotta get back to it. Could you close the door on the way out?"

I do as instructed.

This grief thing is unknown to me. I don't know what I'm supposed to do with it. People are here and then they're gone and everything seems so fragile. What if it is all fragile? That's terrifying!

I hurry to the living room. Kitchen. No one else is in the house. Go outside. Walk to the pottery barn. Erika's inside with a fresh new canvas on her easel. She's got music playing loudly and is totally wrapped up in her focus. I shouldn't interrupt. Back out quietly.

Check the barn. Tango's leaning over the worktable with a welding helmet and thick gloves and leather apron as sparks spatter around him from the torch and metals. Probably should apologize but maybe I shouldn't disturb him. He might burn himself.

I walk back to the house and make myself a cuppa with Agnes's tea set. Now what am I supposed to do? Everyone is working on something creative and I'm supposed to be creative, but nothing is happening.

I add a second teacup to the tray with Agnes's tea set and take a picture with my phone and, I shouldn't but, I send it to Erika. She won't get it anyway. Can't hear the phone over her music and wouldn't stop in the middle of her painting even if she could.

Sip the tea and pretend to enjoy it. How can people live out here? We're in the middle of nowhere. I can't even hop out to a store or movie theater or cafe. I can't bring my laptop into a coffee house and pretend I'm doing something important. This is so boring! I need a job! I need clients to call or money to make or someone to tell me what to do!

On cue Erika taps on my door. "'ello, luv. Time for a cuppa?"

And I get teary and with a squeaky, frustrated voice moan, "Why is everyone good at doing their own stuff but me!? I'm stuck here with nothing to do! I hate it!"

Erika puts her arm around me and lets me sob for a moment, then sits, pours herself a cuppa, and points at the pieces of the ceramic figures.

"What happen'd tae these?"

"They got broke—I broke them. I want to fix them but I don't know if I should glue them back as they were, or mix and match and turn them into something else. What do you think?"

"Sounds like a metaphor o' yer life. What'd *ye* think?"

"I don't know. Everything is too hard to figure out!" I whine.

"Right, lass. Ye are in an existential crisis. 'tis a grand thing! Let's tackle the easy bit first. What ye want is tae not feel each decision is final. If ye use a glue like rubber cement it's sticky an' dries strong, but 'tis nae permanent. Ye can glue an' pull apart and glue and change agin. So, put these lot back as t'were, o' stick them all in one grand creature. Change when 'er ye like. I've got a jar stashed in me packin boxes. When I find it, 'tis yers."

I look at the pieces. "That glue sounds perfect. That way I don't have to choose."

"There ye go! First problem solved! On tae the next. Ye've been to school and did the assignments and made the grades and learned about film-makin' and art and I cannae remember the lot of it, but ye 'ave the temperament o' the poly-creative, but no experience in self-motivation. School coddles ye. As did yer job wi' finance. 'Ad to be on time, wear serious threads, cover yer ferntickles, and they certainly didnae gee ye latitude to come an' go as ye pleased or decide tae make a mud figure instead o' a load o' cash."

"I get that, but I don't know HOW!"

"The films ye did o' scatterings ye didnae ask how te make 'em. The mud figure ye didnae ask how te build. Ye know HOW, ye just dinnea know WHAT."

"Okay, WHAT?"

Erika takes a long sip of tea. "Ye've got the cuppa steepin' doon. Well done."

I sip mine and it *is* just right. "What should I do?"

Erika tells me of how I was energized to do this work for the

Ashes-to-Ashes assignments and business. She suggests that until I find my "art legs" I should think of how to improve the different elements of the business. "What could ye make better?"

I stare at my tea cup, then the teapot. "Okay, we don't know if these unknown or neglected ashes should be scattered or left in containers. But if they come in a decaying box like that one found behind the jars of preserves, then if we don't scatter them, we should build nice urns for them."

"Nice urns out of what?"

"Ceramic, cement, wood, metal, even found objects like the plastic Smokey-the-Bear for Mrs. Rudinski. Anything that respects them."

"Good. What else?"

"If we end up with a lot of urns, they can't just be stored in a shed, they have to have a position of being honored. Like a wall of niches. Could be outside, but covered from the elements."

"Okay, and what's the wall built of?"

"Could be adobe. We could even make the adobe bricks. Could be a mix of adobe and stone and wood and cement."

"And what if a lad were wantin' to 'ave 'eir ashes incorporated intae somethin' else? I'd want tae be turned intae a birdbath."

"Oh, yes! We could make prototypes of everything we can think of for incorporating ashes. Clay figures of the departed, bird baths, planters, anything! Make these and put them on the website."

Erika smiles at me. "Shall I get a pencil tae write it all doon, or will ye remember?"

I hop from my chair and open my laptop. "Gonna get it written out now. So many ideas! This is great!" I start my notes—*urns, niche wall, prototype objects i.e. birdbath*—and don't even notice Erika leave.

DIFFERENT

THE DAY PASSES QUICKLY and Prestonia ends up with many

drawings of the niche wall and urn ideas and *objet d'ash*. Some ideas she figures she can do and some she'll need Tango or Erika to make.

Anxious to share the ideas, she hurries to the barn in hopes that Tango will be there. He is, busy arranging bits of junk. Captain lifts his head from his perch on the pile of mattresses and gives his tail a thump in greeting.

"Tango, can I talk with you about something important?"

He lowers his head to stare at the worktable. "Do we have to?"

Prestonia finds this perturbing. "I'd like to."

Tango sighs, eyes still focused on the tabletop. "I know what it's about."

"You do?"

He nods. "This—us—it couldn't work. We both know that."

His words hit her hard and hurt.

Still not daring to look at her, he continues. "We're worlds apart. You couldn't find more different people."

"Is this because I didn't know the package was yours?!"

"Prestonia, please, just go."

"Is this because—what did you say?—I never mind my own business?"

"I really don't want to get into it—"

"Into *what*? What are you trying to tell me?"

He looks at her directly. "I'm trying to tell you that we've been circling around this—you and me—pretending that there's something there, and it is not fun or fair. I'm the one who's gonna lose."

Prestonia shakes her head angrily. "I—I—I don't know what you're—"

"You don't see me as—enough."

"I never said that."

He stares hard at her. "You didn't have to. It's clear. And—guess what!? You're right! I'm *not* enough! Not for you, not for anyone!"

"I never said *anything* against you!"

"You make judgments about everyone and *worse*, you stick to them. Back when we met outside of Trader Joe's, it was written all over your face."

"You don't know what I thought! Are you a fucking mind-reader?"

Captain moves off of the mattress pile and slinks toward the door.

Tango watches his dog leave and angrily steps closer to Prestonia. "Bottom line is—you're someone and I'm no one. You grew up white, upperclass with two successful parents, privilege and everything, and I grew up mixed-race, in poverty with a single-mom on welfare. You went to college and I never finished high school. You got a job in finance and I got kicked out of the army. You flourished and I wasted years avoiding life—"

"Do you want a pity-party? Boo-hoo—"

"I don't want your pity. I DON'T WANT ANYTHING FROM YOU!"

This silences them both. Prestonia trembles, red faced.

Tango softens. "Prestonia, listen. I'm telling the truth. It's better to never start, than to have to end. The more you get to know me, the less you'll like." He looks down at the wooden, sawdust-covered floor. "I don't want my opinion of myself to become your opinion of me."

Prestonia stares at him, confused, and hurt, then slowly turns and steps out the door. Tango's head slumps and he steadies himself with one hand on the worktable and the other covering his mouth. A sound makes him turn.

Prestonia stomps back in with her hands on her hips. "I *did* judge you when I saw you at Trader Joe's, and I *did* judge you at the bridge and in that jail. Who wouldn't!? But *you* judge me! You think I'm a dilettante."

"Please, go away."

"You think I'm a fucking spoiled dilettante! See! I'm a mind reader, too!"

Tango glares at her. "You think you know more than everyone else. You've had a lot of schooling, but don't assume you know what I think or that I'm ignorant. I learned from living and I'm a lot fuckin' wiser than you in your ivory tower."

"Ivory tower!?"

"You look down on everyone from there and you've chosen to stay there because you're scared, but you don't notice how isolated it is in your safe-comfy-privileged tower."

"What safe-comfy-privileged tower?!" Prestonia holds her arms out, spinning to include the whole barn, the whole ranch. "What do you think all *this* is? It's *all* new. I'm TRYING!"

Tango turns away from her. "Try fuckin' harder."

After fuming and cursing and making serious ultimatums in her head, Prestonia enters the house and stomps into the living room murmuring, "Fuck him and his—" She stops abruptly, seeing Bob and Erika sitting there.

Bob smiles a bit awkwardly. "Everything okay?"

Red-faced, Prestonia nods vigorously.

He continues. "Erika says you have some great new ideas for *Ashes-to-Ashes*."

"I—I—do." Prestonia says, trying to act normal.

Erika squints at her. "Sure t'ings 're okay, lass?"

"Yeah. Yeah. Sure. Fine. Let me—just give me a minute." And she hurries down the hall to her bedroom.

Bob and Erika look at each other with concern.

"Trouble in paradise," Bob whispers.

"Aye. Looks tae be."

The moment Prestonia enters from the hallway with her laptop, Tango enters from the kitchen. Seeing each other, they both freeze. Dragon and Captain casually trot in past their humans. Dragon jumps onto the couch and Captain drops beside Daisy on the spotted cowhide.

"Ah, good. Now we're all here." Bob says. "*Ashes-to-Ashes* meeting will come to order. Prestonia, you have the floor. Please share your new ideas."

Prestonia sits beside Dragon and opens her computer, trying to pretend that nothing's wrong.

Tango sits on the opposite side of the room, staring out the large window to the courtyard.

Prestonia clears her throat. "I've written some ideas down. Made some drawings. We'll need to produce prototypes."

Prestonia shows her drawings and lists and everyone, but Tango, is effusive with praise. Even Dragon gives her nose a kiss.

Erika suggests they update the website with the new aspect of the business—taking care of forgotten ashes.

"We'll be like a Lost-and-Found for ashes," Prestonia says.

"Probably lots are lost and few are found. We could help," says Bob. "If we get lost ashes we can create a database of everything we know about them. Might even reunite some folks with their departed kin."

Tango grows interested. "That would be good. For Clayton. Maybe even Mawmaw and Papaw."

Erika looks around the room. "How d'ye want tae word the new service?"

Bob gets teary and says, "I want a name that honors my Luna. Can we do that?"

They all gaze at the floor or ceiling or courtyard, thinking.

"Can we do it like my name Thibodeaux?" Tango asks. "Tango, Hotel, India, etcetera—"

"Do the whole name for us, luv."

Prestonia turns away as Tango recites, "Tango-Hotel-India-Bravo-Oscar-Delta-Echo-Alpha-Uniform-Xray."

"Ye do that grand, lad, tanks."

Tango resumes his thought. "I don't mean using the military alphabet, but the letters of Luna's name all meaning different words."

"Luna as an acronym?" Bob asks.

Tango nods, "Like Lost—Unknown—Neglected—Ashes. LUNA"

Bob and Erika nod at Tango and his brilliance. Prestonia pets Dragon so roughly that he yelps and jumps off the couch to curl with the other dogs on the cowhide.

Erika adds, "Lost—Unknown—Neglected—Ash—*Sanctuary*.

LUNAS."

Bob waves finger to disagree. "Not every person's ashes are lost or unknown or neglected. Some are known and cared for. Luna among them."

Tango adds, "*Loved*—Unknown—Neglected—Ash—Sanctuary."

Bob wipes his eyes. "It's perfect."

Prestonia glares at Tango and he gives her a quick smile that reads like a wince.

"I'll redo the website," Erika says, glancing at Bob like—*What's up with the kids?*

"I'll weld a sign for the front gate," Tango says.

Erika stands and puts her hand out, palm down. "Come on, off yer arses. Ye've seen it in the sportin' events. Whose 'and be next?"

The others stand and Tango puts his hand on Erika's. Prestonia starts but pulls back. Bob gestures for her to continue with, "Ladies first." And she puts her hand on Tango's. They have a flash of anger at each other, then Bob adds his hand, saying, "To partners in LUNAS!"

"Partners in Lunas!" they all yell and Prestonia and Tango quickly yank their hands away. The two older folks glance again at each other.

Prestonia's phone dings and she listens to the message. "Person wants ashes scattered in Brooklyn, New York."

Tango quickly says, "I'm sure you can manage by yourself. I've got lots to take care of here."

Prestonia smiles stiffly. "Sure, of course. I'll take care of it. Better this way."

Tango calls Captain and steps out of the room. Erika tips her head at Bob and he excuses himself, walking stiffly out.

As Prestonia closes her laptop, Erika moves beside her. "What's up wi' ye? Ye tangle wi' Tango?"

"Why is everything everyone's business?"

"On account o' we care."

"Well, stop. I've got a lot to do to prepare for this trip to New

York."

It's clear Erika wants to say more yet she just smiles and pats Prestonia's arm. "Right. Understood, luv. But let me ask, ye been tae the city afore?"

Upon hearing a "No," Erika suggests that Prestonia schedule a full day in the city beyond the two travel days. "There's no end of things to do. I'm sure some of it would interest that young polycreative who took so many semesters in so many things."

Prestonia agrees to add a day to her trip—if only to have more time away from Tango.

TO BROOKLYN

AS I GET IN TOUCH with the person wanting the ashes scattered in Brooklyn, I fume about Tango. I can't believe he's not going with me. He won't talk or even look at me. He probably thinks I should apologize, but he should apologize to me.

I talk with Patrick. He's the assistant of the client who's in Canada directing a film and can't break away to handle this. The director's grandmother died in an assisted living home in California and she wanted her ashes scattered where she was born, in Brooklyn. She had very specific wishes and he wants me to take care of them. The assistant says he'll send the money electronically and overnight me the ashes, address, key to her place, and special instructions. He tells me to call as soon as I get to the location and he'll talk me through the rest. The second I give him the bank info, the money comes shooting in.

I ask the name of the client, but Patrick says that will remain confidential. I ask the name of the deceased in hopes of finding out the name of the director. Patrick only divulges "Miriam."

Once the assistant sends me the tracking information for my overnight package, I choose the flights to NY and send that info back. In a while Patrick sends the airline ticket. I'm feeling extremely mad about Tango's withdrawing from me. Maybe being apart will make him want to replay the *A Room With a View* moment when I return. Or maybe being apart will let me get over my inane crush.

Before I go to bed I wander out to the kitchen. No one is around and the only lights are a dim nightlight by the sink. I wonder if I'll ever be happy again.

The FedEx package comes in the morning. Inside there's a package that has ASSIGNMENT—OPEN AT LOCATION written on it and a cardboard box that indicates it's TSA airline safe with a red sticker saying Cremated Remains. I pack everything in my carry-on and step out to the barn. Tango is welding again. I tap on the door and he turns and flips up his helmet.

"Sorry to interrupt, Tango, but I'm off to do this job and I wondered if I could ask you a favor."

Tango nods. He's really being aloof.

"Could you take care of Dragon for me?"

"Sure."

"Okay," I say, waiting a moment, hoping he'll wish me *bon voyage*, but he flips down his helmet and returns to his work.

Fine. See if I care. I'm outta here.

Drive to Santa Fe then Albuquerque and board the plane to NY. I'm surprised to find my ticket is for first class. I sit at the back of that section in a very cushy chair and get to watch the people stepping down the aisle to the cheap seats. There's the lovey-dovey couple that'll be divorced after this honeymoon. Here's the stockbroker who's doing insider trading. Now the kid with his gadgets and earbuds and tattoos and piercings and he's petrified to have someone know he's clueless. The wife traveling to see if her husband is having an affair on his business trips. And dropping in the seat in front of me, this old dude with the scraggly hair, leather jacket, and sunglasses, pretending he's some wanna-be rock star.

When the doors are closed and the plane takes off, the flight goes over the Rockies like when I went to Wyoming but continues on for hours. Finally we move along the edge of the ocean for a while and then I see it. The entire New York City skyline. I can make out the Empire State Building but that's all I know. We circle and go over more water and lots of buildings crammed together but it looks very different than Los Angeles did. More vertical for sure.

As we're getting ready to land, the stewardess walks down the aisle, checking our seatbelts. She pauses at the man in front of me and I hear her whisper, "Such an honor to have you on our flight. I'm a huge fan. Can I get you to sign this to Loraine?" Fucking guy *is* a rock star.

I stare out of the window thinking of the people I made snap judgments about as they entered the plane. It's instant and unconscious and entirely unfair. Tango said I make judgments about people and he's right. I made so many about him. Homeless bum, violent killer, ignorant nobody. I made judgements about Erika that she knitted or painted kittens. And my neighbor Alberto was a gang-banger. Rooster was a murderer. Bob, an boring old scientist I couldn't relate to. I assume the worst about people and don't even make an effort to find out if I'm wrong. Tango is right. Maybe it is time that I tried harder.

WHILE SHE'S AWAY

TANGO KNOWS what's going on. He's felt this forever. He knows he's guilty and knows she's going to make him pay. He knows this from his Mother. He knows it started way before that stormy night when he didn't go after the urns of Mawmaw and Papaw, but that's when it got specific. Before that he was just a bad boy and stupid child. But when those ashes floated off he graduated to LOSER and WORTHLESS FUCKUP.

A great gaping hole of sadness envelops him. He climbed onto the roof of the barn and watched the car leave and wondered if she would turn back. Wondered if she would know he didn't mean what he said. Wondered if she would forgive him, but the car didn't turn back. It went on and on until it disappeared into distance.

A cry came from him unbidden atop that barn. A soul-broken cry and way off, acres away, the cry is heard. Ello saunters out of her doublewide trailer to her vast garden and collects several herbs. She brings them inside and then opens her sacred room. Dried plants hang from the wires running across the ceiling. Along the shelves on the walls are jars filled with dark seeds, ancient pods, crinkled mushrooms, and brittle leaves. She collects a concoction of ingredients, closes her eyes for what might be a prayer, and steps out. In the trailer's small kitchen, she puts on the kettle, crushes several fresh herbs using her well worn mortar and pestle, pulverizes several dried elements in her coffee grinder, slips the mix into a cup, adds boiling water, and covers the cup with a saucer to steep. She gets in her pickup truck and rumbles out. Up her mile-long driveway, across the three miles of road. Turning down Luna's driveway, she thinks how nice it is not to have to dodge the downed tree, and circles around the spiral labyrinth, swirls past the pottery shed and green house and skids to a stop at the barn.

"Tango, I thought I told you to stay off roofs," Ello yells. "Come down."

And he does. "You heard me?"

"Doesn't matter. We've got to go. Super important."

Tango doesn't question her. He hops into the passenger seat and they take off, back up to the road, across to her drive, down to her home.

She opens the door to the doublewide trailer. "Do not go thinking all of us live in tepees or some such."

Tango nods at the warning and joins her inside.

"We're gonna have guests so get comfy. Out back is where the chairs be. In the shade so we don't scorch. You ready to mingle?"

Tango gestures for her to lead the way. She puts a hand on his chest to stop him and offers the cup of the well-steeped tea.

"Shouldn't be too hot, so drink up. I don't give a shit if it tastes bad. It's not for your mouth but your being."

Tango drinks it all and sets the cup down on the counter like —*what's next?*

"Not *what's* next?—*Who's* next?" Ello smiles and whispers, "Everyone."

SCATTERING MIRIAM IN BROOKLYN

LA GUARDIA AIRPORT is huge and it's very cool inside. Looks like something from the movie *2001*. White and sleek and modern. I follow the taxi icons until I get out to where there is a line of them. A guy takes my address and points me to the next car in line. It's very efficient and feels safe.

I take the taxi to the address but there's no building, just a large vacant lot between two gleaming high-rises. I tell the driver to wait and immediately call Patrick.

"I think you gave me the wrong address," I say.

"You should be looking at a vacant lot between two modern skyscrapers. Call me back after you open the assignment package."

I pay the driver and step out with my luggage and gear.

A chain link fence surrounds the empty lot. The ground has some trash where people tossed coffee cups and burger wrappers but mainly it's a block long, scraggly grass-covered space. A few burnt timbers lie about the grounds.

I open my "assignment package" feeling like I'm in a *Mission Impossible* movie. There's a phone and an envelope and plastic gloves in the package with instructions to unlock the fence gate and go inside and make a call on that phone.

Patrick answers on the first ring. "You made it. Good. You're inside the lot?"

"Uh-huh."

"So you can see it's not quite a house anymore. Miriam grew up in what was this house. Her parents bought it in the 1890s. When she was in her eighties the developers started offering her money to sell. She didn't want to. They kept the pressure up and she kept refusing. One night, her place caught on fire. She made it out as soon as the alarms went off, but the house was totaled. Fire was blamed on the stove being left on, but Miriam never used the stove, preferring her toaster oven. She even had the gas line to it toggled off so she couldn't accidentally lean against a nob and turn it on, so she knew it was arson. But who believes an old woman? Now, with no home, her grandson arranged for her to live in an assisted living spot near him in California. She deeded her property over to him and told him never to sell. If you knew this director, you'd know he always makes films about the underdog fighting the powerful. Oops, sorry, forget I said that. Anyway, the phone has a map tracking app set up so I can see your movements. You should put the earbuds in so your hands are free as I will be telling you to scatter the ashes in a certain pattern. You will walk slowly so I can direct you and I may say stop, don't scatter for the next few steps, and then start again. Okay?"

"How do you want me to film it?" I ask.

"Don't film it. Please, definitely don't film it. And if anyone tries to stop you or ask questions, you'll find an envelope in the package with a permit from the Brooklyn borough supervisor."

I agree to whatever this is.

"Okay, please open the box of cremains and un-do the twist tie."

I do. These are not the normal looking cremains. The normal greyish white is cluttered with what look like little bits of multi-colored grains. Or seeds. "What is all that?" I ask.

"Nothing dangerous. Nothing toxic."

"Should I have gloves?"

"You will not be harmed in any way by touching this, but there are plastic gloves in the envelope for your comfort."

I put on the gloves.

"Okay, please walk to the far side of the lot and I'll tell you when to stop."

I walk through the grass and as I near the fence he says, "Stop. Take two steps North. No the other North. Good. We'll go slowly but try to scatter the ashes evenly. Not too much at once."

I scoop out my first handful.

"While scattering, walk four steps and curve with five steps in a tight hairpin movement back to the left, overlapping your path—good—keep going, and now start hair-pinning to the right and—perfect, cross your path again and three more steps and stop. Now turn around in place. You'll backtrack and then do a sharp curve to the left—good and stop—spin in place—backtrack and curve again to the left and now to the right curving—"

This goes on and on. I imagine I'm drawing some intricate vision. Maybe even writing something like *Miriam*. I don't know. It's way too hard to visualize from my vantage point. He has me stop and start again in another spot. It's totally weird doing this. Like I'm a robot on remote control and can't tell what my mission is.

"How much do you have left?" Patrick asks.

"Not much. Like three steps?"

"Okay. Take five steps to the East. No the other East. You'll turn and head for the lower fence. Just two steps of scattering."

I do.

"Now take another step forward and dump anything left in that one spot by your feet."

I do.

"Great! Well done! I'm going to ask you to not put this on the *Ashes-to-Ashes* web site. I'll write you a great review but we'll keep quiet about the whole thing. Please be sure to take your belongings and lock the gate behind you. Thank you so much!"

And he hangs up.

That was weirdly exhausting. I pack everything and step out and lock the gate.

EVERYONE

TANGO WATCHES the small fire swirling in the fire pit. This old woman is really strange, he thinks—*I want to respect her beliefs*

but I wonder how long I have to sit here.
"Mind your manners," Mama hisses at him.
Tango turns to her. She's wearing her favorite muumuu and has the ever-present plastic cup of wine in her hand.
"Mama?" he asks.
"Get yer ass over to help Mawmaw and Papaw. They don't got their chairs."
Tango shrinks several feet and he's eight years old. He stumbles over the rocky ground.
"Idiot," comments Mama.
Mawmaw and Papaw are sitting on the desert scrub, wet and dripping. They bob their heads together as if they are the floating urns he saw drift off.
"I'm sorry, Mawmaw and Papaw! I lost you."
Mawmaw opens her mouth and a fish drops out. She smiles and leans close. "No harm done. We did some fine travelin'. Through the Gulf, down south to the Panama Canal, that was sumpin' to see, a seventh wonder, tru dat then out to the Pacific and played with dolphins an' whales all the way to Hawaii."
"I should have dove in to save you!"
"You was a baby, Leon," Mawmaw gurgles.
Papaw exhales strands of seaweed. "You can't save no one as a chile."
Mawmaw adds, "—but you did. You save you mama."
Tango turns to his mother.
She's bubbling as if boiling. Looks about to explode.
"Mama, I'm sorry!"
And she melts like a candle or cube of sugar under hot water and shrinks, sinking into the soil as a wet stain. From that stain rises a vision in light. This glowing woman smiles and waves Tango closer. He recognizes her from pictures. The woman was his Mama before she got fat and angry. She wears an old-fashioned dress and her hair is piled high on her head.
"Leon, I were bad to you but ain't no cause f'you being bad to y'self. My wrong ain't right. You a man now. A good man, fars I'kin tell. So you make a forward path and quit the ol'times. They ain't

nothin' but grief and my no-count meanness. Take to the new times, hear?"

Tango drops to his knees before her. "I hear you, Mama. You forgive me, then?"

His mother shakes her head sadly. "You don't got nothing needing to forgive. You been the best. And you saved my life. You a hero, Leon. It's me that wants *you's* forgiveness. Can you forgive your Mama for the hurt she done you?"

Tango looks baffled. "Me forgive you?"

"I's askin'. Please. C'n you try?"

He stares at the figure. It keeps fluctuating from the young woman to the older over-weight woman he knew well. He sees her pain and sorrow and guilt and fears.

"I do, Mama. I forgive you."

And Mama's figure swirls into a green tornado of light and whooshes up into the sky and sprinkles down bits of shining glitter and Tango collapses, sobbing into the sandy ground.

Behind him, Ello sighs with relief, like she might have been worried about how this could go.

AFTER BROOKLYN

WALKING TWO BLOCKS brings me to a crowded wide street and I test the thing I've seen in movies. I raise my arm and ZOOM a taxi swerves to the curb in front of me. Step in and I say my script line, "Midtown Manhattan" and we're off. I look at the driver and his license clipped to the visor. My guess is he's from India. Will he even know how to take me there? What if he tries to scam me, will I know?

Don't be an arse, Erika says in my brain and another tickle tells me this is exactly the kind of judgmental shit Tango told me to try harder about.

"This is my first time in New York," I say. "What do you think I should see?"

The man looks at me in the mirror. "What are you interested

in?"

"Architecture, film—"

"You want to see the Chrysler building. It's a beautiful example of Art Deco."

"Can you take me there?"

"With pleasure, miss."

That was easy.

And we go through more of Brooklyn and I see the New York skyline up ahead but there's a lot of water to cross and I don't see a bridge and then we drive into a tunnel. It takes me no time to realize this is not like tunnels of Southern California. The longest one I've ever been in, on Second Street in downtown LA, took about ten seconds to go through. It was near that stupid Superior Court. You can't see the end of this tunnel. We might be stuck in a Twilight Zone Episode—Grandpa Cheswick did a few of those—and this is hell and we'll drive for eternity.

It's two lanes going the same way and divided by plastic posts and tiled in pee-yellow and the cars seem to be driving too fast for this space and I wonder if one crashes and goes through the wall will the water we're under come crashing in? And what about the air? With all these cars, won't we die of carbon monoxide poisoning? I guess people have driven here for ages so they've probably figured this out, but it's super bizarre anyway. And we're in here for forever! I don't know how long because I keep looking for the light at the end of the tunnel, but there is none.

My driver must notice something because he says, "Don't worry, miss. It's completely safe. And we're almost out."

I know he wouldn't have said this if I hadn't told him I was new here. Being friendly may be a good thing.

We start curving and then curve back the other way and finally there's the shine of daylight on the tiles and we exit into glare and granite stone walls.

And then we're up on the street. This is Manhattan. Corridors of buildings. People and taxis and shops and buses and it is chaotic and people are waiting to cross inches from the headlights of the taxi, daring us to hit them, and bicycles are trying to get killed by every vehicle and no one seems to care about rules of the road. Every second someone honks, including my driver.

We slalom in and out of traffic and we slide to the curb and the view is of an incredible tall Art Deco doorway. I peer out the window for a skyward view.

"The Chrysler building. You'll love it." my driver says.

I pay and exit with my luggage and the cab zooms off. I'm not going to be happy lugging around my luggage for long. After this I'll find a hotel and dump everything before exploring more. I've got a lot to see.

Enter the massive lobby. It's very dark inside but in a rich, warm way. The floors, with herringbone patterns made of mixes of brown and ochre marble, reflect the glow of the tall columns with vertical lights. Footsteps and conversations bounce around the cavernous room. Massive Art Deco stripes of lights fill entire walls over the entrance ways. I back to the wall made from natural patterns in dark amber and mahogany marble. My fingers spread across the cool smooth stone and I feel the many, many years of labor and artistry that went into this building. Everything was done for beauty. We don't seem to do that anymore. High above me a mural dances with patterns across the ceiling, warm with oranges and yellows and images of workers, airplanes, what looks like Progress. I feel like I'm in the movies *The Great Gatsby* or *Metropolis*. Everything is so right for the time. The clock. The elevator sign. The fonts of the directory. Such a thrill! I move to the elevators. The doors have different colored wood inlays with stainless steel designs among them.

A guard steps up to me. "Only the lobby is open to the public, miss."

I nod and step away so he won't think I'm trying to sneak up, though I'd like to.

I explore the grandeur of it all for an hour and then my day catches up with me so I look in my phone for a nearby hotel. There are many in walking distance. Lots for lots of money. I pick one and start walking. Wow. People really don't care if you're walking toward them on the sidewalk. They're all on their phones and I have to keep dodging them. Dang! That dog almost tripped me! And the owner seems to think that's my fault.

There are sirens everywhere. Are they all police racing to a shooting or something? This place is supposed to be dangerous.

But, even in the chaos, walking here is like being in a movie. So many movies! Is it *Midnight Cowboy*, or *Inside Llewyn Davis*, or *The French Connection*, or *A Complete Unknown*, or *Breakfast at Tiffany's*?

I get to the hotel and it's not quite like the pictures. The pictures on line must have been shot with a wide-angle lens so everything looked expansive. The lobby is the size of my living room in Eagle Rock and that was a tiny house. But, I'm here, and too tired to keep walking with luggage.

The clerk is friendly in a I'm-paid-to-be-friendly-but-they-don't-pay-me-enough-to-mean-it way. Or maybe that's just how people are in this city. I've heard they're mean—or maybe—

"I like your hair," I say.

The clerk's eyes shine and a smile blooms on her face. "Thank you. Enjoy your stay and let me know if you need anything."

This feels like a magic trick. I wave to her and step to the elevator. It's the size of a shower stall. Up to the twelfth floor. The hallway is very sharp-edged looking and reminds me of the offices of Goldman Sachs. That seems so long ago. It feels sterile but I'm not going to keep looking. Slide in the room card. Try again. And flip it and try and the little light clicks green. Push in to the smells of disinfectant and a sprayed scent probably named Misty Forest or Ocean Clouds. The room is tiny. I suppose every hotel room in New York is tiny. There's room for the bed and a one-foot passage way around the foot of the bed to the window. It's quite a view. Buildings in every direction and people walking down below. Cars honking and buses and taxis and the street has a big white arrow and the letters *ONLY* for a right turn. Big letters. Seen from above.

I call and Patrick answers.

"What does it spell?" I ask.

"I'll send you the map of your route. You did a great job by the way. I was going to do it, but when I did a test run, I was so bad at it I made a complete mess."

He hangs up and a text comes in. A picture of a map of the vacant lot between the two skyscrapers. In cursive writing, the route I took spells out:

fuck you!

Another text comes in. *Those were wildflower seeds mixed in with the ashes. Should be a colorful display in the spring.*

I text back: *I'm so happy to have been part of this. Please send me pictures when the sentiment blooms.*

A thumbs up comes back.

It's already too late to do more sight-seeing. I'm glad Erika suggested I stay another day. What with waking early, driving to Albuquerque, flying to NY, scattering ashes, traveling under the water in a tunnel, seeing the lobby of the Chrysler building, and walking here, I'm exhausted.

The hotel has a rooftop bar/cafe. I take an elevator up there. It's kind of trendy in a young-people-only way. Like the Avalon was. Everyone is with someone and I know the score—they won't be trying to engage with me. I could try my magic trick but I'm tired and don't really want to engage. I order a glass of wine and sit at the cushioned chair closest to the building edge. The street must go East and West because I can see all the way down to the orange glow of sunset bouncing on the cars and pavement and lighting the windows of the buildings edging the street. It's beautiful in a really unnatural way.

The sounds don't really change as night falls. This must be *The City That Never Sleeps*. There are still sirens, honks, humming sounds from all the buildings' air conditioners, and screeching tires and shouts and passing music and too many conversations. I don't think I could take it as a regular thing.

My phone says it's 10:07. So it's only 8:07 in New Mexico. Wonder what Bob is doing now. Playing guitar? What about Erika? Is she painting? And Ello? Is she at her place or visiting?

Maybe Captain and Daisy and Dragon are curled up together. It's nice to think about all of them.

Just them?

Okay. I wonder what Tango's doing now.

TANGO CRIES

IT MUST BE HOURS of sobbing before Tango lifts his head from the desert dust and blinks. Ello is smoking a pipe and rocking in a rusty metal rocking chair. The chair makes a slow squeak every time she pushes back on it.

Tango wipes his face with the back of his hands.

"Here." Ello pours water onto a towel and hands him the wet cloth.

He wipes his face and neck and arms. "That was not your store-brand tea."

Ello smiles and hands him a large jug of water. "Drink as much as you can."

As Tango drinks, Ello watches him. "You lost a lot."

"Yeah, I need this water. Sweating, crying..."

"No, you lost a lot of the things inside that were stuck. They're gone now. They're no longer in your face."

Tango cocks his head like Captain would, examining how he feels inside. "It's clearer. More room. Like open space."

Ello laughs puffs of smoke from her pipe.

"You think that's why I like being outside?" Tango asks. "Because I didn't have any space inside?"

Wagging her finger at Tango, Ello says, "I saw you have a book by Pema Chödrön. You know what that wise woman says? *Don't put a story-line on everything.*"

Setting down her pipe, Ello gestures for Tango to get off the ground. "Don't talk to anyone about what you experienced for a while. Let it steep in you and make itself a home in your heart. You can tell the dogs but no human. I'll drive you back now."

"I'll walk back. My body wants to move."

Ello stands and puts her wrinkled hands on his strong shoulders and looks up into his eyes. "Don't forget. You are absolutely wonderful."

He breathes that in and smiles like he believes it.

It takes a while to walk all the way from Ello's doublewide to the road. With each step his back straightens and his shoulders lift and his chest widens. By the time he gets there, he's got an entirely different posture from the hunched man he was. The sun is down and the sky's a darkening expanse. The same expanse he feels inside. *Ello's right,* he thinks. *A lot has left and there's more room for me.*

He whistles for Captain and hopes it carries across the dark desert. In a few minutes, he hears the galloping of paws on gravel and the big dog bounds up, leaping at him, and swirling with joy.

"I'll tell you all about it, Captain. Only you and Dragon and Daisy."

Turning at Luna's ceramic mailbox, he walks down past where they cut the tree blocking the road, kicks sawdust in remembrance of a good day's work, moves to the orchard and plucks an apple and bites hard. The sweet crunch explodes flavor in his mouth. Has he ever tasted food before? He packs his sleeping bag and stuffs his belongings in his duffel bag and takes the back way, far from the house where the kitchen glows and laughter scatters out, past the greenhouse, behind the pottery shed, and around to the barn. As he pulls the big door wide, thunder rolls.

"Good thing we're sleeping inside tonight, Captain. We might do that from now on. This barn is expansive and has its mojo workin'."

The rain starts and thunder booms. Tango spreads his sleeping bag on the pile of the old rejected mattresses.

"Hop up."

And Captain does. Dragon, wet from the now pounding deluge, rockets into the barn and onto the bed, giving Tango scolding barks for spending the day away.

Tango slides into the sleeping bag and props himself up with his duffle bag. "Okay, Captain. Dragon. You ready? Let me tell you what happened."

NEW YORK EXPLORATION

I'M SITTING WITH TANGO at the top of the ferris wheel. Black sky around us. We keep looking like we want to kiss except I tell him I'm a bad person. I'm surprised I'm telling him this. He turns into James Dean. James Dean and I kiss and we both quickly turn away, knowing it's the wrong thing to do.

I wake and stare at the smoke alarm on the ceiling. Around it, shimmers dance from the nighttime glow of streetlights and lit windows in the buildings across the way.

Why did I dream that? It's a weirdly familiar scenario. I open my phone and google James Dean Ferris Wheel. The movie scene comes right up. *East of Eden*. He's with Julie Harris on the ferris wheel and she says she's a bad person. But in the film, he's the character who thinks he's bad. So what is my dream telling me? That Tango thinks he's bad? James Dean's character wasn't bad, he was only treated as if he was and believed it. Did that happen to Tango?

I close my eyes, hoping for another dream like that.

Dawn wakes me. It's a wonder it can find a way through the maze of buildings blocking its path. The bedside clock says 6:30. So that means 4:30 New Mexico time. I'm not getting up. I close the curtains and slide back into bed and sleep.

A horrible pounding wakes me at eight. Peek through the curtains and men in hardhats are jack-hammering holes in the street. I doubt this will stop anytime soon.

Go up to the rooftop cafe. They don't have tea so I settle for coffee. I look up where the Guggenheim Museum is and where the Metropolitan Museum of Art is and where there are plays that might be something with good acting as opposed to singing.

My first stop will be the Frank Lloyd Wright-designed Guggenheim Museum.

As I walk to the museum, I near a sunken doorway with a man curled in a sleeping bag. Tango wouldn't last here. He needs quiet and nature. The man opens his eyes, dead-like, not making contact with mine, and holds out a greasy palm. I dig in my purse for a bill. It's a twenty. I guess knowing Tango, I should, so I do. The dead eyes spark alive and he smiles, gapped-toothed and friendly. "Thank you, Miss!" I think Tango would approve.

Up ahead is a cultural icon. A hotdog stand with a yellow and blue Sabrett umbrella. I've seen this in lots of movies. It's a must-have NY experience. The man running it has on a filthy apron over a white t-shirt. He's got a scary five-o'clock shadow and looks like he's a mafia hit man. He stares at me like I'm supposed to do something. Since I don't, he puts his hands up in exasperation—"Whadyuh want?!"

Okay, Prestonia, be brave. "I've seen these stands in so many movies but I've never been to New York and I knew I had to try one of these hotdogs. Can you suggest what I should get?"

"Acourse, sweethaat. I alwiz dink duh waydago is sauerkraut, onions, and mustud. Soun goot?"

"It does."

"Okay, bu youdonlike, I make ye sumpin else."

And I almost start crying with the way this magic works.

He makes the hotdog and hands it to me on a square of foil. Before I can do anything, he threatens me with, "You tryit 'ere."

I take a bite. The hot dog skin pops and squirts meaty-salty liquid across my mouth. Then the sauerkraut and onions and mustard kick in. The combination of flavors is perfect. "That's the best hotdog I ever had!"

Once again the hands come up. "WhadItellyuh?"

I open my wallet.

"Ondaouse, sweethaat. Enjoy yuh stay."

I walk along the edge of Central Park toward 88th street eating my treat. There are lots of real dogs, not hot, and squirrels and pigeons. It makes me glad to see them.

The Guggenheim is gorgeous from the outside. Like a layer

cake with the biggest piece on top. An inverse pyramid. Inside, I'm stunned by the size of the space. Spiraling corridors around this huge central room with a massive spiderweb skylight at the top. But where's the art?

A guard suggests I take the elevator to the top and so I do. Exiting the elevator I'm on the ramp and one side is the huge drop to the center of the building and the other side—*there's* the art. I move down the sloping circular walkway and look. There's a Picasso of a bird on a tree. It looks like the ravens on the trees at Luna's place. Keep walking. Not everything is of interest to me and I can't study each one if I have only today. So it's okay to pick and choose.

Egon Schiele's painting of an old man reminds me so much of Bob. He's tall and bent but still with a deep vibrancy. Walk farther, spiraling down. Oh! A beautiful Franz Marc painting called "White Bull." The bull is curled in on itself like the way Dragon does when he's sleeping. There are some works that strike me immediately. A Paul Cézanne landscape "Bibémus" looks very much like the New Mexico desert. Red rocks, scrubby trees, clouds against blue. I can almost hear the humming insects and feel the dry air. Keep going down, swirling past art that doesn't catch my eye—Wait! That one's like the view from Luna's kitchen window! Pierre Bonnard's "Dining Room on the Garden." It looks so peaceful and inviting. Almost like Erika's about to serve me a cuppa. That makes me want tea.

Back onto the street. I should have more to eat than a hotdog. I could go to Little Italy or I could go to Chinatown. For some reason I feel like Chinatown would be best and I know they'll have black tea. It's pretty far south and I am scared of the subways because there are so many movies of bad things happening on them so I try my hand at hailing another cab. It works again and I say "Chinatown" like I'm Jack Nicholson.

Chinatown's colorful and noisy and bustling with people walking every which way, some even talking in Chinese. I'm about to go into a restaurant when a shop window pulls at me.

The bell rings as I go in. I'm greeted by a pretty Asian woman.

"I'd like to see your Buddha statues," I say.

They have many. Most of them are of the thin man sitting in a yoga pose meditating. Some are of a fat man laughing. There are a few of the thin man reclining on his side with his head propped up on his hand. This reminds me of Tango on his sleeping bag under the mulberry tree.

I get a small stone one. The one that looks the most like Tango. The woman asks if it's a present and when I nod, she wraps it in blue tissue paper and places it in a golden box with a gold ribbon and slips it into a cute paper sack. I'm going to be embarrassed to give it to Tango!

The lunch is great and not like the Chinese food I'm used to. We do have "authentic" places in Los Angeles, but I didn't really experiment back then. I guess I'm moving away of my comfort zone! The staff doesn't speak a lot of English and I point at pictures in the menu to order. I must not have seen one of the pictures clearly because it ends up being chicken feet. I consider covering them with a napkin and ignoring them but instead, I ask how to eat them. The staff surrounds me trying to explain with gestures and we do a lot of laughing.

The Metropolitan Museum of Art is next and it's huge and I go to the Impressionists and the Abstract Expressionists and those alone get me exhausted. You really can't look at art all day.

I walk through the Renaissance halls quickly but stop short in front of a painting of a man in the black tunic with the white ruffled collar. Typical Renaissance style for a noble, but this is a Black man. He could be Tango. The card says *Portrait of Juan de Pareja* by Velázquez 1650. It also says the man was Velázquez's slave, but he's painted with the humanity and honor of any of Velázquez's rich patrons. I sit on a bench and stare. In my head, I ask Juan de Pareja, *What should I say to Tango when I get back? How will we figure out what to do or not to do?* The eyes of this man look at me with understanding, just like Tango's. I stand from the bench and take a step close to the painting. You could touch that cheek and feel the warmth—

"Get back, young lady," a guard barks, moving to protect the art from me.

"I understand. This is my first time here and—"

"Back up now!"

I guess the magic doesn't always work.

Before leaving, I slip into the Museum gift shop and buy a small print of the *Portrait of Juan de Pareja*.

On the street, I walk a block then pause mid-sidewalk to check the street sign and a young woman financial-advisor-type yells, "OUTTA MY FUCKING WAY, BITCH." I recognize her shoes, business suit, hair, and demeanor. She's exactly ME a few months ago. I almost want to tell her that there are other options, but I don't. I just backup to a building's wall so I'll be out of the flow of important people moving fast and watch her disappear in the throng. I'm so happy not to be her!

It's already dinner time and if I'm going to see a show on-or-off Broadway, I've got to do it now, so I start walking but I realize I'm so tired I'll probably fall asleep at a play, so I end up at my hotel and I ride the elevator to the cafe bar, and order a burger and fries for an obscene price, and take it down to my room, and prop up the pillows and stretch out on the bed with my dinner on one side of me and Tango's present open so the Buddha lounges on the other side and though I can hardly keep my eyes open, I gaze at the print of Juan de Pareja. He's darker than Tango and has a beard, mustache, and Afro hairstyle, but the rest of him is very similar. Strong, proud, empathetic, inquisitive, challenging, gorgeous—

I'm in Velázquez's studio. A massive room of activity. Canvases, Models. Draped fabric. Someone is yelling.

Several apprentices and slaves, including Juan de Pareja are painting detailed portraits. I step toward Juan and hope he'll recognize me from gazing at his painting at the museum.

"Señor Juan," I say, "you look like someone who knows about life and loss and might give me advice."

The man glares at me. "You know nothing."

"I understand our different lives. I accept you."

The painter spits on the paint-encrusted floor. "You flatter yourself. You don't accept me. I recognize respect and you don't own it for me or yourself or anyone else. Do you like this painting? It's mine. See how it differs from Velázquez's. He still won't paint me as I am. Nor can you see me as I am."

Now I'm facing the mirror reflecting the Spanish king and queen in Velázquez's *Las Meninas*. Tango, hunched shouldered, lumbers in front of the child princess, her servants, and entourage. He stops in front of me, opens his shirt, and gestures to his body, daring me to paint him. I would but, why is the top of this room so dark? Why is there a vast void above? I turn to Tango to ask this and the entire world drips, melting like the running slop of a Francis Bacon painting.

INSIDE CHANGES

PRESTONIA JERKS AWAKE. *Fuckin' dreams! This was not as good as the Ferris wheel one!*

After exhaling those visions, she cleans her barely-eaten, somewhat-squashed burger and fries from the bed, packs Tango's Buddha present and her belongings, takes a cab to La Guardia, and gets on the plane for her nearly-six-hour flight to Albuquerque, as Tango works on finishing his two welding projects.

Erika drops in the barn to see him, bringing tea and scones.

"'ere, luv. 'eard ye workin' but didnae see ye in the kechen, so thought ye might be needin' sustenance."

"Thanks, Erika."

She scrutinizes his face like she did back in the Los Angeles County Jail. "Ye've changed. Somthin' happened."

Tango smiles at her. "You and Ello sure can see into a person."

Erika laughs, "'Course we can. We're witches. Women who know too much 're always witches."

Tango takes a bite of a scone, stops, pushes it to the side of his mouth so he can talk. "It's—dense. Too hard for a muffin and too soft for a cookie."

"'Tis a scone. And the texture is that o' a scone. Ye can like it or ferget me e'r bringin' ye breaky agan."

"I like it, I like it," Tango says, munching with exaggerated pleasure.

As Tango washes down the scone with a big gulp of tea, Erika looks at the worktable, tilting her head and trying to make out what he's made. "What is this lot?"

"You'll see when it's up."

"Okay, Mister Secret Man. Enjoy yer dense scones!" She steps to the big sliding door. "Ye know Prestonia 'tis back tonight."

Tango nods, returning to his work. "I know."

"Ye happy aboot 'er return?"

Tango turns to Erika with a smile. "I'm happy about everything now. Didn't you see that when you peered inside me?"

Erika glares in mock anger, raises her fist at him, and stomps out the door.

BACK TO LUNA'S

I CAN HARDLY keep my eyes open! And having no street lights on these desert roads makes it harder to drive. All I see is the road right in front of my headlights. What with the delayed flight and the long drive from Albuquerque, past Santa Fe, and up to Ojo Caliente, I've got not an ounce of life left in me. Hope I don't get lost finding the—ah! the ceramic mailbox—but there's something new. Tall wooden beams on each side of the driveway hold up a sign. I click on the brights to see it clearer. Metal welded letters spell: LUNAS. It's hard to see well but it looks like each letter is unique and beautiful. I get tearful driving under it.

As I drive past the orchard, I look over to see if Tango is visible in his spot under the apple trees. Slow down to scour each tree but there is no sign of his sleeping bag or any of his things. Fear grips my stomach and I realize he might be gone. We were terrible to each other when I left. Maybe he had enough of me and vanished after finishing the sign. Oh please. Please don't be gone.

I park beside the labyrinth and a projectile of fur hits my lap the moment I open the door.

"Dragon! I missed you!"

He's squiggling and wiggling like he missed me, too. Maybe I can have someone else scatter ashes in the future. I don't want to make these trips without my pal.

Erika steps out of the adobe house to greet me. "Jesus, Mary, 'n' Joseph, ye look done in, luv."

"I am. A long trip. Can I tell you about it later? I'm too tired to talk."

"'course, lass. I'll get ye a bowl o' the soup Bob and me concocted. A mix o' Mulligatawny and tortilla soups."

She grabs my suitcase and leads me into the house. Down past the painting she made just for me. Past Bob's closed door and past Erika's room and down to the windowed room at the end of the hall. As she sets the suitcase on my bed, I ask, "Everyone okay?" Not daring to question if Tango is gone.

She smiles and pats my arm. "We're grand. More than grand now that yer 'ome. I'm sure Bob—and Tango—'ill be delighted to see ye in the morrow."

Dragon hops on the bed and snuggles and cuddles and whines with joy as I smother him with kisses. After we both calm down, I turn on Agnes's burro lamp and there's the formica table with its chairs and the mud-figure and the pinecone and pieces of the rooster and hen salt-and-pepper shakers and the broken toothpick-holder dog and the super-glue and beside them sits a jar of rubber cement. A wave of relief sweeps over me. This feels like home.

Erika brings in the soup and delivers a kiss to the top of my head and closes the door quietly. I eat, letting the soup comfort me and the room nourish me and thoughts of tomorrow bring me hope.

LONG NIGHT

TANGO WATCHED from the barn as Prestonia drove up and was taken inside by Erika. Now he waits, staring at the warm glow of the kitchen windows. Maybe she'll come out to greet him. But he was mean when she left. Maybe he should go greet her. Yes, he should make the move.

He puts a palm out to Captain and whispers, "Stay." The dog, stretched out on the sleeping bag atop the mattresses, opens one eye to the palm, then closes it. He's not even slightly inclined to disobey.

Tango starts toward the house, steps past the greenhouse, the pottery shed, over the spirals of the labyrinth and—the kitchen light goes out. He stops, waiting. No sign of anyone. He moves to the porch and peers in the window. Only the nightlight over the sink is on. He steps next to Prestonia's car and touches the warm hood. Continues on around to the side of the adobe. Those windows are dark. Continues around the next corner to the end of the house, the room with windows on three sides. All dark.

Tango doesn't get near. He doesn't want to be a creep. But he stands there by the Tamarisk tree and tries to send his greeting. Tries to send his apology. Tries to send his love and regrets.

TANGO'S PRESENT

WHEN I COME OUT of my room I feel so rested and glad to be here. In the corner of the living room is a large pile of packages. Post office, Fed Ex, and UPS. Return addresses with unknown names and funeral homes. Are these all ashes?

Bob's gravely voice answers, "LUNAS website for the Loved, Unknown, Neglected Ash Sanctuary has really been busy. Lots of people have ashes they don't know what to do with. We were written up in the Santa Fe newspaper and I know that story is going to spread. Get ready."

I give him a hug.

"Good trip?"

I wobble my head with wide eyes like the overwhelmed person I was there.

He laughs and says, "Can't wait to hear. You tell us when you're ready."

After my cuppa ritual, I re-wrap the present for Tango, put it back in the little cute paper sack, and start toward the barn.

The sliding door is open as usual but I don't hear welding or hammering, only my pounding heart. I step in and Captain hops from the mattresses where Tango is lying on his side, shirtless, reading, his head propped up on his palm, *just like the reclining Buddha pose.*

I can't help but laugh.

As Captain greets me, Tango looks up and quickly hops off the bed and puts on a shirt. "Oh! Sorry, I—I—welcome back!"

"Thank you, and before we say anything else, I'm sorry for being a jerk before I left."

Tango puts a hand on his chest. "I'm sorry, too, but why the laughing?"

"The way you were on the bed," I say, and hold out the paper sack. "This's for you."

Tango steps toward me looking bewildered. "For me?"

I nod and he pulls the gift out of the sack. His eyes widen holding the gold box tied with the gold ribbon. "I like it already!"

The ribbon is carefully undone and the lid lifted. He pulls the blue tissue out and gently unfolds it. One hand moves to cover his mouth as he looks at the reclining statue. He keeps shaking his head, tears in his eyes, glancing up at me and turning the figure in his fingers.

"Never. Never. Never had a present that fit before."

He pulls me close for a one-arm hug, but before I can enjoy it he breaks away and goes back to looking at the statue. "Buddha relaxing. I'm going to keep it by the bed to remember how to be. Thank you so much, Prestonia!"

The one-arm hug has disarmed me and I look around to distract myself. "I didn't see your stuff in the orchard. You moved?"

He grins, gesturing to his mattress palace. "Did you know that these strange puffy things are softer than sleeping on the ground?"

"And you're in a place with a roof and walls. Better during a thunderstorm. No flooding."

"Yeah, that little brave boy is okay now. He made it out a hero."

I look at him. There is something different about him. He looks much calmer and at peace and he's even standing straighter.

"Something happened while I was gone?" I ask.

"Yes, but it started way back when Agnes Sloan spoke to me on the Colorado bridge. Isn't it strange?" Tango says. "That you and I would not be here in New Mexico, would not have met, would not be creating new futures, except for one person's generosity. Agnes Sloan."

"Tango, speaking of Agnes, I'm kind of embarrassed but—I hope she wouldn't mind—when I left LA, I took some—I went to the carousel and took some of what might be a mix of her and maybe a little of her wife Tracy and dirt. You think she's mind?"

"I don't think she was that sort. You want to scatter her?"

I nod.

"And film it?"

"No, this is private. Just you and me."

He smiles. "I know a spot. Meet you back here in half an hour. This is important, so I have to change."

I hurry out. I've got to change, too.

SCATTERING AGNES AGAIN

PRESTONIA PUTS ON the shirt she's never worn. The vintage, silky, pale-blue one with the yellow polkadots. It's funny, and that's how she wants to be from now on. Now into the black mid-calf capri pants that Brent wouldn't let her wear. She slips on simple shoes that go with those kind of pants. A nice beatnik look. The beat generation women sometimes wore bright red lipstick. It's been a while since she wore any makeup. She searches through her bags and finds a deep red one. The effect is perfect.

She thinks, *I would fit well in Bob's mid-century modern house, and I'd fit well in a New Mexican adobe house. This is me.*

Tango dresses in the clothes he bought while shopping with Bob in Santa Fe. He said one little thing about Bob's clothes not fitting too well and a moment later they were in a second-hand clothing store. Not thrift-store second hand, but vintage, with a focus on Western wear. He got three shirts, two pants, boots, and a hat.

He slides into the black cowboy shirt with the mother-of-pear snaps and red piping around the pockets and shoulders. Pulls up blue jeans that fit. And pushes into pointy-toed black cowboy boots.

As he combs his hair, Prestonia knocks. He turns and they both freeze.

"You look like—yourself, in a new way," Tango says with his heart fluttering among the words.

Prestonia points at him, trying to get her mouth to work. "You—you also."

Nothing more can they manage. Tango leads them out and they walk with Captain and Dragon swirling around them—away from the homestead, toward distant tall trees.

Silently, side by side, they walk. Keeping the pace. Easy but with purpose. Both think it would be a perfect time to be holding hands, but neither makes the move.

At the tall cottonwood trees, they step down among the ancient trunks toward the sound of rushing water. The arroyo's full from the recent storms. Grasses, wildflowers, even cattails surround the banks.

Tango looks at Prestonia. "Good?"

"Perfect."

She lifts the jar of the Griffith Park mix. "Where?"

Tango looks around. He looks up across the tree canopy. He checks out all directions and steps to a large cottonwood. "Here. She'll get afternoon shade, but sun in the morning. Good view of the sky, but protection from the rain. Close enough to hear the water but not get washed away."

Prestonia nods because she can't talk. She twists her mouth to keep the tears in.

They go to the spot and Tango kneels and carefully moves several stones at the base of the tree. Prestonia kneels beside him and hands him the jar. He opens it and hands it back.

Prestonia takes a deep breath and sprinkles some of the mix of dirt and ash. "Thank you, Agnes Sloan, for giving us so much. You've changed our lives." She passes the jar to Tango.

He scatters the ashes in a slow arc. "The gift you gave me, saved my life. The gift you gave me, opened a whole new world. The gift you gave me, made me a better person. Thank you for what you gave me and thank you for introducing me to Prestonia and for changing her life as well. Because of you, we have an entirely new future."

As he speaks, Prestonia's eyes overflow, cascading tears over her freckles and off her chin to join the polka dots on her shirt—even as half her brain wonders why she isn't as eloquent. Tango sets down the empty jar and puts his arm around her. They silently cry until WHAM!—Captain and Dragon leap at them. They're knocked backwards and the dogs tumble around, kicking up dirt and ash and breaking the spell of sorrow.

As Tango arranges a circle of rocks around Agnes's spot, Prestonia watches him work. "You said Agnes had huevos, Tango. What did you mean by that?"

"She struck me as brave, with grit, and determination."

"You're like that. You've changed your life completely. To do that, you gotta have huevos."

Tango stands and holds out a hand to Prestonia. "Seems like Agnes spread her huevos to both of us."

Prestonia takes his hand, he pulls her up, and they walk back toward the barn.

At the house, Erika sits with Bob on the porch. She squints at the two figures in the distance and gives Bob a pat on the arm, flicking her head to the couple.

Bob looks where she's indicating, then makes that triangle with two fingers and his thumb, and peeks through the pinhole. "Holding hands."

"Aye."

"'Bout time."

"That's feckin' right."

At the barn, Tango asks if he can show Prestonia something. She follows him in.

At the welding table is a sculpture. He lifts it and stands it on the ground. It's a figure. Feet made of a garden trowel and a metal pasta fork. One leg a welded strand of different-sized crescent wrenches. The other leg a conglomeration of rusted cans and gears. Atop the legs, a bicycle seat for hips. Then what looks like part of a radiator with the fan as the chest. Thick spring for the neck. An antique car headlight for the face and a upside down silver champagne bucket on top of that. Arms of welded chain reach up to hold a tray skyward as if presenting something to the gods.

"This is amazing, Tango! I just came from New York and the works I saw—nothing had the heart of this! You're an artist!"

Tango smiles broadly. "It's for Clayton." He goes to his bedside and lifts Clayton's urn and sets it on the tray at the top. Raising the ashes to the gods.

Prestonia is awed by the sculpture and sentiment. "I know Clayton'd love it. You really honored him. You've been carrying him for a long time. You knew him well?"

"He's a stranger."

"I can't imagine anyone helping a stranger like you have."

"I can." Tango smiles at Prestonia. "You'll have to help me find a spot for his sculpture."

"I will. Maybe by the fire pit."

"But not now. I've got a lot to prepare. I'm making dinner

tonight."

"*You're* making dinner?" The minute she says this she regrets it. "I did it again. I'm sorry. Why *couldn't* you cook?"

"You caught it, so thank you. And I find that cooking is just like welding. Combining elements with heat. Ello's coming over. Be ready at six pm. But you can't come in the kitchen until I call. Now git!"

And Prestonia skips out of the barn with her heart fluttering like a sparrow in a bird bath.

GLUE

I SKIP ALL THE WAY around the labyrinth and into the house. In my room, I set out all the pieces of the salt-and-pepper shakers and toothpick-holder. Parts of dog, hen, and rooster. I start arranging them on the tabletop. The rooster head on the left, the dog head on the right. Body of the rooster with the hen head coming from its chest. Leg of dog, leg of rooster, leg of hen. Dog ear hanging down as a fig-leaf at the crotch. Hen tail-feathers as a head-dress. Dog tail rising as an antennae from the rooster's beak. It's funny and I like it. These figures are never going to be what they were. They're going to be something entirely new.

I push aside Erika's rubber cement and grab the super-glue—this is gonna be permanent!

SPECIAL DINNER AND MAGIC HOUR

TANGO HAS EVERYONE promise not to enter the kitchen or living room and starts cooking. When he's done, exactly at six pm, he rings the triangle bell he made and everyone comes in. Erika smiles, sniffing the air.

"I kin smell what ye've done, lad. 'Tis a grand surprise."

Ello smells as well. "Navajo blood sausage."

"Haggis," Erika corrects. "Made wi' lamb and grains stuffed in a sheep's tummy."

Ello nods. "Like I said, Navajo blood sausage."

Prestonia comes in from her back room and blushes at Tango's warm smile. Everyone's ushered into the living room to a long table made of boards nailed across two sawhorses covered with a southwest style cloth. It's set with ceramic plates and trays and cups made by Luna and loaded with a smorgasbord of food.

Erika laughs at the spread. "T'is perfect, Tango luv. Haggis, neeps and tatties. Scottish salmon, meat pie, scones even, and ye didnae forget the Scotch, I see."

Tango grins and give her a hug. "I wanted to repay that New Orleans dinner you gave me."

They all maneuver around the table, somehow steering Prestonia to sit beside Tango. The bottle of Scotch is passed, with Tango filling his glass with water, and once everyone's got something, Erika raises her drink to the table of friends. "To ye all. T'is a rare thing ye've done and are set to do. I'm proud tae be in the mix."

Everything is enjoyed by everyone except the Haggis, which is only relished by Erika and Ello.

"Now, Prestonia, luv. When d'we get to 'ere o' yer adventures in the Big Apple?"

"And when can we see your latest scattering of ashes film?" Bob asks.

"There is no film," Prestonia says. "They want it private, and I understand why."

She explains how Miriam wouldn't sell her house even when it was flanked by sky-rises and how it was burned down by arson and how Miriam's had specific plans of how she wanted her ashes scattered in that vacant lot. Prestonia explains how the guy on the phone directed her every step. "So after I was done I asked what all the back and forth and loops meant. He sent me the map of my movements. I'll show you."

She opens the texted photo and it's passed around the table to great laughter.

"But what did you scatter?" Tango asks. "I'm sure Miriam's

ashes wouldn't be the message she was hoping for."

"You're right. The ashes were mixed with wildflower seeds. It will be a beautiful *fuck you* in the spring."

"Crackin' idea. Maybe w'different word options. I'll be sure t'add that tae the LUNAS website. "

Bob looks to Ello. "Speaking of Luna, what can you tell me about my daughter. You knew her here. Was she happy?"

This brings silence and a solemnity to the table.

Ello peers at Bob, like she's seeing how much he can handle. Decision made, she says, "Luna was frustrated by her name, like it meant she was only a reflecting body, not creating light herself. It felt too predictive. She told me she came from especially accomplished parents. A JPL scientist who was getting vehicles on the moon and a mother who decorated sets for some of the greatest movies. Luna had this mental block about all they'd done which made her unable to do anything. She felt unimportant. A nobody. She came to New Mexico to find a place she could be on her own. She floundered at first but little by little she discovered her own path. Sculpture, ceramics, painting, welding, planting."

Tango looks at Prestonia. She smiles in a tentative way with a little shrug. He peers at her intently, then nods.

"Prestonia was somewhat like that," says Tango to the group. "I don't know her parents but if she had a mental block, it was being good at something that made a lot of money. As if that mattered. She was brought up to be one thing but the real, passionate self couldn't be squashed and, even when she tried, she couldn't smother her creativity."

Prestonia looks at him like she's amazed at his understanding. Really she's looking at him like—*When the fuck are we going to kiss?*

Bob coughs and stands. He walks to the niche in the wall and lifts his wife's metal fish-shaped urn. "I want a cement bench. I want to have my ashes and my wife's ashes combined and mixed into concrete and formed into a bench. I want the bench facing west to watch the sunset. I want it off to the side of Luna's spiral so she doesn't feel we're watching her. Okay?"

Erika stands and shakes his hand. "I've done cement sculptures and will research about incorporating ashes. You will have your bench and you will pick that spot yourself."

Ello stands and touches both their arms. "But first I'm driving you over to my place to see the new baby goats. Sun's setting soon so we've got to hurry. And, Erika, I'll want to show you my healing herbs, as I expect you'll be learning the medicine-woman-ways soon enough."

Prestonia and Tango stand and Erika turns to them. "Ye are nae comin'. Dishes tae be cleaned. Dinnae ye think we cannae tell if ye shirk the job. An' be sure te pack any left over neeps and tatties. I'll be wantin' them for brecky."

They leave with Daisy. Captain and Dragon remain behind watching Tango and Prestonia move all the dishes and platters to the kitchen. The dogs concentrate as dishes are sorted. What's good is put in containers and they get to lick out the rest. Tango scrapes scraps from a dish onto the dogs' platter and hands the plate to Prestonia to wash.

"You know they did this on purpose," Tango says.

"To get us alone."

He hands her another dish. "I'm glad of it."

"Me, too."

"You think they're outside watching?" Tango asks.

Prestonia's eyes widen. "That would be really fucked up."

And they both move to the door and open it together. There's no one there but they're closer than ever. Each heart is pounding with anticipation. Each one hopes and despairs at the same time. Tango closes the door and Prestonia steps back to the sink. They stay at that distance as if to protect themselves from anything rash.

There is a long awkward silence. Dragon and Captain look back and forth between the two humans.

Tango takes in a deep breath and, "We talked about it. Our differences—"

Prestonia puts her hand up to stop him. "We *are* different. I have really come to see that. You're someone who's kind and warm and cares about people and dogs and who is artistic and uniquely creative and brave and finds solutions and who maybe never was given a chance, but made something incredibly wonderful of himself despite that. I'm a mess. I'm not considerate of other people like you are. And you wouldn't want to know what goes on in my head. I'm judgmental and opinionated and think unkind things about everyone. I'm trying, but all the thoughts are still there. I'm—" She pauses trying to hold back the shame and finally chokes out, "—I'm not really—a good person."

Tango slowly shakes his head. "You can have all the thoughts you want, but it's how you *act* that matters. No one sees your thoughts but you, and, as I'm learning from Pema the Buddhist with the smiling face, *thoughts are not reality*. What is real, is what you do. You rescue the dogs of a stranger, bailing them out of an animal shelter. You bring that jailed stranger home to a backyard sanctuary. You employ him. You create moving and caring films while scattering ashes of strangers. You fight against pink joggers. You care about art and creativity and dogs and Erika and Bob and Agnes Sloan—a dead woman you never met! I see Prestonia, who, in spite of what she thinks of herself, is a really good person."

Prestonia wipes tears from her eyes. Tango takes a step toward her but Prestonia puts up a hand to stop him.

He steps back to the door and asks, "How long have we known each other from that day I talked with you about Agnes in the Trader Joe's parking lot?"

"I went off to scatter her ashes at the carousel right after that so—" Prestonia swipes on her phone and counts—"a little over eight weeks."

"How long did you know that ex-boyfriend Brent before you —got involved?"

"I met him the day I started at the firm. He took me to dinner. We had everything in common—grew up in LA, went to UCLA, studied finance—we fit, so that was it."

"How long?"

"A day."

"You had a lot of external things in common, but probably not much internal."

Prestonia nods. "I know what you're saying."

"I mean, you and that dude—"

"—that asshole—"

"—that asshole had finance in common, but you and I—we've had *being homeless* in common."

Prestonia smiles. "True. But—I'm scared, Tango."

Tango steps close to her. "I'm also scared."

They don't dare look at each other, both staring at the soapy water.

Prestonia exhales sharply. "I wish we didn't have to think so much. I wish we could go back to that moment I got out of the car and you were running across the field."

Tango slowly, tentatively, takes her hand. She looks up at him, into those caring amber eyes as he says, "If we're creating an entirely new future, we can create an entirely new past."

And he leads her out the door, and to her car, and, leaving her there, starts trotting toward the barn. Captain and Dragon move to the porch and exchange a look.

Prestonia is trembling as she opens the car door and sits. She takes a deep breath. The great expanse between the barn and her car is lit with what she knows—from her semester studying film—is called Magic Hour. The magic time when the sun is setting or has just set and the light is golden and the shadows are long and everything is beautifully backlit. She steps out of the car and pulls her shirt from sticking to her back. Across the field, a figure is running from the barn. He's shirtless and passes the greenhouse and the pottery shed and he's getting closer and she smiles, watching him leap across the spiraling paths of the labyrinth, and she replays his words from down in the arroyo those many weeks ago, *Brace yourself,* and she does, grinning as he reaches her, arms surrounding, lifting and spinning and she's held tightly with Tango's skin wonderfully everywhere, and he sets her down sliding along his chest and he touches her cheek with one hand and the small of her back with the other, and she cups his face and their lips meet as strangers but quickly find they're already lovers, and they create a new past even as they're writing this new future.

And Captain and Dragon circle in the dirt, drop to the ground, and sigh contentedly.

THE END

And unlike in the movies, Tango and Prestonia don't stop after the final shot of THE END or FIN and they keep going during the credits and long after the audience has left and even in a book, as the reader turns that last page, these two don't stop but instead, when they need to, they lie down, and that leads to more magic and they're not constrained by what you or I think will happen and so they do what they want. And it's wonderful.

WITH GRATITUDE

Thank you to all those in the Writing Circle Group of Santa Fe's La Farge Library. Your support and comments and enthusiasm carried this story forward week after week.

Thank you to Anne Anthony, Charles Baumert, and Chris Coulson for your notes and editorial suggestions.

Susan Emshwiller wears several hats: filmmaker, playwright, screenwriter, director, novelist, actress, artist, teacher, and improvisational carpenter. She lives with her husband and dogs in Santa Fe, NM, where she enjoys inventing stories and backyard contraptions.

www.ingramcontent.com/pod-product-compliance
Lightning Source LLC
LaVergne TN
LVHW091703070526
838199LV00050B/2266